DIE VOLUME 1:
FANTASY HEARTBREAKER

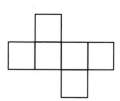

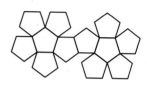

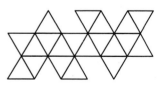

DIE VOLUME 1: FANTASY HEARTBREAKER

KIERON GILLEN
Writer

STEPHANIE HANS
Artist

CLAYTON COWLES
Letterer

RIAN HUGHES
Designer

CHRISSY WILLIAMS
Editor

IMAGE COMICS, INC.
Robert Kirkman: Chief Operating Officer
Erik Larsen: Chief Financial Officer
Todd McFarlane: President
Marc Silvestri: Chief Executive Officer
Jim Valentino: Vice President
Eric Stephenson: Publisher / Chief Creative Officer
Corey Hart: Director of Sales
Jeff Boison: Director of Publishing Planning, Book Trade Sales
Chris Ross: Director of Digital Sales
Jeff Stang: Director of Specialty Sales
Kat Salazar: Director of PR & Marketing
Drew Gill: Art Director
Heather Doornink: Production Director
Nicole Lapalme: Controller
imagecomics.com

ISBN, Standard Edition: 978-1-5343-1270-8
ISBN, Forbidden Planet/Big Bang/Jetpack Exclusive: 978-1-5343-1437-5
ISBN, Travelling Man Exclusive: 978-1-5343-1438-2
ISBN, Diamond SDCC 2019 Exclusive: 978-1-5343-1454-2

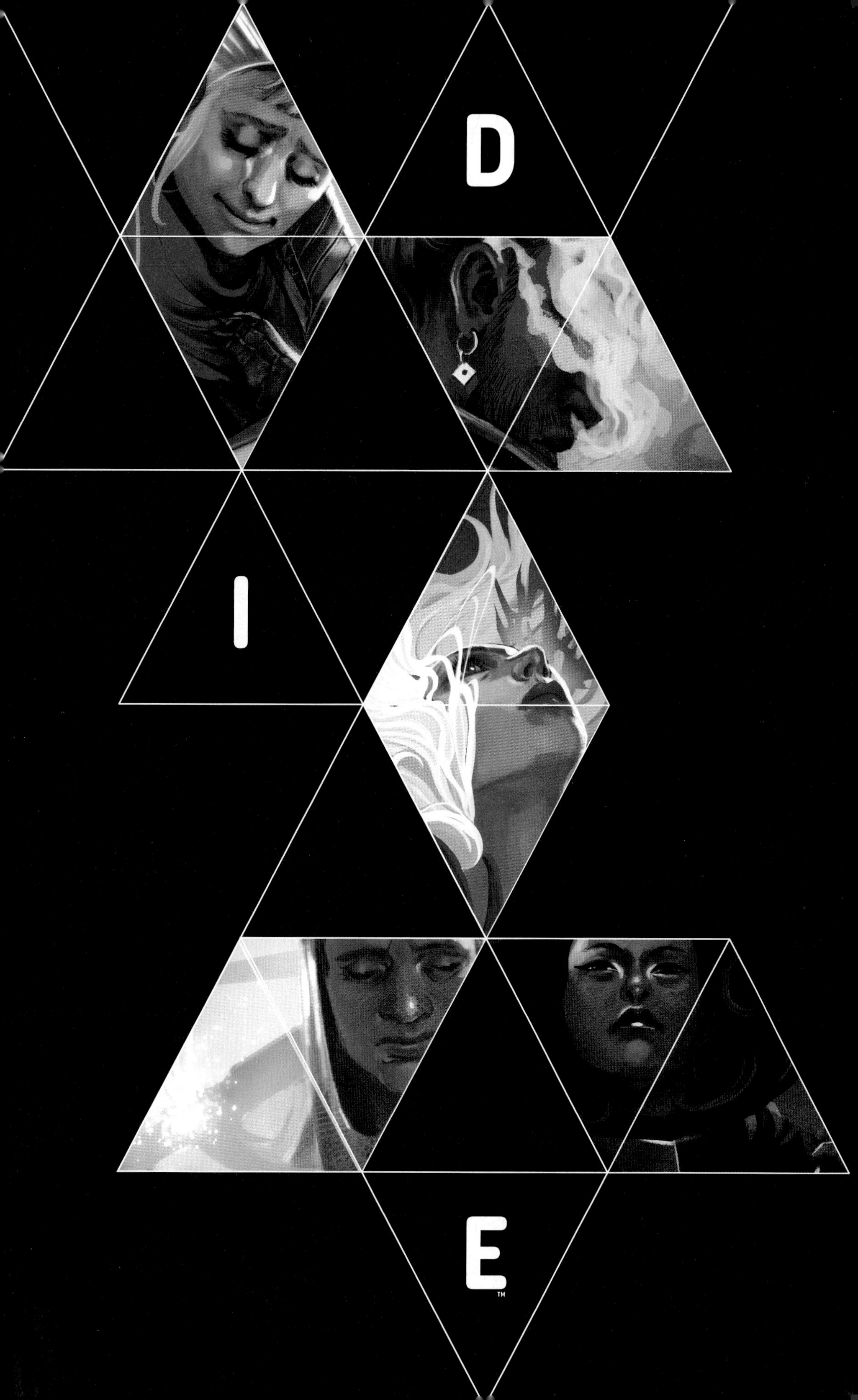
D
I
E™

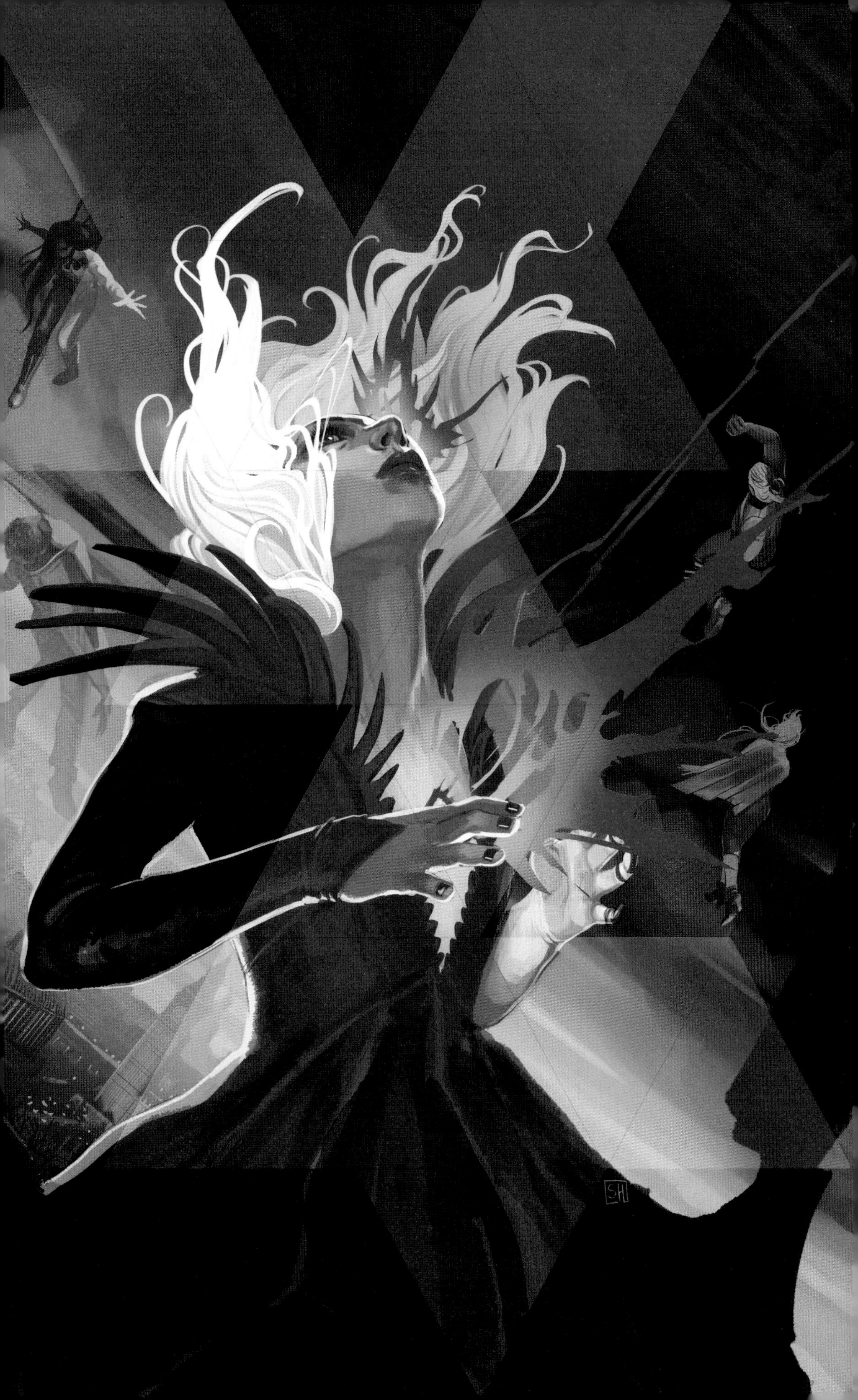

1:
THE PARTY

"I am not at all sure that the tendency
to treat this whole thing as a kind of
vast game is really good - certainly
not for me, who finds that kind of thing
only too fatally attractive."
– *JRR Tolkien*

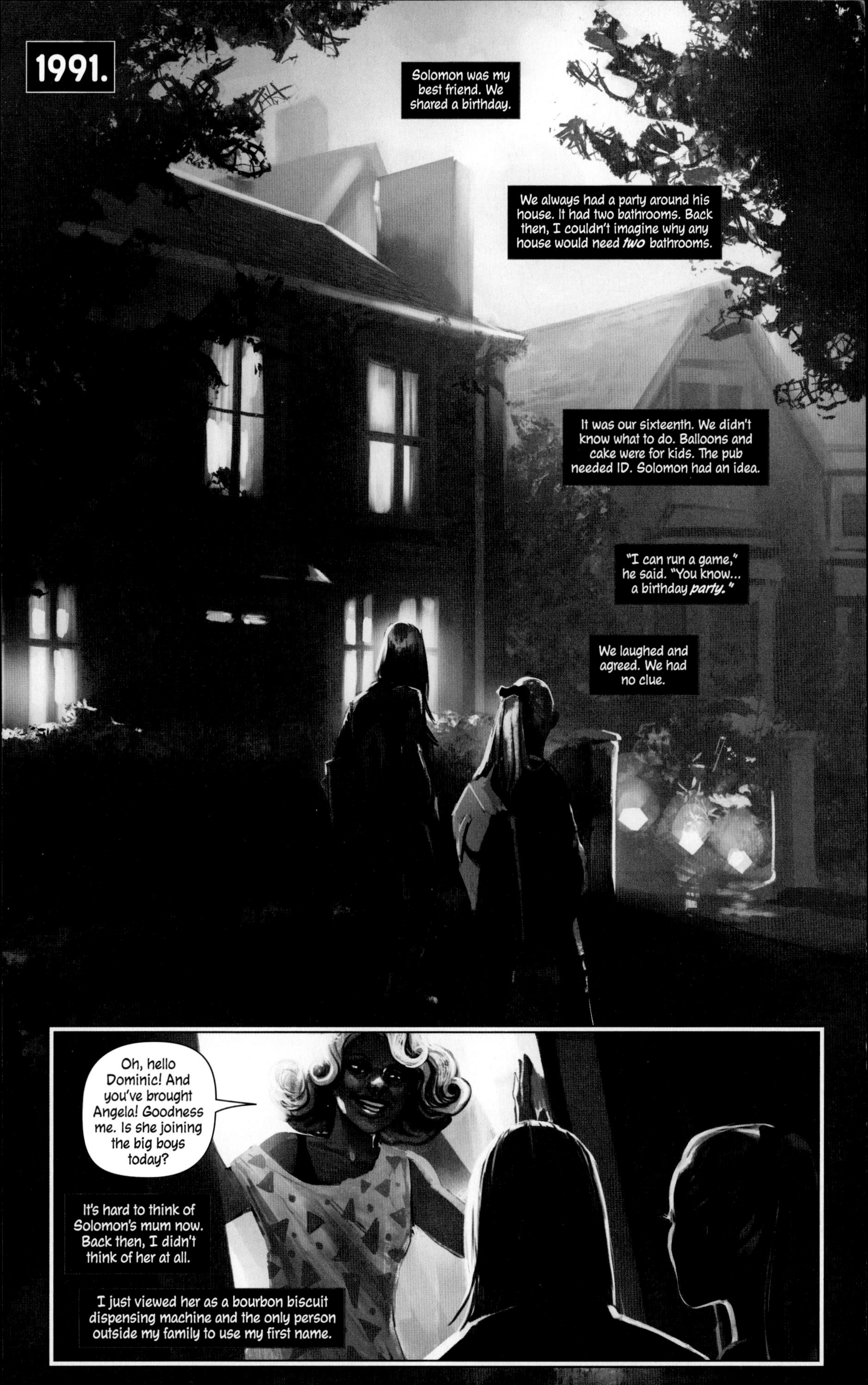
1991.
Solomon was my best friend. We shared a birthday.
We always had a party around his house. It had two bathrooms. Back then, I couldn't imagine why any house would need *two* bathrooms.
It was our sixteenth. We didn't know what to do. Balloons and cake were for kids. The pub needed ID. Solomon had an idea.
"I can run a game," he said. "You know... a birthday *party.*"
We laughed and agreed. We had no clue.
Oh, hello Dominic! And you've brought Angela! Goodness me. Is she joining the big boys today?
It's hard to think of Solomon's mum now. Back then, I didn't think of her at all.
I just viewed her as a bourbon biscuit dispensing machine and the only person outside my family to use my first name.

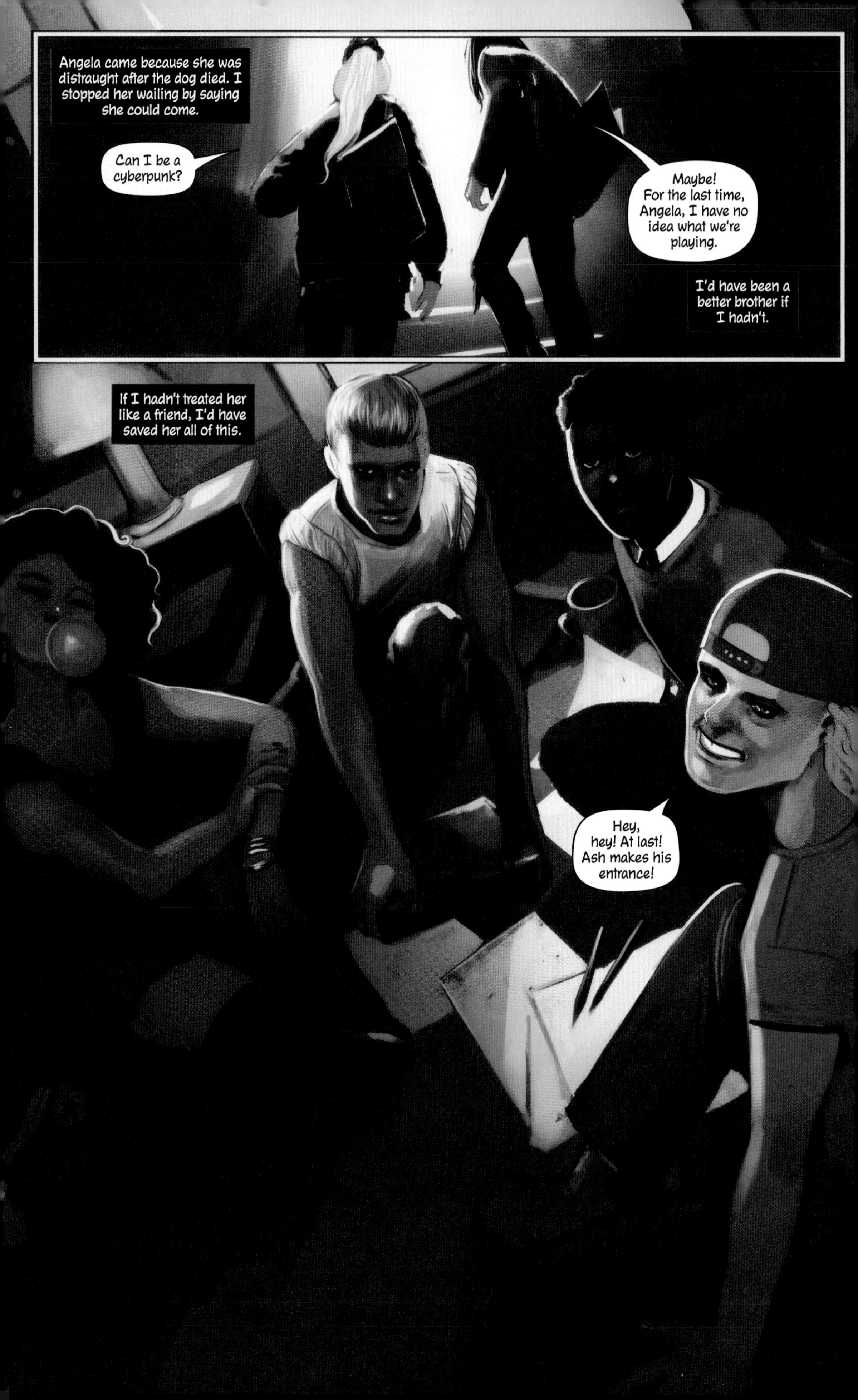
Angela came because she was distraught after the dog died. I stopped her wailing by saying she could come.
Can I be a cyberpunk?
Maybe! For the last time, Angela, I have no idea what we're playing.
I'd have been a better brother if I hadn't.
If I hadn't treated her like a friend, I'd have saved her all of this.
Hey, hey! At last! Ash makes his entrance!

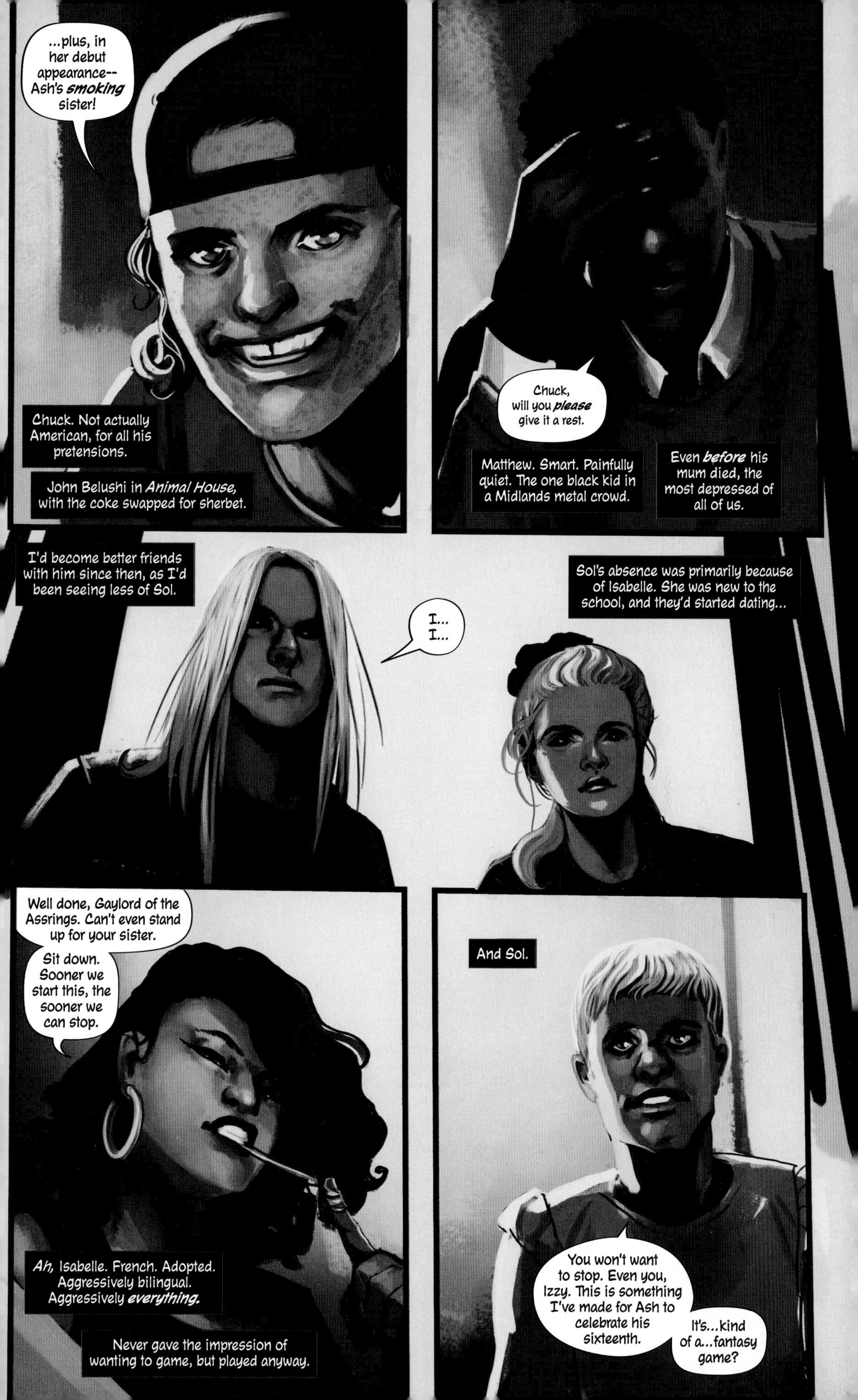
...plus, in her debut appearance-- Ash's *smoking* sister!
Chuck. Not actually American, for all his pretensions.
John Belushi in *Animal House,* with the coke swapped for sherbet.
Chuck, will you *please* give it a rest.
Matthew. Smart. Painfully quiet. The one black kid in a Midlands metal crowd.
Even *before* his mum died, the most depressed of all of us.
I'd become better friends with him since then, as I'd been seeing less of Sol.
I... I...
Sol's absence was primarily because of Isabelle. She was new to the school, and they'd started dating...
Well done, Gaylord of the Assrings. Can't even stand up for your sister.
Sit down. Sooner we start this, the sooner we can stop.
Ah, Isabelle. French. Adopted. Aggressively bilingual. Aggressively *everything.*
Never gave the impression of wanting to game, but played anyway.
And Sol.
You won't want to stop. Even you, Izzy. This is something I've made for Ash to celebrate his sixteenth.
It's...kind of a...fantasy game?

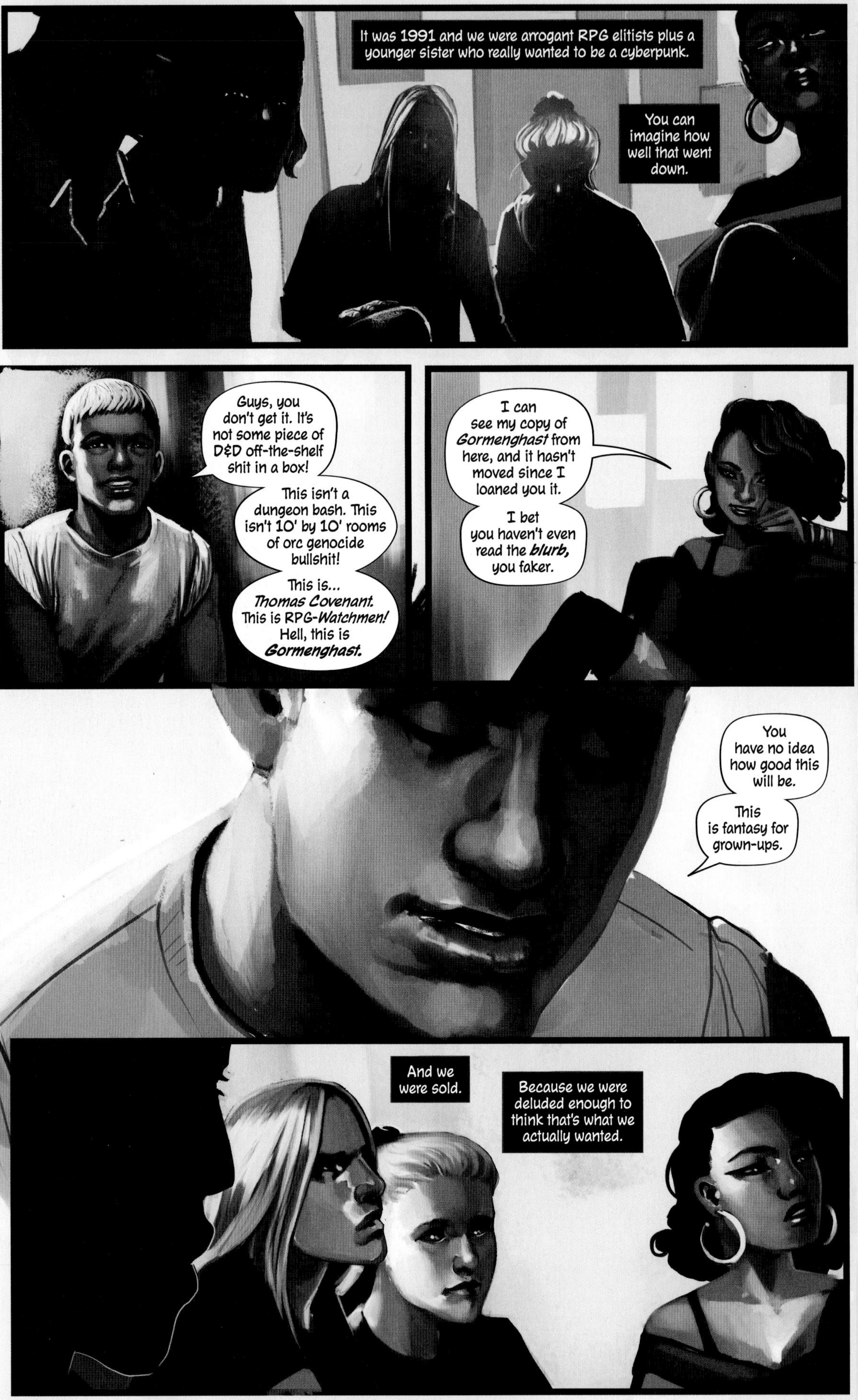
It was 1991 and we were arrogant RPG elitists plus a younger sister who really wanted to be a cyberpunk.
You can imagine how well that went down.
Guys, you don't get it. It's not some piece of D&D off-the-shelf shit in a box!
This isn't a dungeon bash. This isn't 10' by 10' rooms of orc genocide bullshit!
This is... *Thomas Covenant.* This is RPG-*Watchmen!* Hell, this is ***Gormenghast.***
I can see my copy of *Gormenghast* from here, and it hasn't moved since I loaned you it.
I bet you haven't even read the ***blurb,*** you faker.
You have no idea how good this will be.
This is fantasy for grown-ups.
And we were sold.
Because we were deluded enough to think that's what we actually wanted.

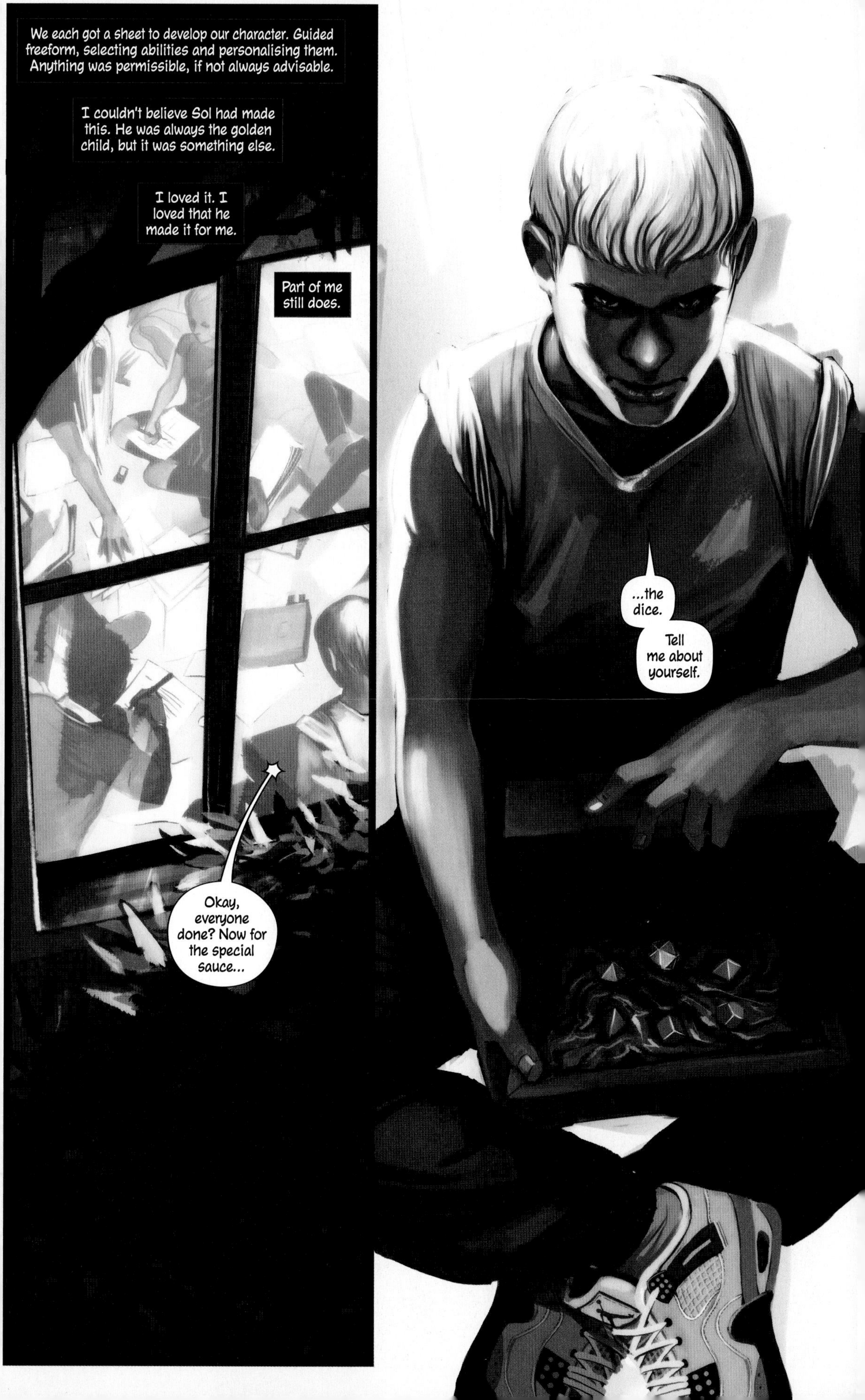
We each got a sheet to develop our character. Guided freeform, selecting abilities and personalising them. Anything was permissible, if not always advisable.
I couldn't believe Sol had made this. He was always the golden child, but it was something else.
I loved it. I loved that he made it for me.
Part of me still does.
Okay, everyone done? Now for the special sauce...
...the dice.
Tell me about yourself.

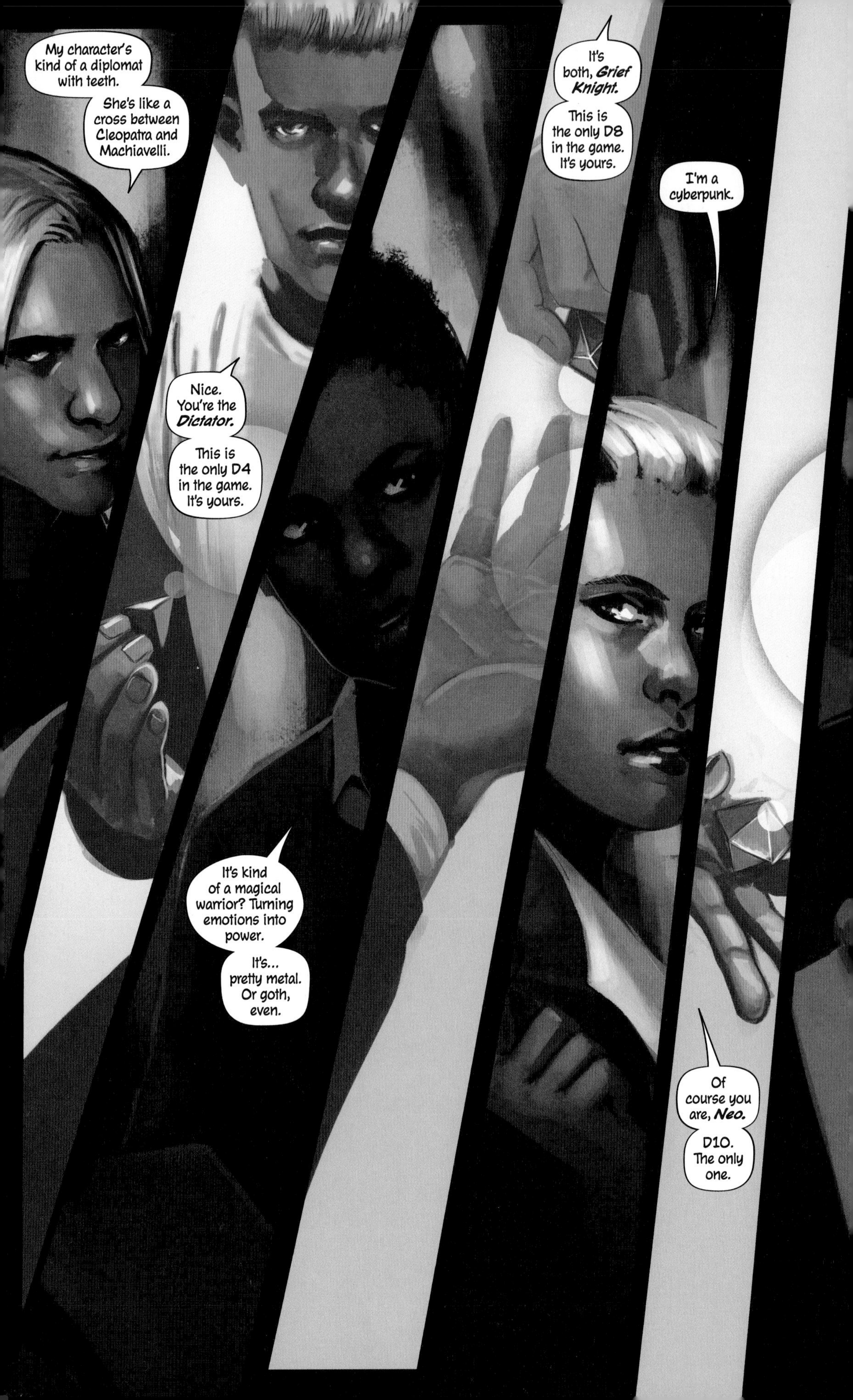
My character's kind of a diplomat with teeth.
She's like a cross between Cleopatra and Machiavelli.
Nice. You're the *Dictator.*
This is the only D4 in the game. It's yours.
It's kind of a magical warrior? Turning emotions into power.
It's... pretty metal. Or goth, even.
It's both, *Grief Knight.*
This is the only D8 in the game. It's yours.
I'm a cyberpunk.
Of course you are, *Neo.*
D10. The only one.

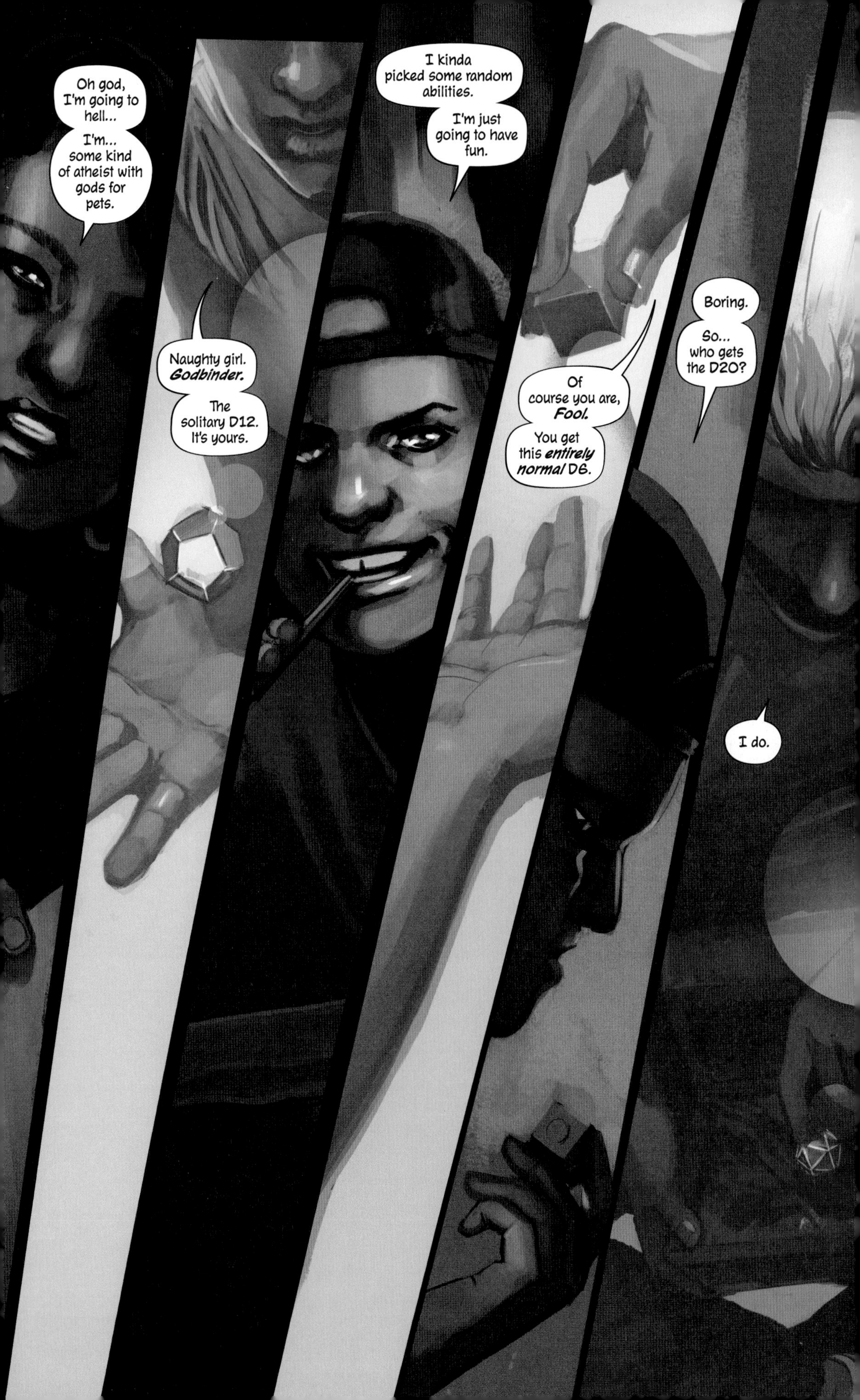

Oh god, I'm going to hell...
I'm... some kind of atheist with gods for pets.
Naughty girl. *Godbinder.*
The solitary D12. It's yours.
I kinda picked some random abilities.
I'm just going to have fun.
Of course you are, *Fool.*
You get this *entirely normal* D6.
Boring.
So... who gets the D20?
I do.

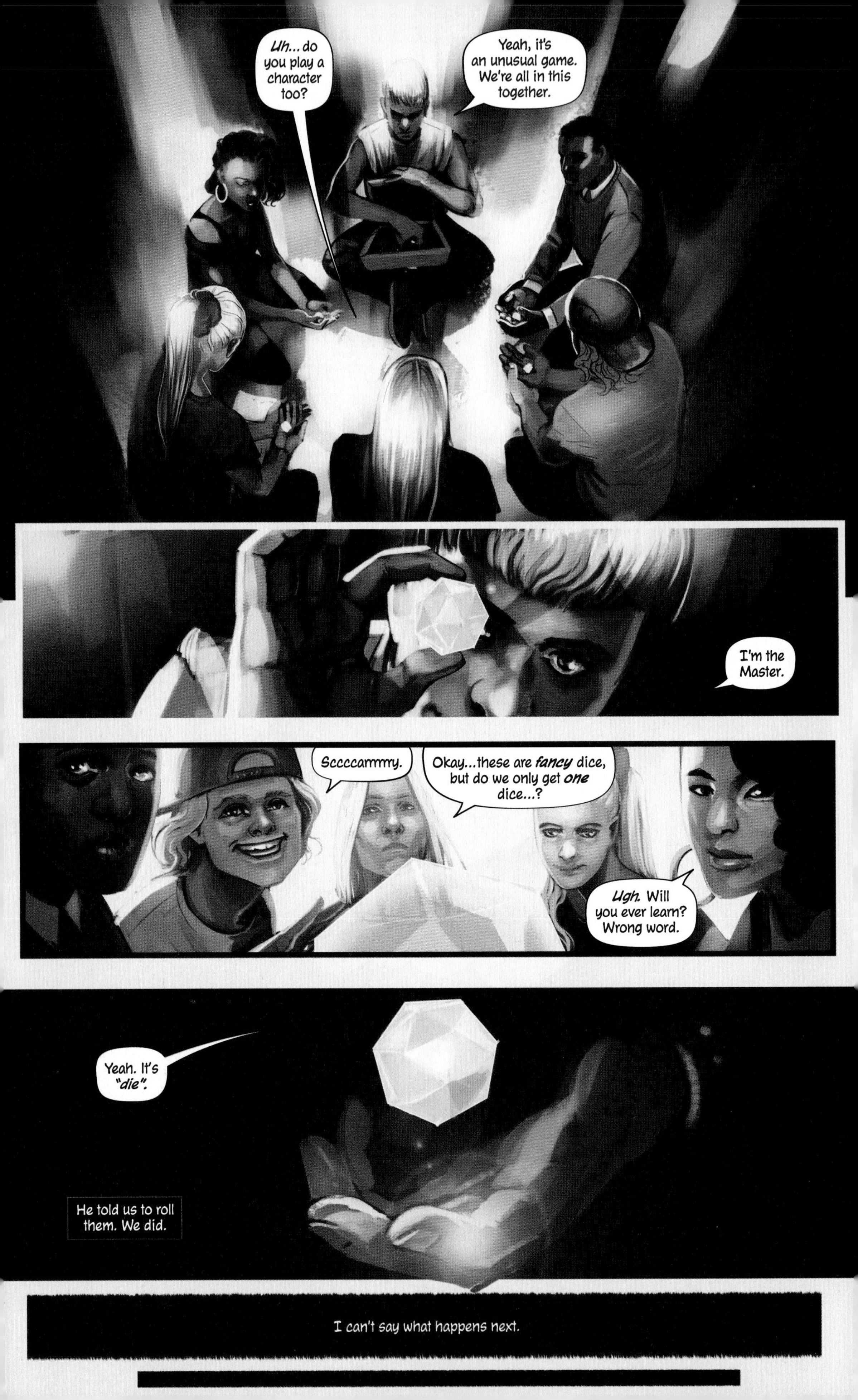
Uh... do you play a character too?
Yeah, it's an unusual game. We're all in this together.
I'm the Master.
Scccarrrry.
Okay...these are fancy dice, but do we only get one dice...?
Ugh. Will you ever learn? Wrong word.
Yeah. It's "die".
He told us to roll them. We did.
I can't say what happens next.
[redacted]

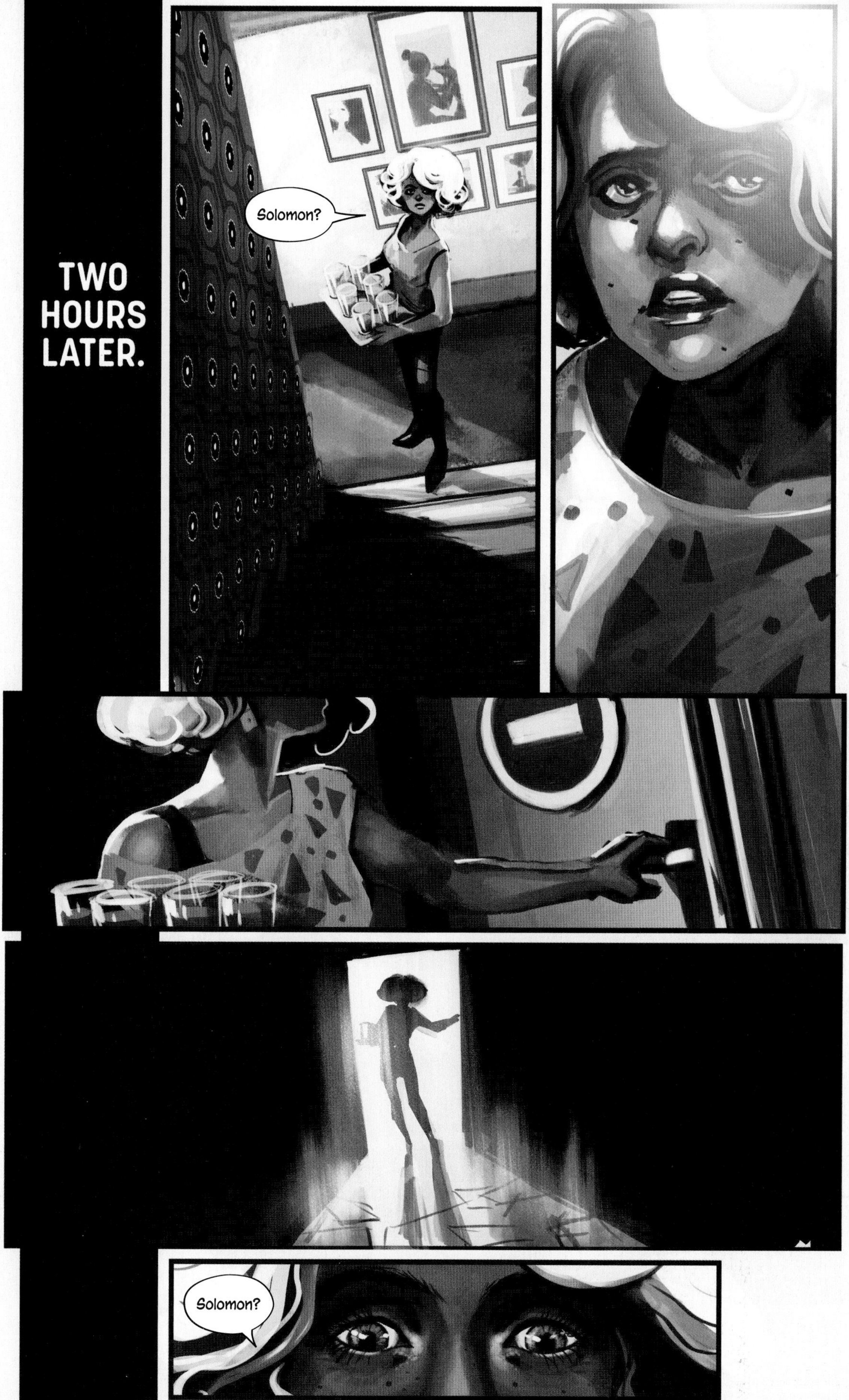
TWO HOURS LATER.
Solomon?
Solomon?

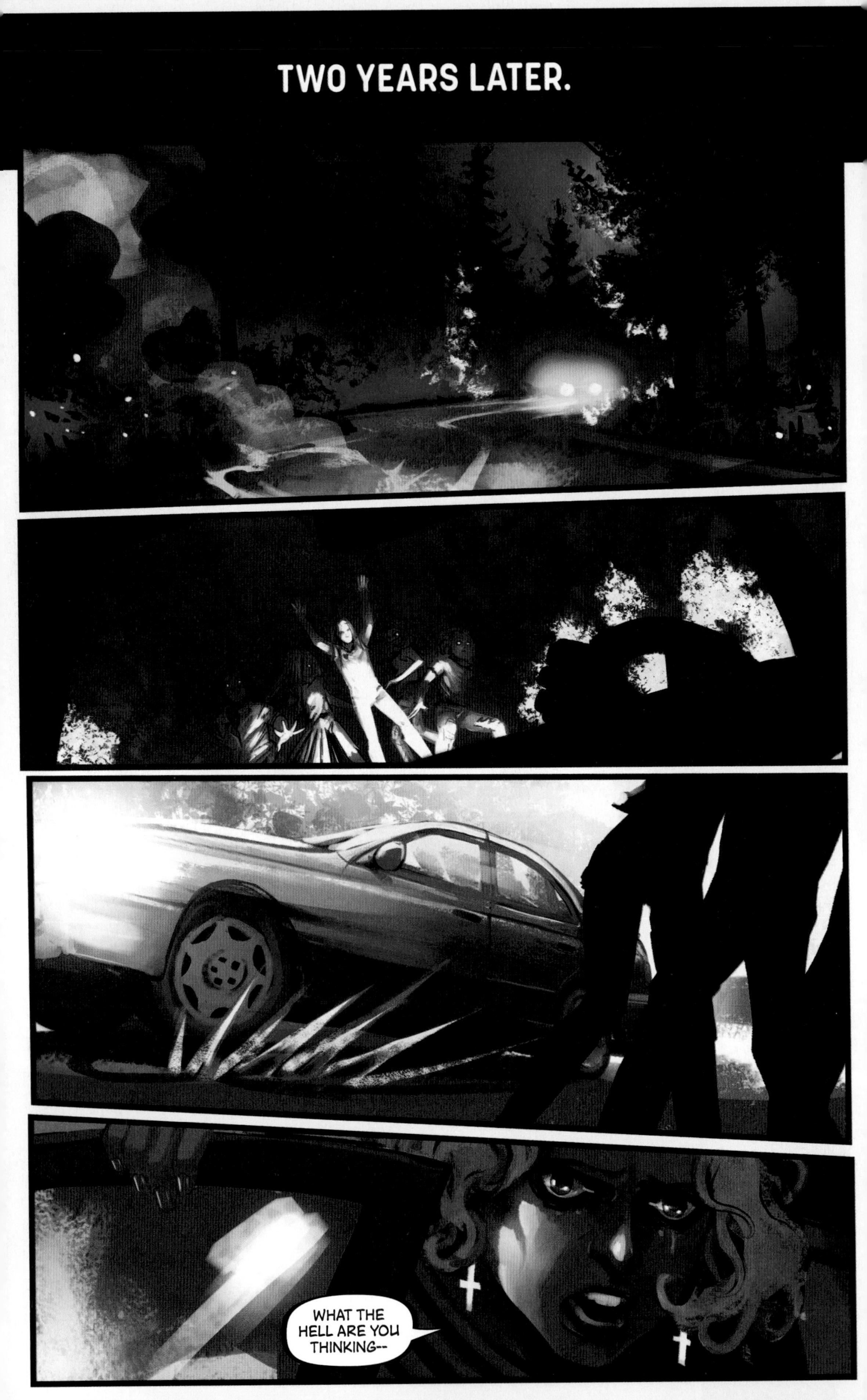
TWO YEARS LATER.
WHAT THE HELL ARE YOU THINKING--

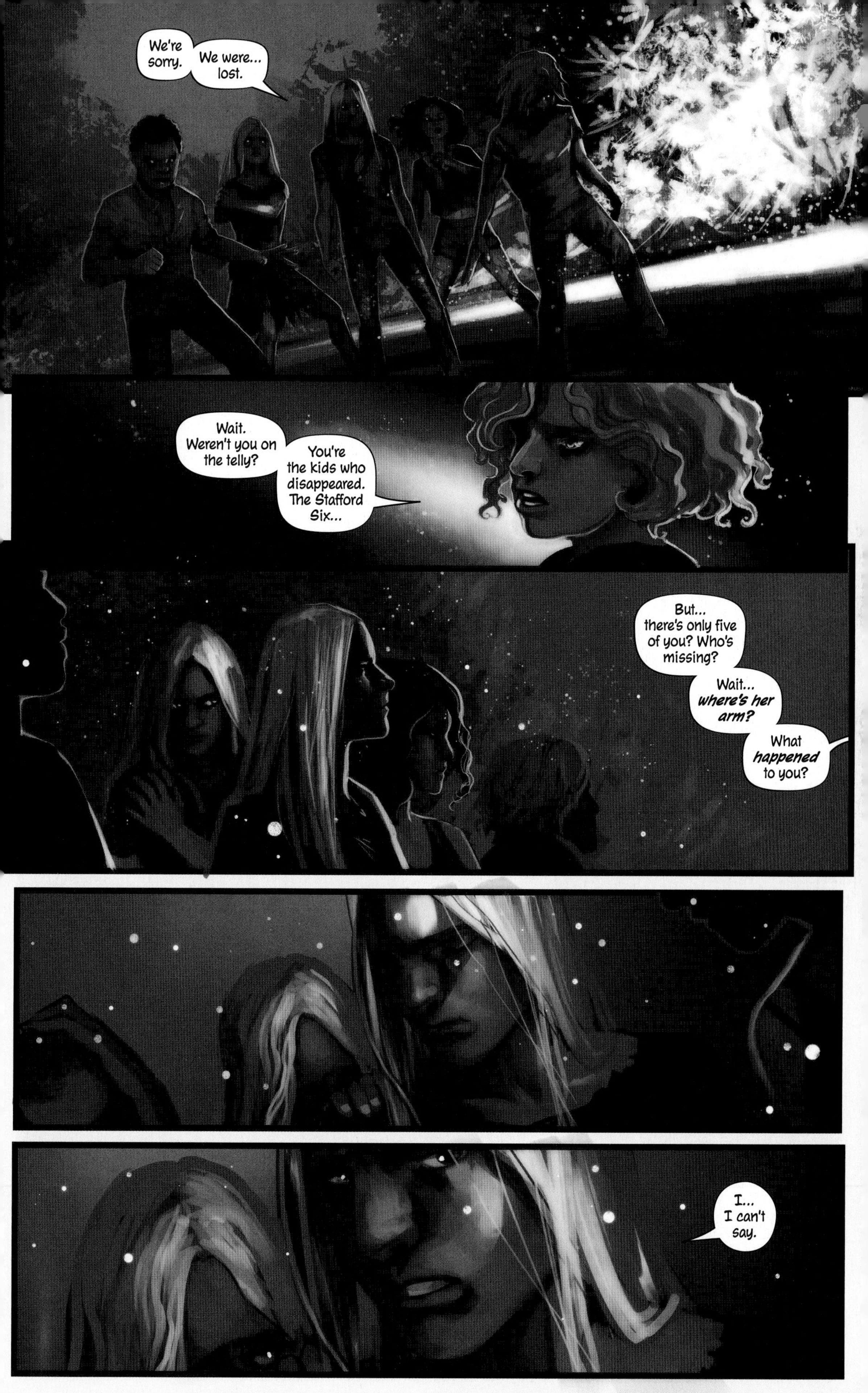
We're sorry.
We were... lost.
Wait. Weren't you on the telly?
You're the kids who disappeared. The Stafford Six...
But... there's only five of you? Who's missing?
Wait... *where's her arm?*
What *happened* to you?
I... I can't say.

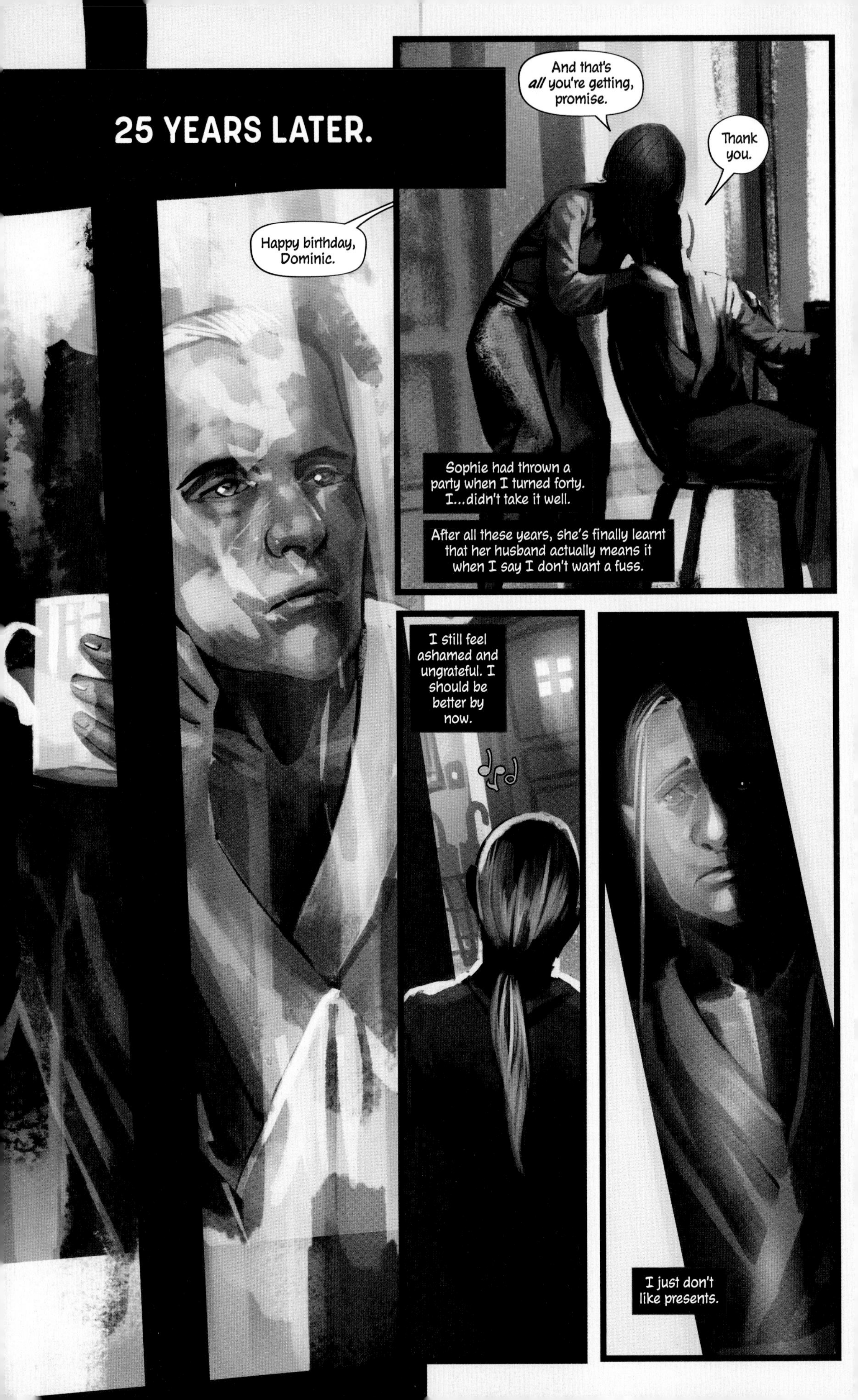
25 YEARS LATER.
Happy birthday, Dominic.
And that's *all* you're getting, promise.
Thank you.
Sophie had thrown a party when I turned forty. I...didn't take it well.
After all these years, she's finally learnt that her husband actually means it when I say I don't want a fuss.
I still feel ashamed and ungrateful. I should be better by now.
I just don't like presents.

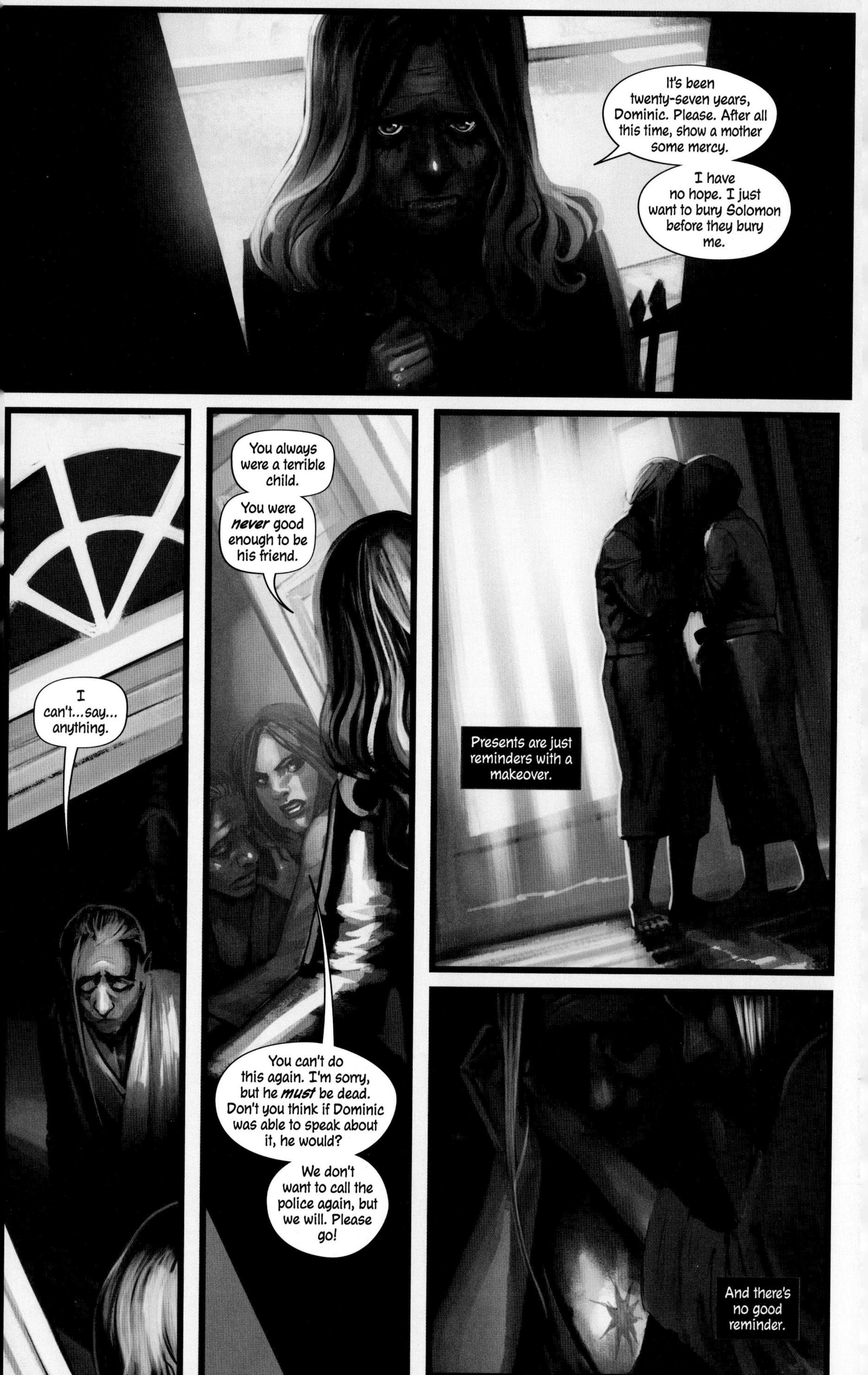
It's been twenty-seven years, Dominic. Please. After all this time, show a mother some mercy.
I have no hope. I just want to bury Solomon before they bury me.
I can't...say... anything.
You always were a terrible child.
You were never good enough to be his friend.
You can't do this again. I'm sorry, but he must be dead. Don't you think if Dominic was able to speak about it, he would?
We don't want to call the police again, but we will. Please go!
Presents are just reminders with a makeover.
And there's no good reminder.

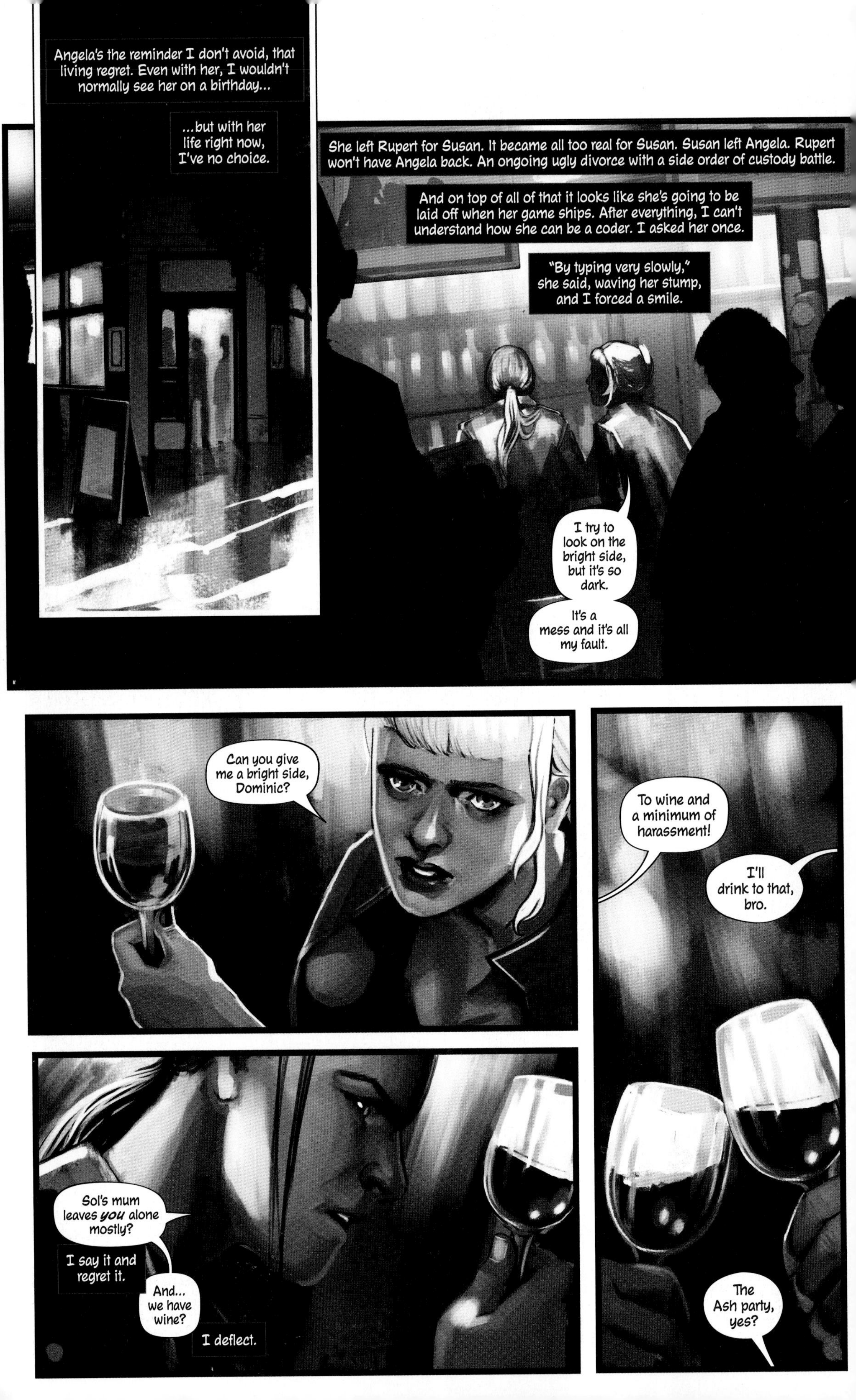
Angela's the reminder I don't avoid, that living regret. Even with her, I wouldn't normally see her on a birthday...
...but with her life right now, I've no choice.
She left Rupert for Susan. It became all too real for Susan. Susan left Angela. Rupert won't have Angela back. An ongoing ugly divorce with a side order of custody battle.
And on top of all of that it looks like she's going to be laid off when her game ships. After everything, I can't understand how she can be a coder. I asked her once.
"By typing very slowly," she said, waving her stump, and I forced a smile.
I try to look on the bright side, but it's so dark.
It's a mess and it's all my fault.
Can you give me a bright side, Dominic?
Sol's mum leaves *you* alone mostly?
I say it and regret it.
And... we have wine?
I deflect.
To wine and a minimum of harassment!
I'll drink to that, bro.
The Ash party, yes?

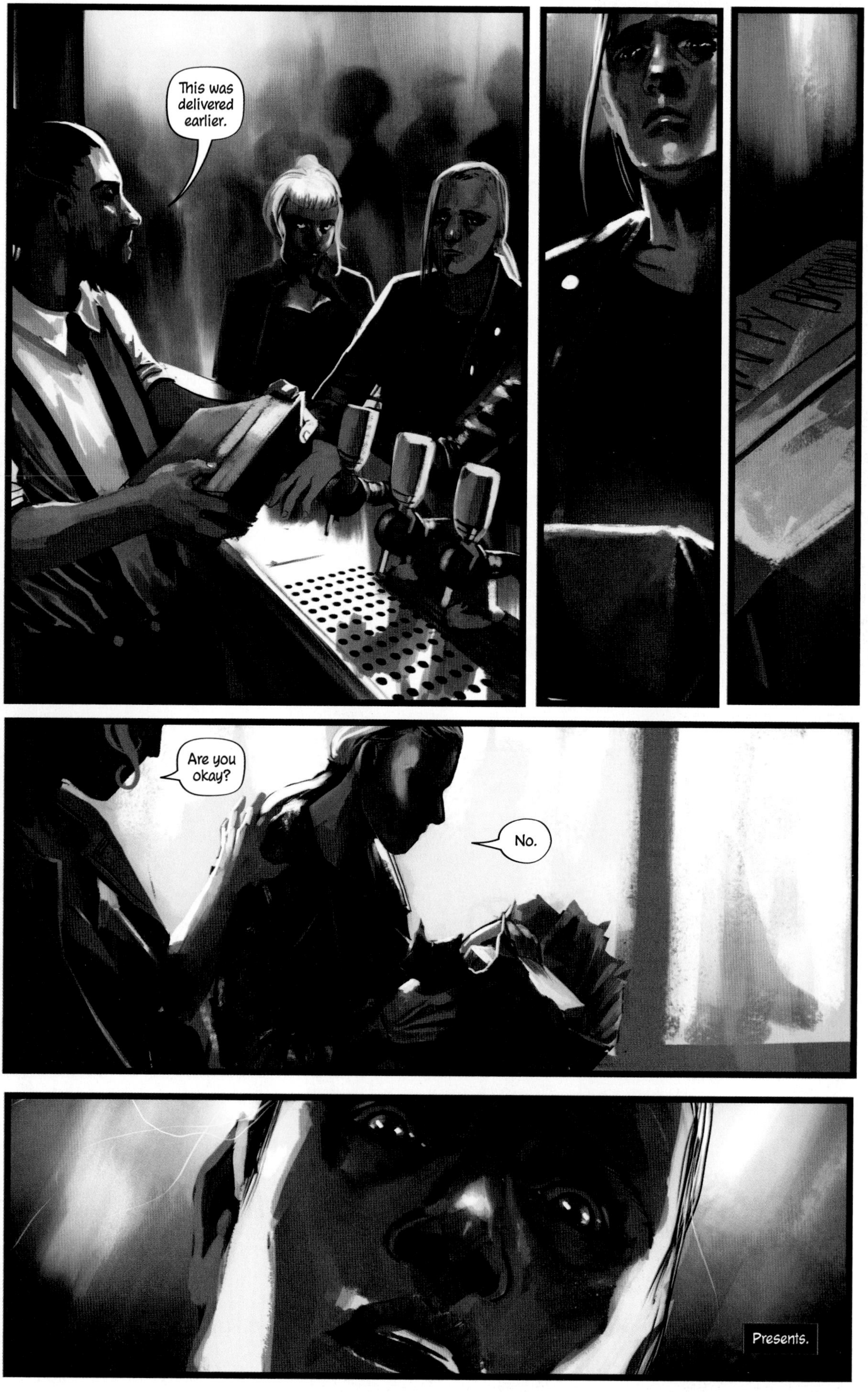
This was delivered earlier.
Are you okay?
No.
Presents.

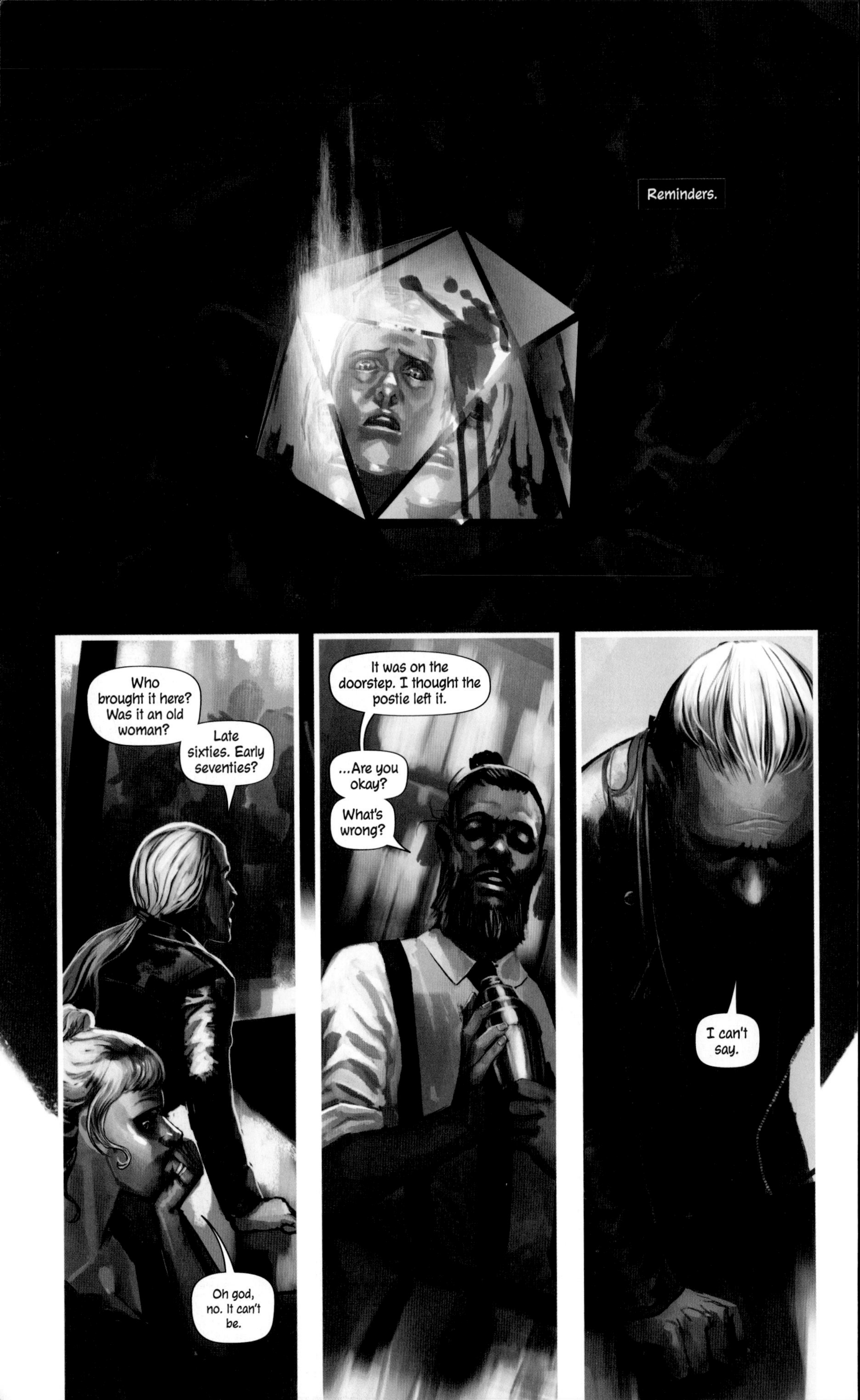
Reminders.
Who brought it here? Was it an old woman?
Late sixties. Early seventies?
Oh god, no. It can't be.
It was on the doorstep. I thought the postie left it.
...Are you okay?
What's wrong?
I can't say.

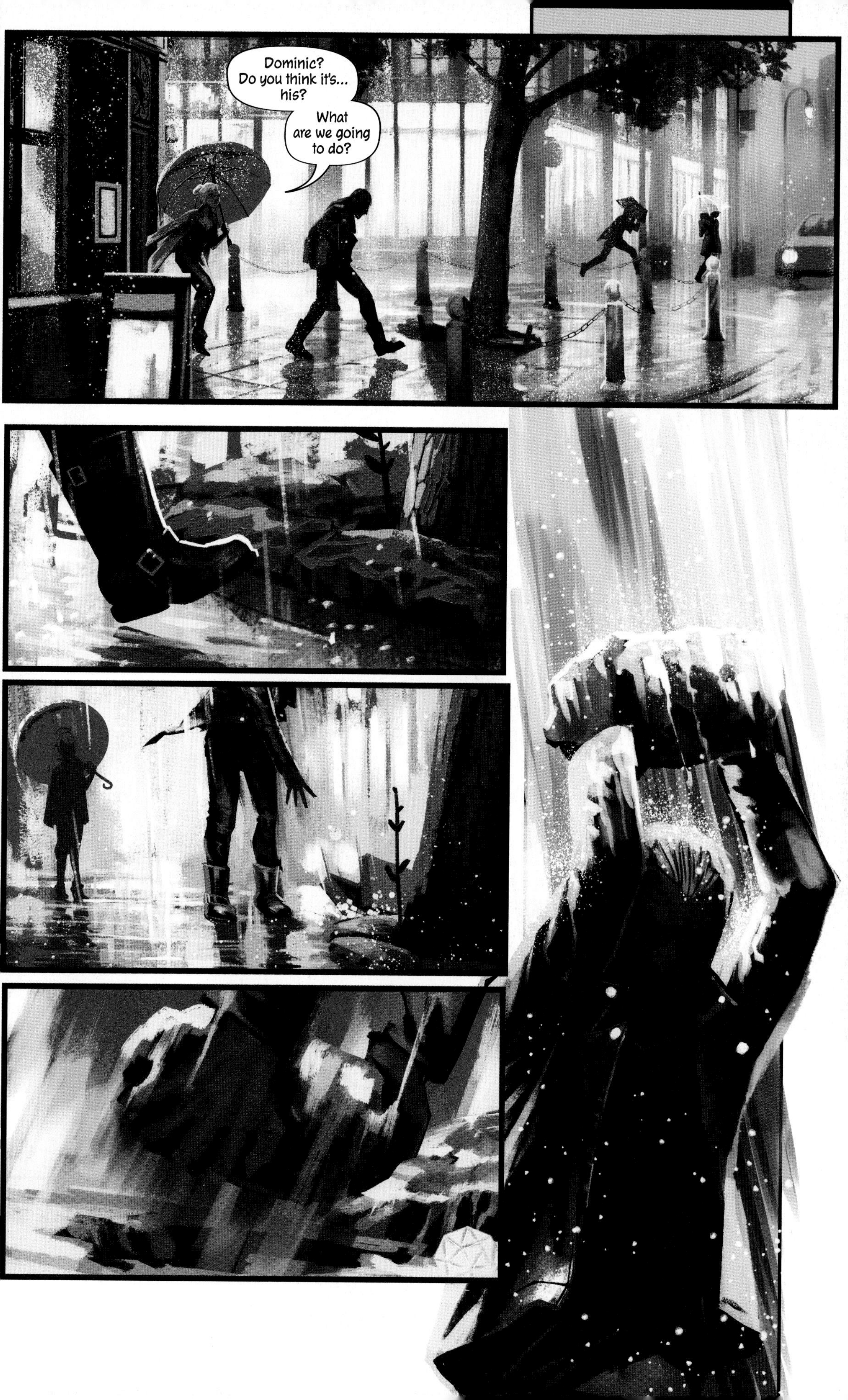
Dominic? Do you think it's... his?
What are we going to do?

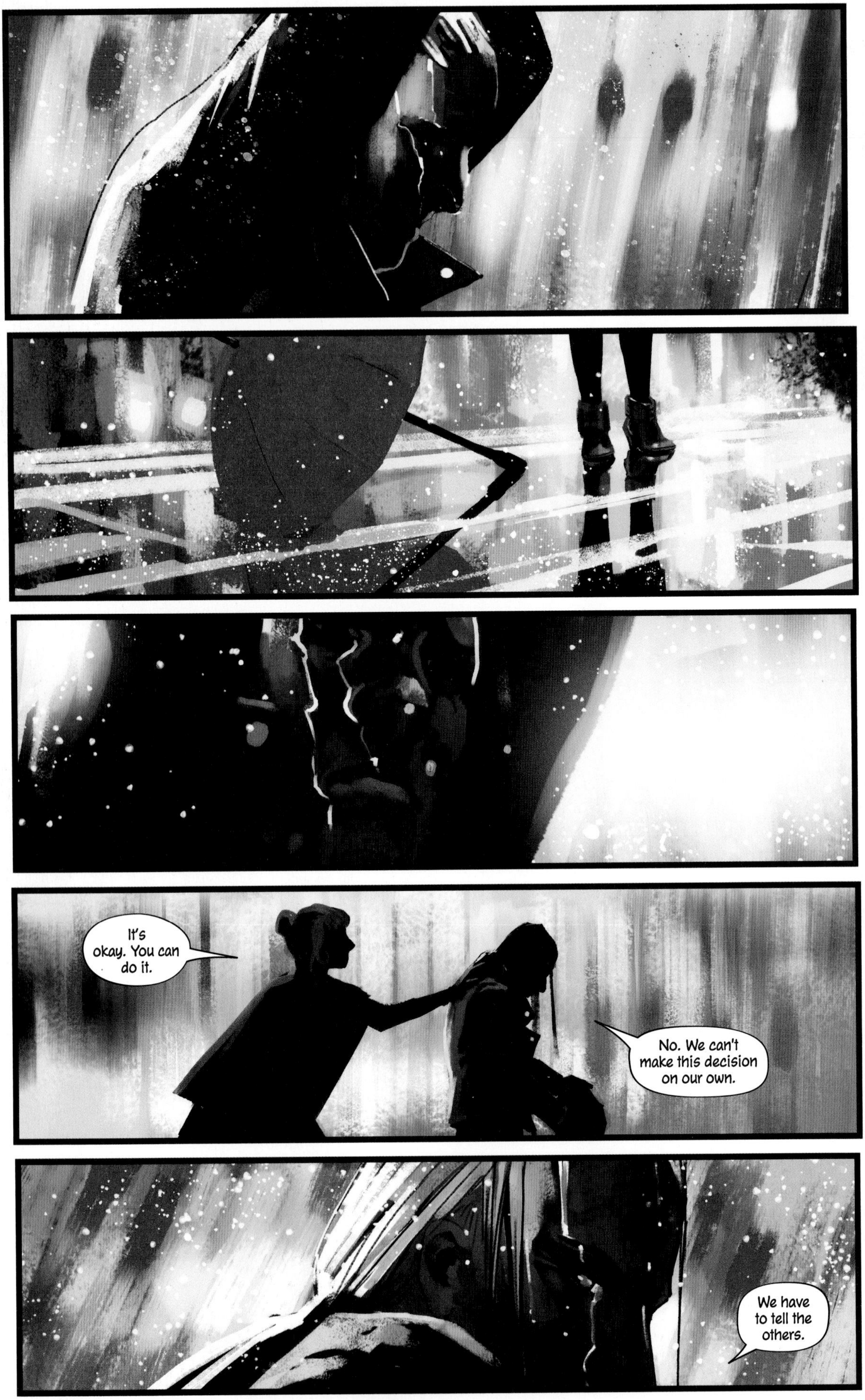
It's okay. You can do it.
No. We can't make this decision on our own.
We have to tell the others.

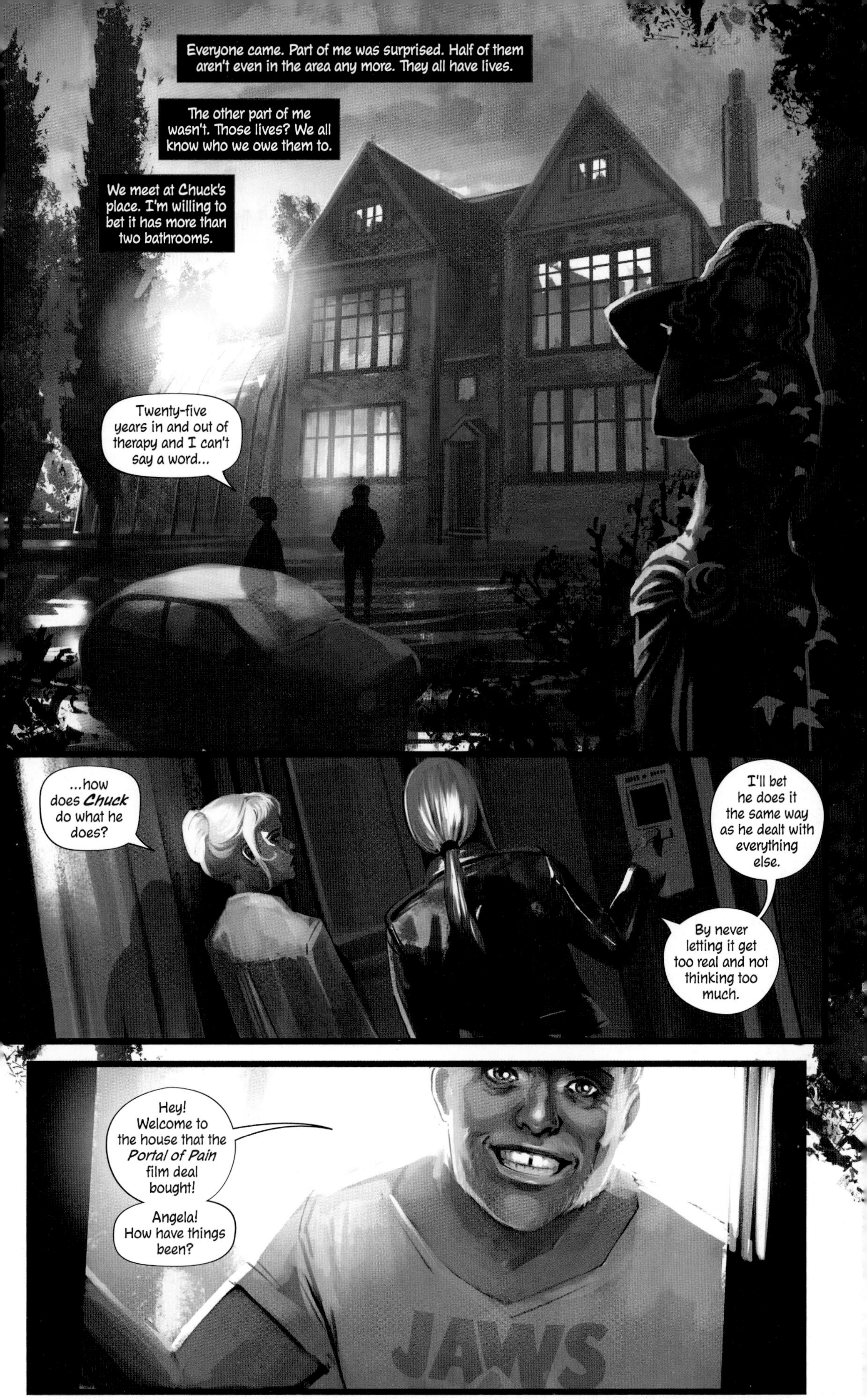
Everyone came. Part of me was surprised. Half of them aren't even in the area any more. They all have lives.
The other part of me wasn't. Those lives? We all know who we owe them to.
We meet at Chuck's place. I'm willing to bet it has more than two bathrooms.
Twenty-five years in and out of therapy and I can't say a word...
...how does *Chuck* do what he does?
I'll bet he does it the same way as he dealt with everything else.
By never letting it get too real and not thinking too much.
Hey! Welcome to the house that the *Portal of Pain* film deal bought!
Angela! How have things been?
JAWS

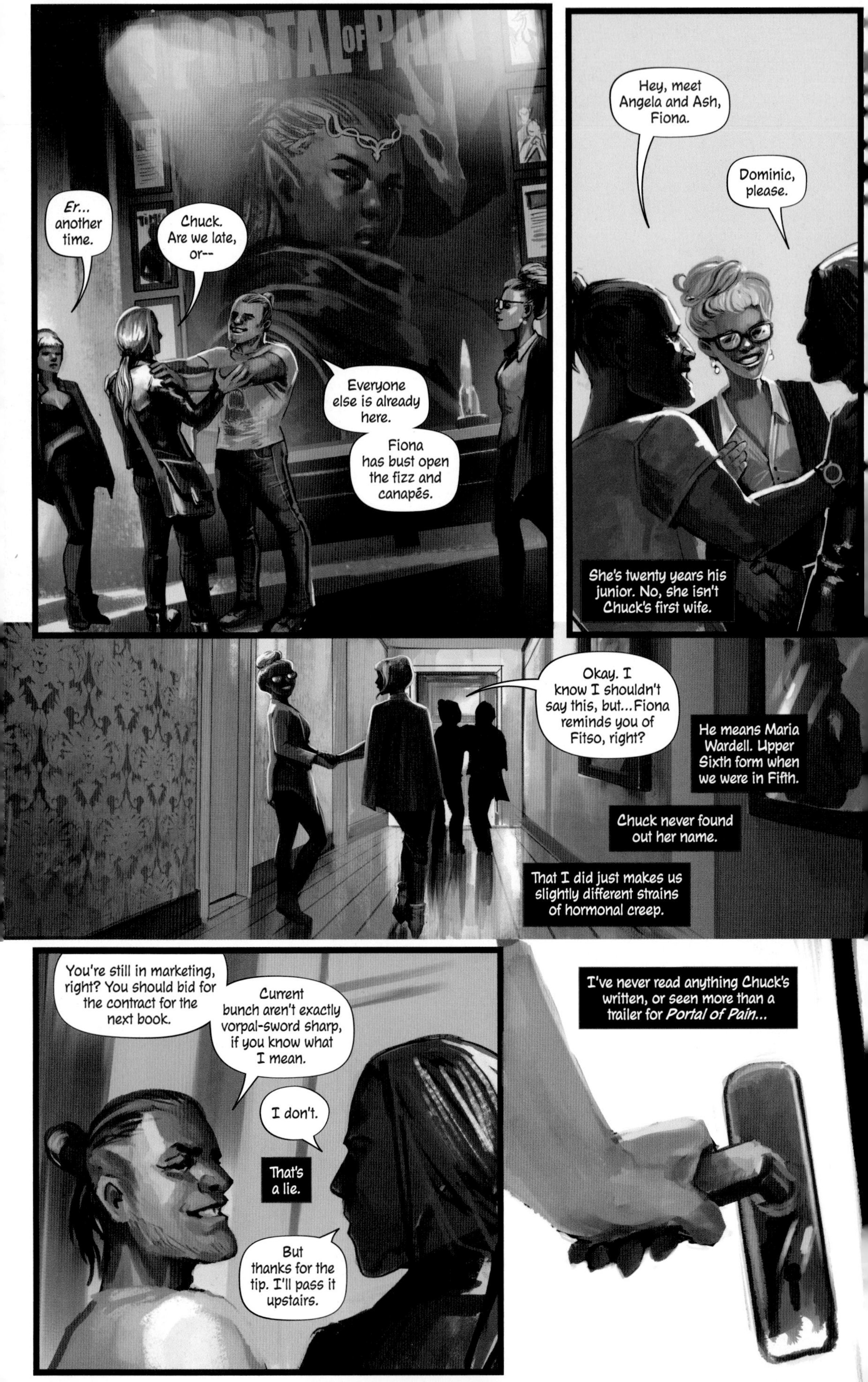
PORTAL OF PAIN
Er... another time.
Chuck. Are we late, or--
Everyone else is already here.
Fiona has bust open the fizz and canapés.
Hey, meet Angela and Ash, Fiona.
Dominic, please.
She's twenty years his junior. No, she isn't Chuck's first wife.
Okay. I know I shouldn't say this, but...Fiona reminds you of Fitso, right?
He means Maria Wardell. Upper Sixth form when we were in Fifth.
Chuck never found out her name.
That I did just makes us slightly different strains of hormonal creep.
You're still in marketing, right? You should bid for the contract for the next book.
Current bunch aren't exactly vorpal-sword sharp, if you know what I mean.
I don't.
That's a lie.
But thanks for the tip. I'll pass it upstairs.
I've never read anything Chuck's written, or seen more than a trailer for *Portal of Pain*...

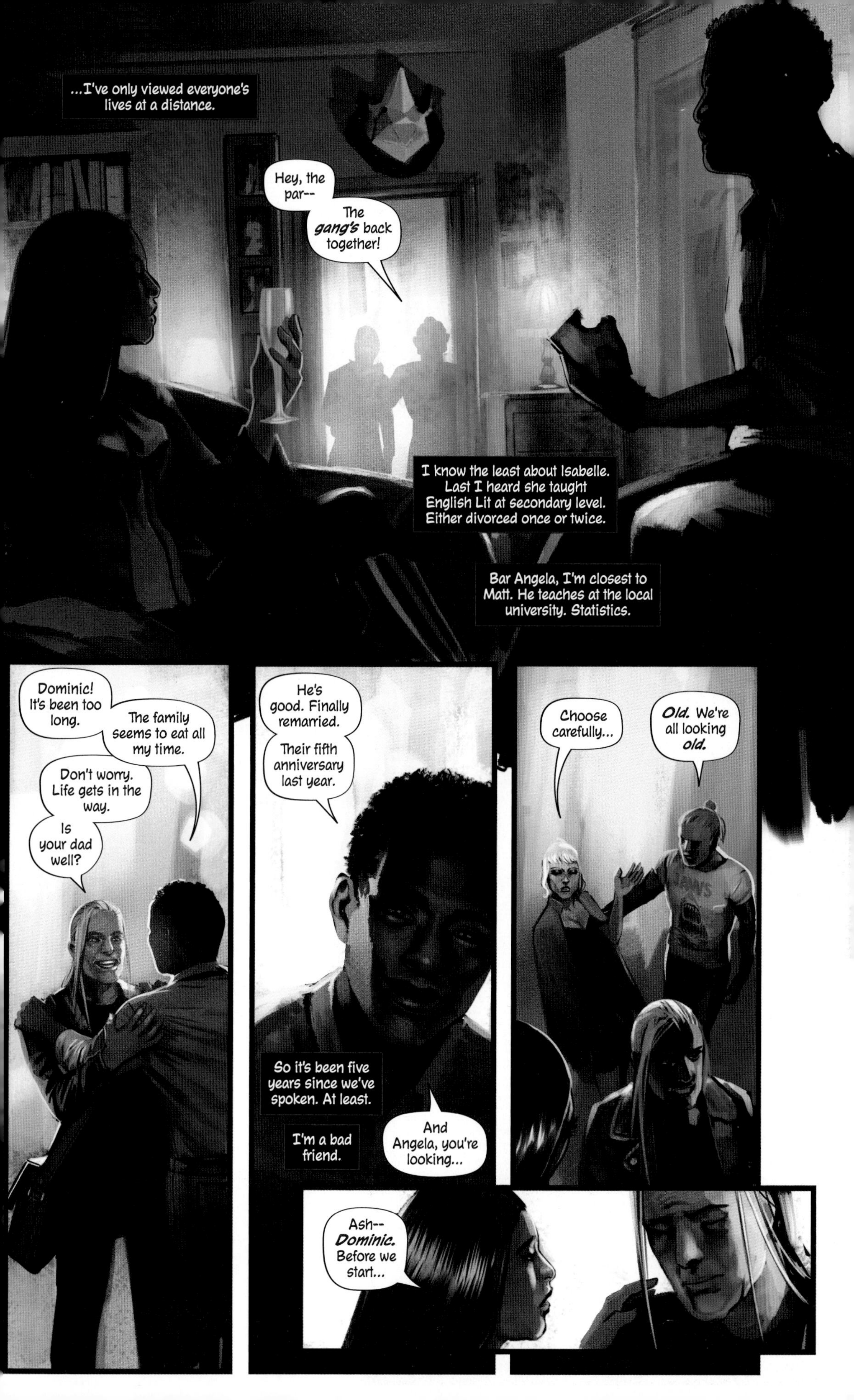
...I've only viewed everyone's lives at a distance.
Hey, the par--
The *gang's* back together!
I know the least about Isabelle. Last I heard she taught English Lit at secondary level. Either divorced once or twice.
Bar Angela, I'm closest to Matt. He teaches at the local university. Statistics.
Dominic! It's been too long.
The family seems to eat all my time.
Don't worry. Life gets in the way.
Is your dad well?
He's good. Finally remarried.
Their fifth anniversary last year.
So it's been five years since we've spoken. At least.
I'm a bad friend.
And Angela, you're looking...
Choose carefully...
Old. We're all looking *old.*
Ash-- *Dominic.* Before we start...

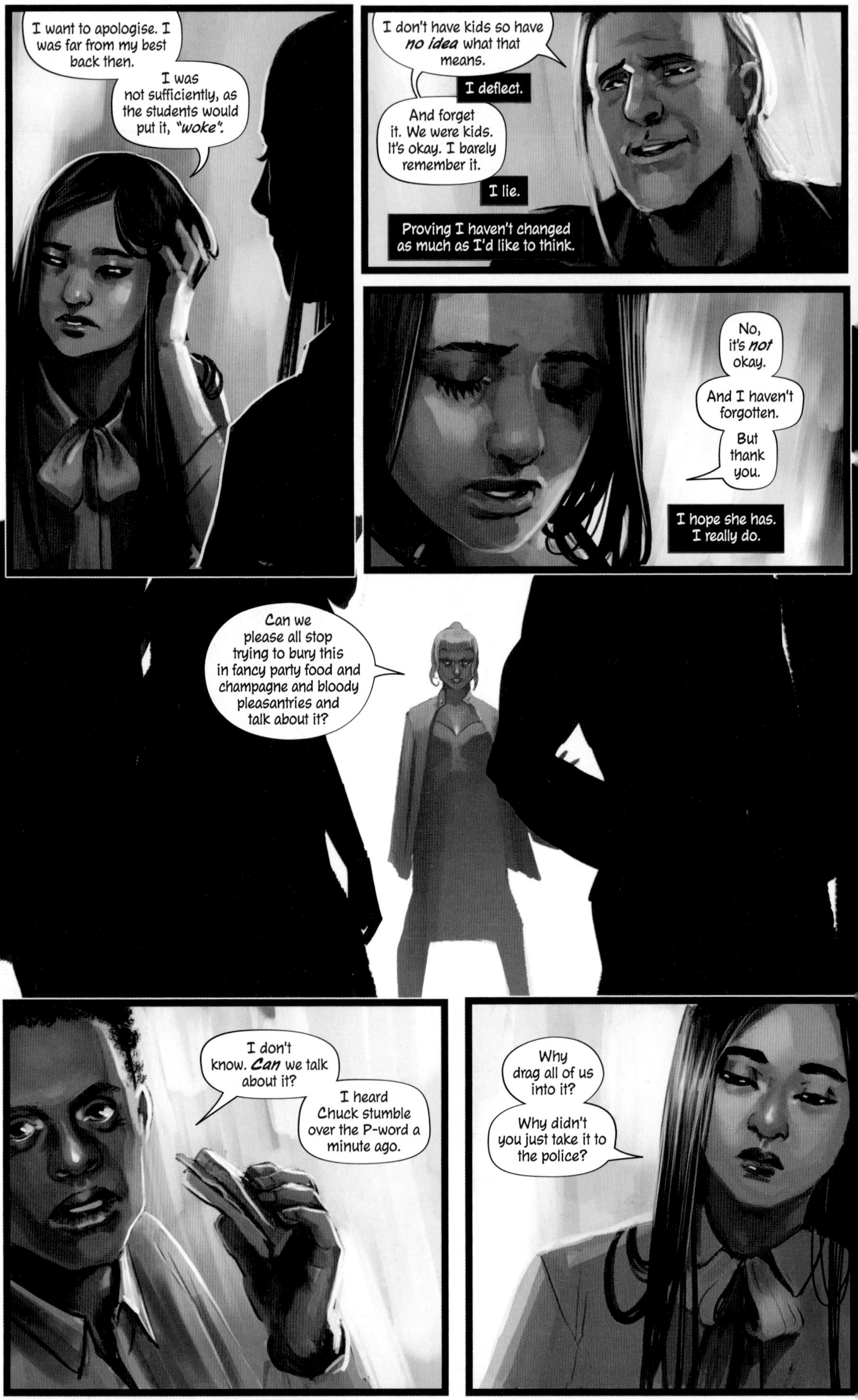

I want to apologise. I was far from my best back then.
I was not sufficiently, as the students would put it, *"woke".*
I don't have kids so have ***no idea*** what that means.
I deflect.
And forget it. We were kids. It's okay. I barely remember it.
I lie.
Proving I haven't changed as much as I'd like to think.
No, it's ***not*** okay.
And I haven't forgotten.
But thank you.
I hope she has. I really do.
Can we please all stop trying to bury this in fancy party food and champagne and bloody pleasantries and talk about it?
I don't know. ***Can*** we talk about it?
I heard Chuck stumble over the P-word a minute ago.
Why drag all of us into it?
Why didn't you just take it to the police?

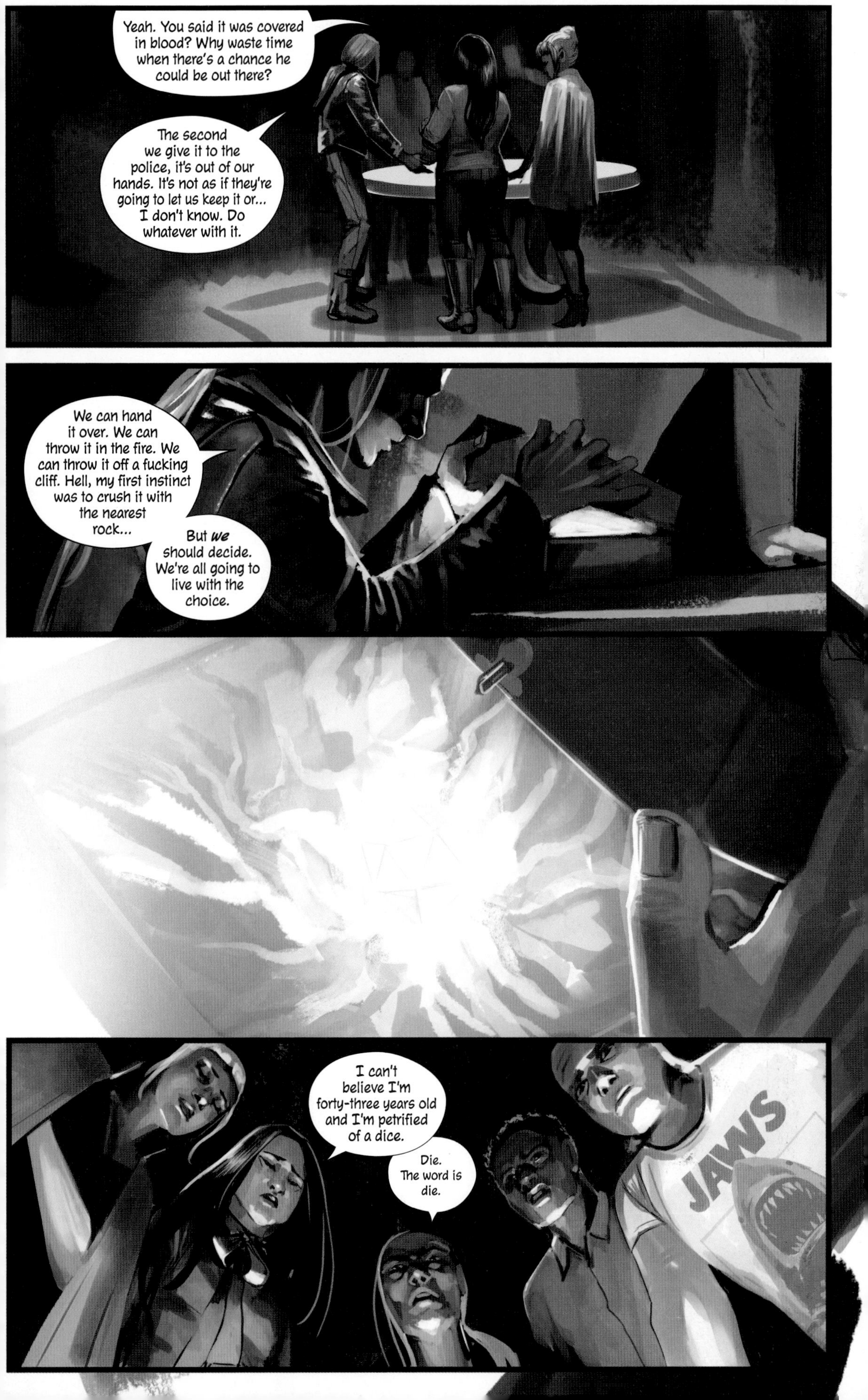
Yeah. You said it was covered in blood? Why waste time when there's a chance he could be out there?
The second we give it to the police, it's out of our hands. It's not as if they're going to let us keep it or... I don't know. Do whatever with it.
We can hand it over. We can throw it in the fire. We can throw it off a fucking cliff. Hell, my first instinct was to crush it with the nearest rock...
But *we* should decide. We're all going to live with the choice.
I can't believe I'm forty-three years old and I'm petrified of a dice.
Die. The word is die.
JAWS

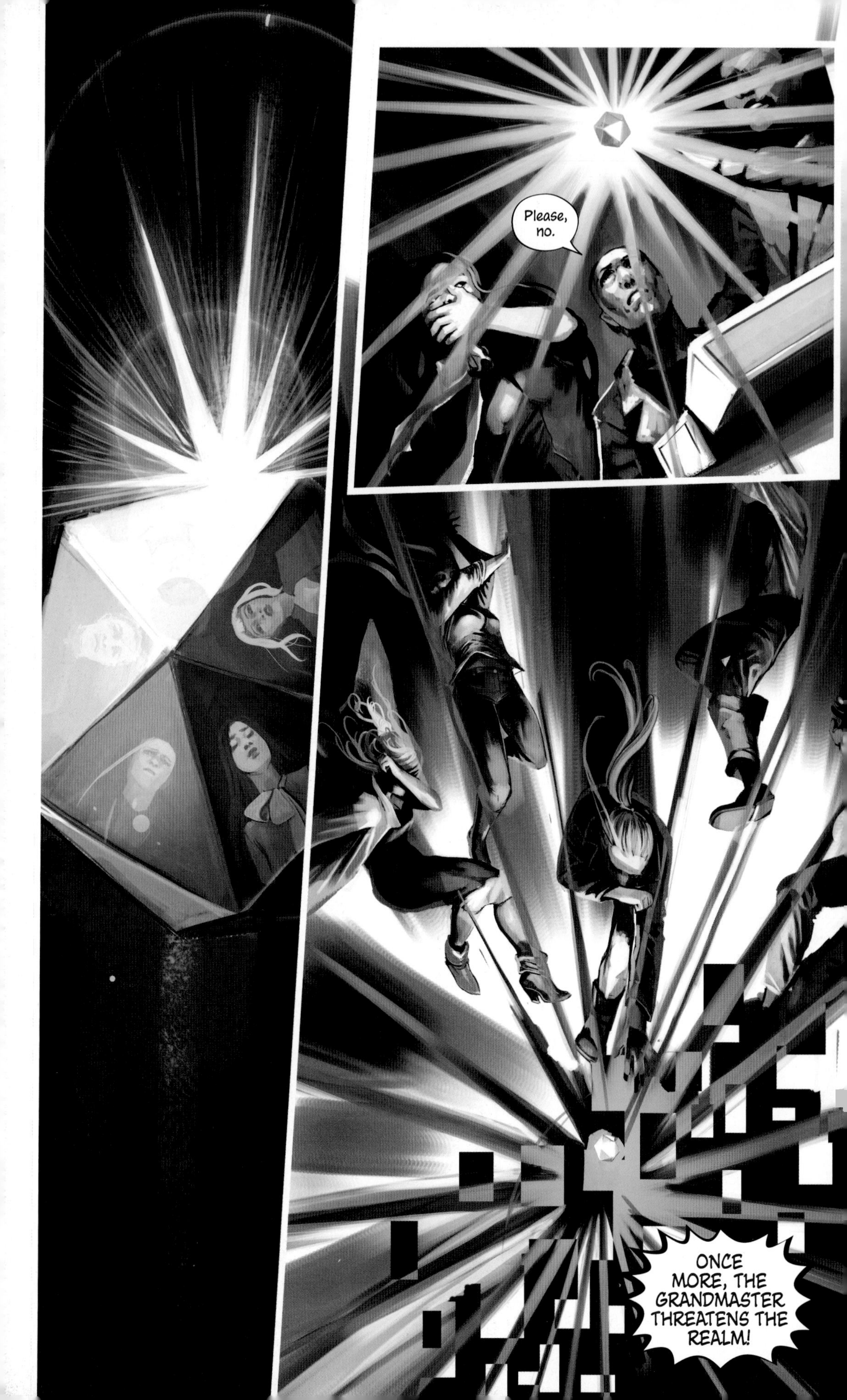
Please, no.
ONCE MORE, THE GRANDMASTER THREATENS THE REALM!

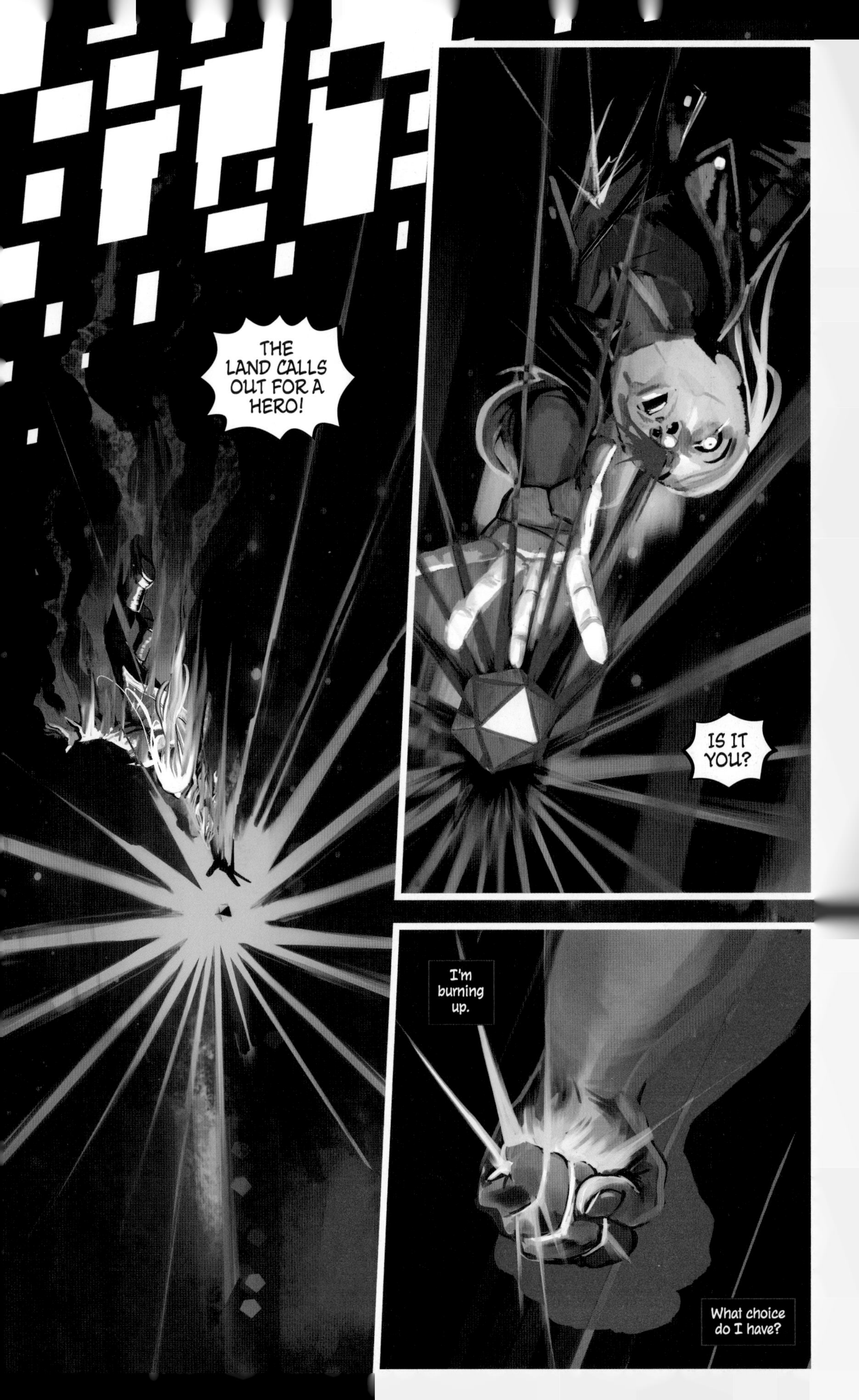
THE LAND CALLS OUT FOR A HERO!
IS IT YOU?
I'm burning up.
What choice do I have?

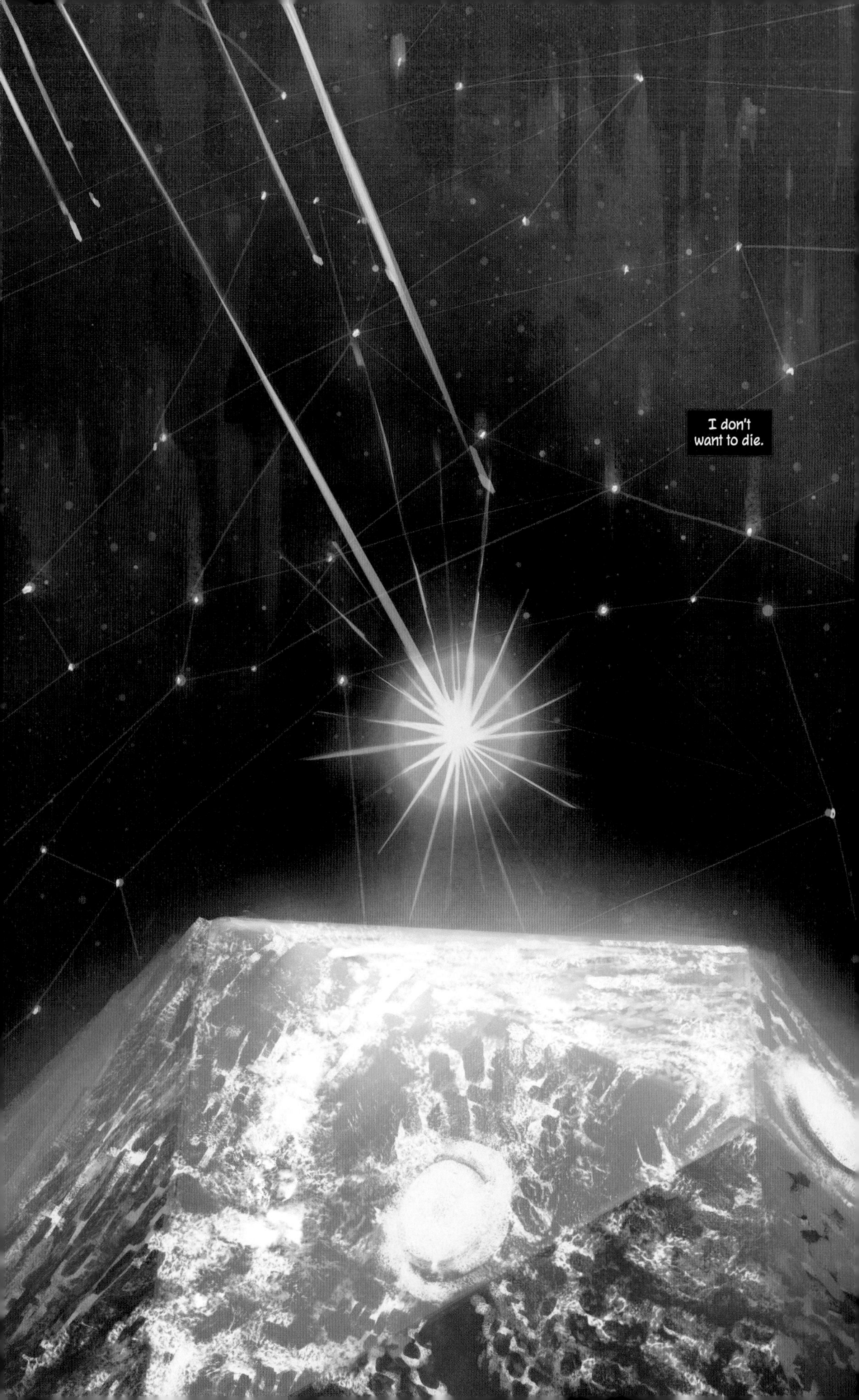
I don't want to die.

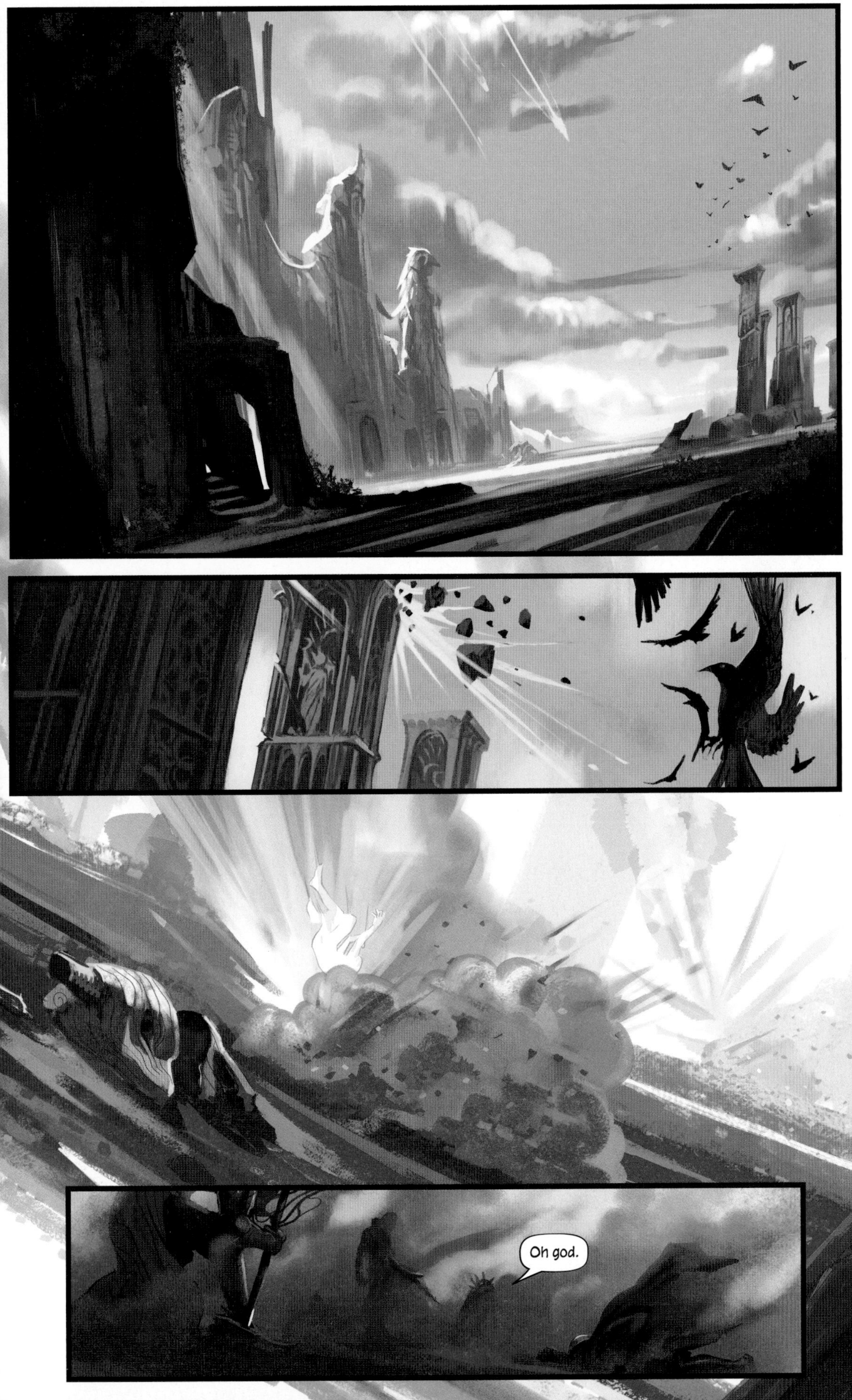
Oh god.

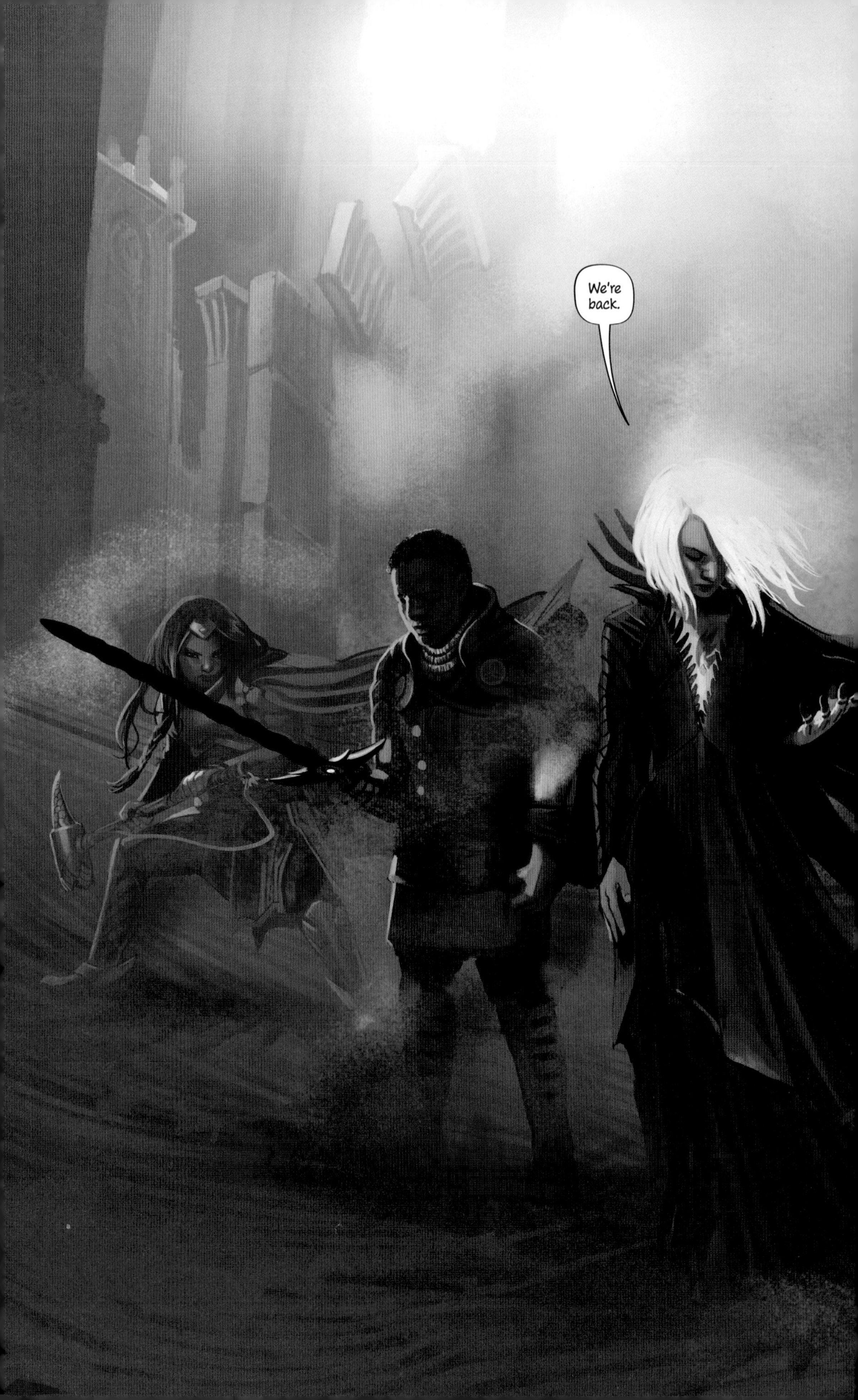
We're back.

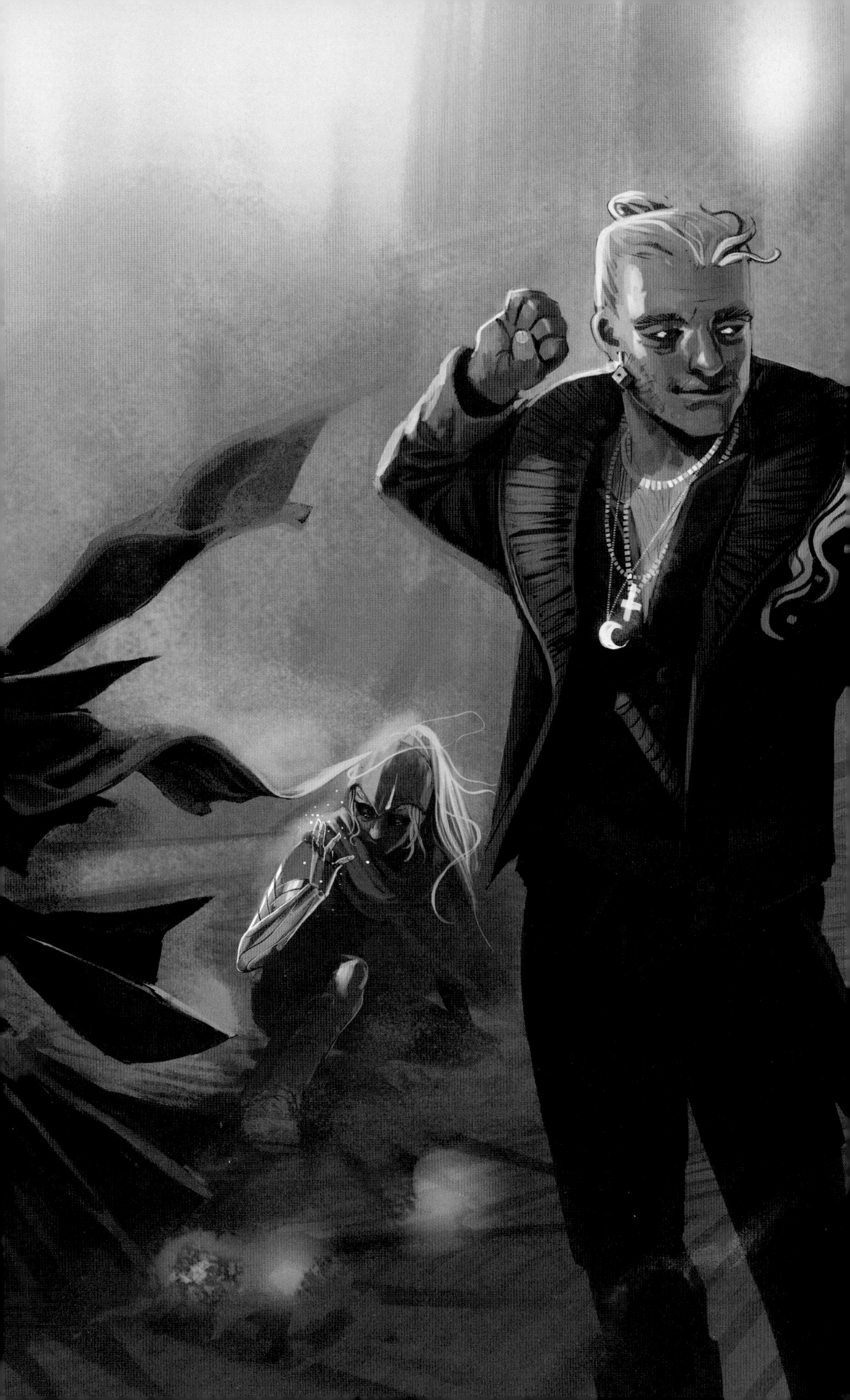

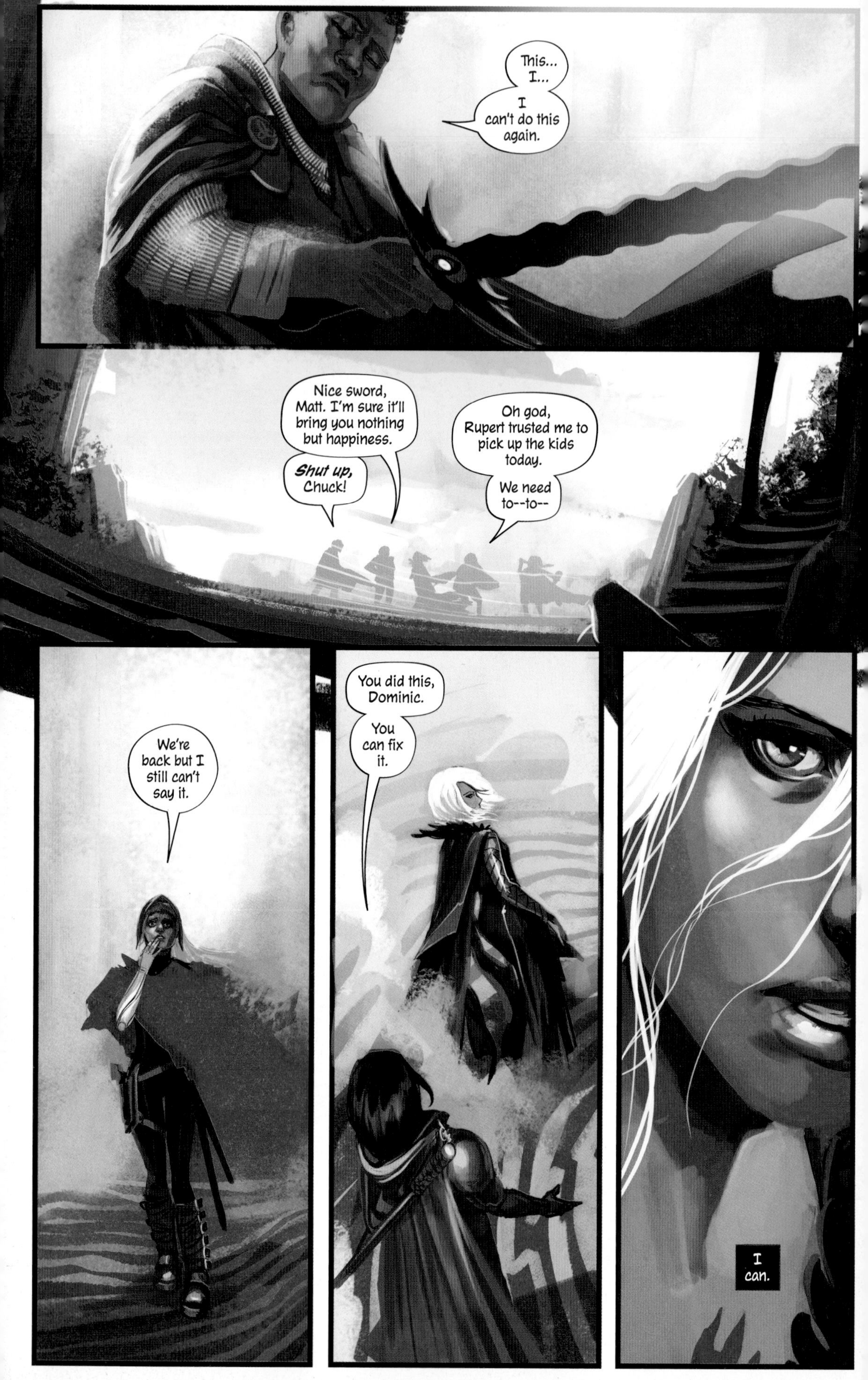
This... I...
I can't do this again.
Nice sword, Matt. I'm sure it'll bring you nothing but happiness.
Shut up, Chuck!
Oh god, Rupert trusted me to pick up the kids today.
We need to--to--
We're back but I still can't say it.
You did this, Dominic.
You can fix it.
I can.

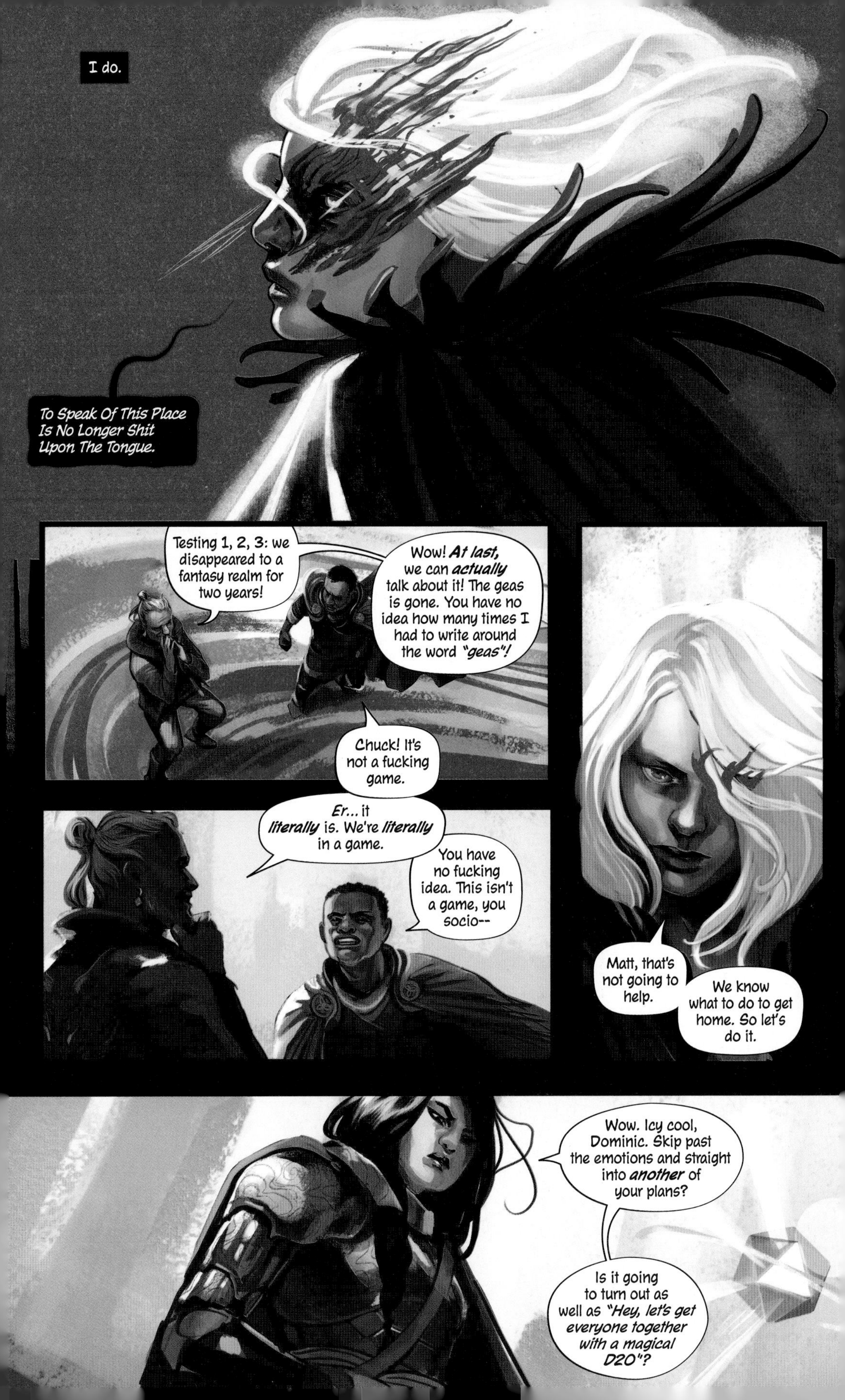
I do.
To Speak Of This Place Is No Longer Shit Upon The Tongue.
Testing 1, 2, 3: we disappeared to a fantasy realm for two years!
Wow! *At last,* we can *actually* talk about it! The geas is gone. You have no idea how many times I had to write around the word *"geas"*!
Chuck! It's not a fucking game.
Er... it *literally* is. We're *literally* in a game.
You have no fucking idea. This isn't a game, you socio--
Matt, that's not going to help.
We know what to do to get home. So let's do it.
Wow. Icy cool, Dominic. Skip past the emotions and straight into *another* of your plans?
Is it going to turn out as well as *"Hey, let's get everyone together with a magical D20"*?

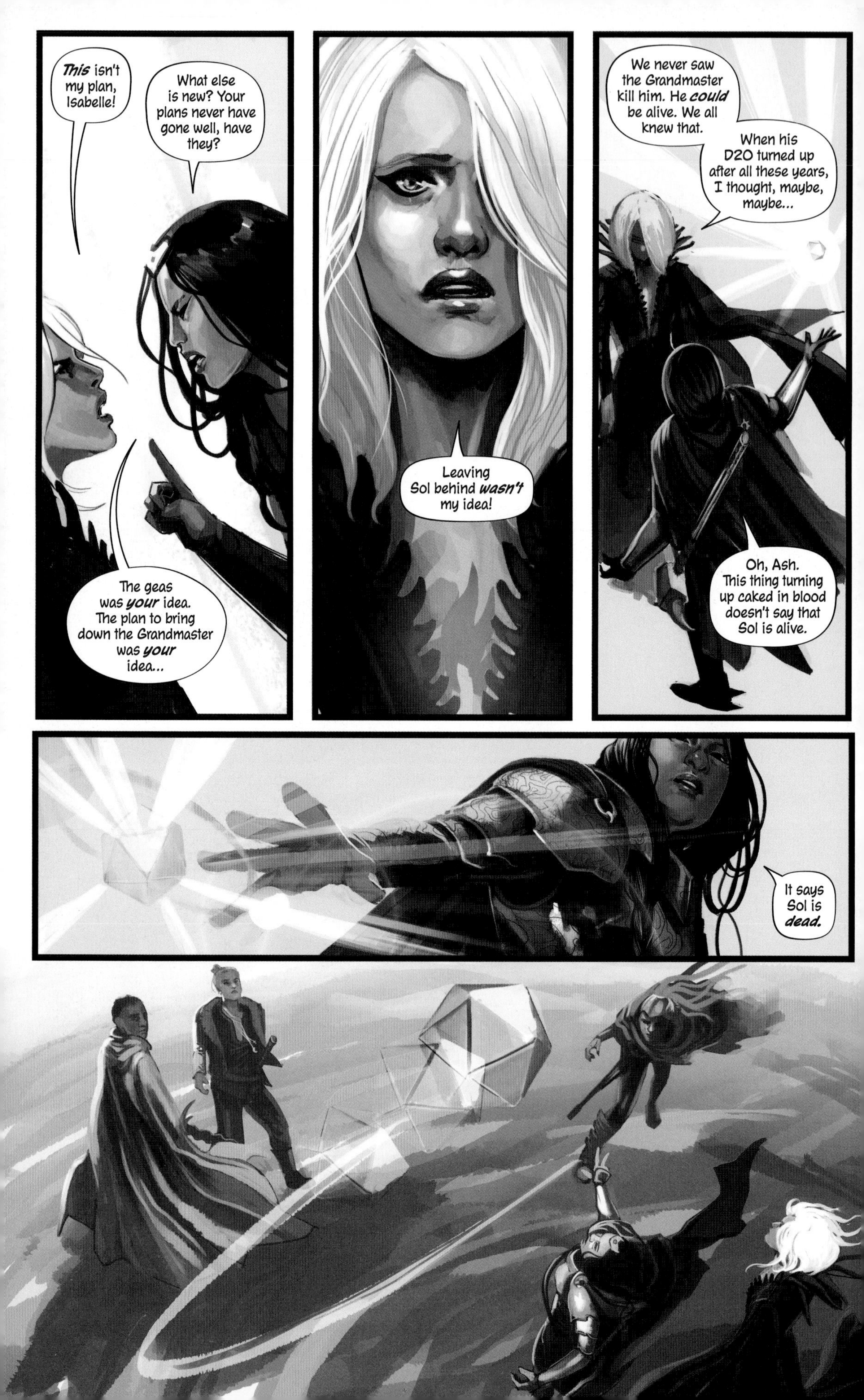
This isn't my plan, Isabelle!
What else is new? Your plans never have gone well, have they?
The geas was your idea. The plan to bring down the Grandmaster was your idea...
Leaving Sol behind wasn't my idea!
We never saw the Grandmaster kill him. He could be alive. We all knew that.
When his D20 turned up after all these years, I thought, maybe, maybe...
Oh, Ash. This thing turning up caked in blood doesn't say that Sol is alive.
It says Sol is dead.

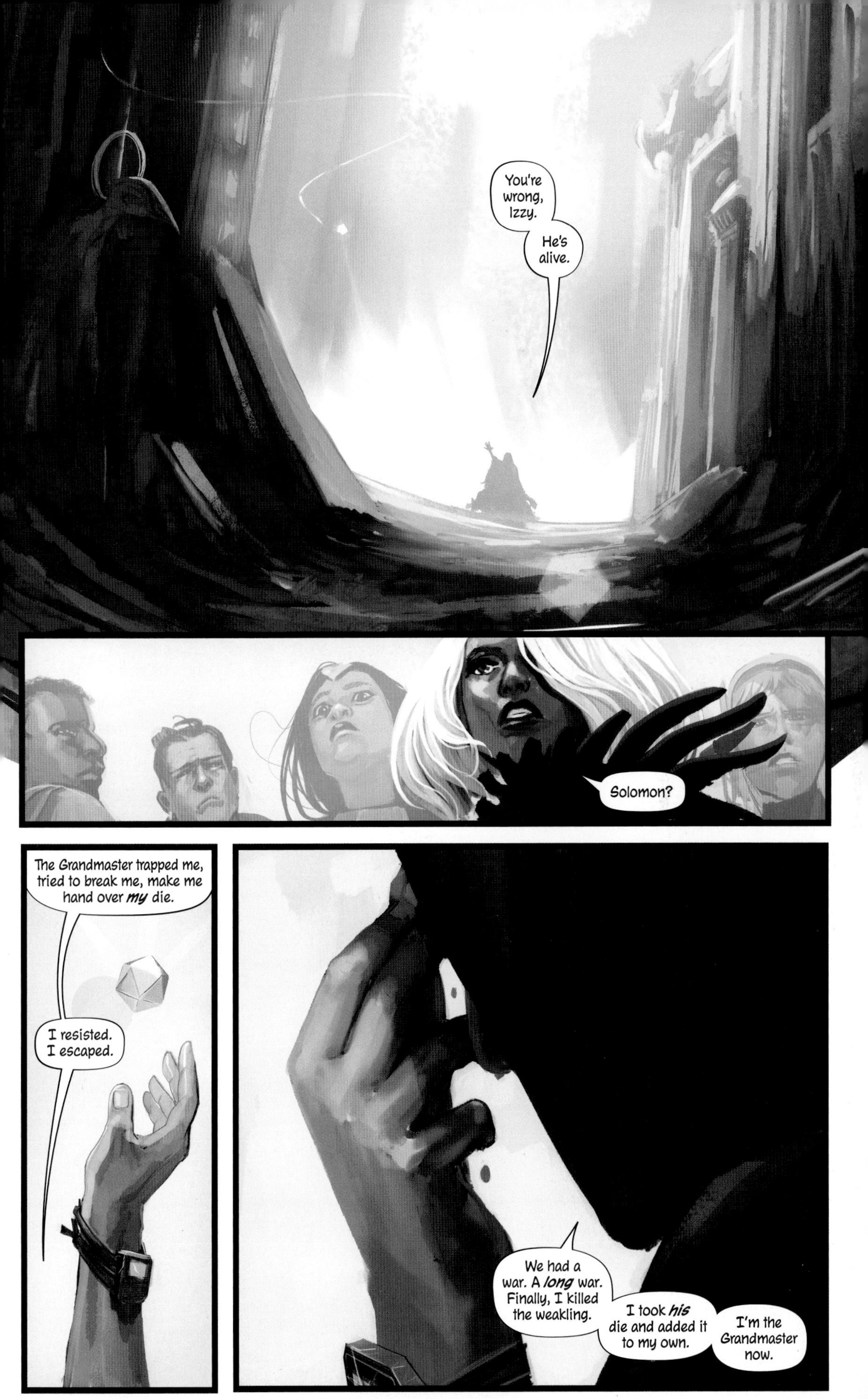
You're wrong, Izzy.
He's alive.
Solomon?
The Grandmaster trapped me, tried to break me, make me hand over *my* die.
I resisted. I escaped.
We had a war. A *long* war. Finally, I killed the weakling.
I took *his* die and added it to my own.
I'm the Grandmaster now.

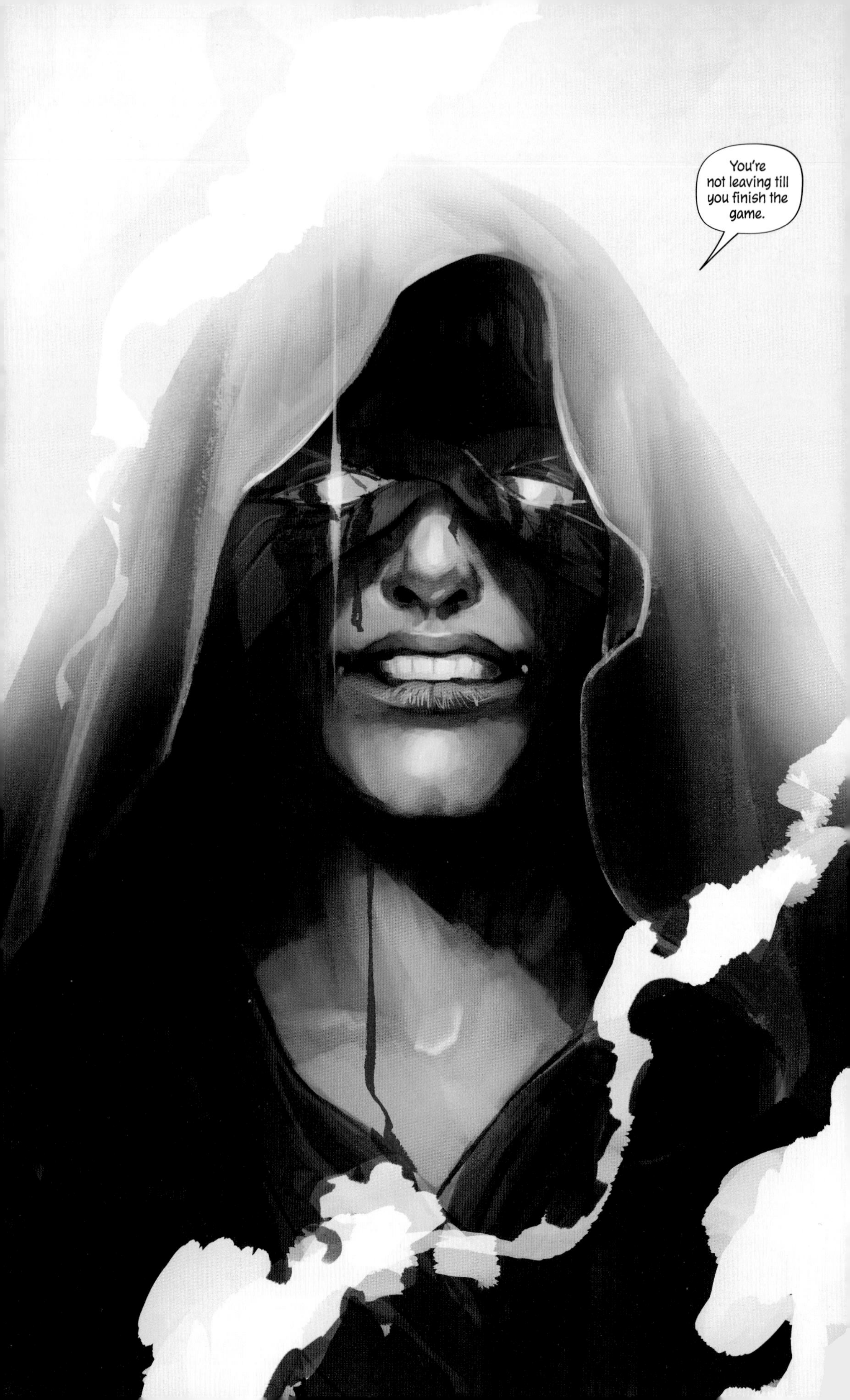
You're not leaving till you finish the game.

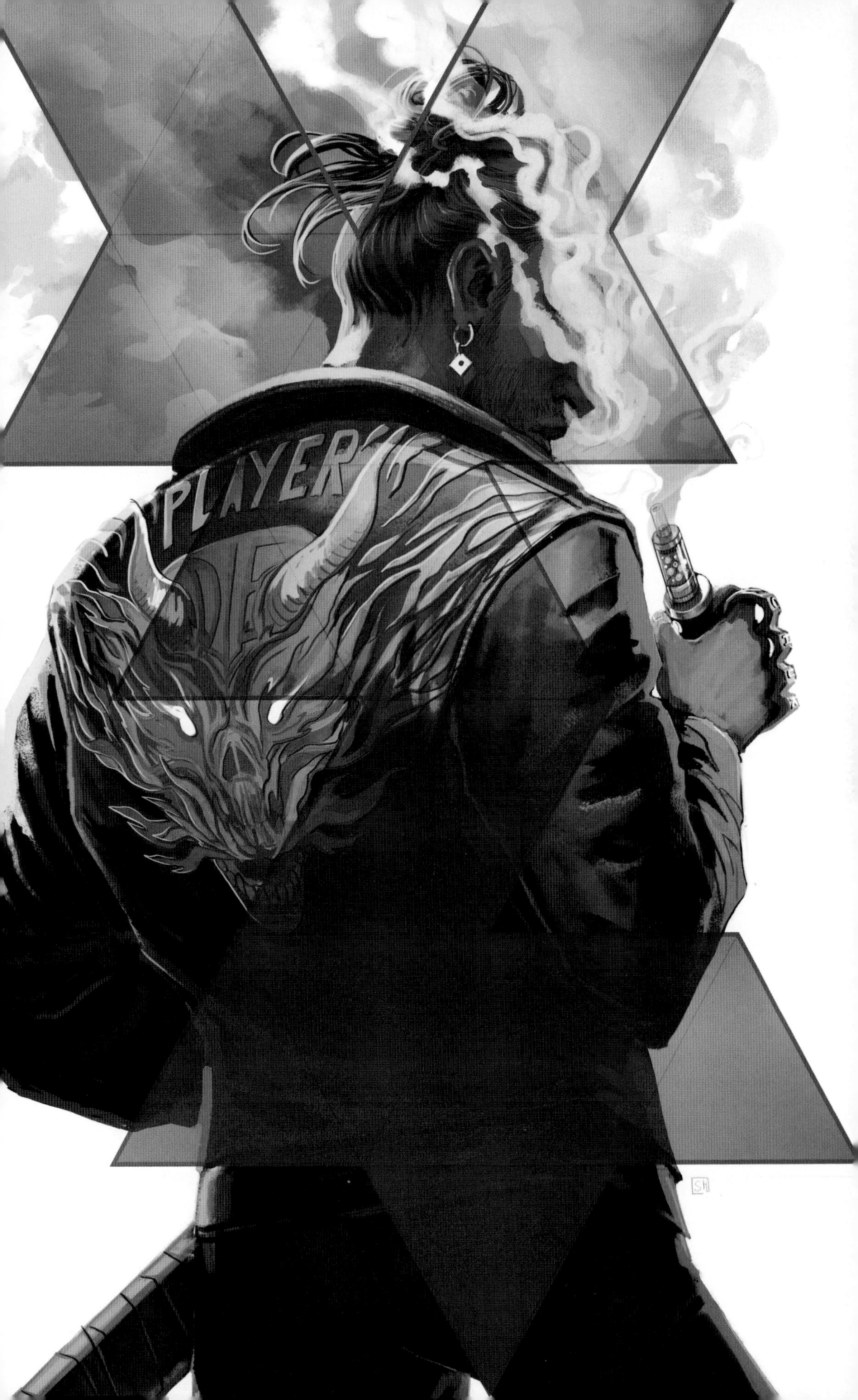
PLAYER

2:
PLAYERS

"Rules? What rules?"
– David Arneson to Gary Gygax, upon being asked for a copy of the rules for the game he just played

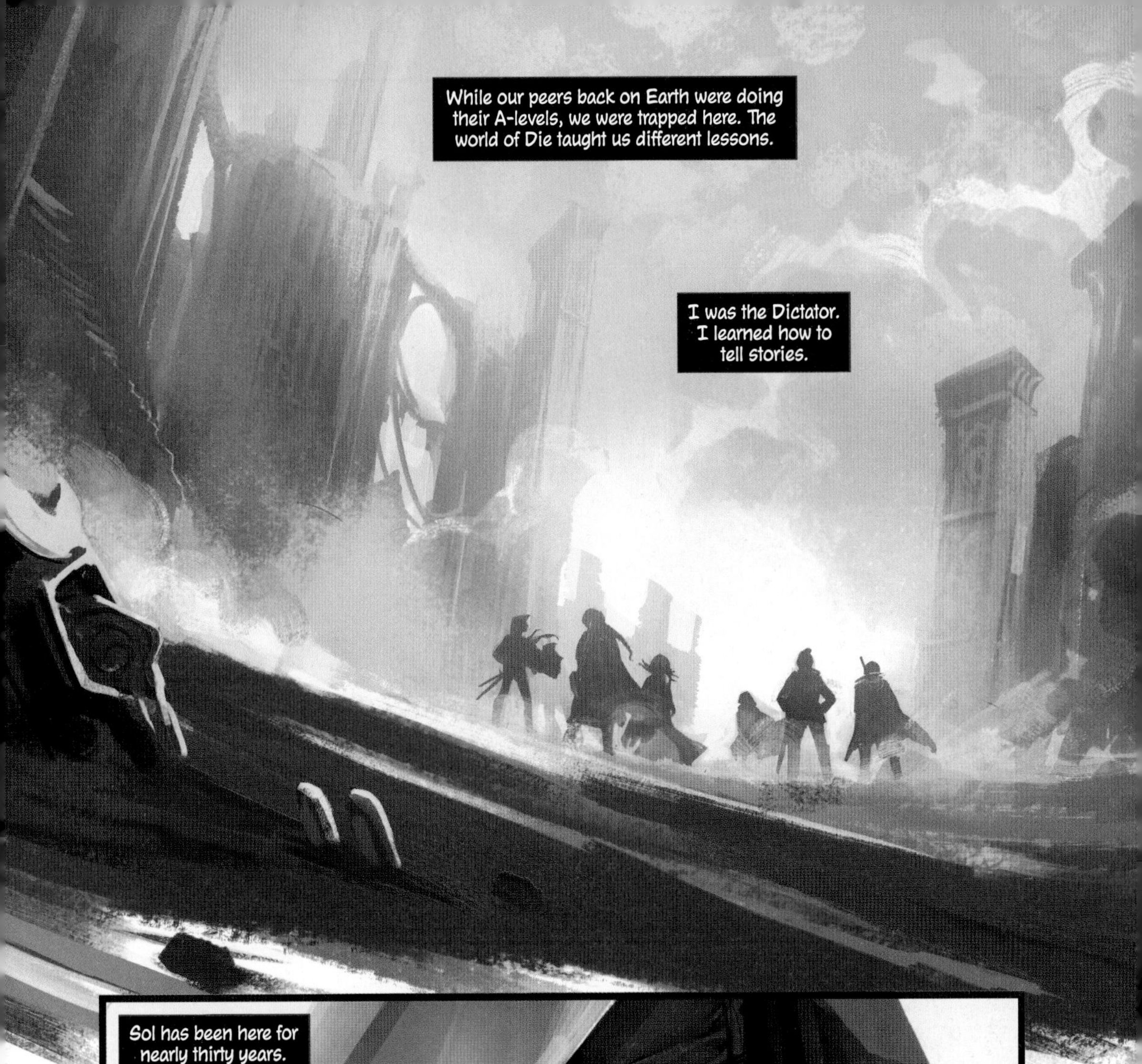
While our peers back on Earth were doing their A-levels, we were trapped here. The world of Die taught us different lessons.
I was the Dictator. I learned how to tell stories.

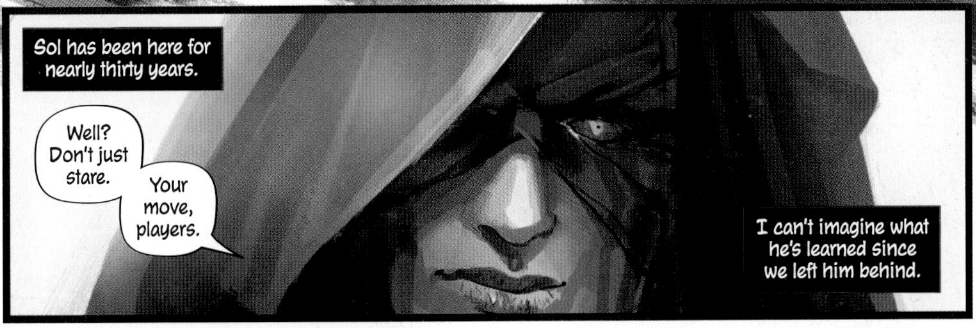
Sol has been here for nearly thirty years.
Well? Don't just stare.
Your move, players.
I can't imagine what he's learned since we left him behind.

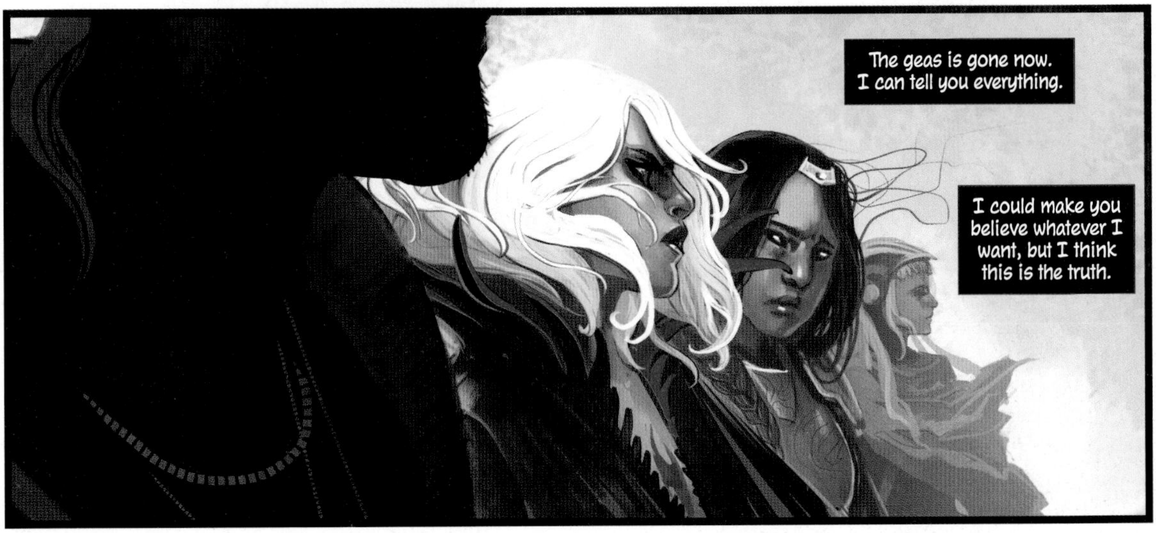
The geas is gone now. I can tell you everything.
I could make you believe whatever I want, but I think this is the truth.

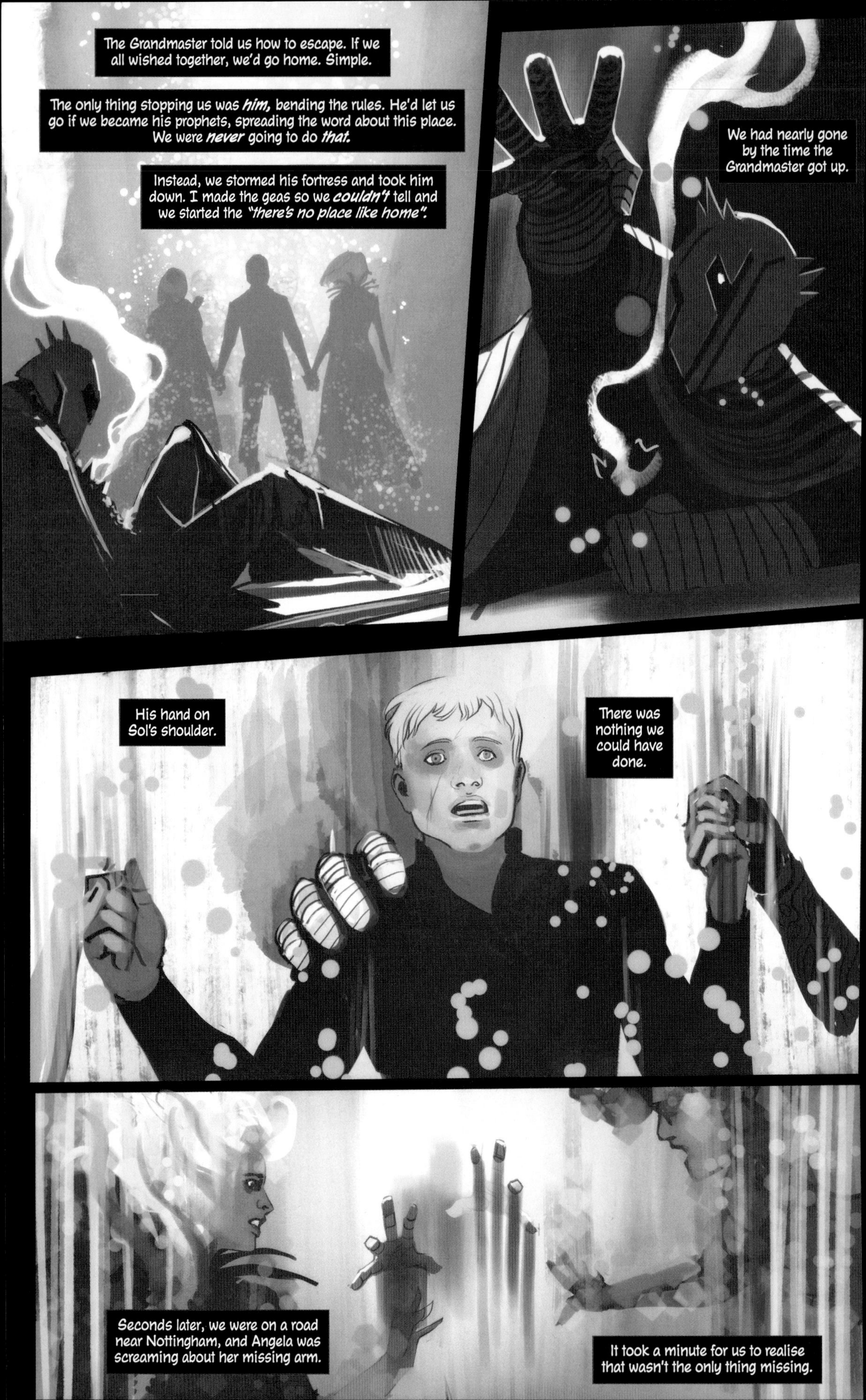
The Grandmaster told us how to escape. If we all wished together, we'd go home. Simple.
The only thing stopping us was *him,* bending the rules. He'd let us go if we became his prophets, spreading the word about this place. We were ***never*** going to do ***that.***
Instead, we stormed his fortress and took him down. I made the geas so we ***couldn't*** tell and we started the ***"there's no place like home".***
We had nearly gone by the time the Grandmaster got up.
His hand on Sol's shoulder.
There was nothing we could have done.
Seconds later, we were on a road near Nottingham, and Angela was screaming about her missing arm.
It took a minute for us to realise that wasn't the only thing missing.

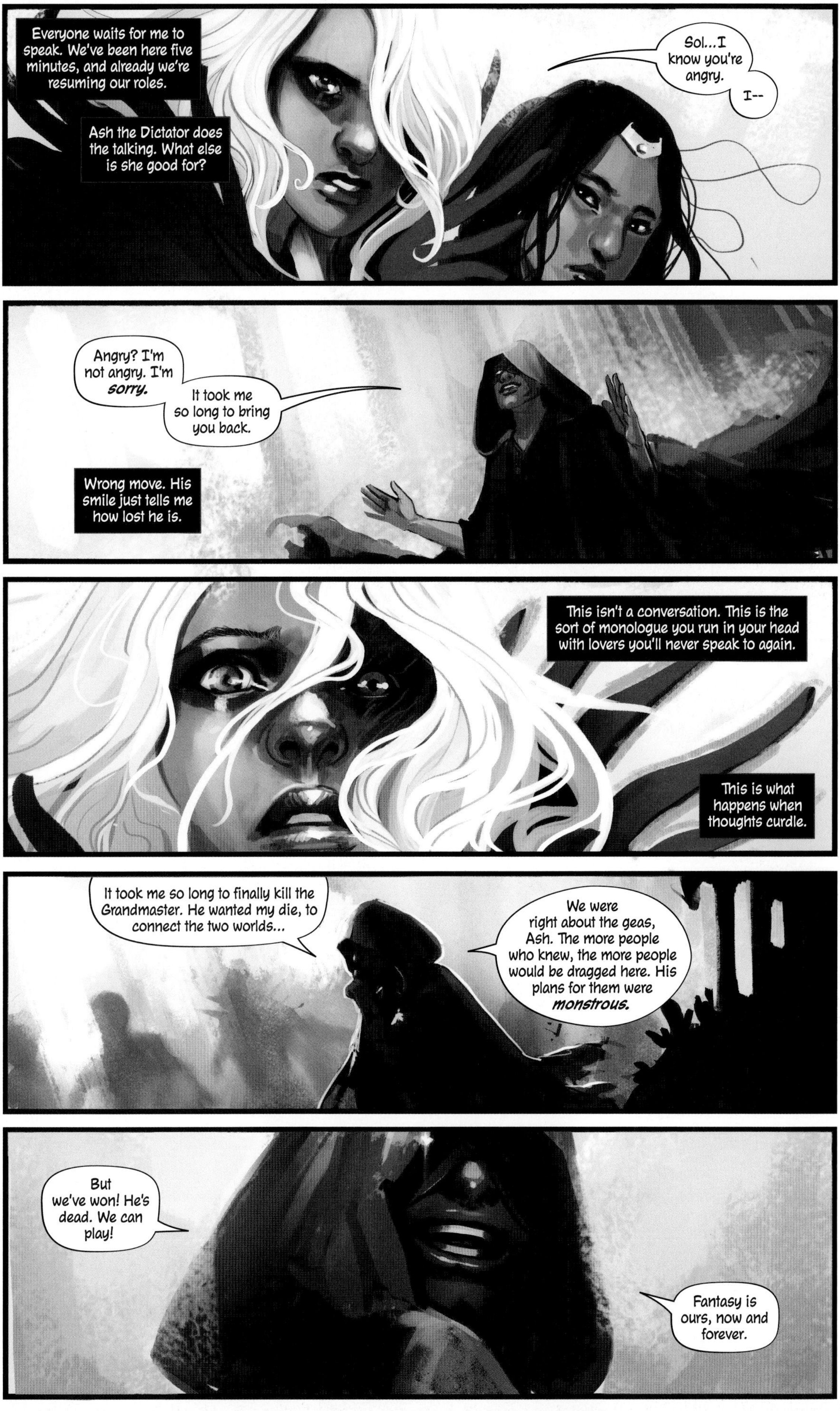
Everyone waits for me to speak. We've been here five minutes, and already we're resuming our roles.
Ash the Dictator does the talking. What else is she good for?
Sol...I know you're angry.
I--
Angry? I'm not angry. I'm *sorry.*
It took me so long to bring you back.
Wrong move. His smile just tells me how lost he is.
This isn't a conversation. This is the sort of monologue you run in your head with lovers you'll never speak to again.
This is what happens when thoughts curdle.
It took me so long to finally kill the Grandmaster. He wanted my die, to connect the two worlds...
We were right about the geas, Ash. The more people who knew, the more people would be dragged here. His plans for them were *monstrous.*
But we've won! He's dead. We can play!
Fantasy is ours, now and forever.

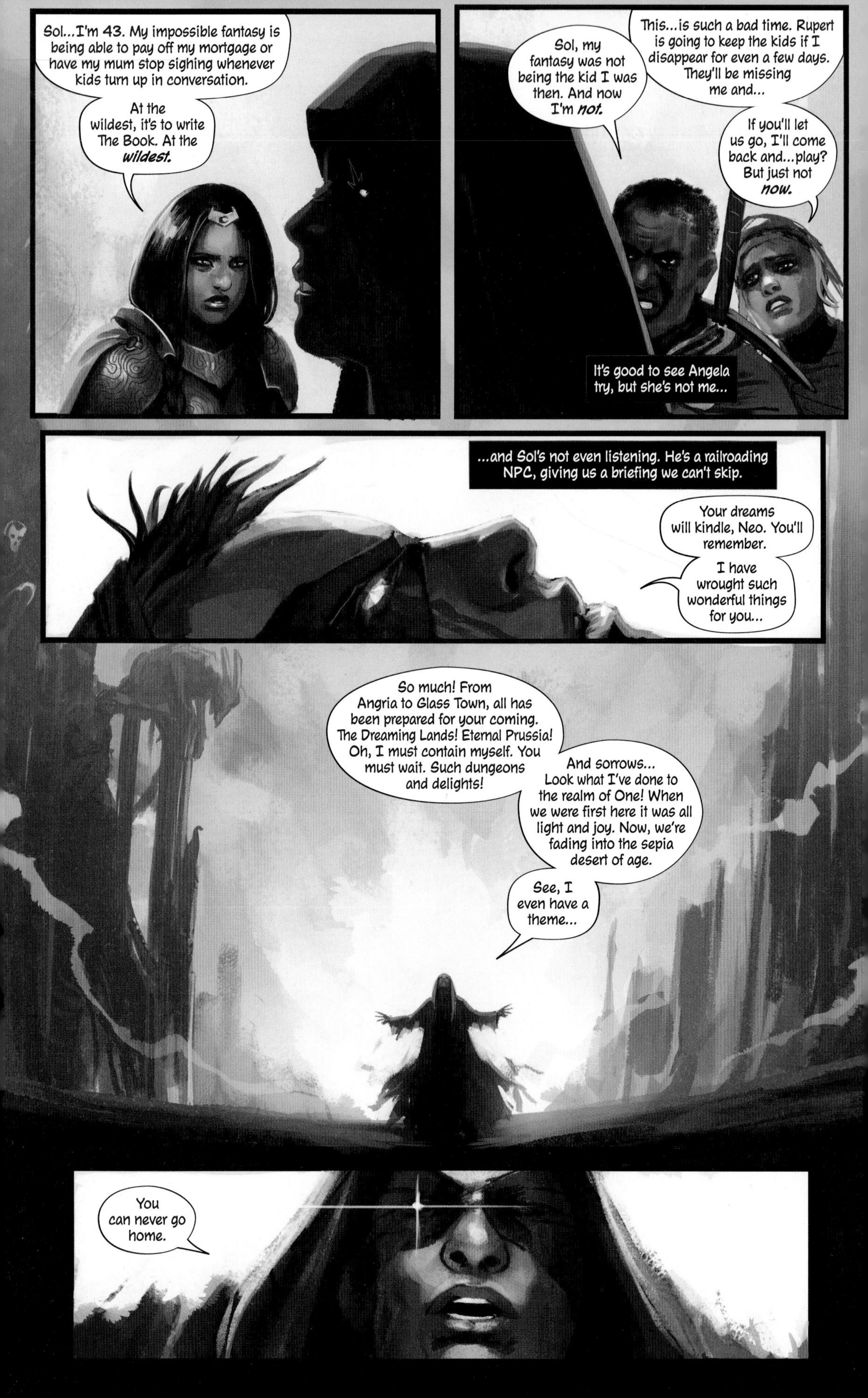

Sol...I'm 43. My impossible fantasy is being able to pay off my mortgage or have my mum stop sighing whenever kids turn up in conversation.
At the wildest, it's to write The Book. At the *wildest.*
Sol, my fantasy was not being the kid I was then. And now I'm *not.*
This...is such a bad time. Rupert is going to keep the kids if I disappear for even a few days. They'll be missing me and...
If you'll let us go, I'll come back and...play? But just not *now.*
It's good to see Angela try, but she's not me...
...and Sol's not even listening. He's a railroading NPC, giving us a briefing we can't skip.
Your dreams will kindle, Neo. You'll remember.
I have wrought such wonderful things for you...
So much! From Angria to Glass Town, all has been prepared for your coming. The Dreaming Lands! Eternal Prussia! Oh, I must contain myself. You must wait. Such dungeons and delights!
And sorrows... Look what I've done to the realm of One! When we were first here it was all light and joy. Now, we're fading into the sepia desert of age.
See, I even have a theme...
You can never go home.

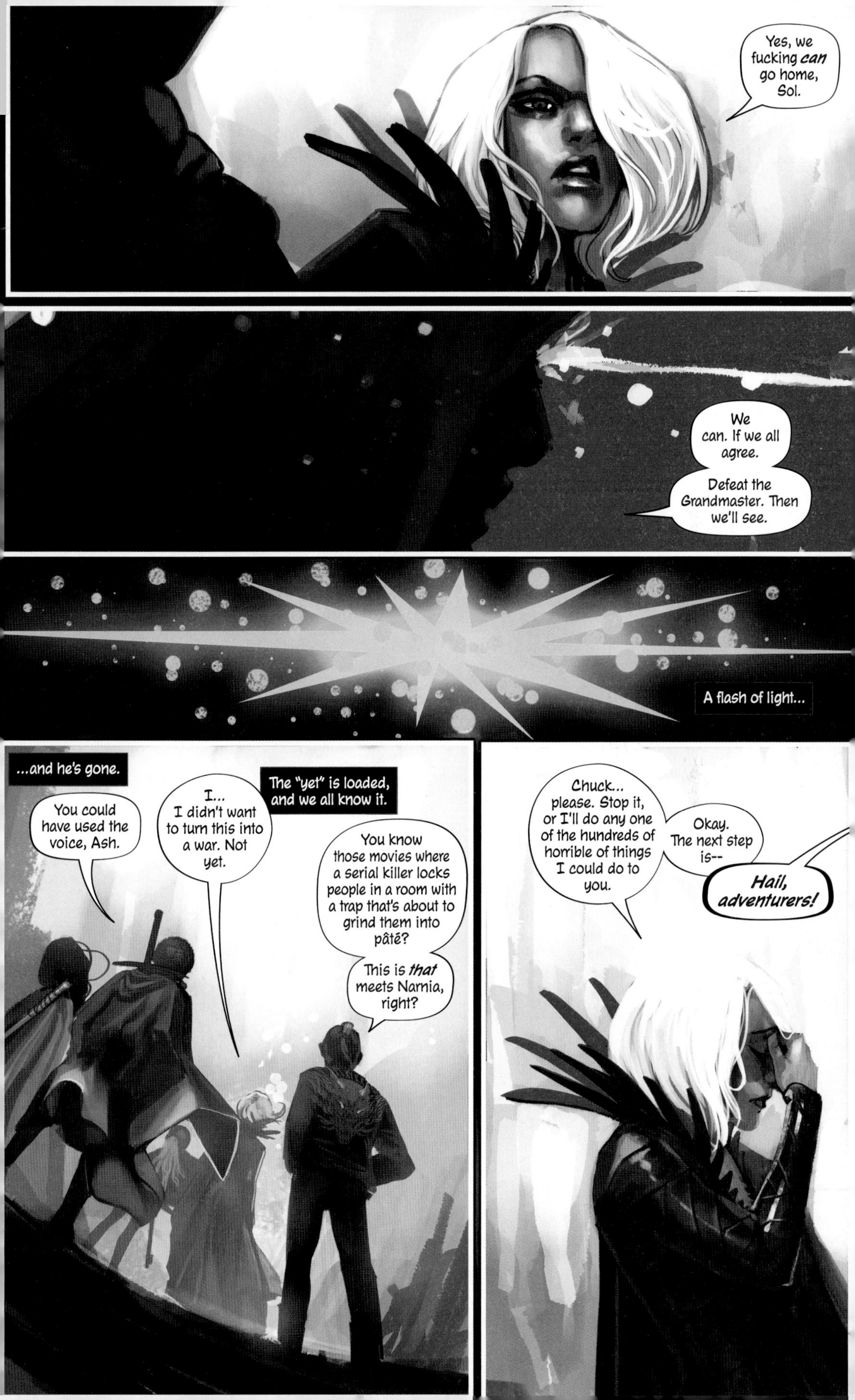
Yes, we fucking *can* go home, Sol.
We can. If we all agree.
Defeat the Grandmaster. Then we'll see.
A flash of light...
...and he's gone.
You could have used the voice, Ash.
I... I didn't want to turn this into a war. Not yet.
The "yet" is loaded, and we all know it.
You know those movies where a serial killer locks people in a room with a trap that's about to grind them into pâté?
This is *that* meets Narnia, right?
Chuck... please. Stop it, or I'll do any one of the hundreds of horrible of things I could do to you.
Okay. The next step is--
Hail, adventurers!

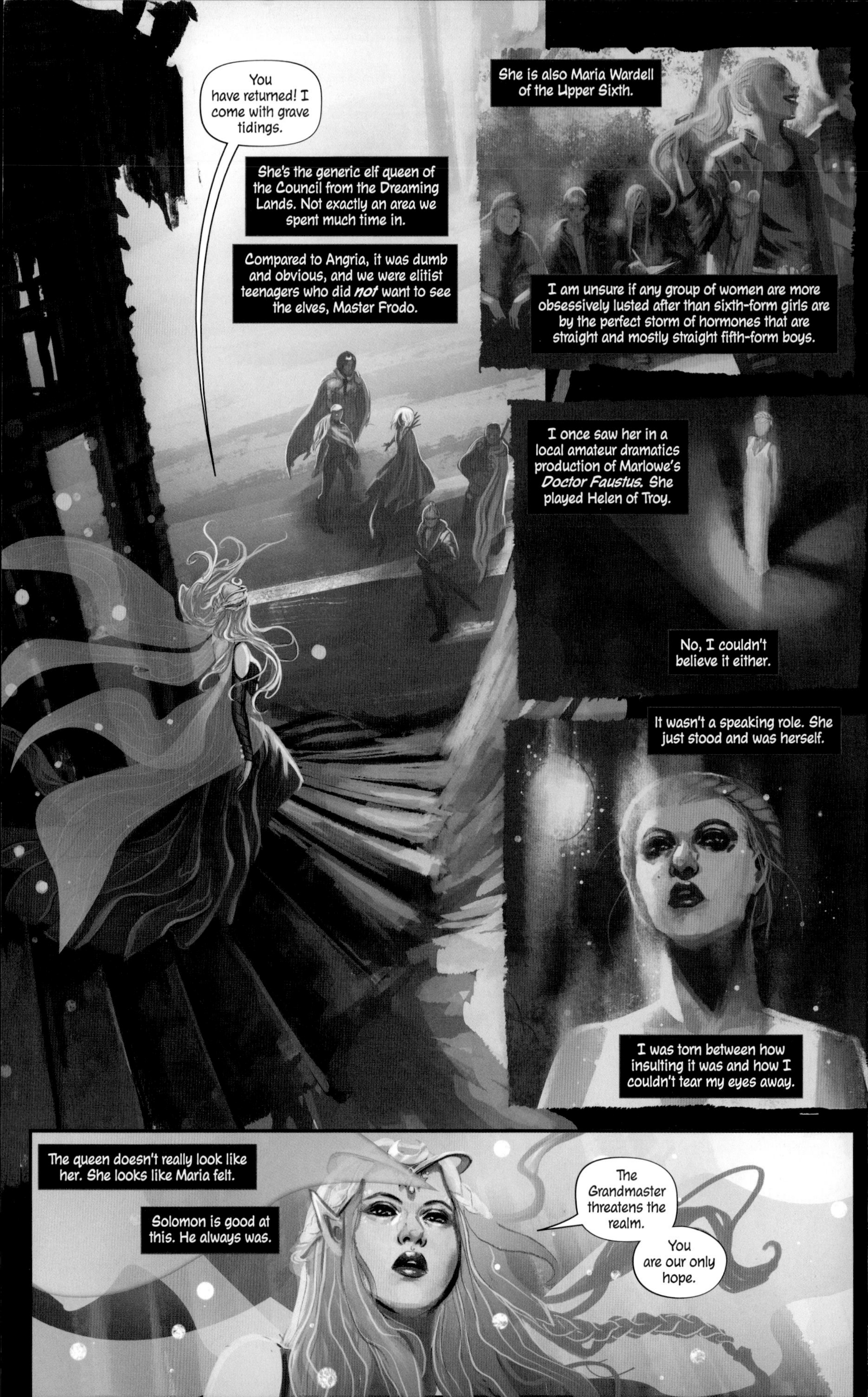
You have returned! I come with grave tidings.
She's the generic elf queen of the Council from the Dreaming Lands. Not exactly an area we spent much time in.
Compared to Angria, it was dumb and obvious, and we were elitist teenagers who did *not* want to see the elves, Master Frodo.
She is also Maria Wardell of the Upper Sixth.
I am unsure if any group of women are more obsessively lusted after than sixth-form girls are by the perfect storm of hormones that are straight and mostly straight fifth-form boys.
I once saw her in a local amateur dramatics production of Marlowe's *Doctor Faustus.* She played Helen of Troy.
No, I couldn't believe it either.
It wasn't a speaking role. She just stood and was herself.
I was torn between how insulting it was and how I couldn't tear my eyes away.
The queen doesn't really look like her. She looks like Maria felt.
Solomon is good at this. He always was.
The Grandmaster threatens the realm.
You are our only hope.

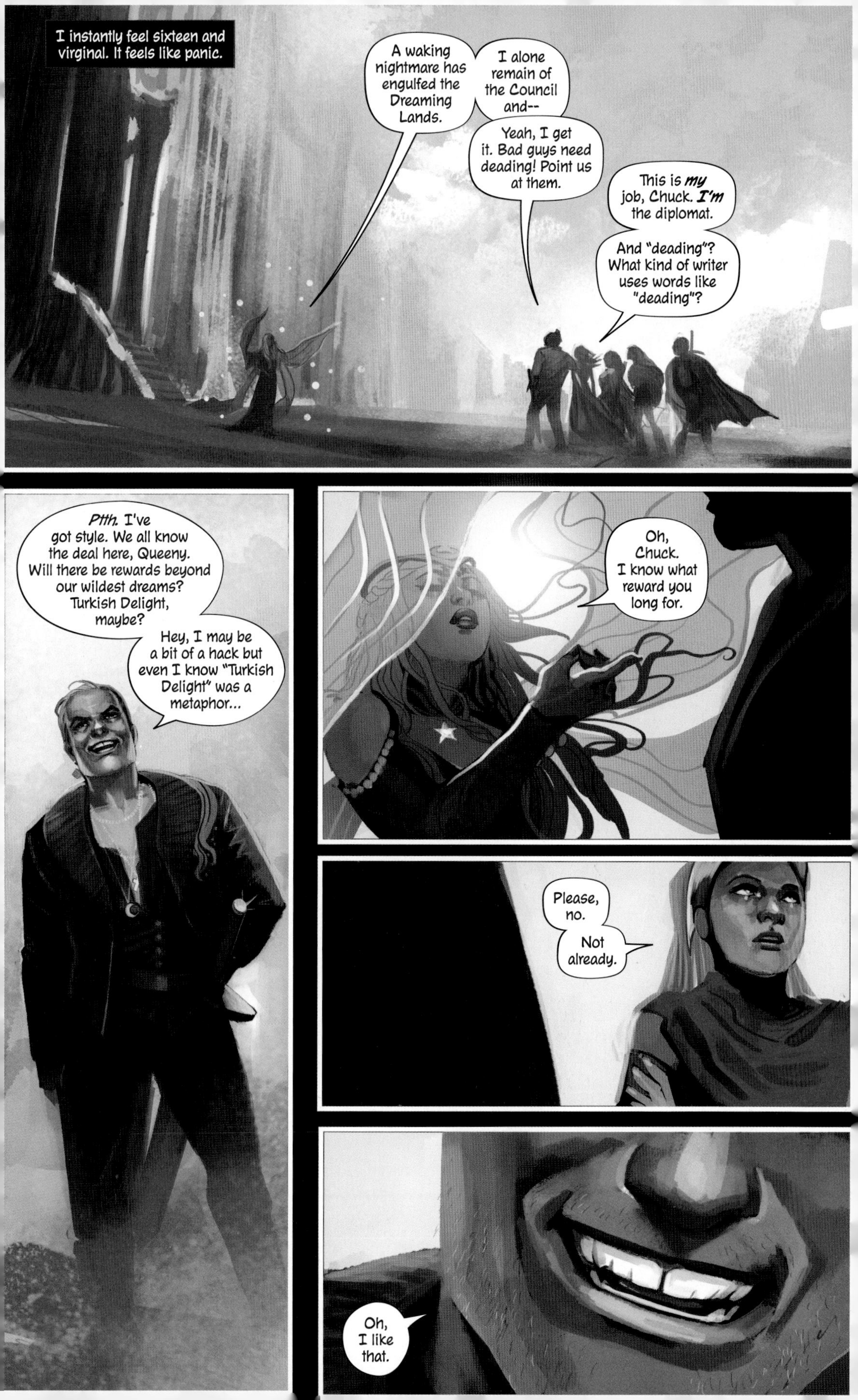
I instantly feel sixteen and virginal. It feels like panic.
A waking nightmare has engulfed the Dreaming Lands.
I alone remain of the Council and--
Yeah, I get it. Bad guys need deading! Point us at them.
This is *my* job, Chuck. ***I'm*** the diplomat.
And "deading"? What kind of writer uses words like "deading"?
Pfft. I've got style. We all know the deal here, Queeny. Will there be rewards beyond our wildest dreams? Turkish Delight, maybe?
Hey, I may be a bit of a hack but even I know "Turkish Delight" was a metaphor...
Oh, Chuck. I know what reward you long for.
Please, no.
Not already.
Oh, I like that.

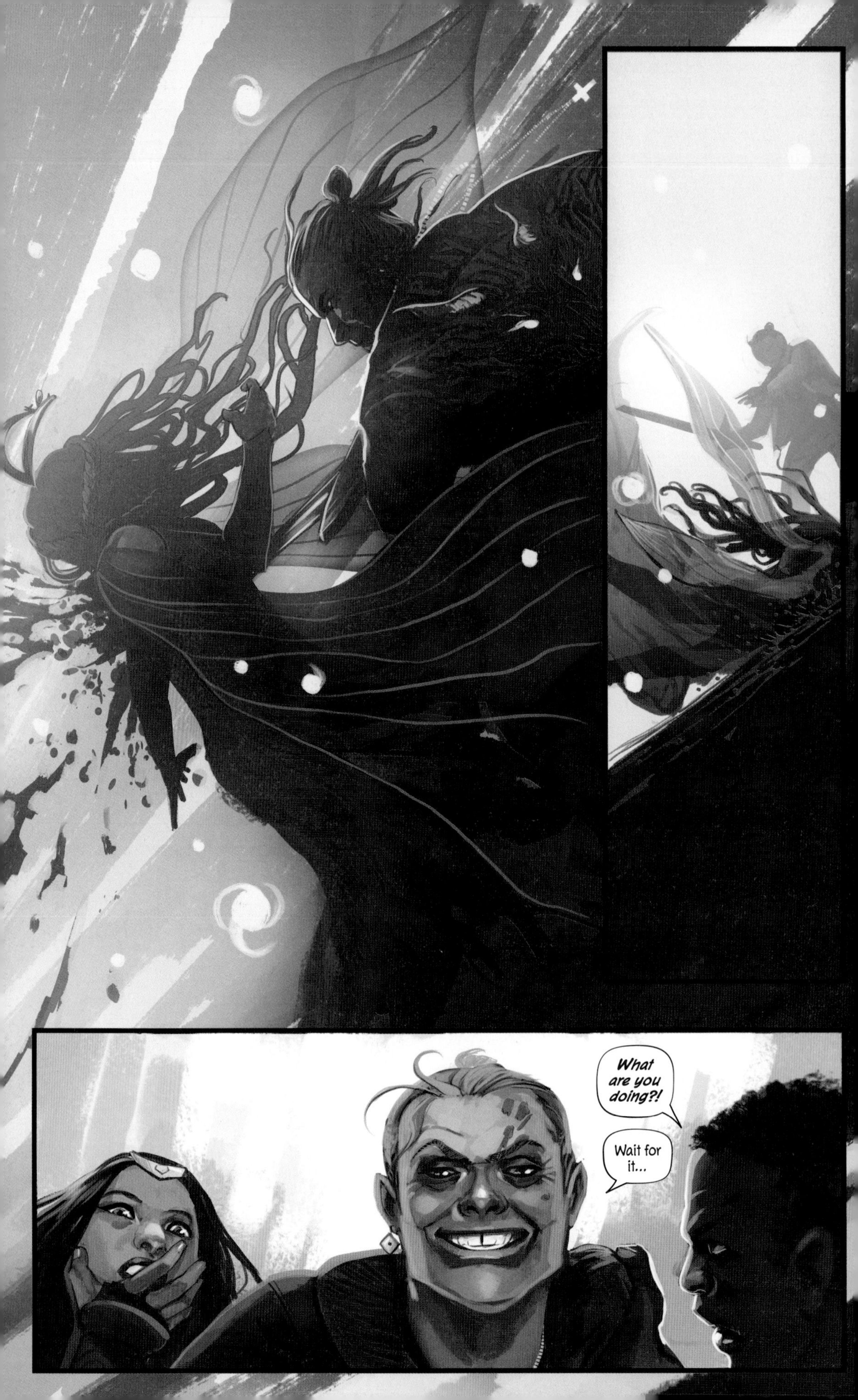
What are you doing?!
Wait for it...

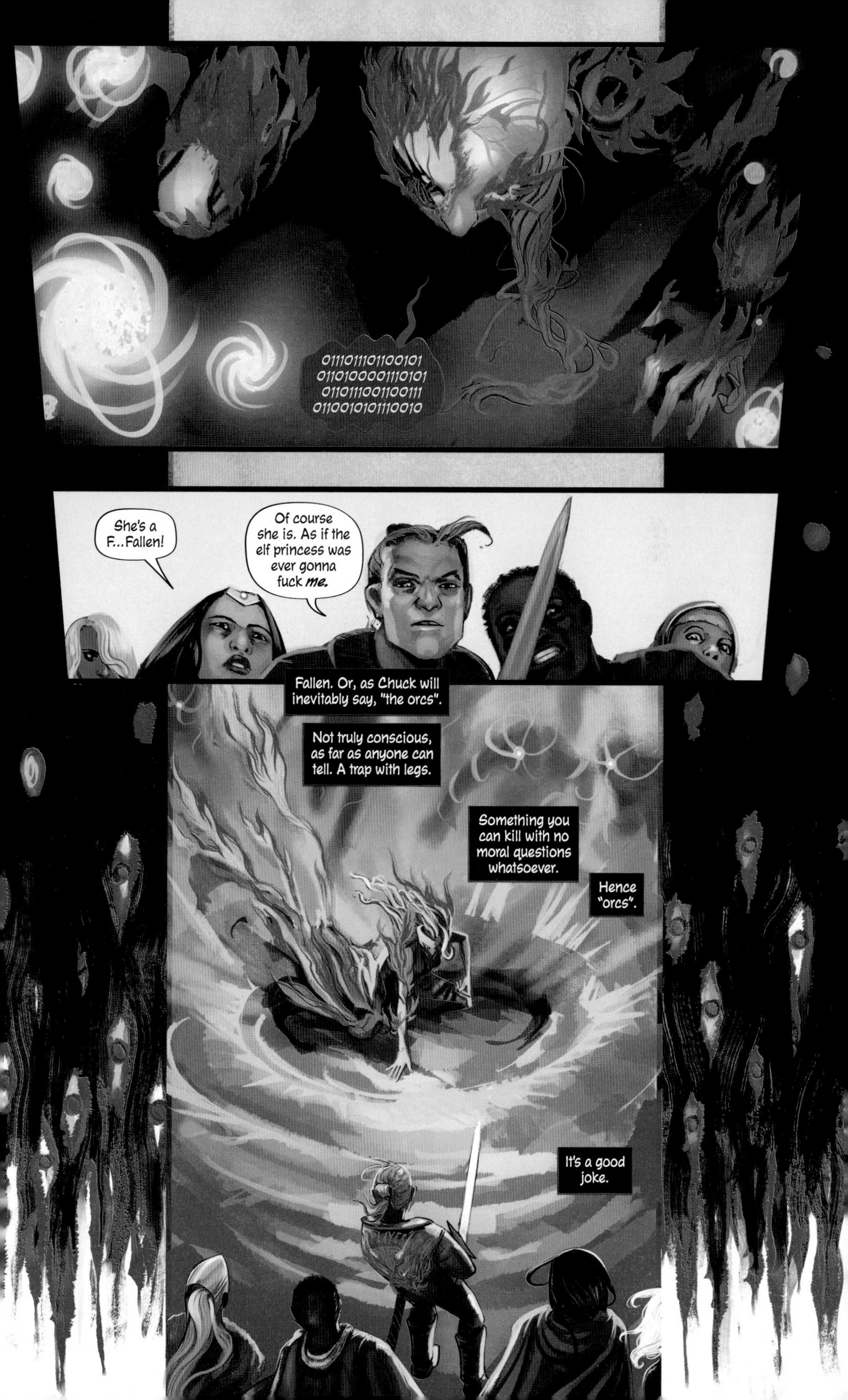

0111011101100101
0110100001110101
0110111001100111
0110010101110010
She's a F...Fallen!
Of course she is. As if the elf princess was ever gonna fuck *me.*
Fallen. Or, as Chuck will inevitably say, "the orcs".
Not truly conscious, as far as anyone can tell. A trap with legs.
Something you can kill with no moral questions whatsoever.
Hence "orcs".
It's a good joke.

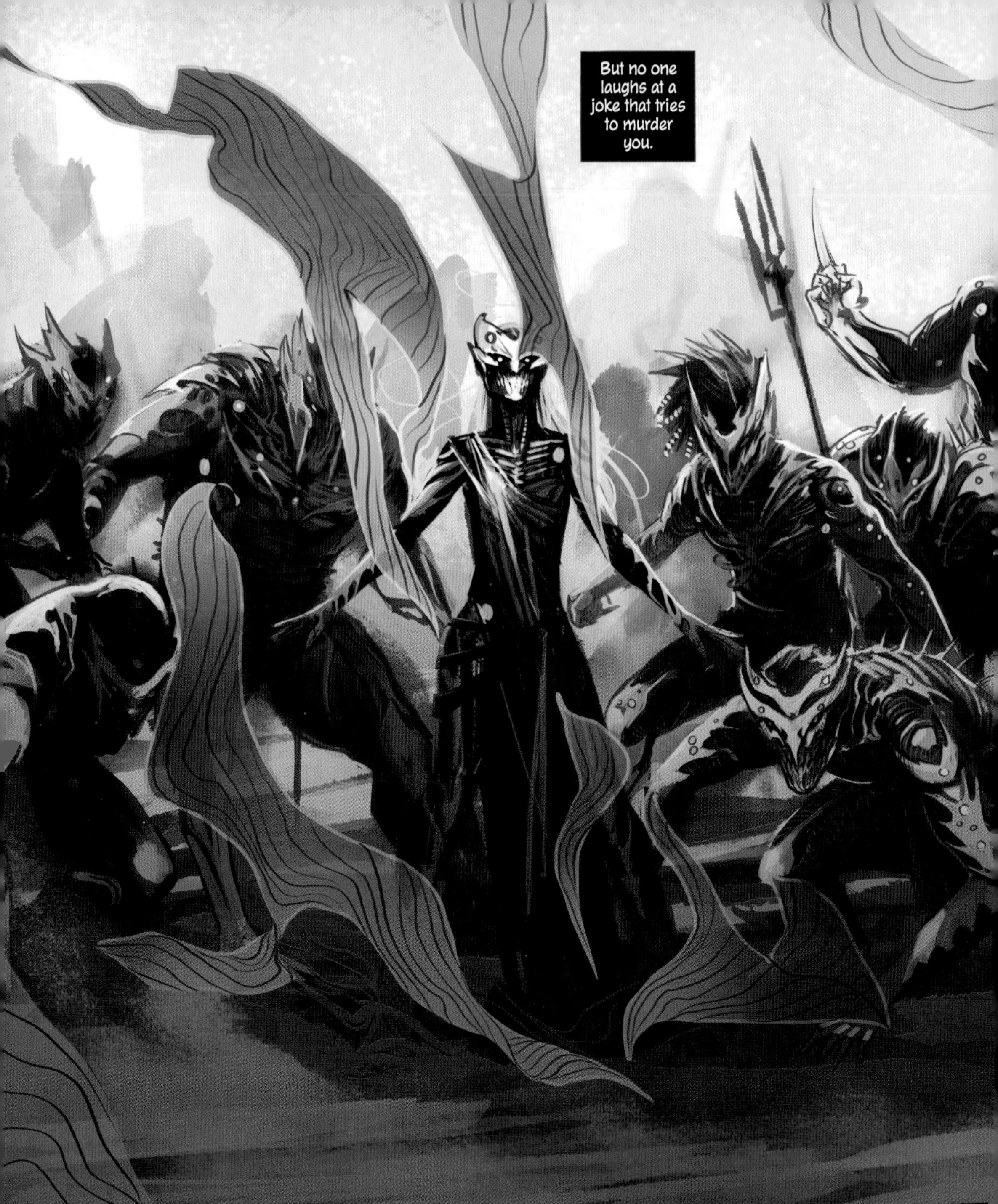
But no one laughs at a joke that tries to murder you.

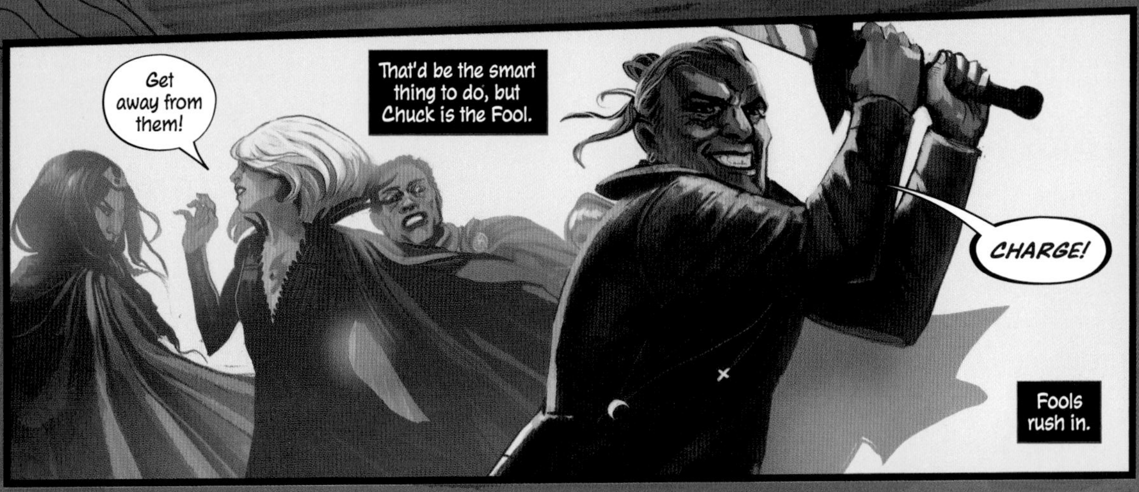
Get away from them!
That'd be the smart thing to do, but Chuck is the Fool.
CHARGE!
Fools rush in.

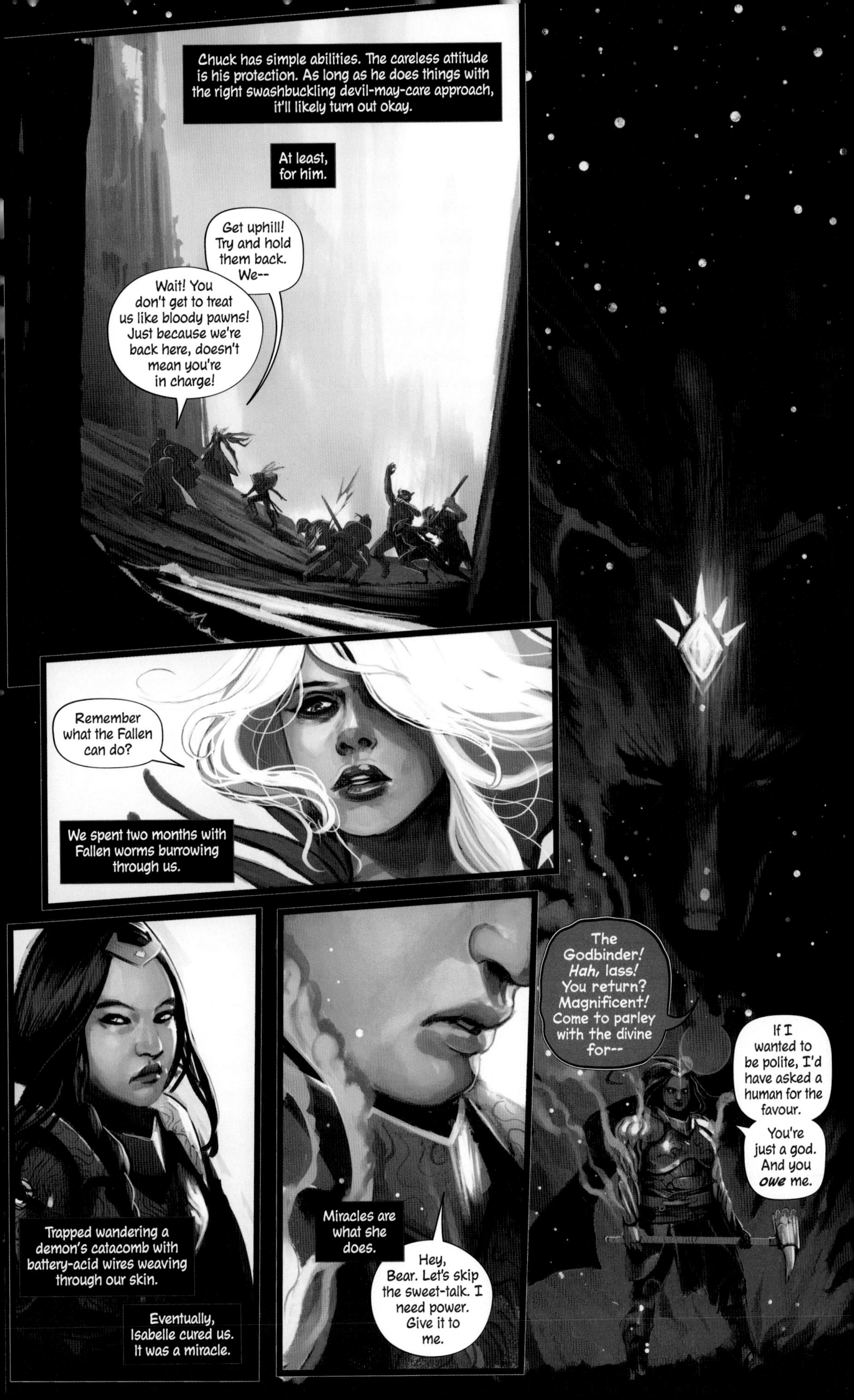
Chuck has simple abilities. The careless attitude is his protection. As long as he does things with the right swashbuckling devil-may-care approach, it'll likely turn out okay.
At least, for him.
Get uphill! Try and hold them back. We--
Wait! You don't get to treat us like bloody pawns! Just because we're back here, doesn't mean you're in charge!
Remember what the Fallen can do?
We spent two months with Fallen worms burrowing through us.
Trapped wandering a demon's catacomb with battery-acid wires weaving through our skin.
Eventually, Isabelle cured us. It was a miracle.
Miracles are what she does.
Hey, Bear. Let's skip the sweet-talk. I need power. Give it to me.
The Godbinder! *Hah*, lass! You return? Magnificent! Come to parley with the divine for--
If I wanted to be polite, I'd have asked a human for the favour.
You're just a god. And you ***owe*** me.

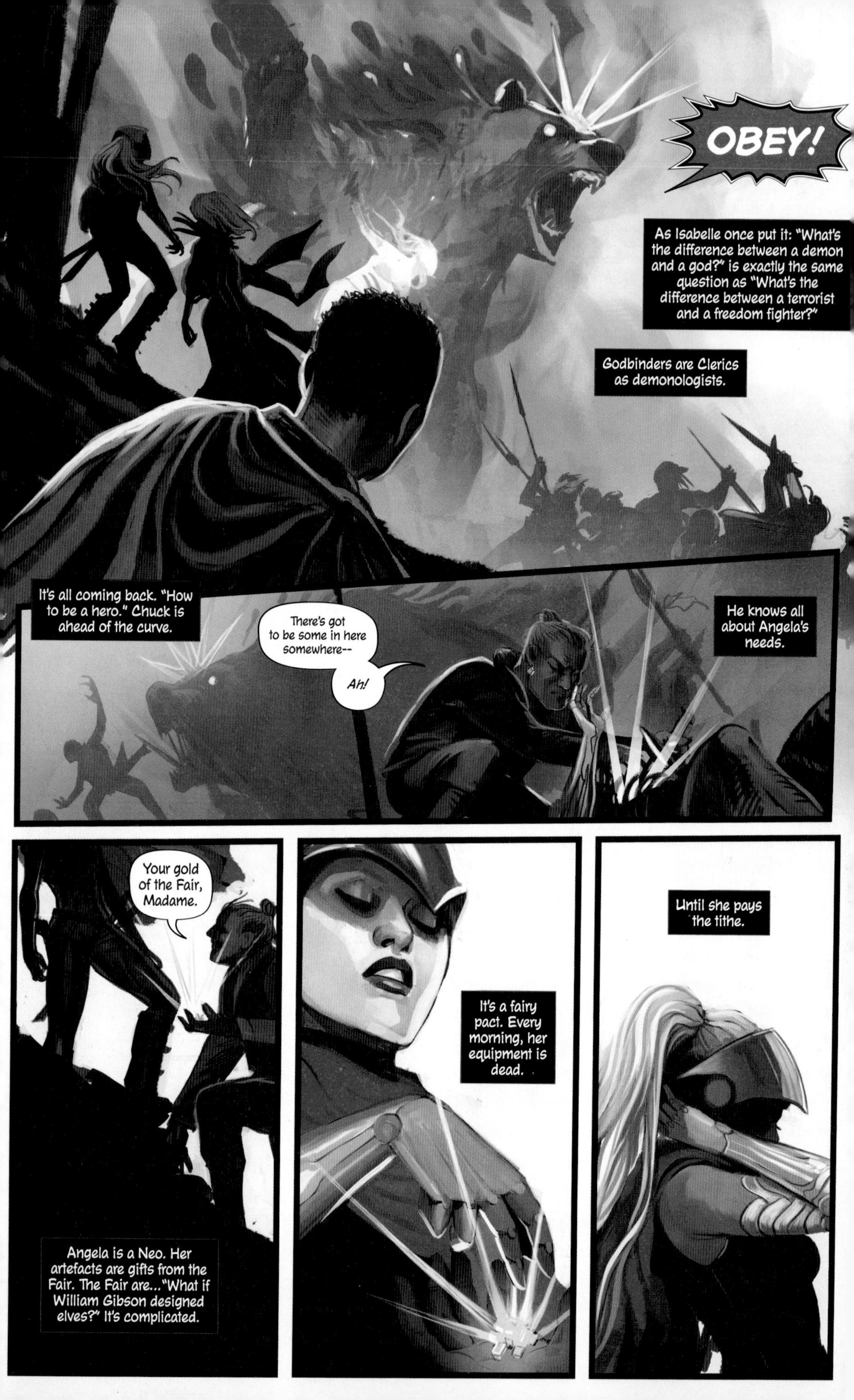
OBEY!
As Isabelle once put it: "What's the difference between a demon and a god?" is exactly the same question as "What's the difference between a terrorist and a freedom fighter?"
Godbinders are Clerics as demonologists.
It's all coming back. "How to be a hero." Chuck is ahead of the curve.
There's got to be some in here somewhere--
Ah!
He knows all about Angela's needs.
Your gold of the Fair, Madame.
Angela is a Neo. Her artefacts are gifts from the Fair. The Fair are..."What if William Gibson designed elves?" It's complicated.
It's a fairy pact. Every morning, her equipment is dead.
Until she pays the tithe.

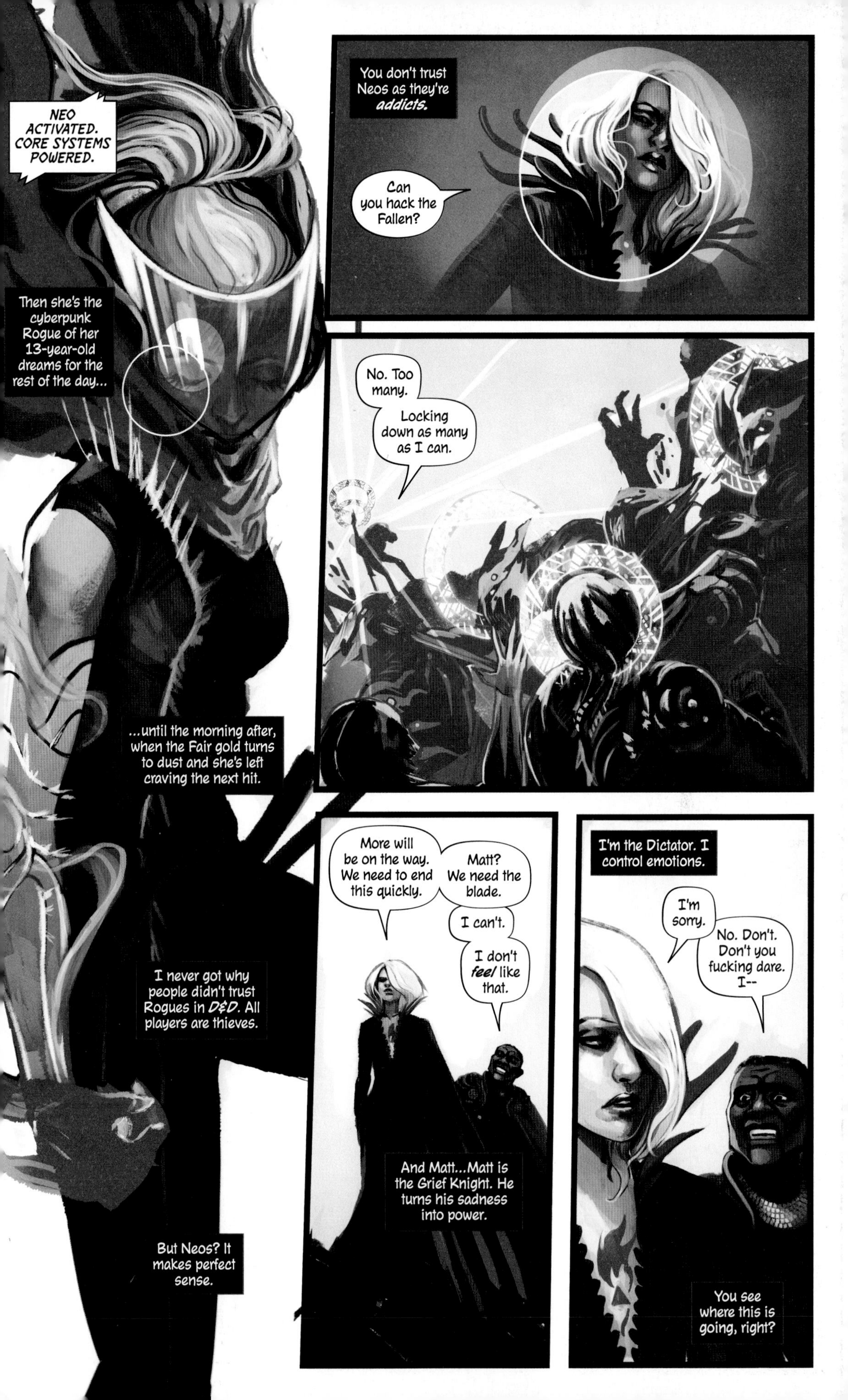

NEO ACTIVATED. CORE SYSTEMS POWERED.
Then she's the cyberpunk Rogue of her 13-year-old dreams for the rest of the day...
You don't trust Neos as they're *addicts.*
Can you hack the Fallen?
No. Too many.
Locking down as many as I can.
...until the morning after, when the Fair gold turns to dust and she's left craving the next hit.
I never got why people didn't trust Rogues in *D&D*. All players are thieves.
But Neos? It makes perfect sense.
More will be on the way. We need to end this quickly.
Matt? We need the blade.
I can't.
I don't *feel* like that.
And Matt...Matt is the Grief Knight. He turns his sadness into power.
I'm the Dictator. I control emotions.
I'm sorry.
No. Don't. Don't you fucking dare. I--
You see where this is going, right?

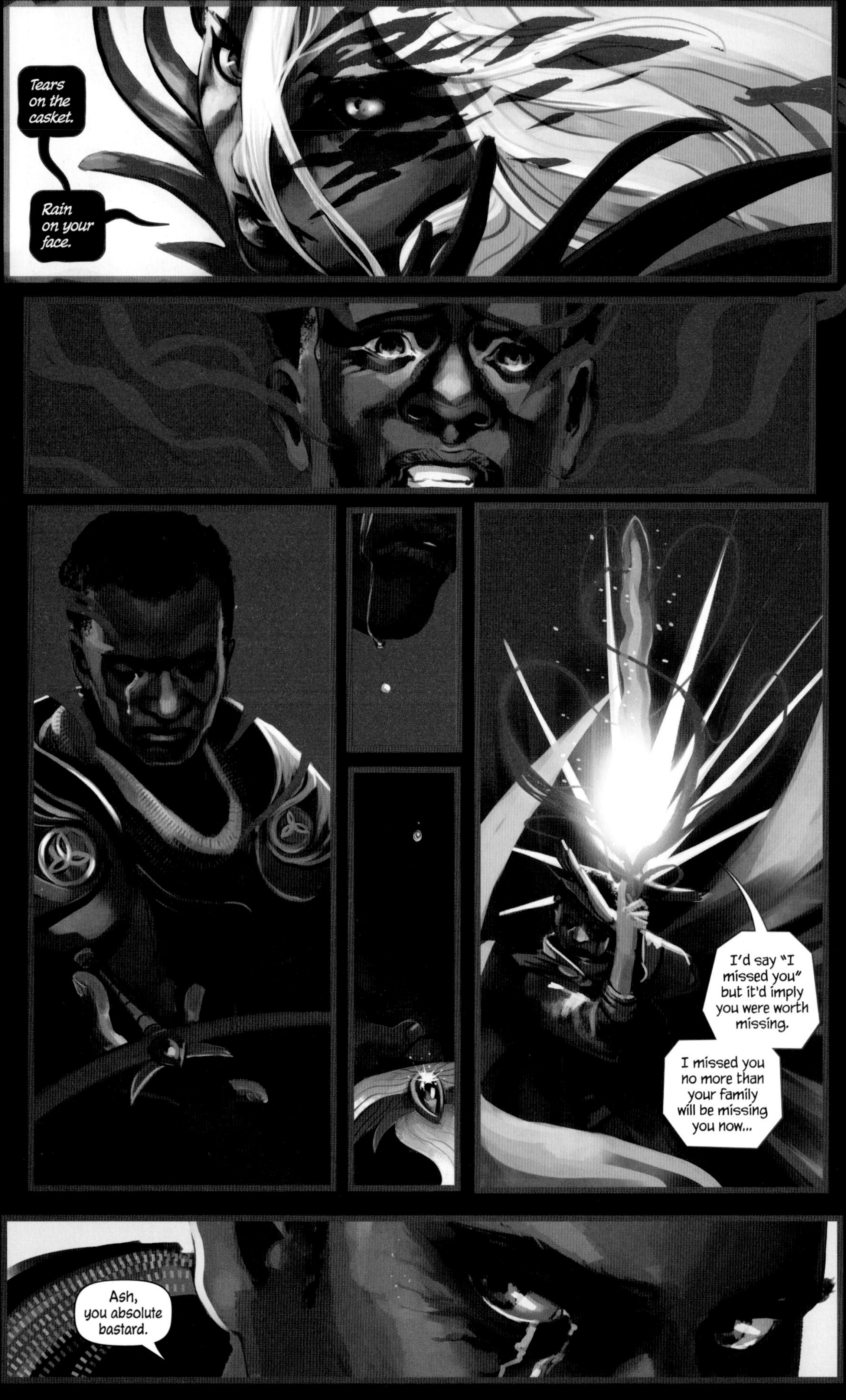

Tears on the casket.
Rain on your face.
I'd say "I missed you" but it'd imply you were worth missing.
I missed you no more than your family will be missing you now...
Ash, you absolute bastard.

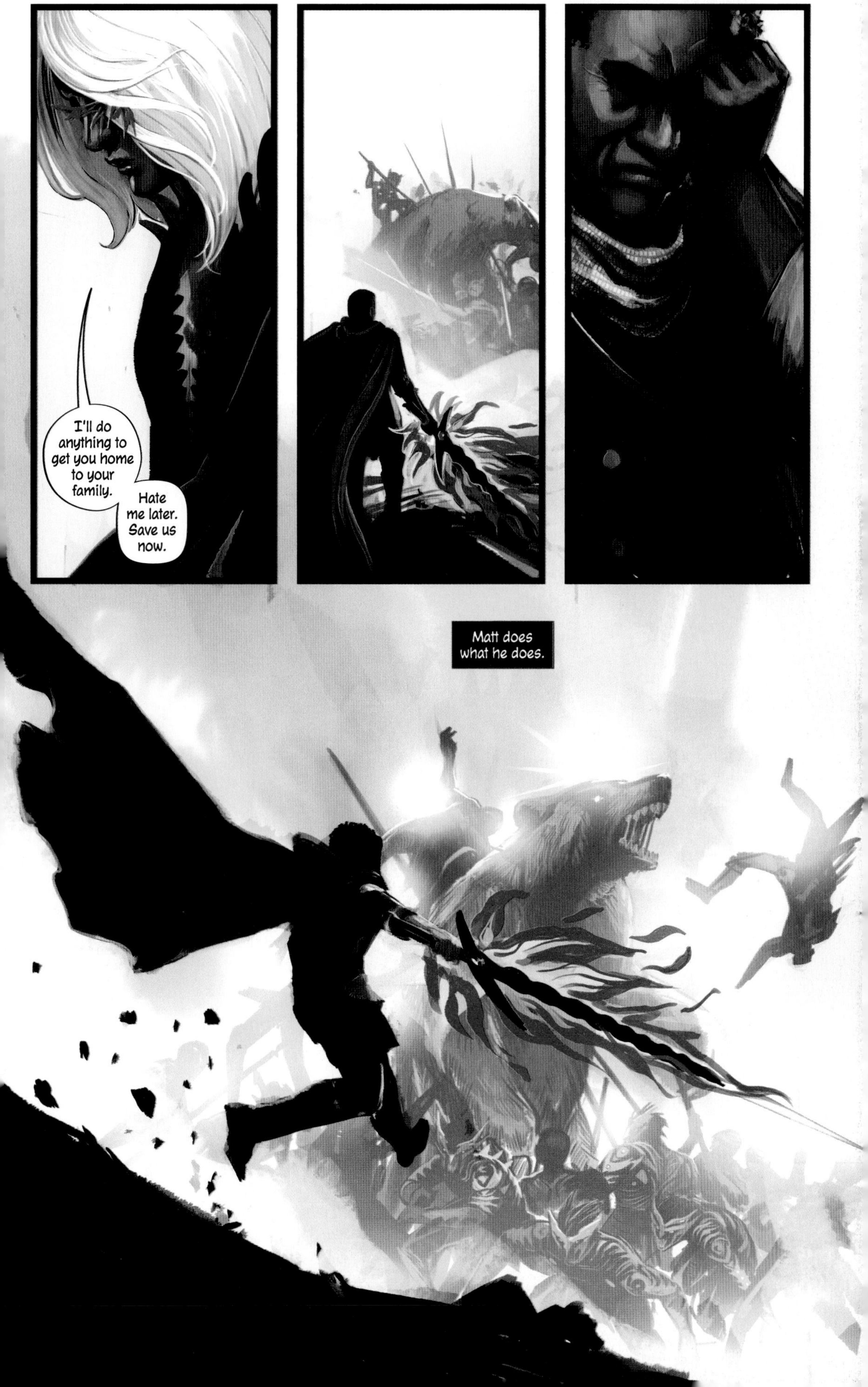
I'll do anything to get you home to your family.
Hate me later. Save us now.
Matt does what he does.

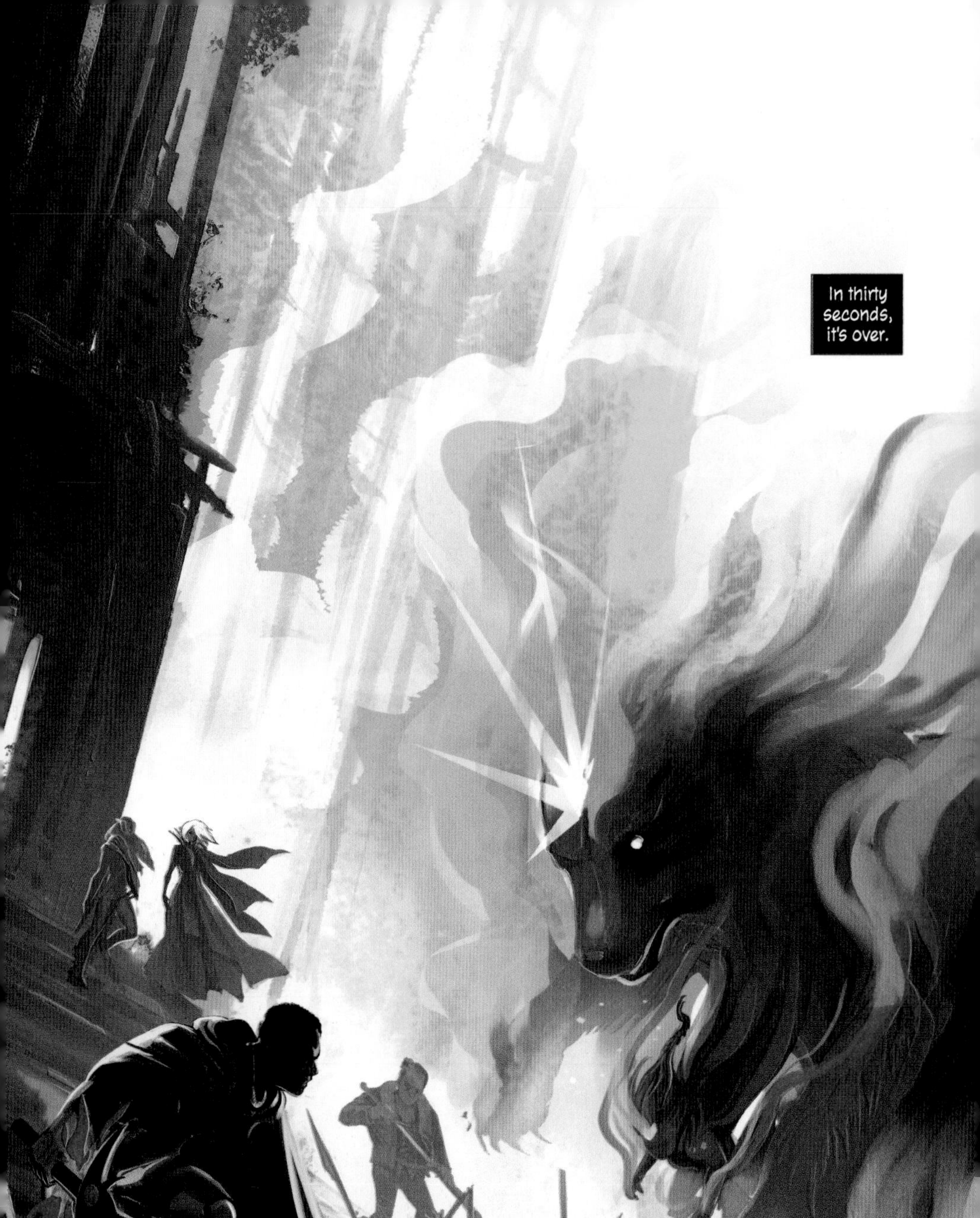
In thirty seconds, it's over.

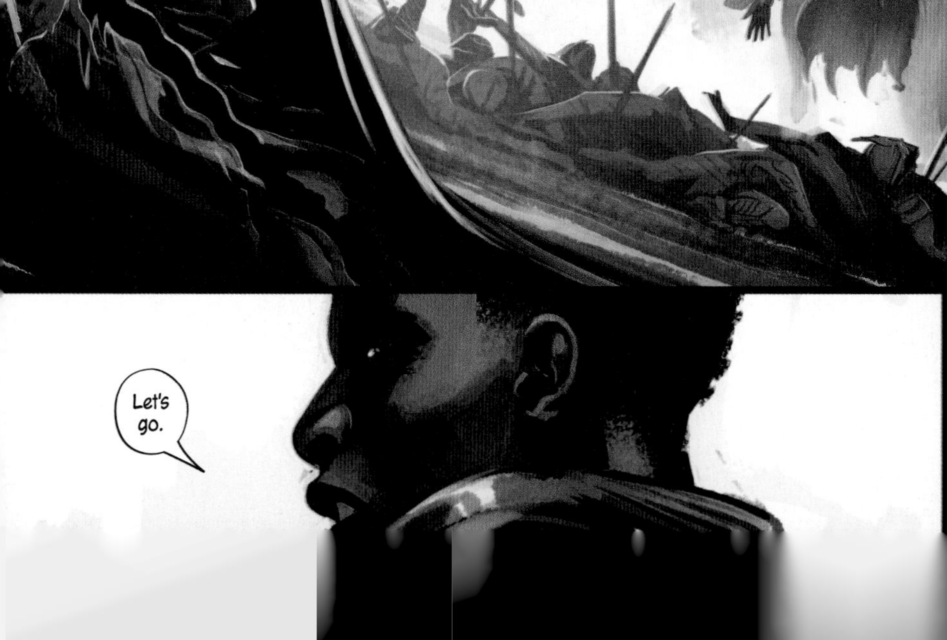
Let's go.

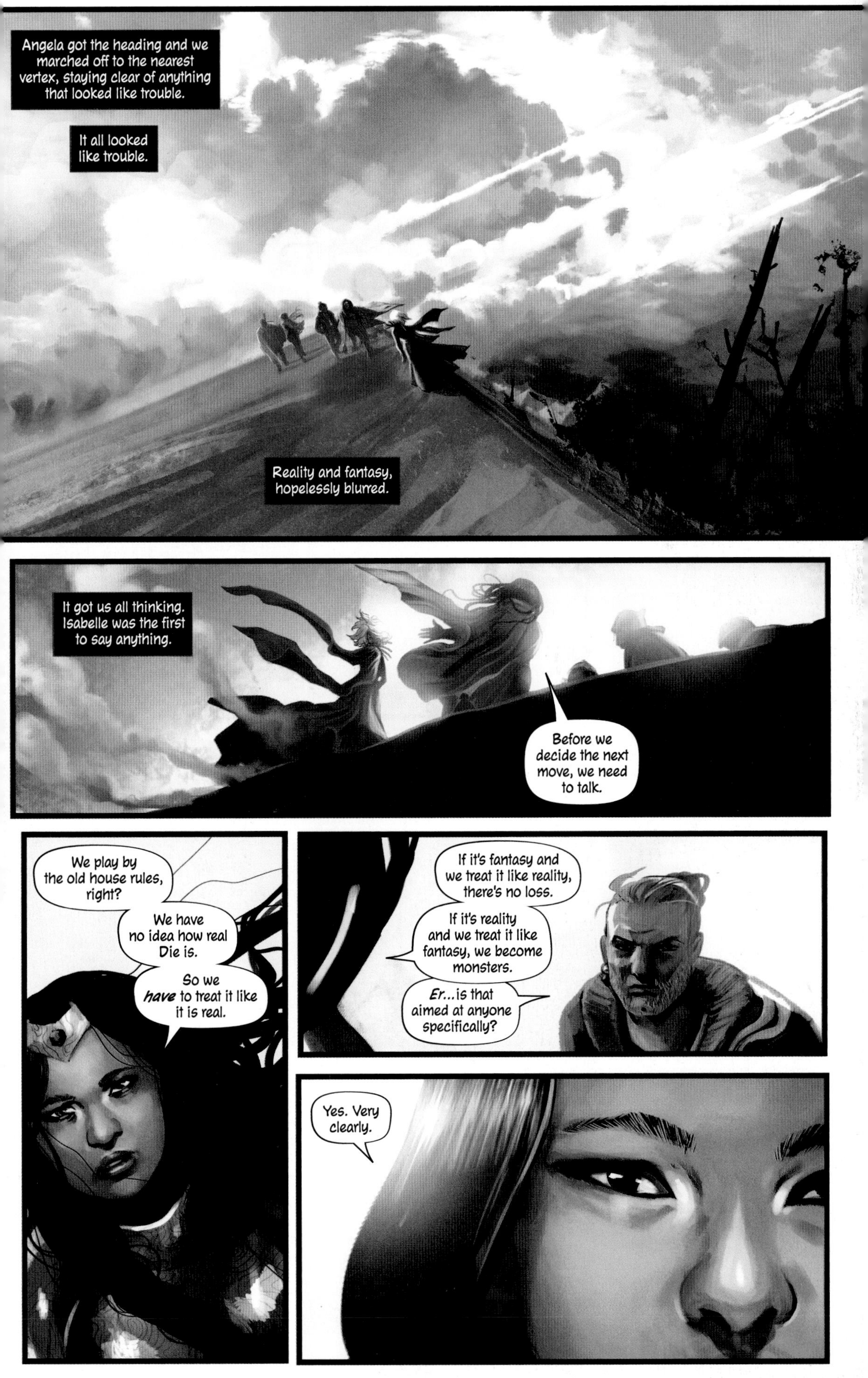
Angela got the heading and we marched off to the nearest vertex, staying clear of anything that looked like trouble.
It all looked like trouble.
Reality and fantasy, hopelessly blurred.
It got us all thinking. Isabelle was the first to say anything.
Before we decide the next move, we need to talk.
We play by the old house rules, right?
We have no idea how real Die is.
So we *have* to treat it like it is real.
If it's fantasy and we treat it like reality, there's no loss.
If it's reality and we treat it like fantasy, we become monsters.
Er...is that aimed at anyone specifically?
Yes. Very clearly.

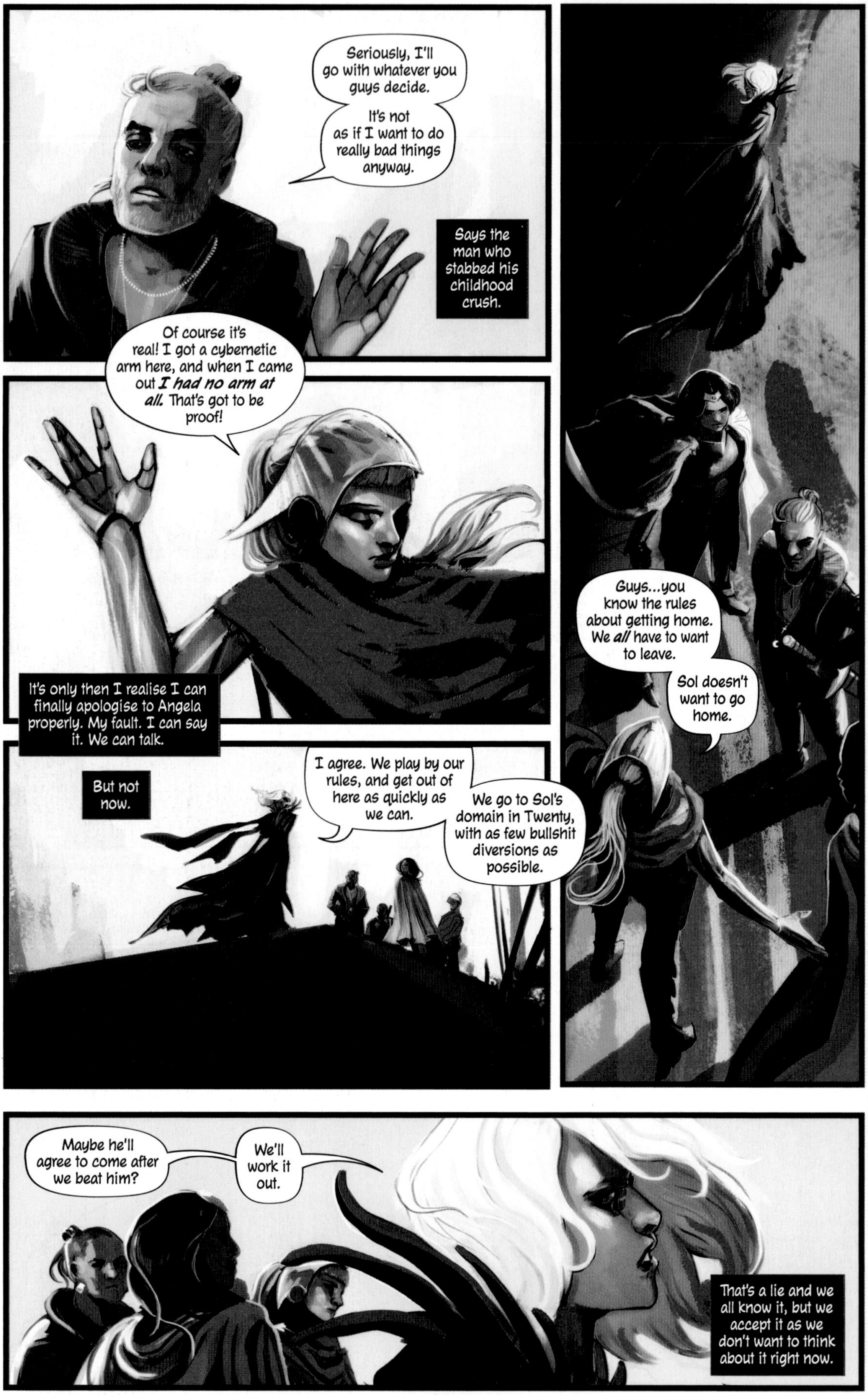
Seriously, I'll go with whatever you guys decide.
It's not as if I want to do really bad things anyway.
Says the man who stabbed his childhood crush.
Of course it's real! I got a cybernetic arm here, and when I came out *I had no arm at all.* That's got to be proof!
It's only then I realise I can finally apologise to Angela properly. My fault. I can say it. We can talk.
But not now.
I agree. We play by our rules, and get out of here as quickly as we can.
We go to Sol's domain in Twenty, with as few bullshit diversions as possible.
Guys...you know the rules about getting home. We *all* have to want to leave.
Sol doesn't want to go home.
Maybe he'll agree to come after we beat him?
We'll work it out.
That's a lie and we all know it, but we accept it as we don't want to think about it right now.

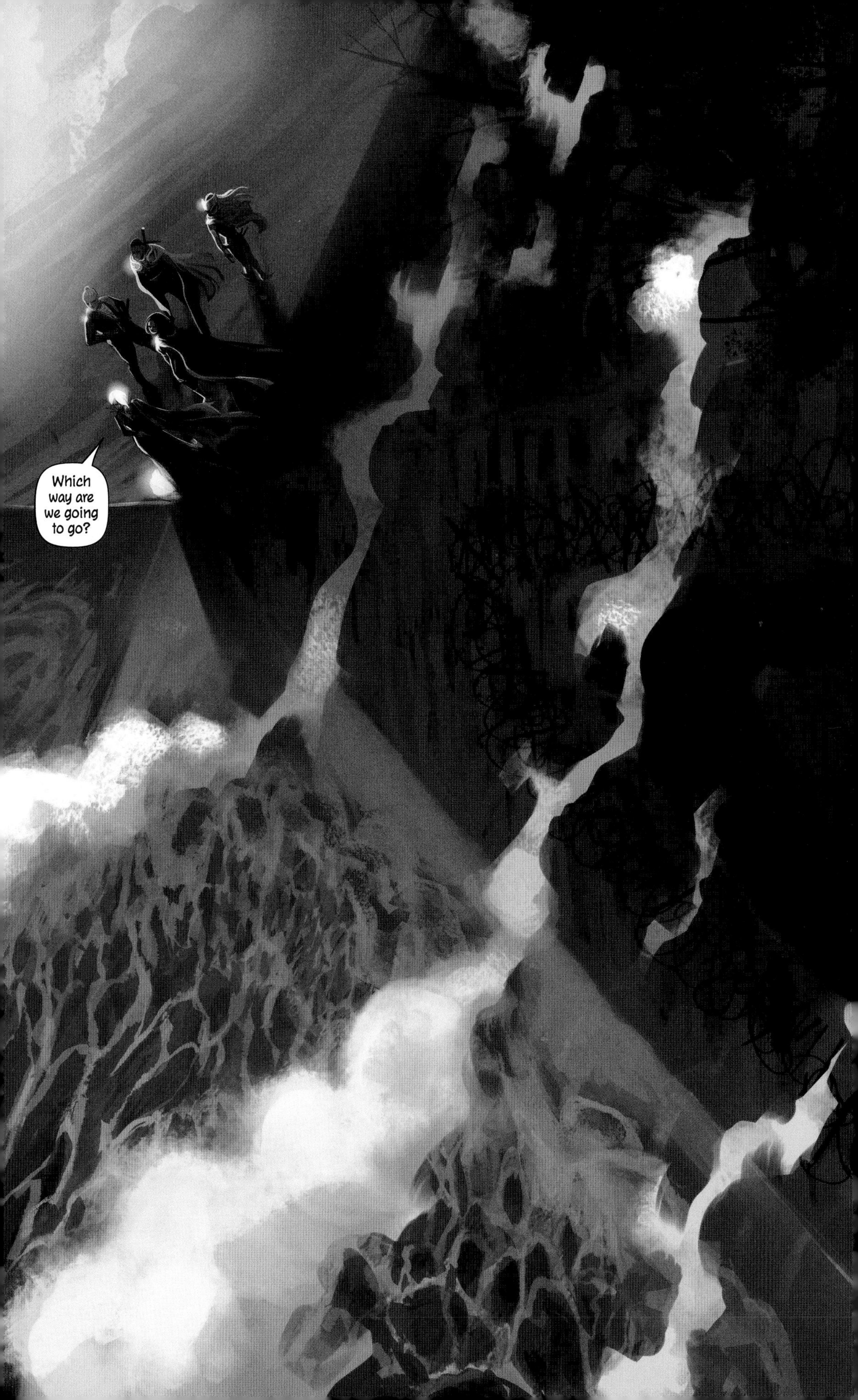
Which way are we going to go?

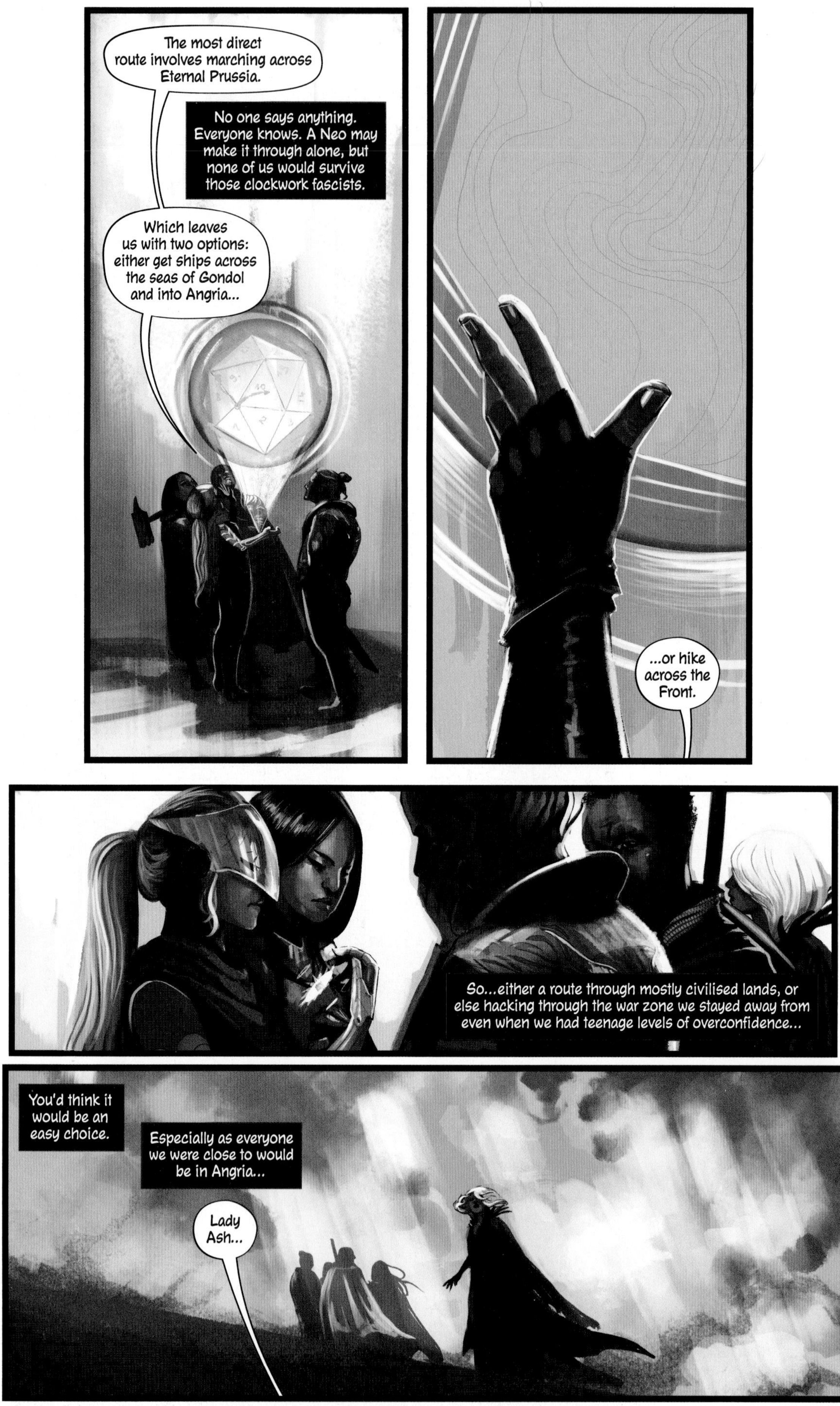

The most direct route involves marching across Eternal Prussia.
No one says anything. Everyone knows. A Neo may make it through alone, but none of us would survive those clockwork fascists.
Which leaves us with two options: either get ships across the seas of Gondol and into Angria...
...or hike across the Front.
So...either a route through mostly civilised lands, or else hacking through the war zone we stayed away from even when we had teenage levels of overconfidence...
You'd think it would be an easy choice.
Especially as everyone we were close to would be in Angria...
Lady Ash...

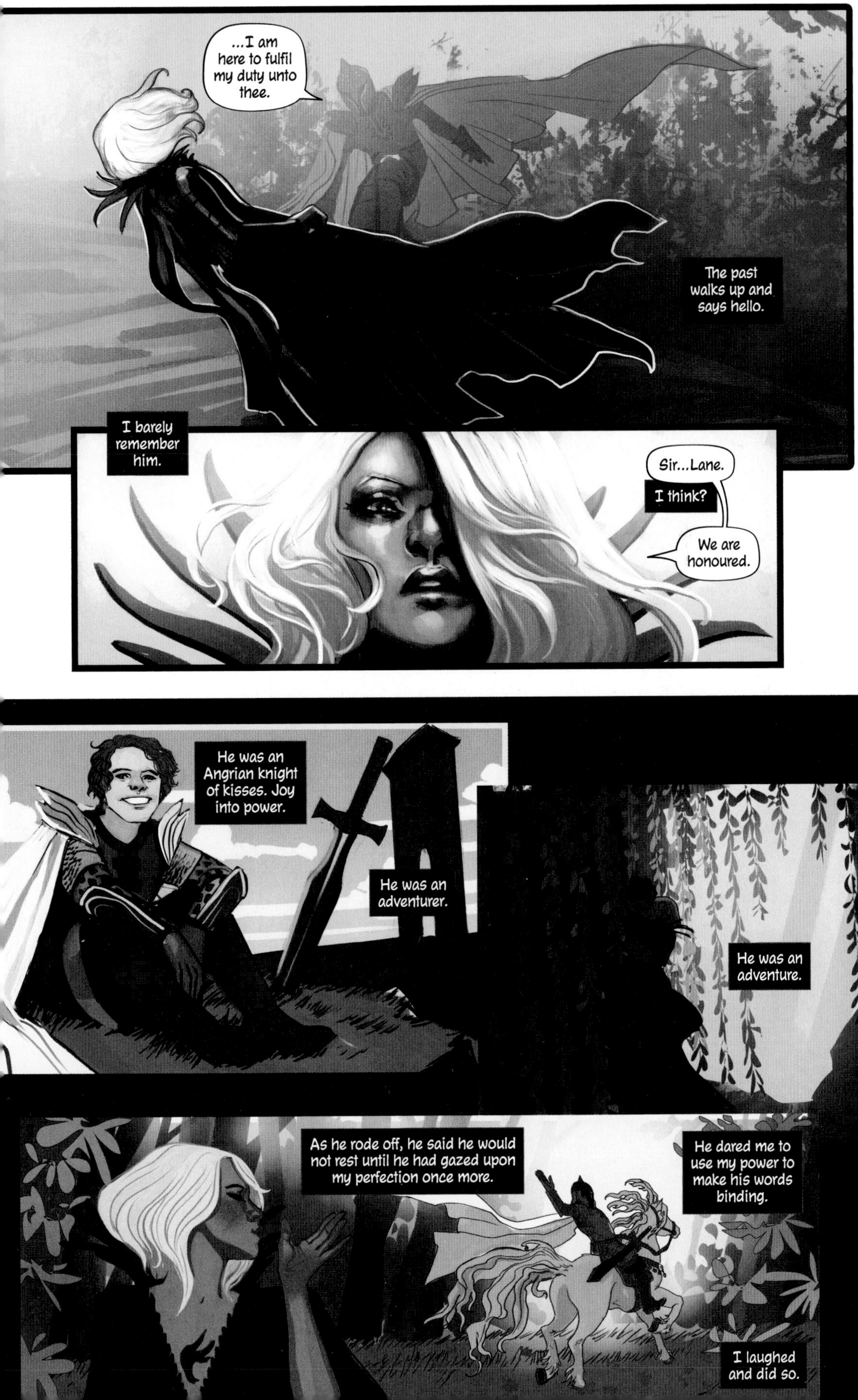
...I am here to fulfil my duty unto thee.
The past walks up and says hello.
I barely remember him.
Sir...Lane.
I think?
We are honoured.
He was an Angrian knight of kisses. Joy into power.
He was an adventurer.
He was an adventure.
As he rode off, he said he would not rest until he had gazed upon my perfection once more.
He dared me to use my power to make his words binding.
I laughed and did so.

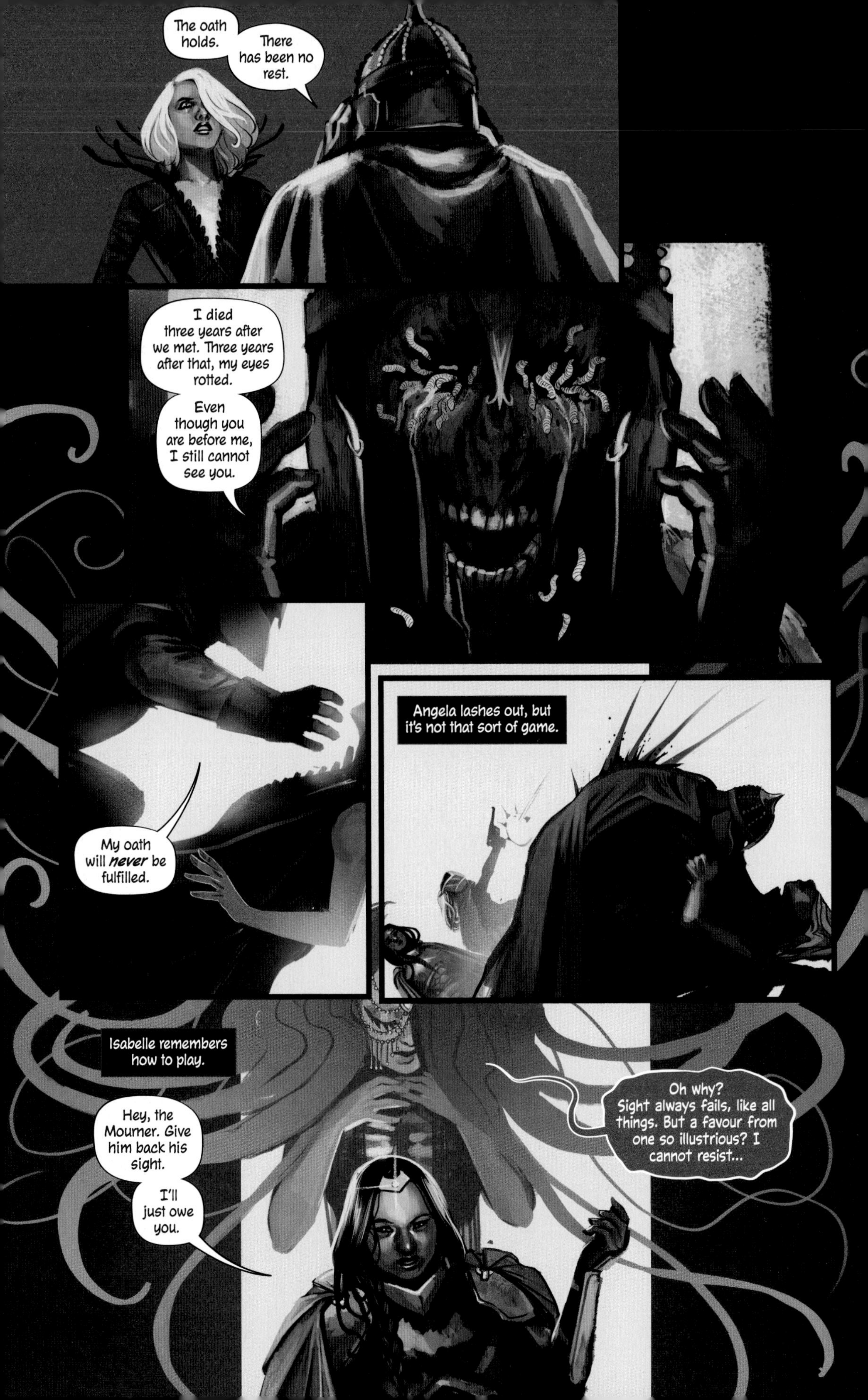
The oath holds.
There has been no rest.
I died three years after we met. Three years after that, my eyes rotted.
Even though you are before me, I still cannot see you.
My oath will ***never*** be fulfilled.
Angela lashes out, but it's not that sort of game.
Isabelle remembers how to play.
Hey, the Mourner. Give him back his sight.
I'll just owe you.
Oh why? Sight always fails, like all things. But a favour from one so illustrious? I cannot resist...

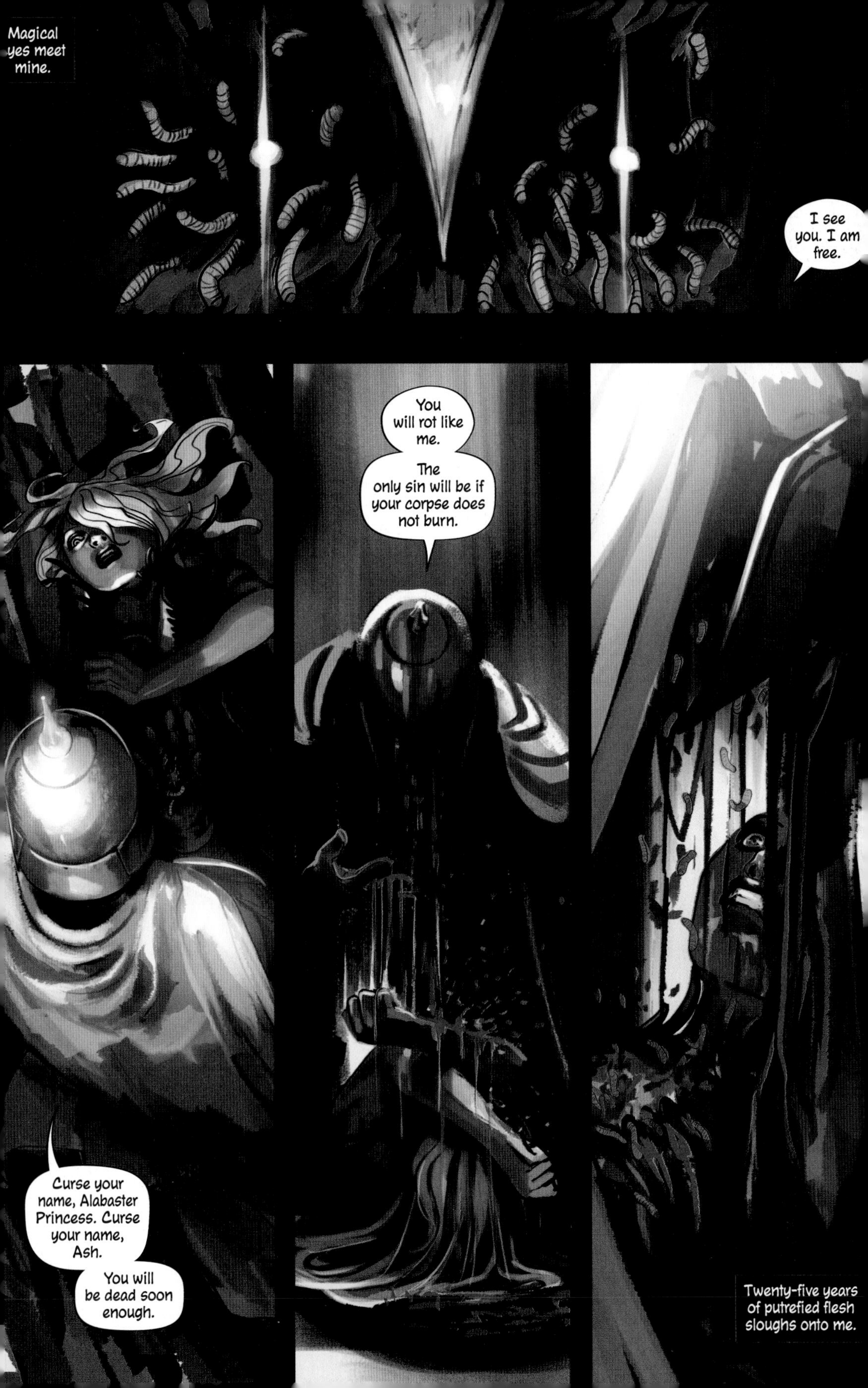
Magical yes meet mine.
I see you. I am free.
Curse your name, Alabaster Princess. Curse your name, Ash.
You will be dead soon enough.
You will rot like me.
The only sin will be if your corpse does not burn.
Twenty-five years of putrefied flesh sloughs onto me.

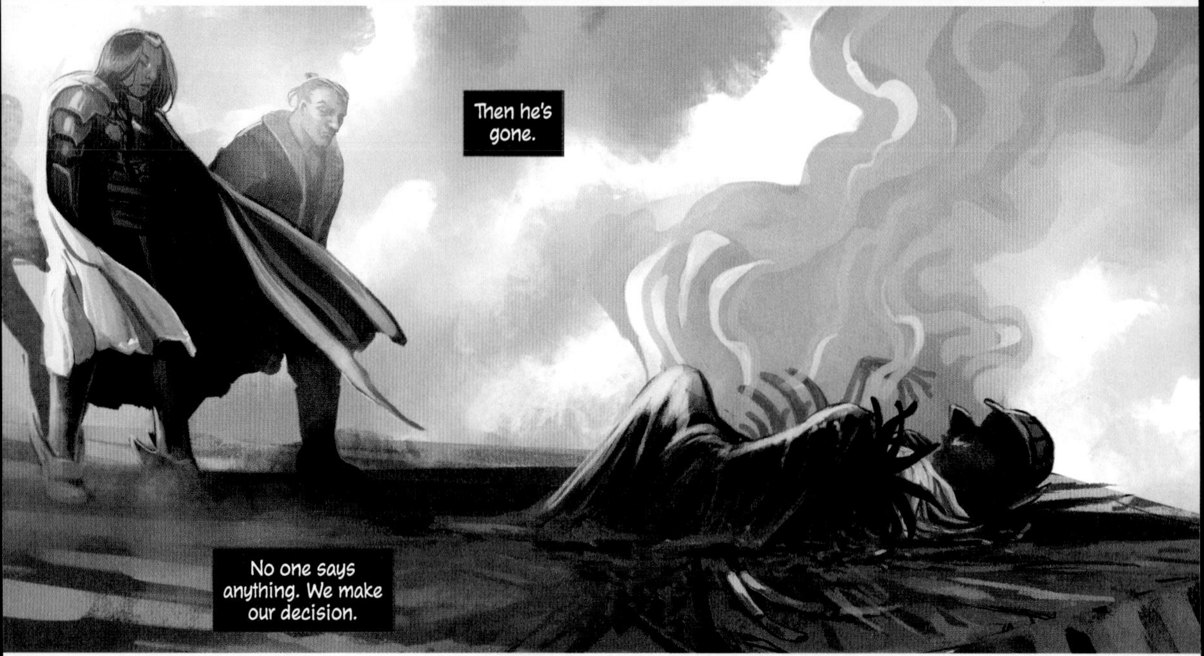
Then he's gone.
No one says anything. We make our decision.

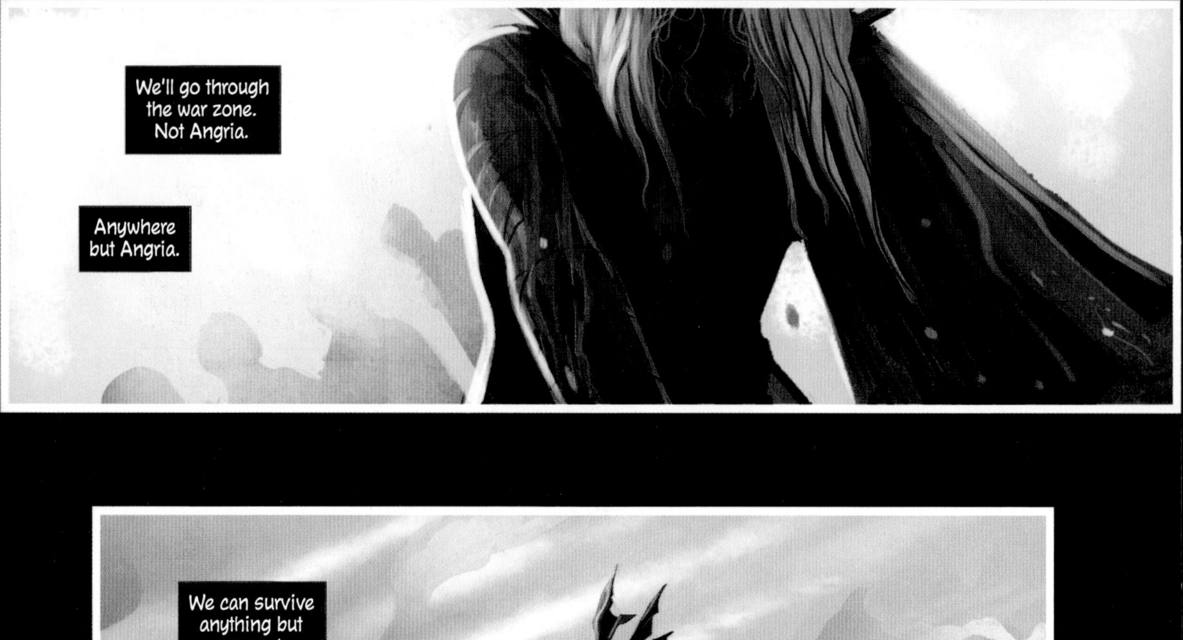
We'll go through the war zone. Not Angria.
Anywhere but Angria.

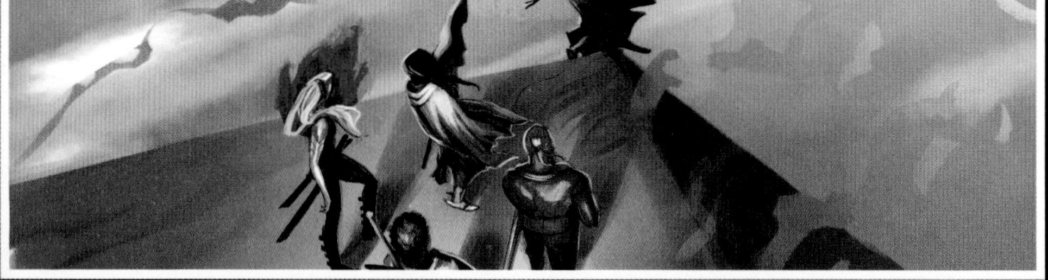
We can survive anything but our past.

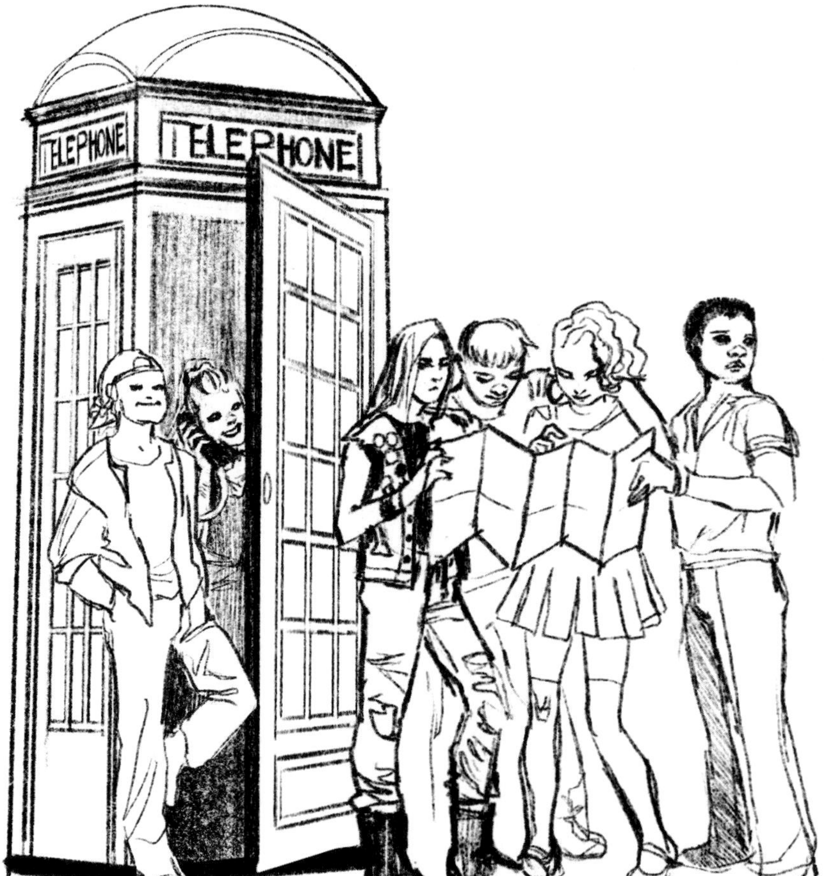
TELEPHONE
TELEPHONE

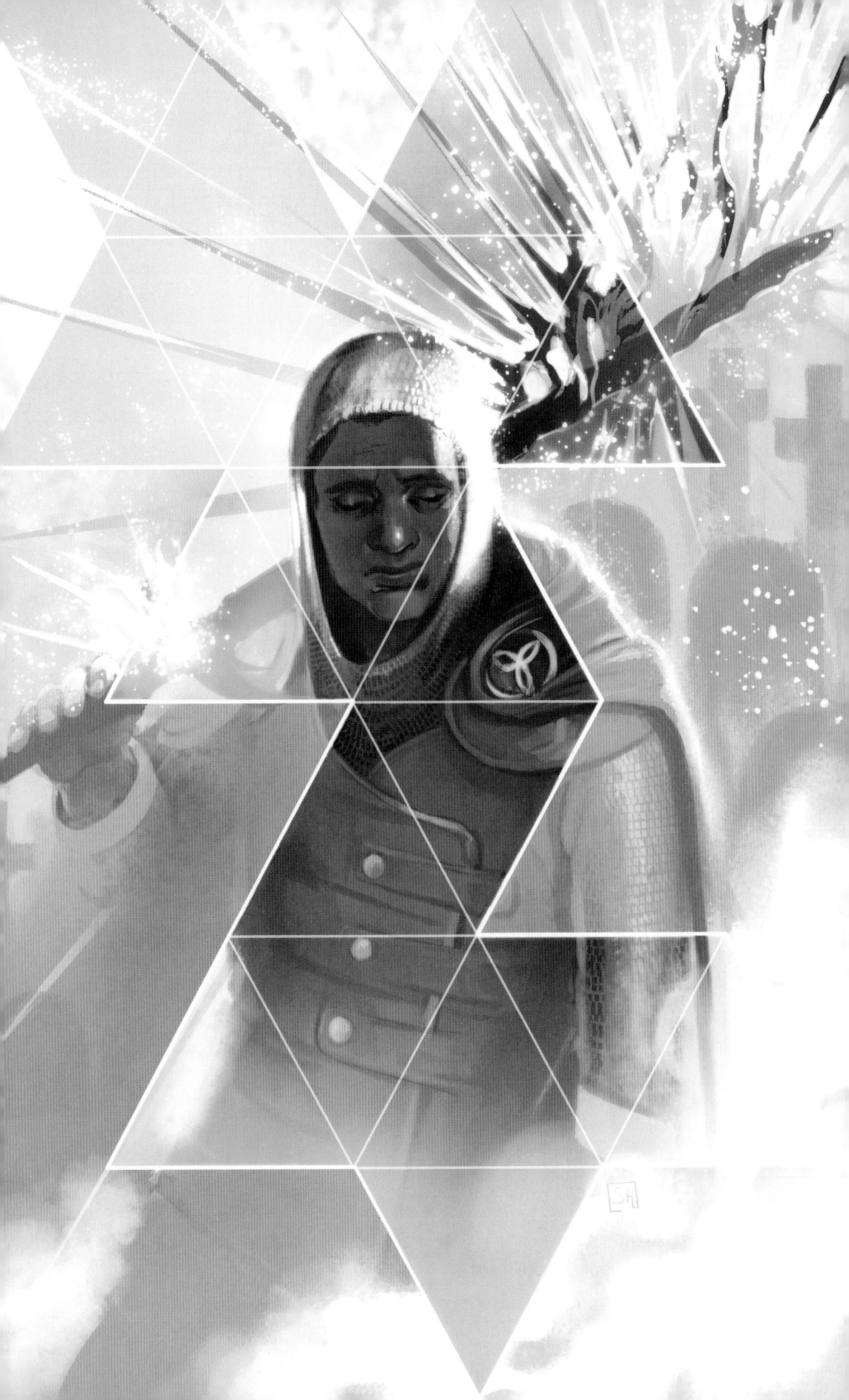

3:
DUNGEONS

"You only have to play at Little Wars
three or four times to realise what a
blundering thing Great War must be."
– *HG Wells*

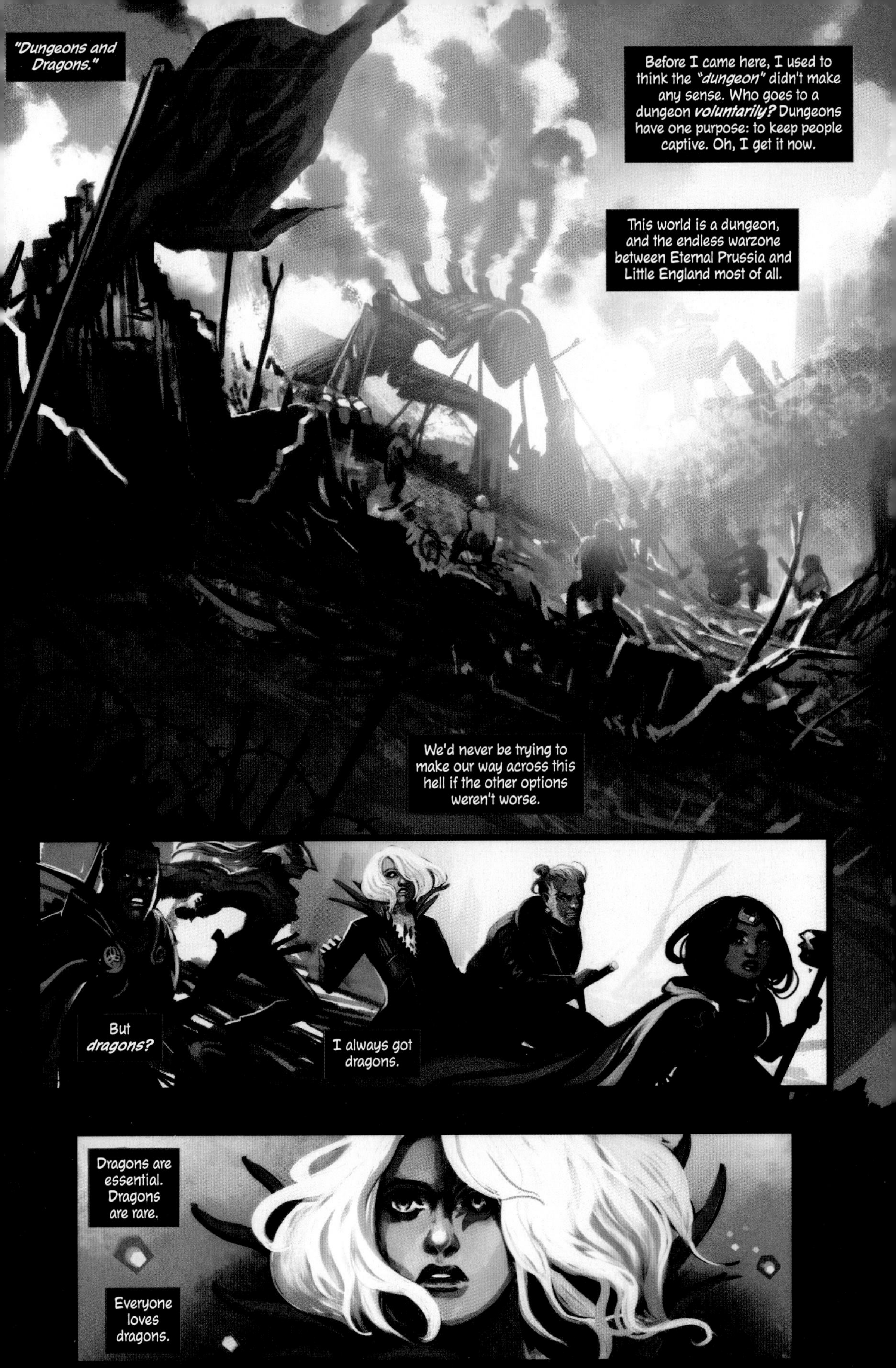
"Dungeons and Dragons."
Before I came here, I used to think the "dungeon" didn't make any sense. Who goes to a dungeon voluntarily? Dungeons have one purpose: to keep people captive. Oh, I get it now.
This world is a dungeon, and the endless warzone between Eternal Prussia and Little England most of all.
We'd never be trying to make our way across this hell if the other options weren't worse.
But dragons?
I always got dragons.
Dragons are essential. Dragons are rare.
Everyone loves dragons.

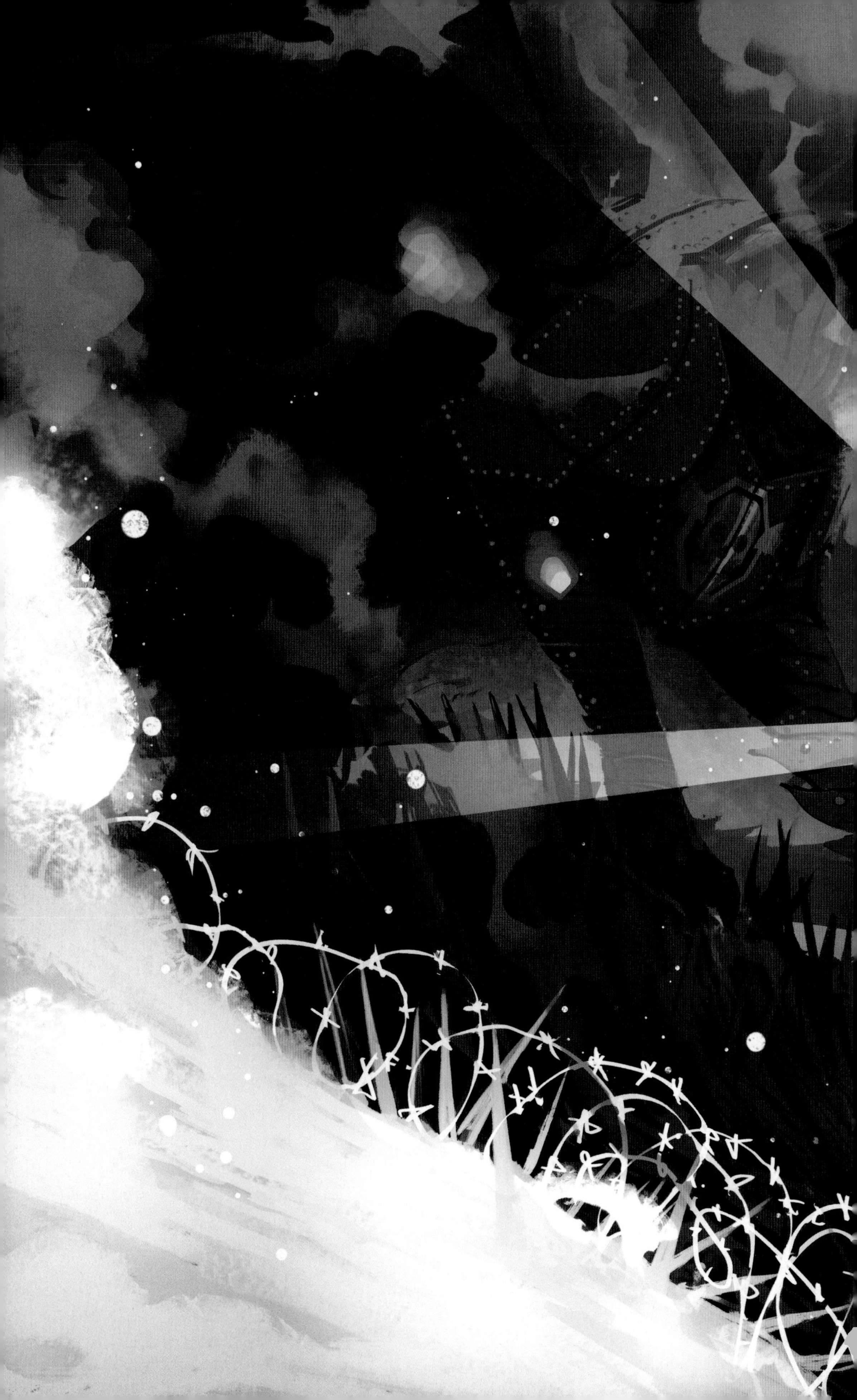

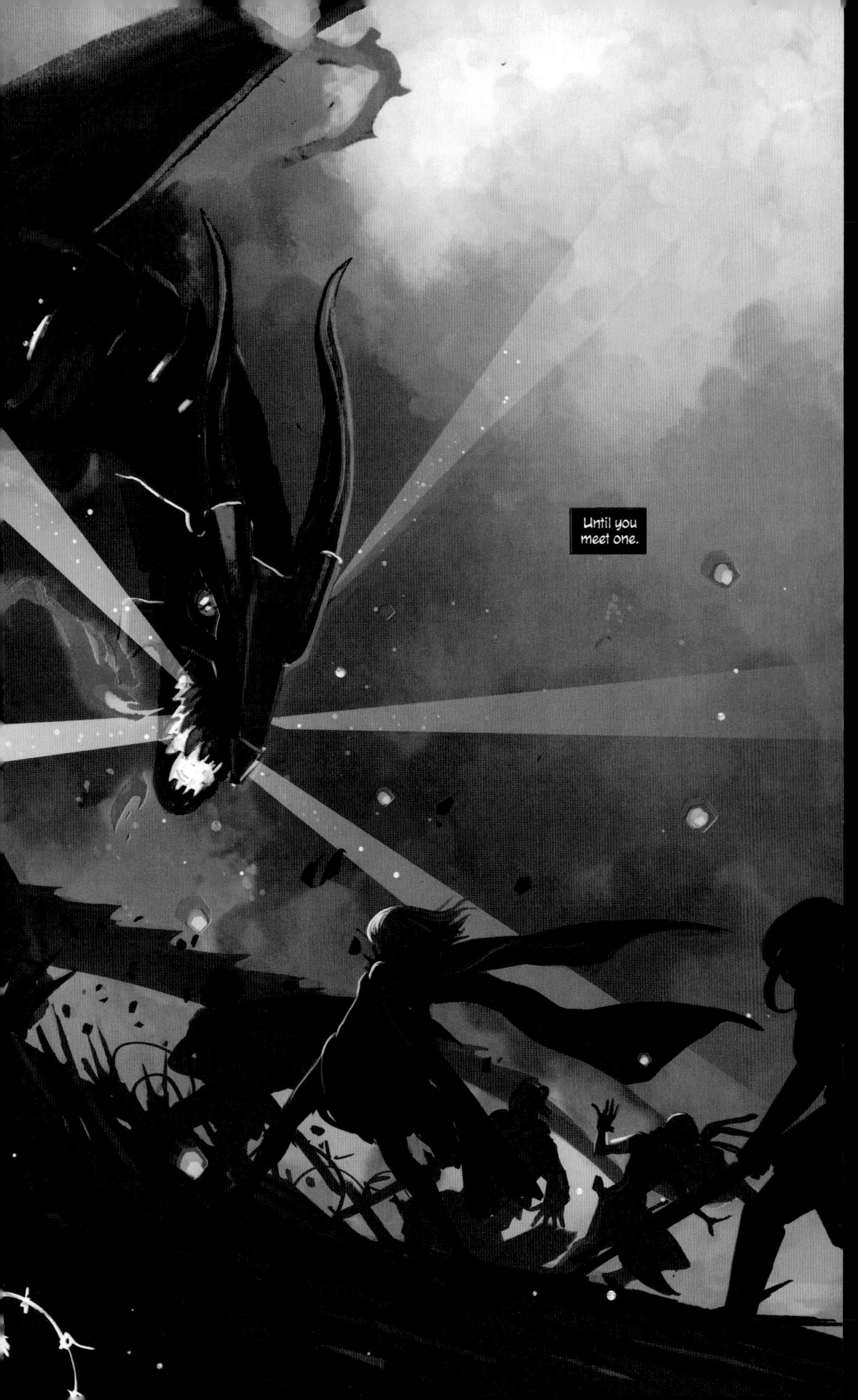
Until you meet one.

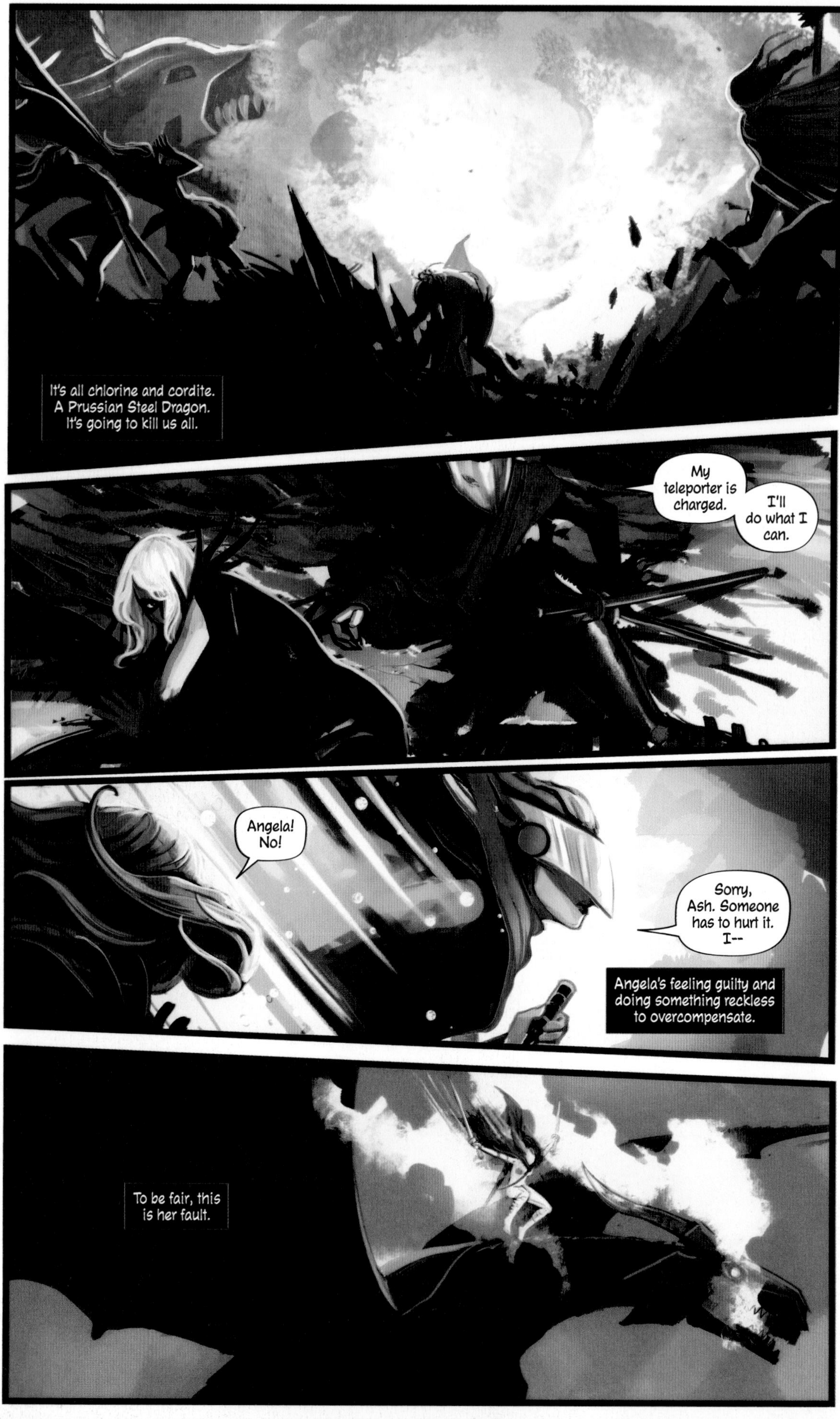
It's all chlorine and cordite. A Prussian Steel Dragon. It's going to kill us all.
My teleporter is charged.
I'll do what I can.
Angela! No!
Sorry, Ash. Someone has to hurt it. I--
Angela's feeling guilty and doing something reckless to overcompensate.
To be fair, this is her fault.

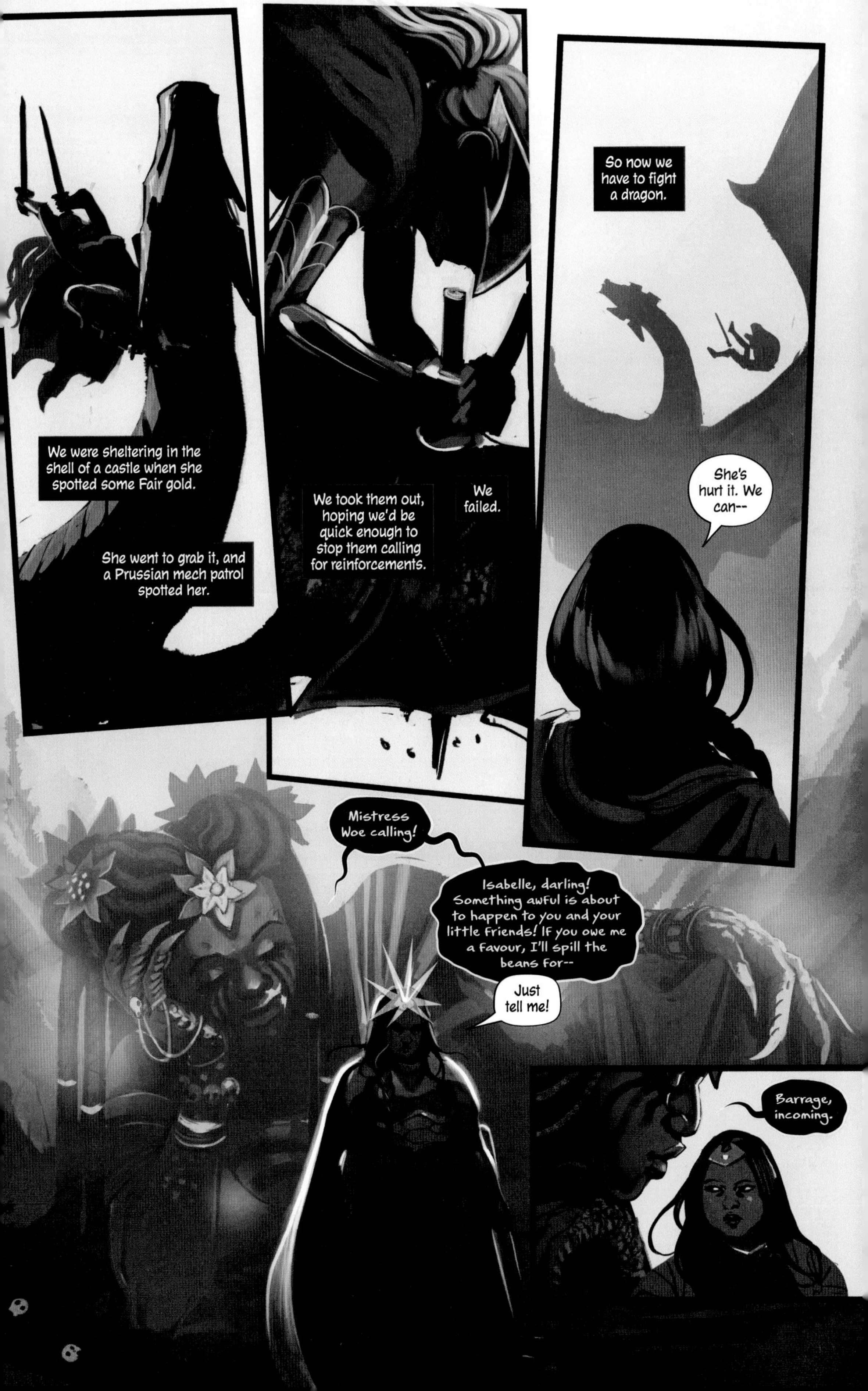
We were sheltering in the shell of a castle when she spotted some Fair gold.
She went to grab it, and a Prussian mech patrol spotted her.
We took them out, hoping we'd be quick enough to stop them calling for reinforcements.
We failed.
So now we have to fight a dragon.
She's hurt it. We can--
Mistress Woe calling!
Isabelle, darling! Something awful is about to happen to you and your little friends! If you owe me a favour, I'll spill the beans for--
Just tell me!
Barrage, incoming.

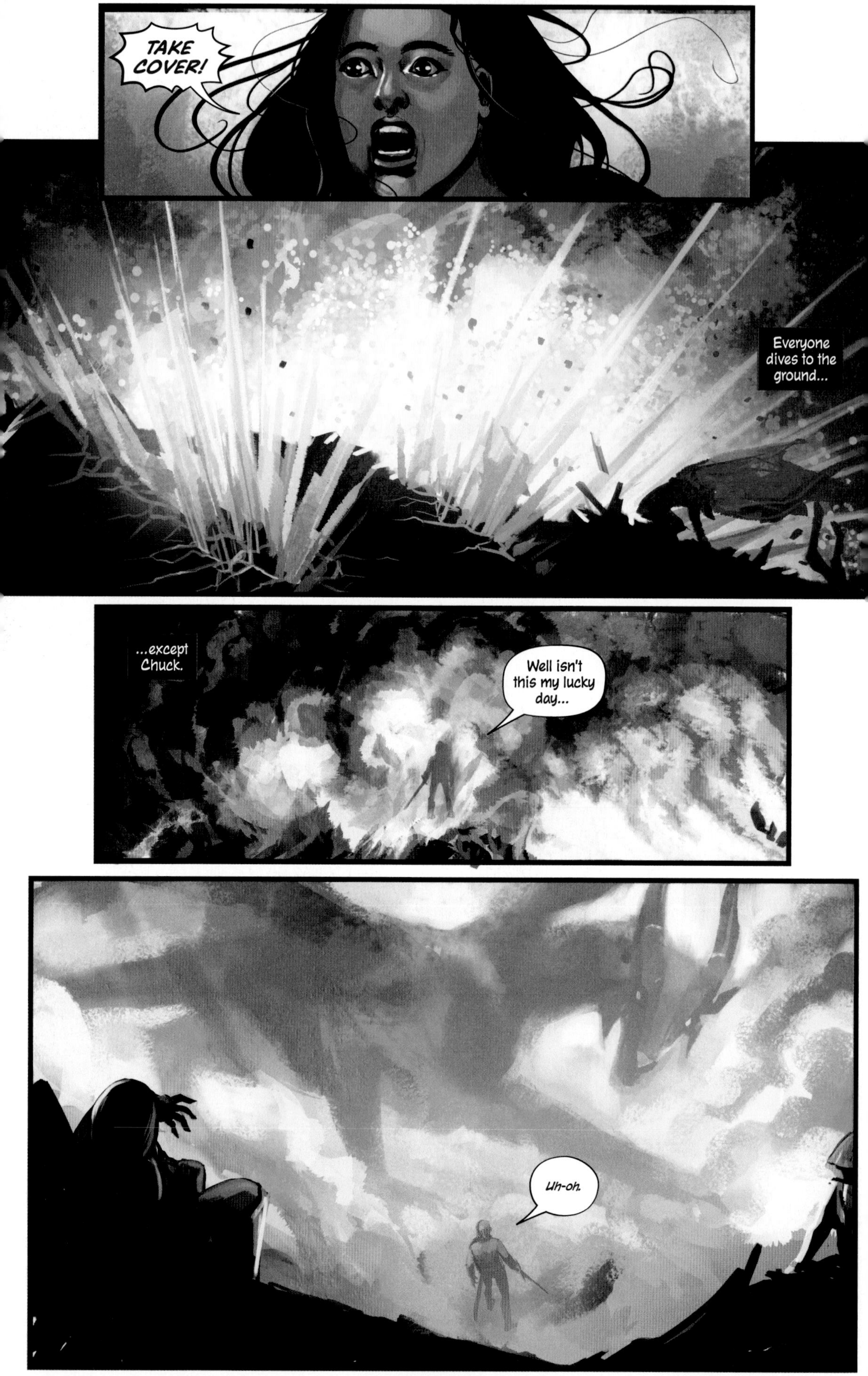
TAKE COVER!
Everyone dives to the ground...
...except Chuck.
Well isn't this my lucky day...
Uh-oh.

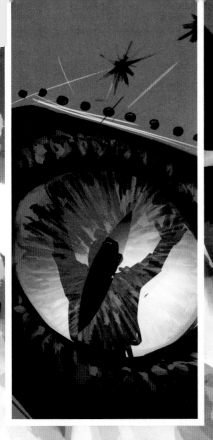

It goes after Chuck as another barrage of God knows what hits.

Lungfuls of gas.

Chaos.

Panic.

Eyes burning.

I've lost everyone.

I am lost.

Sol's eternal wisdom comes back to mind...

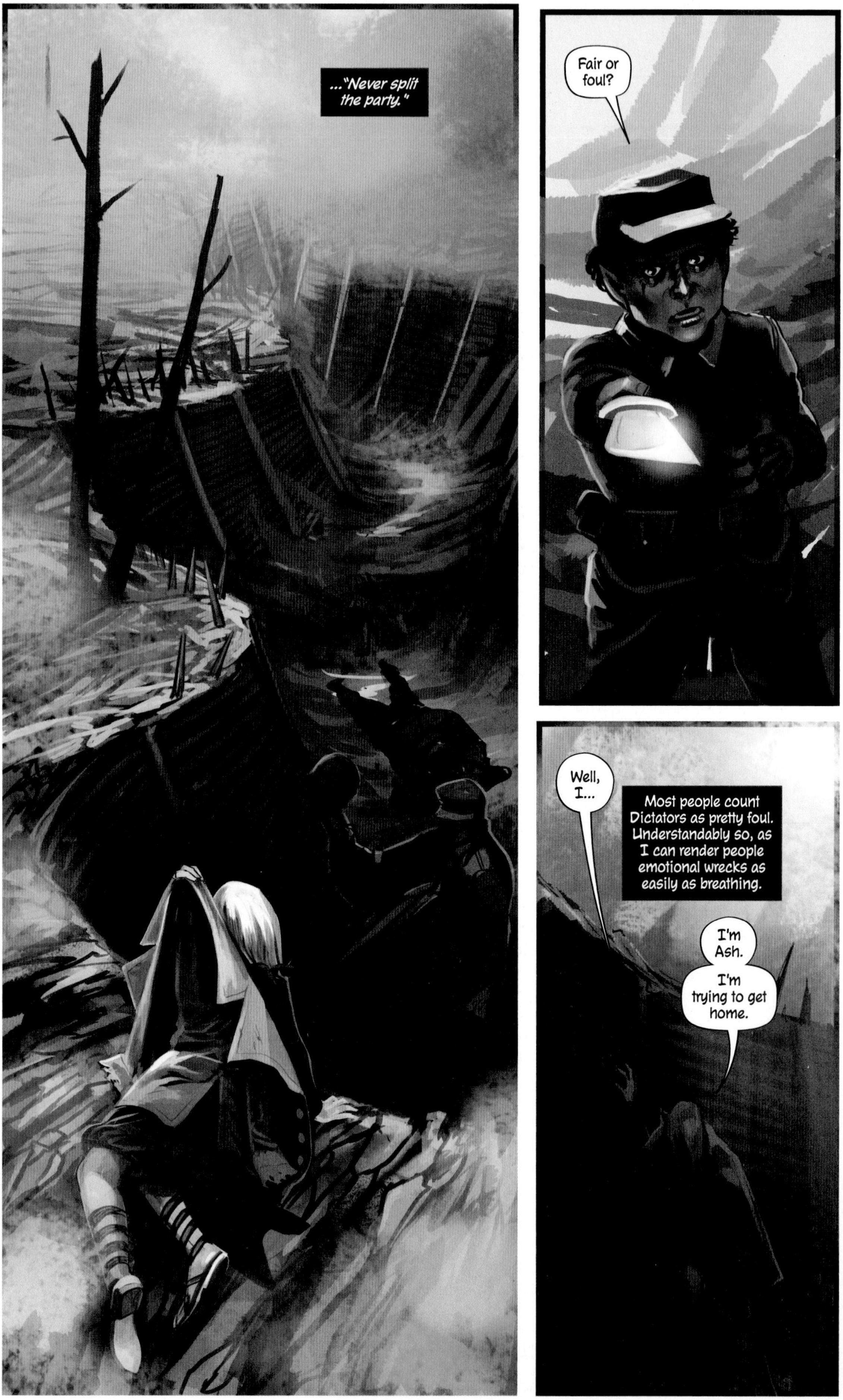
..."Never split the party."
Fair or foul?
Well, I...
Most people count Dictators as pretty foul. Understandably so, as I can render people emotional wrecks as easily as breathing.
I'm Ash.
I'm trying to get home.

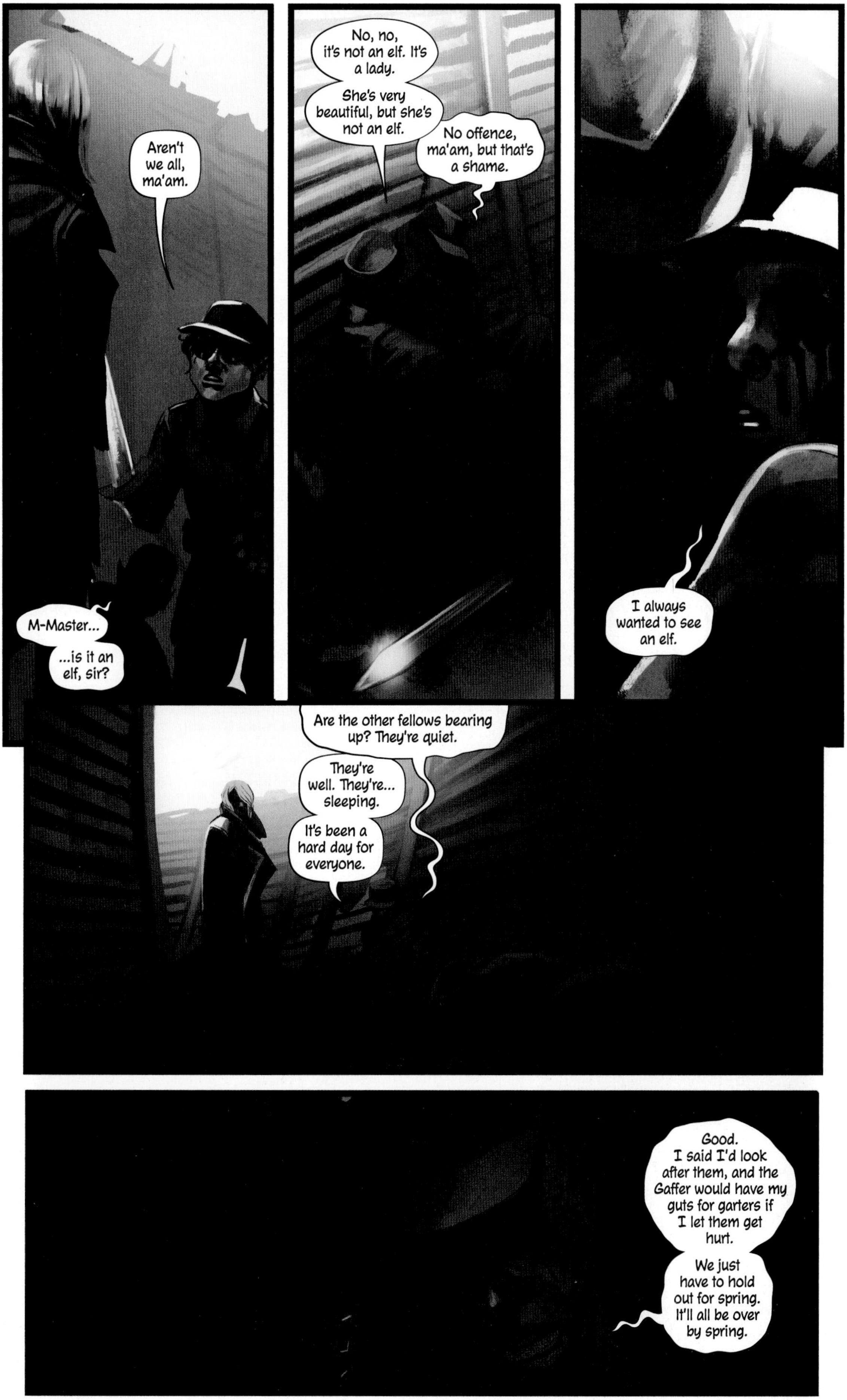
Aren't we all, ma'am.
M-Master...
...is it an elf, sir?
No, no, it's not an elf. It's a lady.
She's very beautiful, but she's not an elf.
No offence, ma'am, but that's a shame.
I always wanted to see an elf.
Are the other fellows bearing up? They're quiet.
They're well. They're... sleeping.
It's been a hard day for everyone.
Good. I said I'd look after them, and the Gaffer would have my guts for garters if I let them get hurt.
We just have to hold out for spring. It'll all be over by spring.

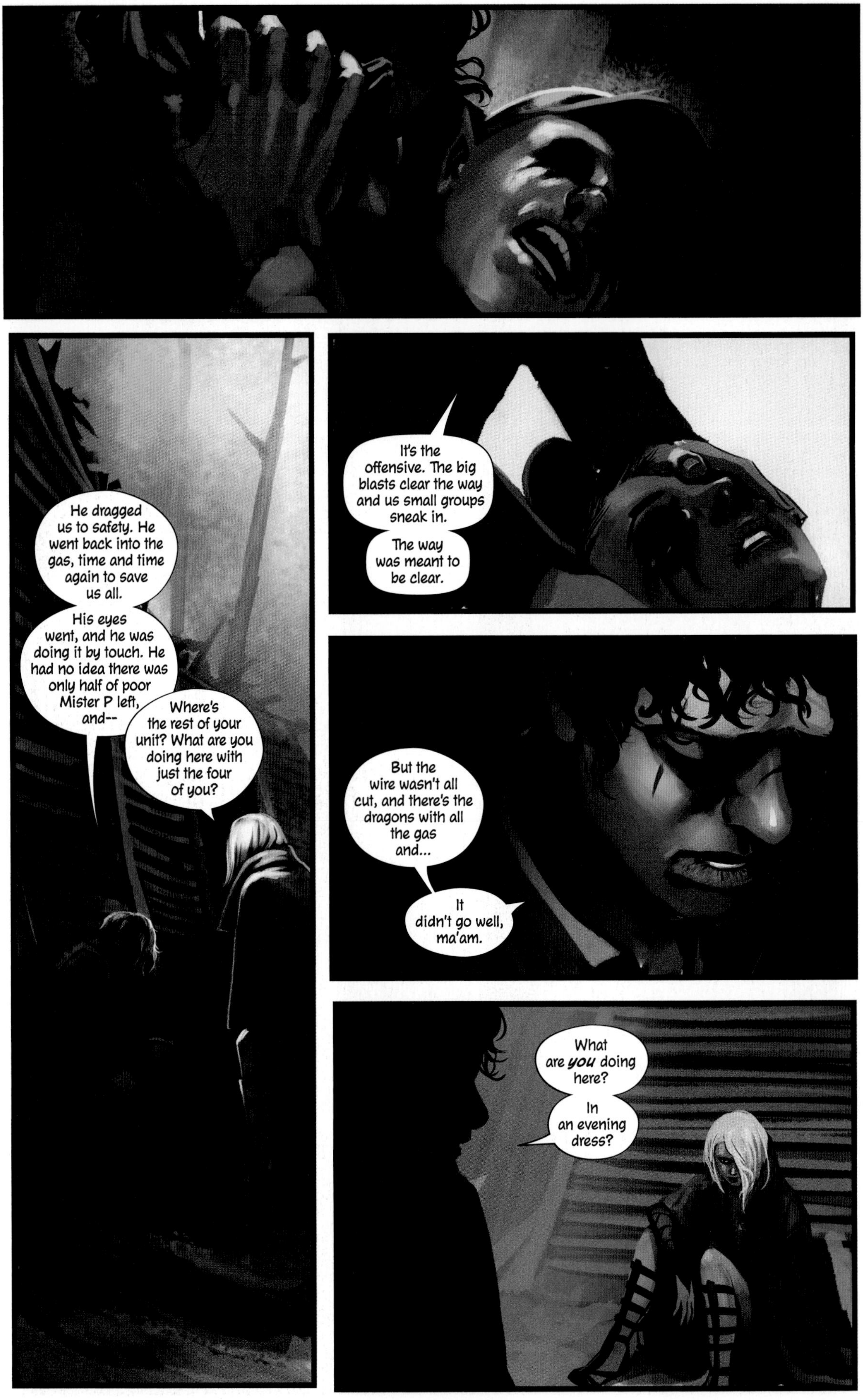
He dragged us to safety. He went back into the gas, time and time again to save us all.
His eyes went, and he was doing it by touch. He had no idea there was only half of poor Mister P left, and--
Where's the rest of your unit? What are you doing here with just the four of you?
It's the offensive. The big blasts clear the way and us small groups sneak in.
The way was meant to be clear.
But the wire wasn't all cut, and there's the dragons with all the gas and...
It didn't go well, ma'am.
What are *you* doing here?
In an evening dress?

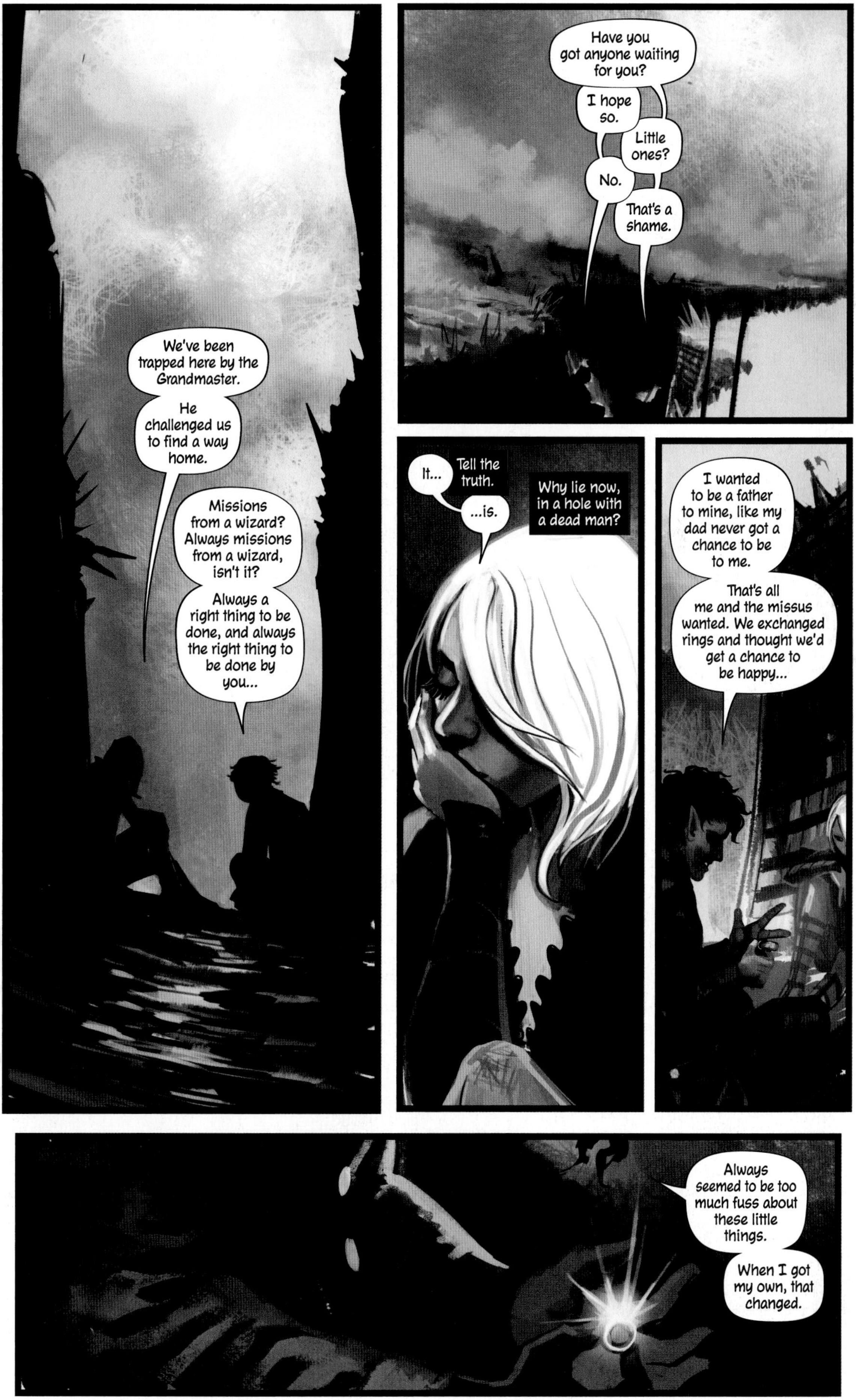

We've been trapped here by the Grandmaster.
He challenged us to find a way home.
Missions from a wizard? Always missions from a wizard, isn't it?
Always a right thing to be done, and always the right thing to be done by you...
Have you got anyone waiting for you?
I hope so.
Little ones?
No.
That's a shame.
Tell the truth.
It...
...is.
Why lie now, in a hole with a dead man?
I wanted to be a father to mine, like my dad never got a chance to be to me.
That's all me and the missus wanted. We exchanged rings and thought we'd get a chance to be happy...
Always seemed to be too much fuss about these little things.
When I got my own, that changed.

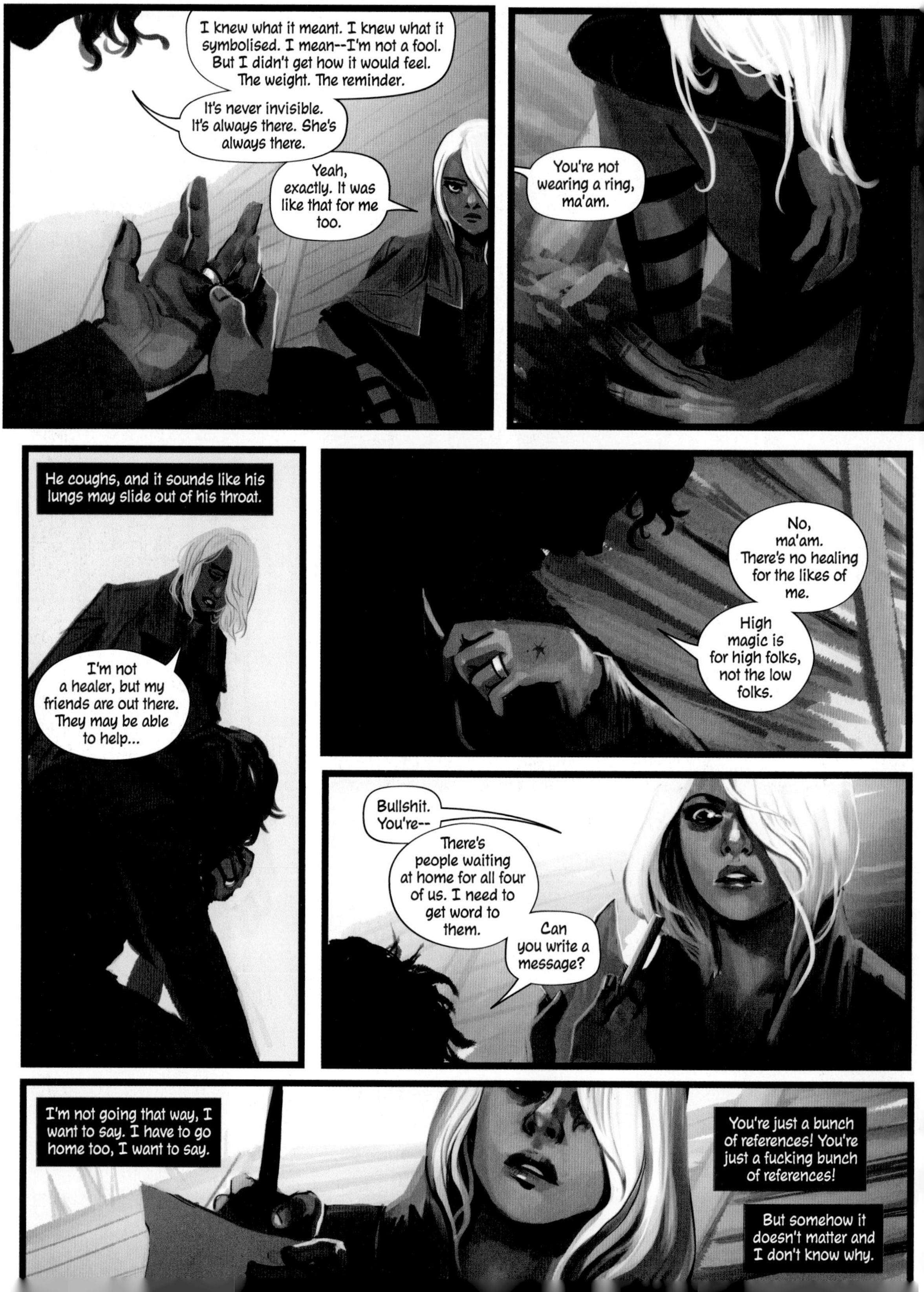
I knew what it meant. I knew what it symbolised. I mean--I'm not a fool. But I didn't get how it would feel. The weight. The reminder.
It's never invisible. It's always there. She's always there.
Yeah, exactly. It was like that for me too.
You're not wearing a ring, ma'am.
He coughs, and it sounds like his lungs may slide out of his throat.
I'm not a healer, but my friends are out there. They may be able to help...
No, ma'am. There's no healing for the likes of me.
High magic is for high folks, not the low folks.
Bullshit. You're--
There's people waiting at home for all four of us. I need to get word to them.
Can you write a message?
I'm not going that way, I want to say. I have to go home too, I want to say.
You're just a bunch of references! You're just a fucking bunch of references!
But somehow it doesn't matter and I don't know why.

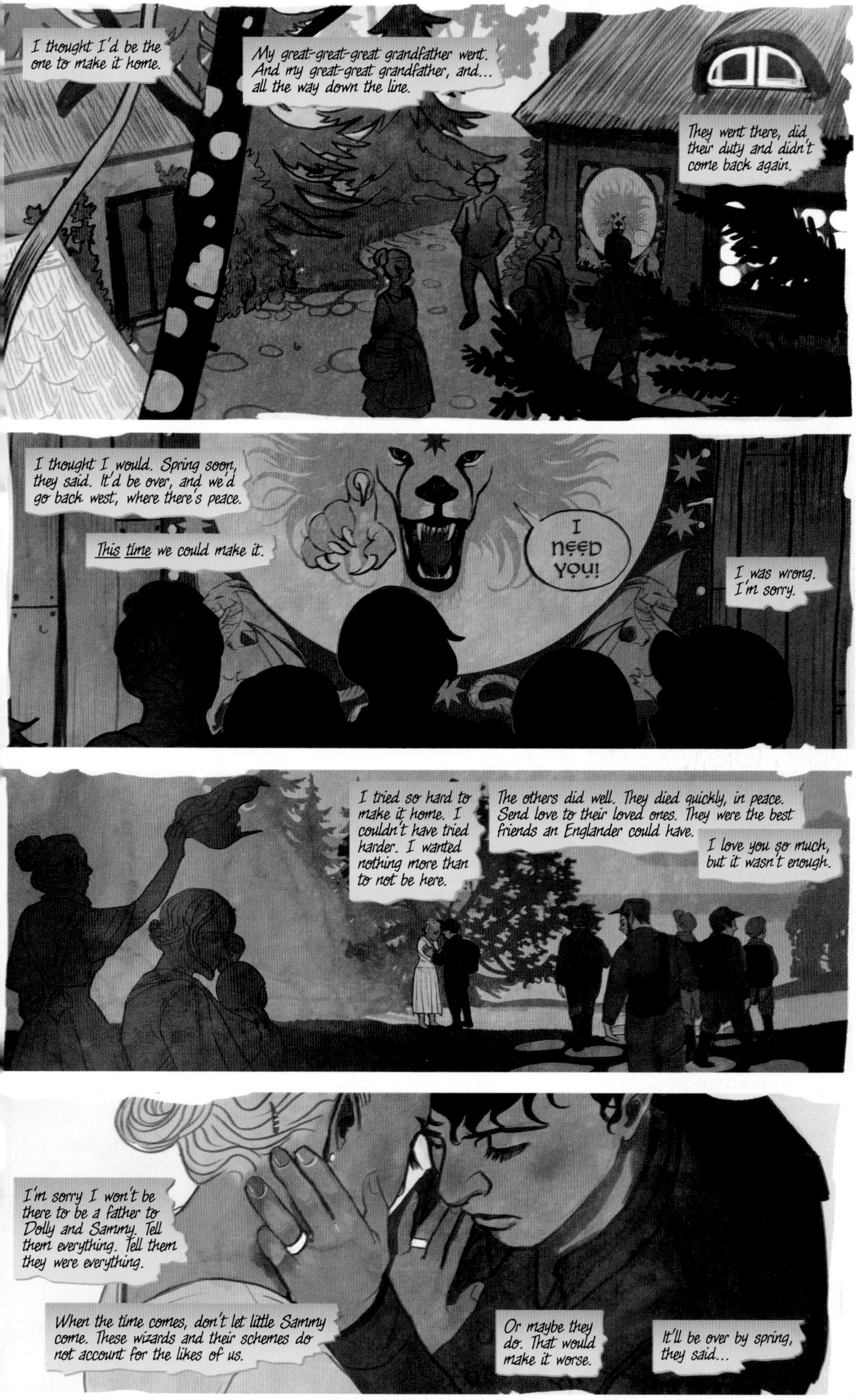
I thought I'd be the one to make it home.
My great-great-great grandfather went. And my great-great grandfather, and... all the way down the line.
They went there, did their duty and didn't come back again.
I thought I would. Spring soon, they said. It'd be over, and we'd go back west, where there's peace.
This time we could make it.
I NEED YOU!
I was wrong. I'm sorry.
I tried so hard to make it home. I couldn't have tried harder. I wanted nothing more than to not be here.
The others did well. They died quickly, in peace. Send love to their loved ones. They were the best friends an Englander could have.
I love you so much, but it wasn't enough.
I'm sorry I won't be there to be a father to Dolly and Sammy. Tell them everything. Tell them they were everything.
When the time comes, don't let little Sammy come. These wizards and their schemes do not account for the likes of us.
Or maybe they do. That would make it worse.
It'll be over by spring, they said...

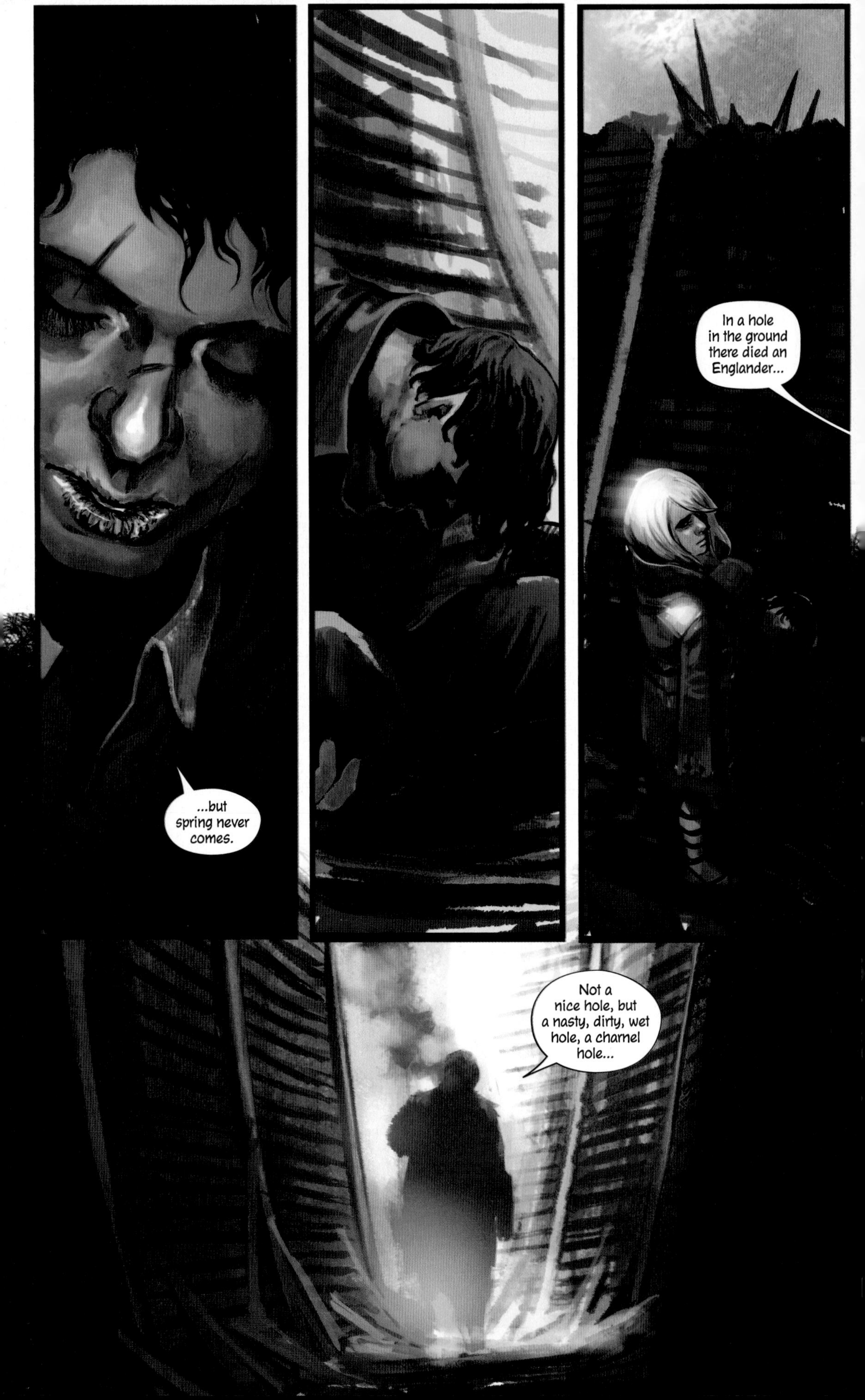
...but spring never comes.
In a hole in the ground there died an Englander...
Not a nice hole, but a nasty, dirty, wet hole, a charnel hole...

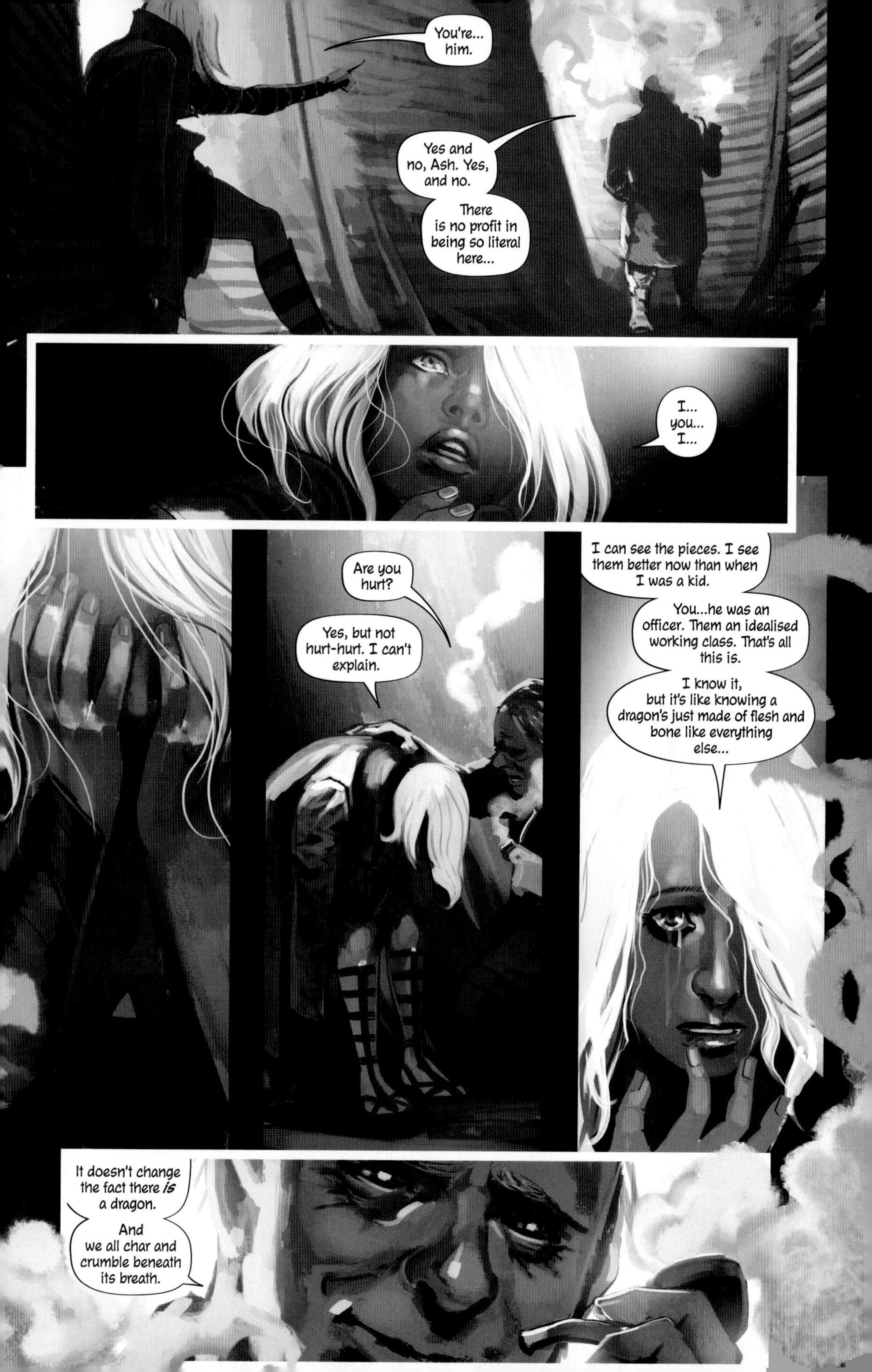
You're... him.
Yes and no, Ash. Yes, and no.
There is no profit in being so literal here...
I... you... I...
Are you hurt?
Yes, but not hurt-hurt. I can't explain.
I can see the pieces. I see them better now than when I was a kid.
You...he was an officer. Them an idealised working class. That's all this is.
I know it, but it's like knowing a dragon's just made of flesh and bone like everything else...
It doesn't change the fact there *is* a dragon.
And we all char and crumble beneath its breath.

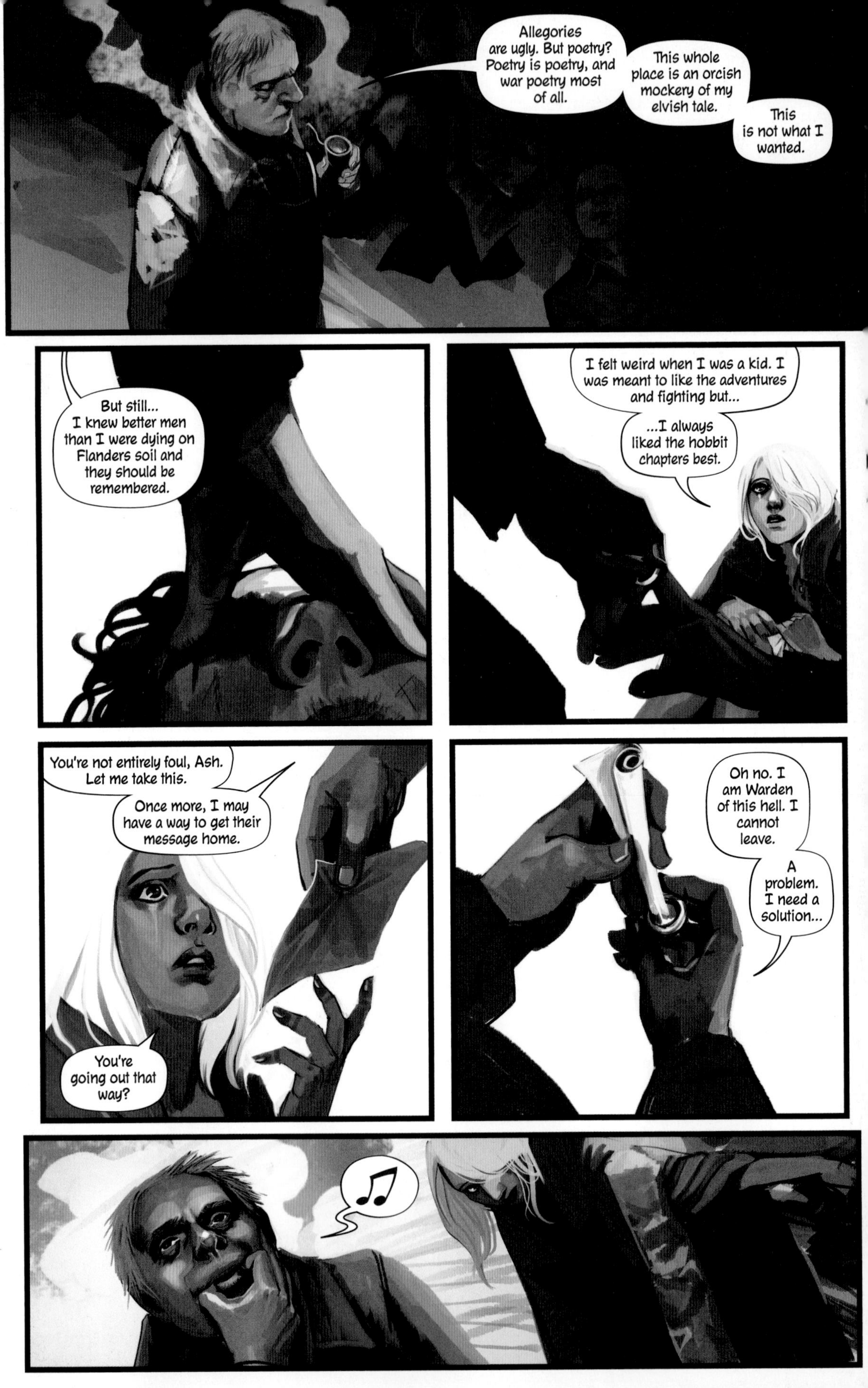
Allegories are ugly. But poetry? Poetry is poetry, and war poetry most of all.
This whole place is an orcish mockery of my elvish tale.
This is not what I wanted.
But still... I knew better men than I were dying on Flanders soil and they should be remembered.
I felt weird when I was a kid. I was meant to like the adventures and fighting but...
...I always liked the hobbit chapters best.
You're not entirely foul, Ash. Let me take this.
Once more, I may have a way to get their message home.
You're going out that way?
Oh no. I am Warden of this hell. I cannot leave.
A problem. I need a solution...

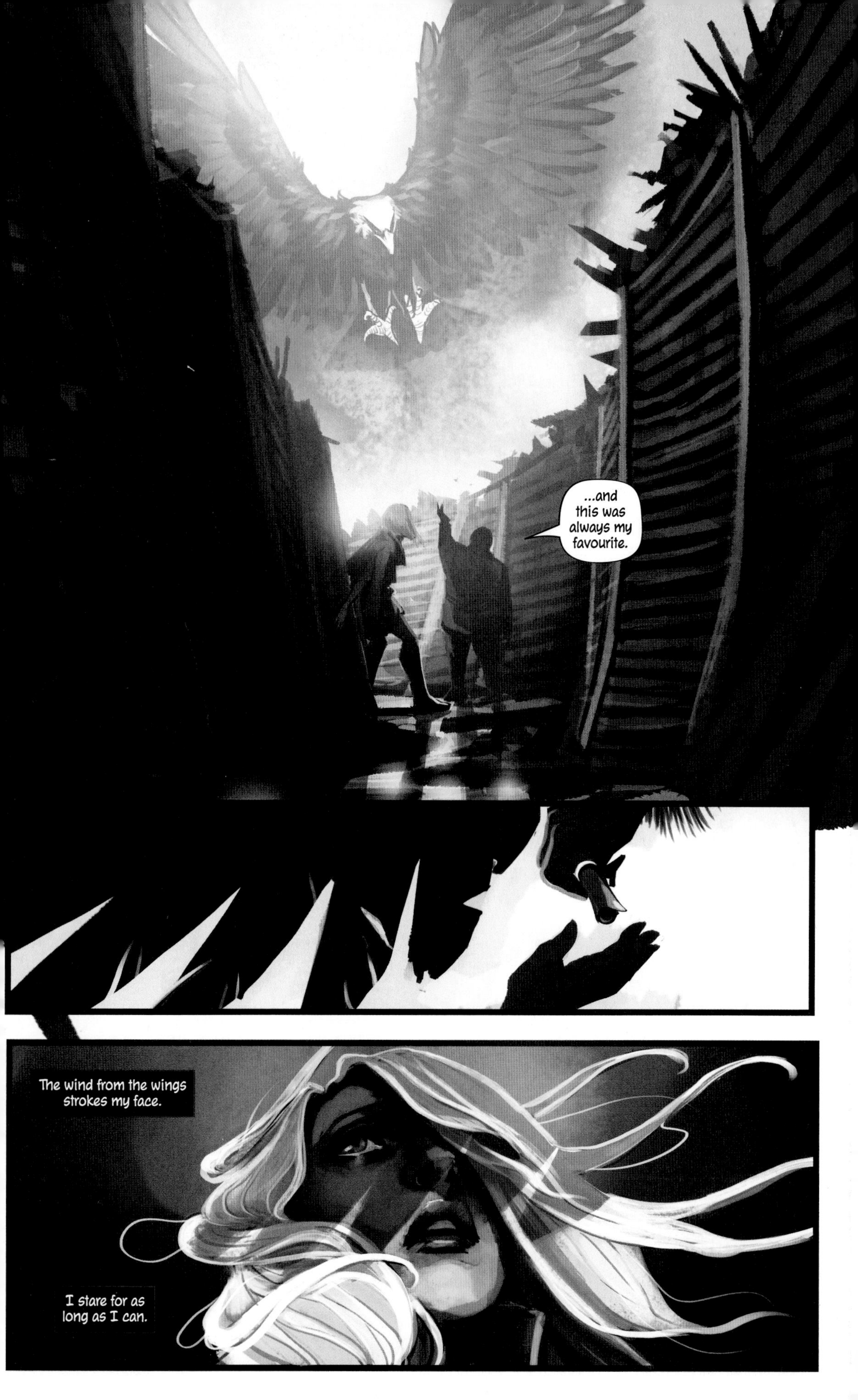
...and this was always my favourite.
The wind from the wings strokes my face.
I stare for as long as I can.

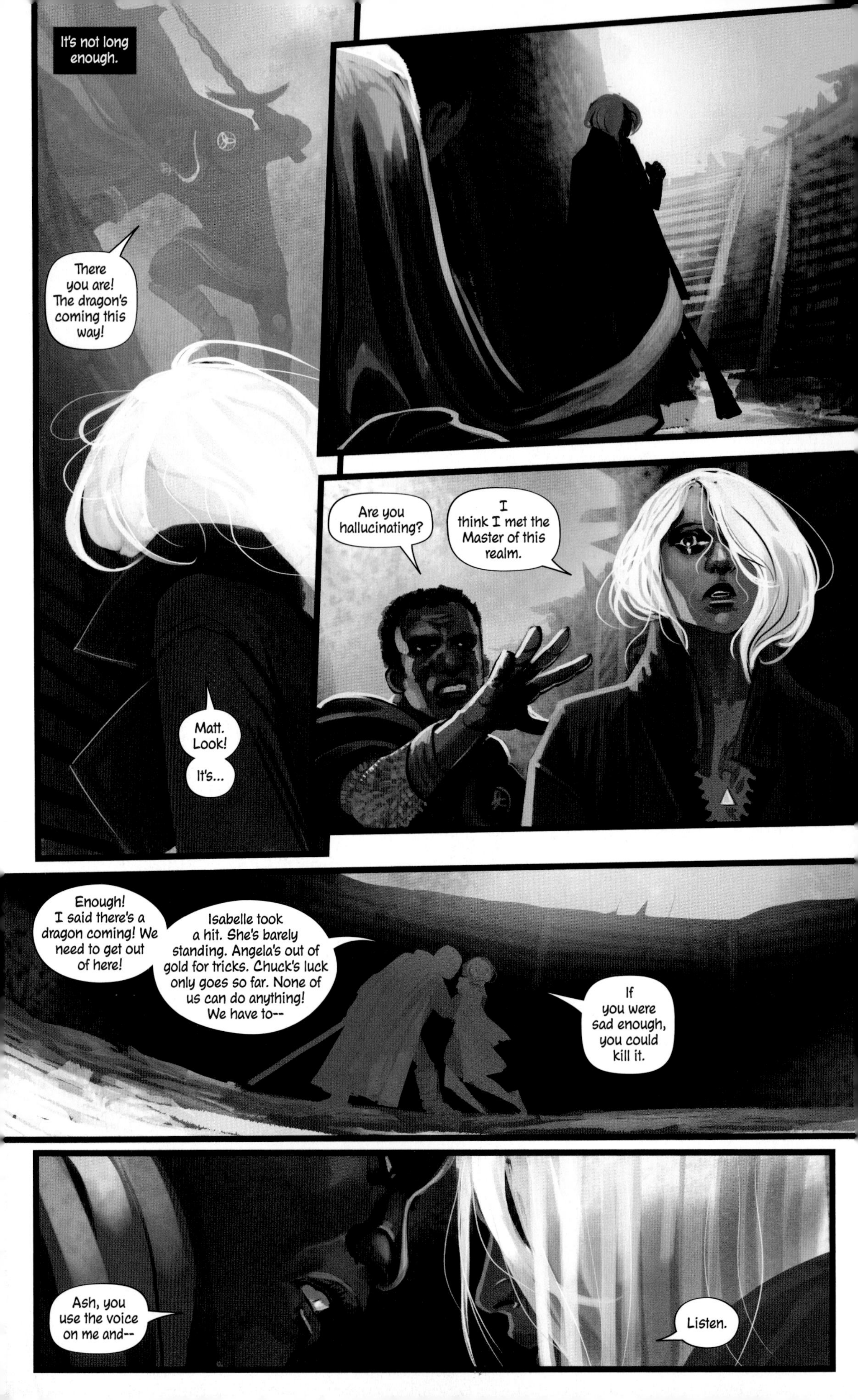
It's not long enough.
There you are! The dragon's coming this way!
Matt. Look!
It's...
Are you hallucinating?
I think I met the Master of this realm.
Enough! I said there's a dragon coming! We need to get out of here!
Isabelle took a hit. She's barely standing. Angela's out of gold for tricks. Chuck's luck only goes so far. None of us can do anything! We have to--
If you were sad enough, you could kill it.
Ash, you use the voice on me and--
Listen.

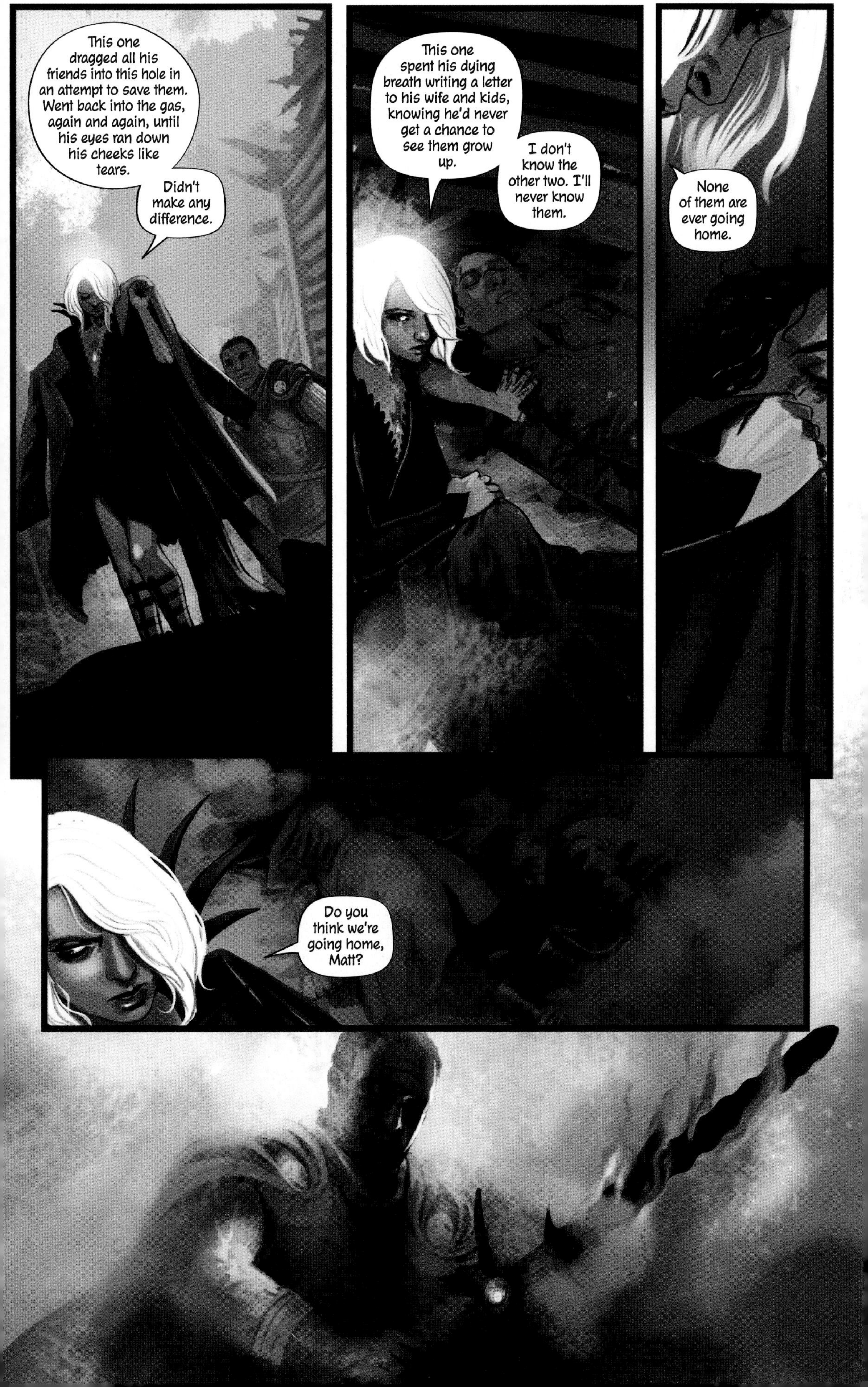
This one dragged all his friends into this hole in an attempt to save them. Went back into the gas, again and again, until his eyes ran down his cheeks like tears.
Didn't make any difference.
This one spent his dying breath writing a letter to his wife and kids, knowing he'd never get a chance to see them grow up.
I don't know the other two. I'll never know them.
None of them are ever going home.
Do you think we're going home, Matt?

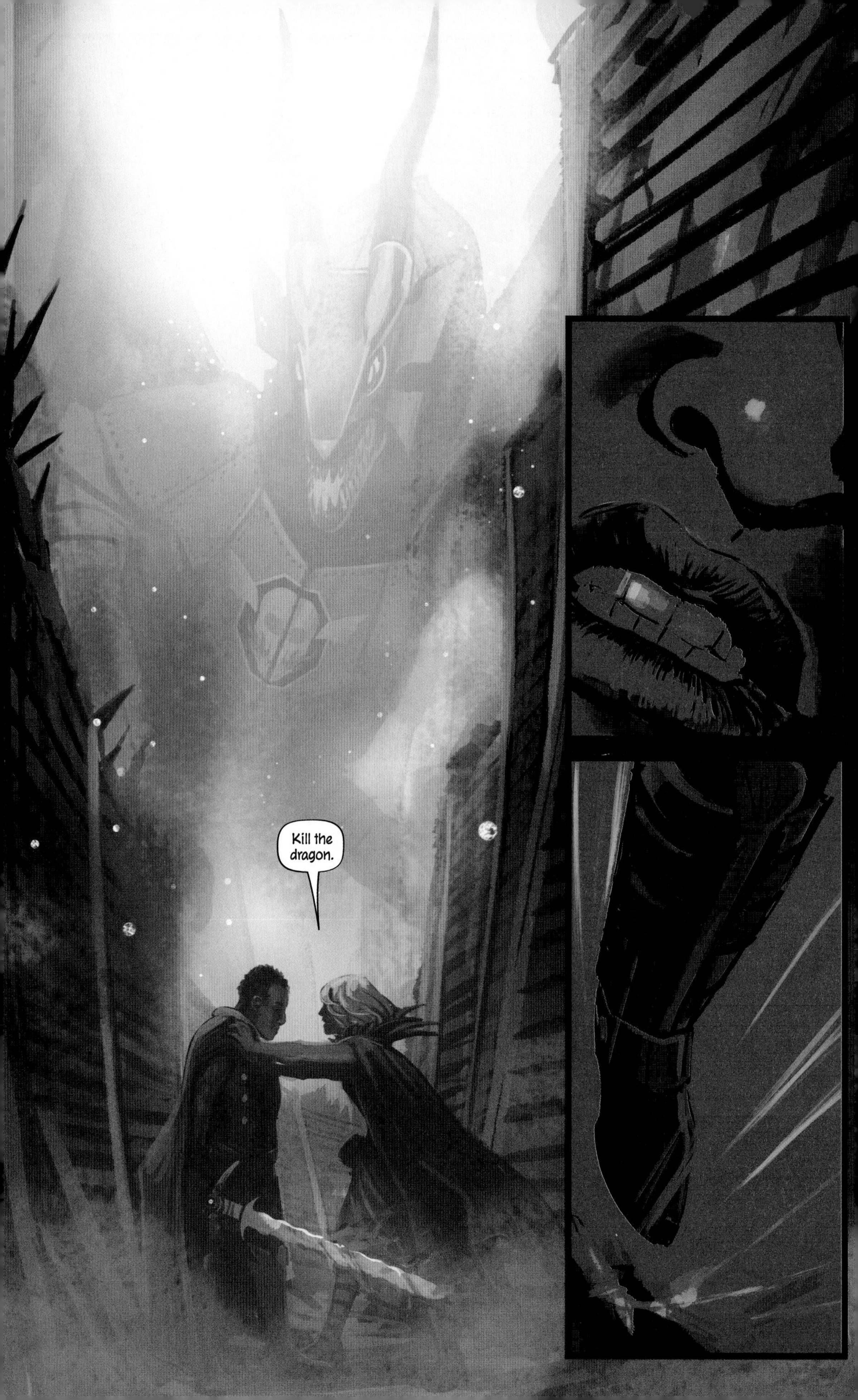
Kill the dragon.

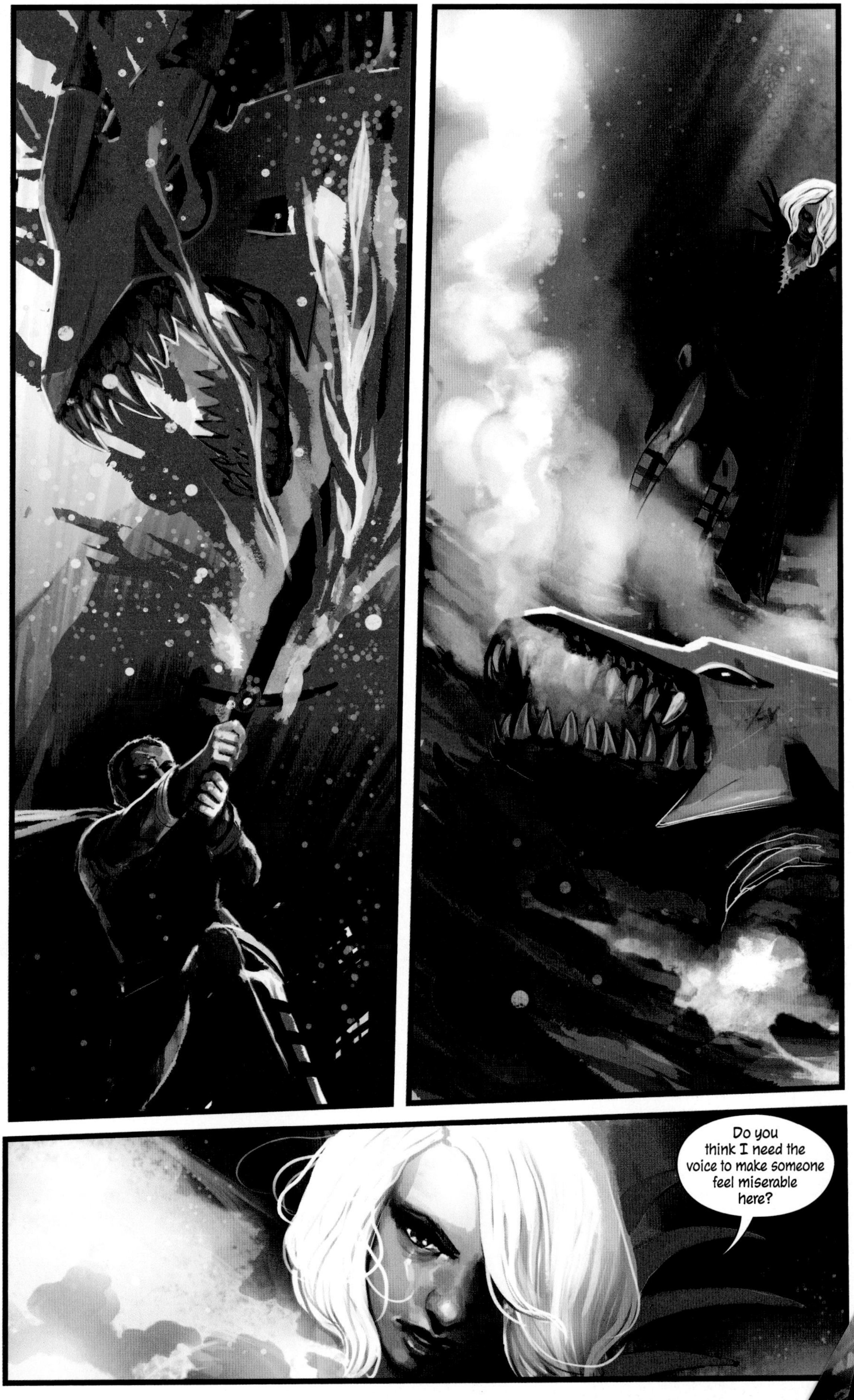
Do you think I need the voice to make someone feel miserable here?

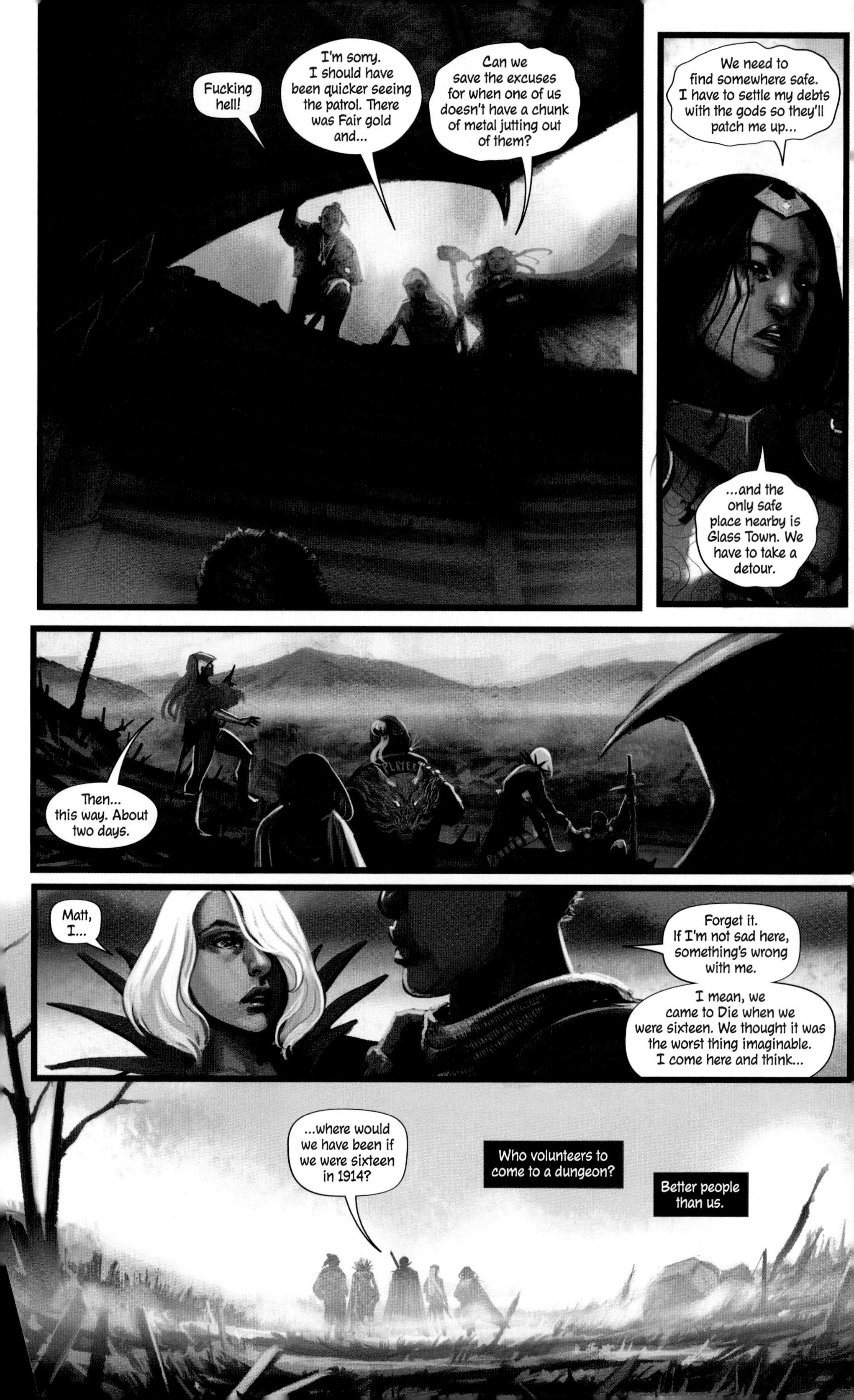

Fucking hell!
I'm sorry. I should have been quicker seeing the patrol. There was Fair gold and...
Can we save the excuses for when one of us doesn't have a chunk of metal jutting out of them?
We need to find somewhere safe. I have to settle my debts with the gods so they'll patch me up...
...and the only safe place nearby is Glass Town. We have to take a detour.
Then... this way. About two days.
Matt, I...
Forget it. If I'm not sad here, something's wrong with me.
I mean, we came to Die when we were sixteen. We thought it was the worst thing imaginable. I come here and think...
...where would we have been if we were sixteen in 1914?
Who volunteers to come to a dungeon?
Better people than us.

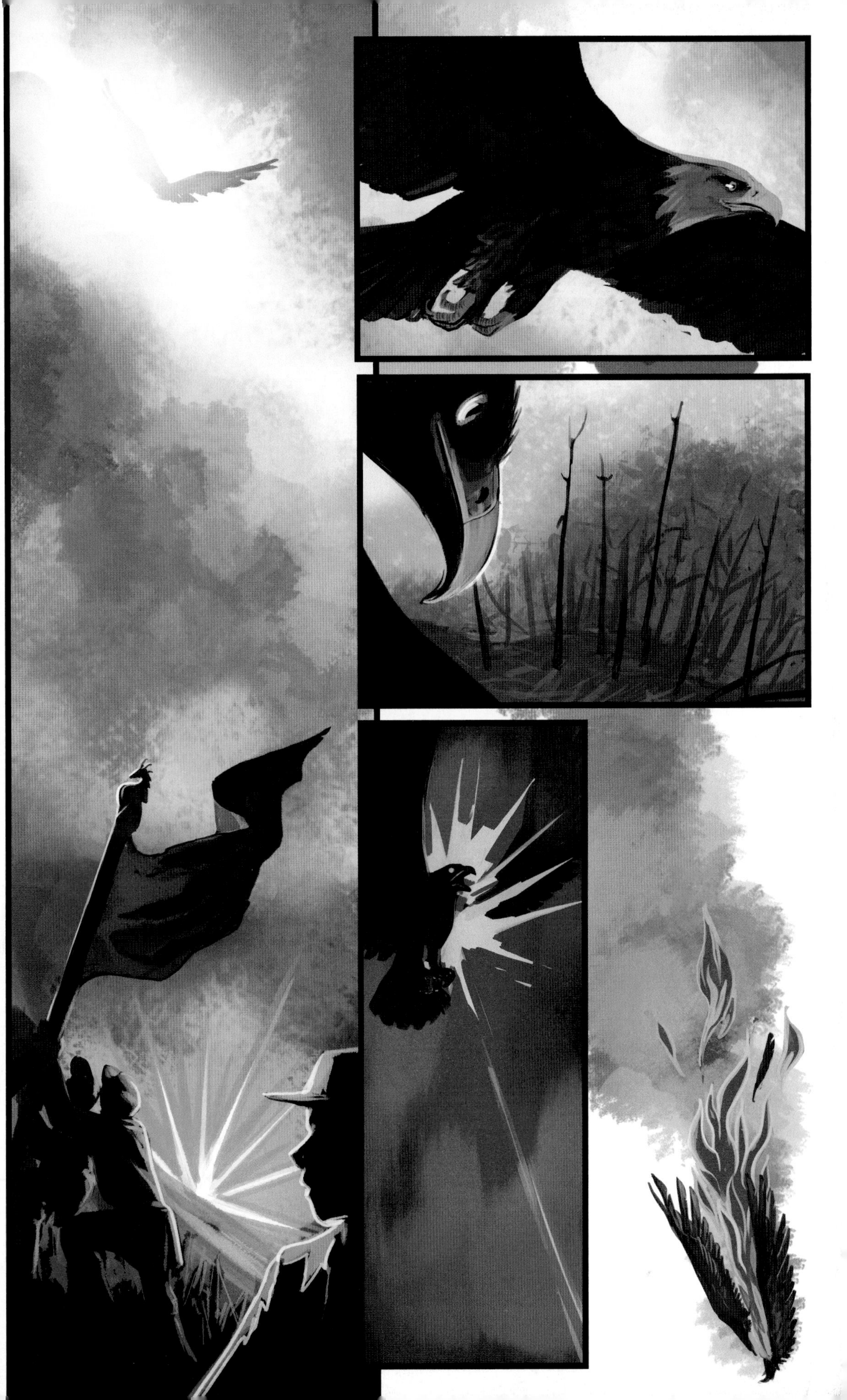

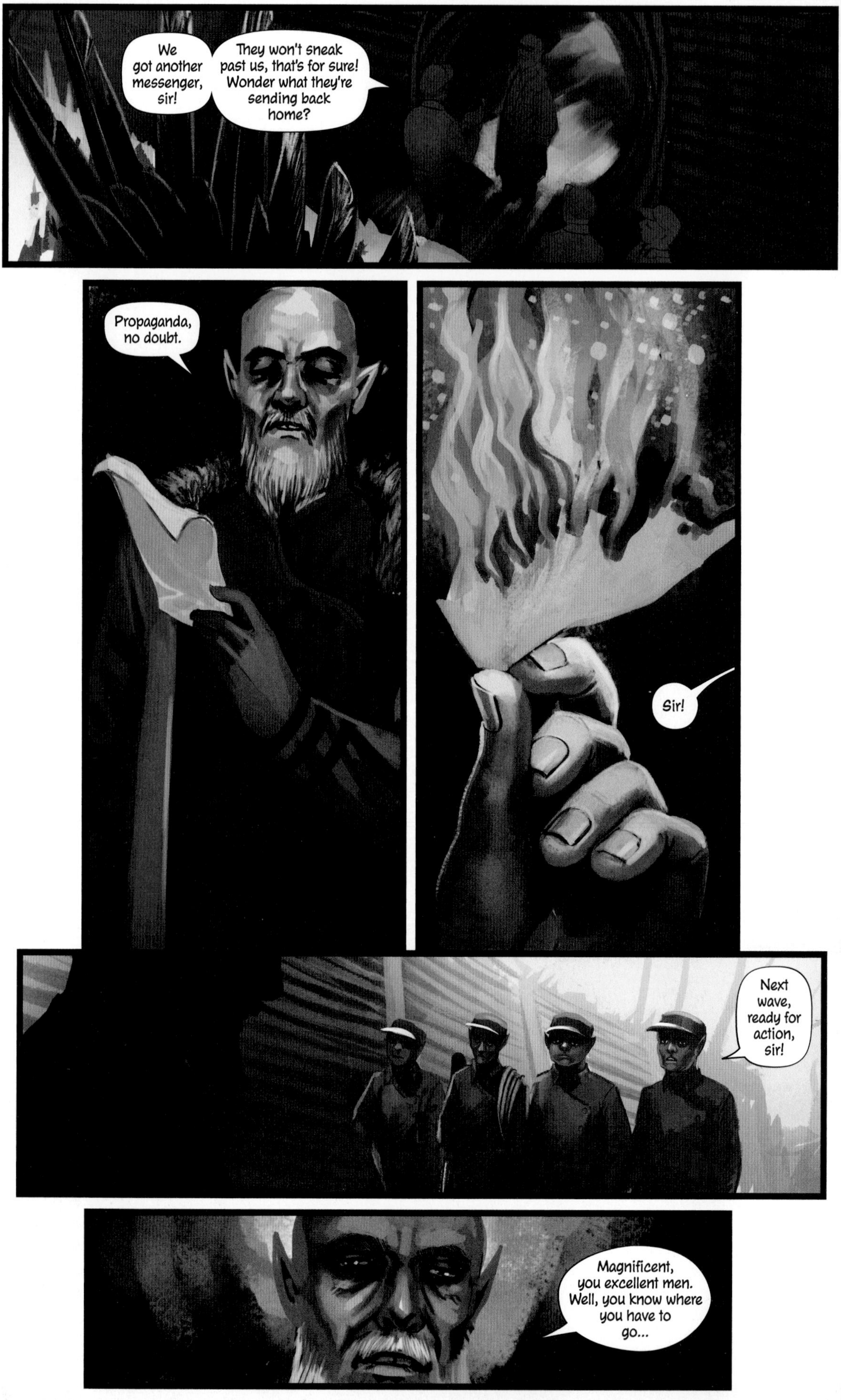
We got another messenger, sir!
They won't sneak past us, that's for sure! Wonder what they're sending back home?
Propaganda, no doubt.
Sir!
Next wave, ready for action, sir!
Magnificent, you excellent men. Well, you know where you have to go...

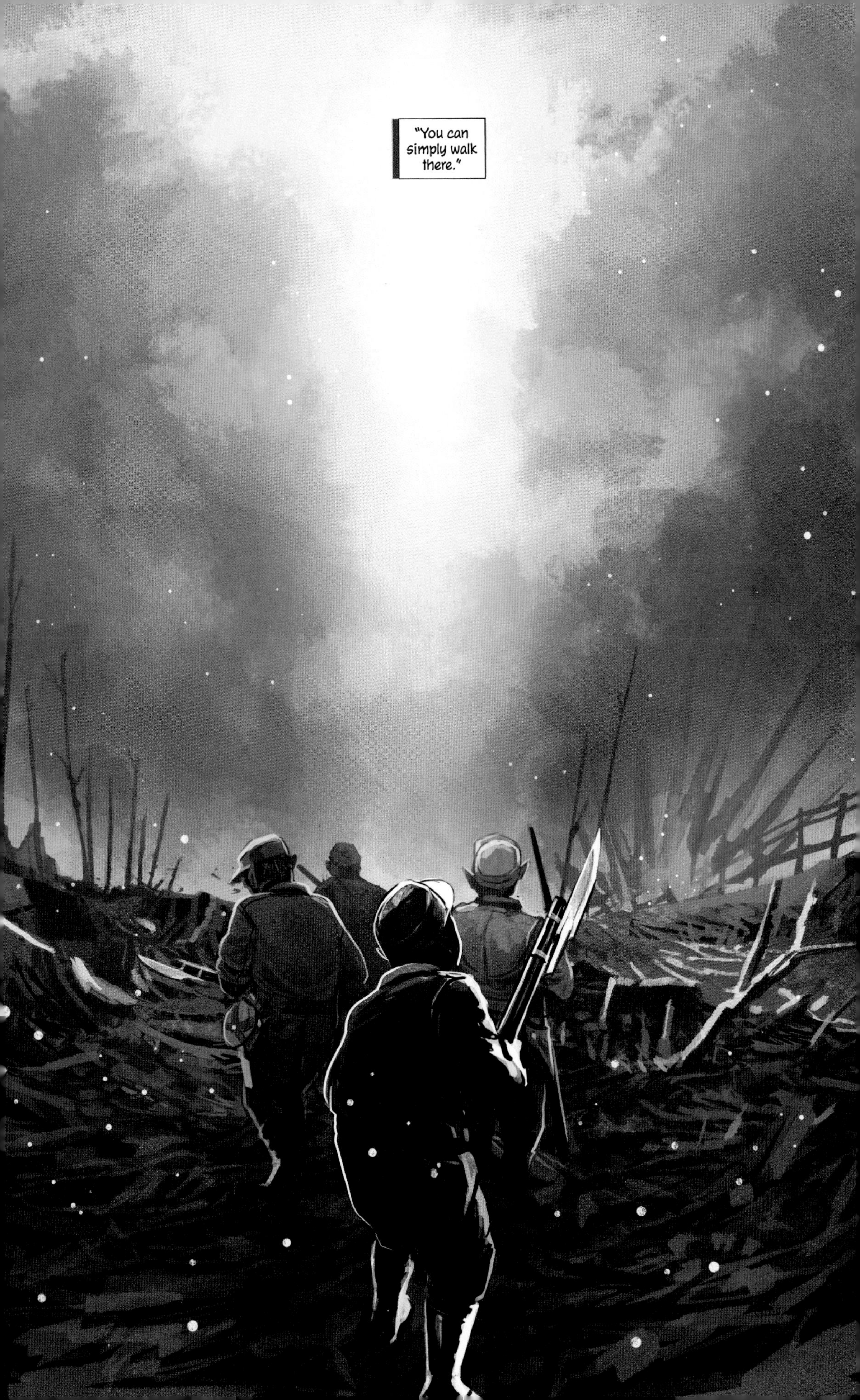
"You can simply walk there."

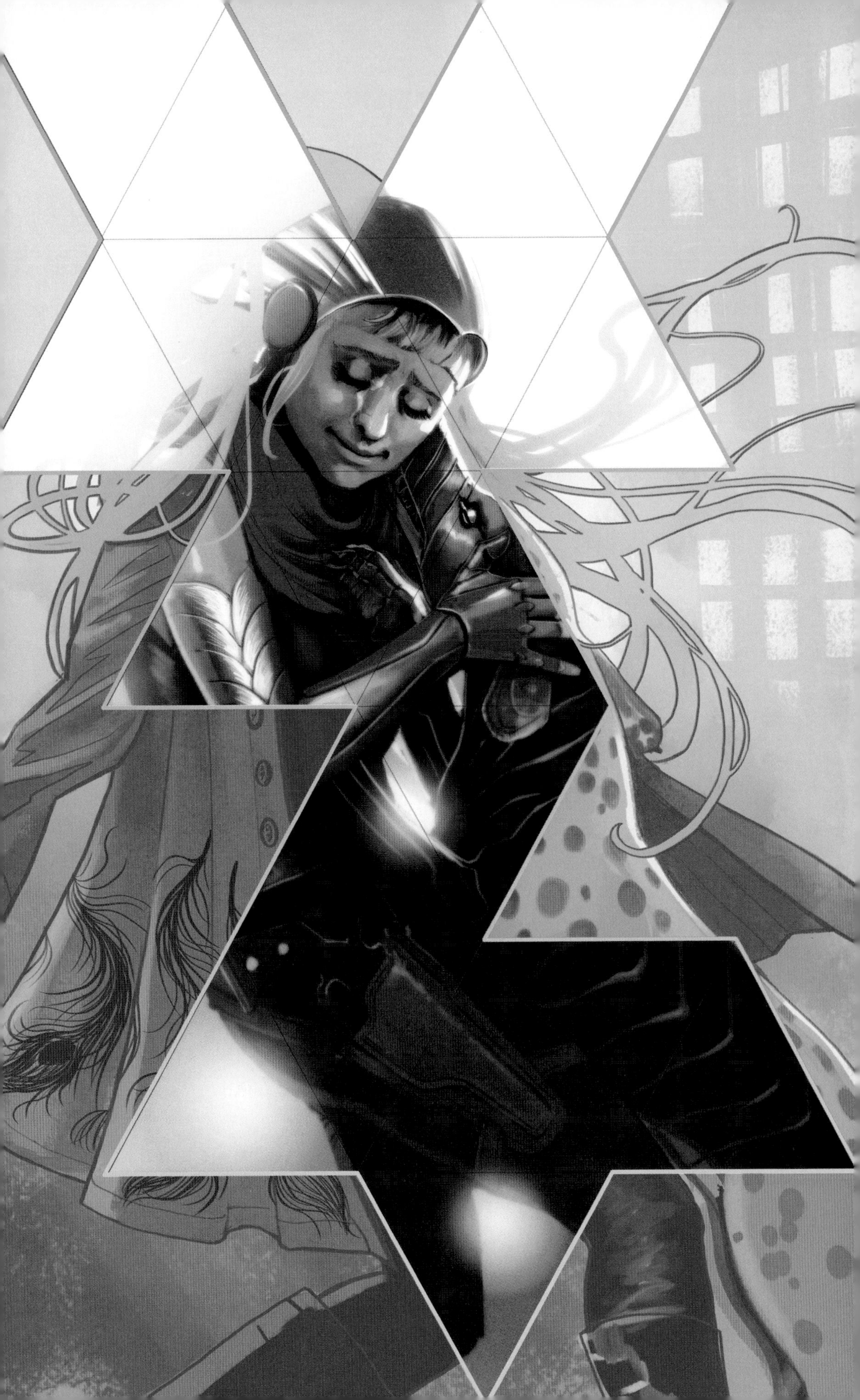

4:
THE INN

"It is not easy to dismiss from my imagination the images which have filled it so long."
– *Charlotte Brontë*

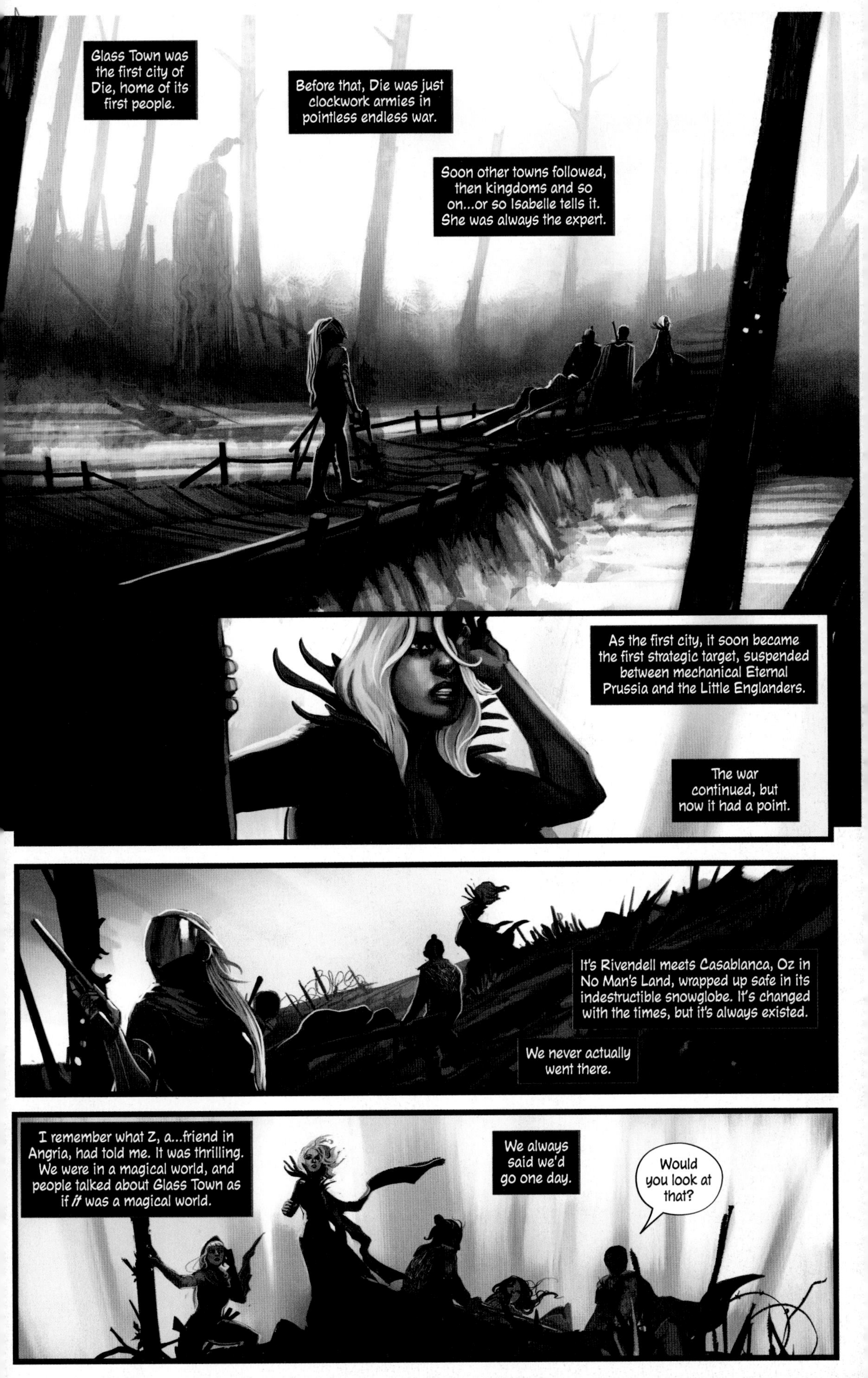
Glass Town was the first city of Die, home of its first people.
Before that, Die was just clockwork armies in pointless endless war.
Soon other towns followed, then kingdoms and so on...or so Isabelle tells it. She was always the expert.
As the first city, it soon became the first strategic target, suspended between mechanical Eternal Prussia and the Little Englanders.
The war continued, but now it had a point.
It's Rivendell meets Casablanca, Oz in No Man's Land, wrapped up safe in its indestructible snowglobe. It's changed with the times, but it's always existed.
We never actually went there.
I remember what Z, a...friend in Angria, had told me. It was thrilling. We were in a magical world, and people talked about Glass Town as if *it* was a magical world.
We always said we'd go one day.
Would you look at that?

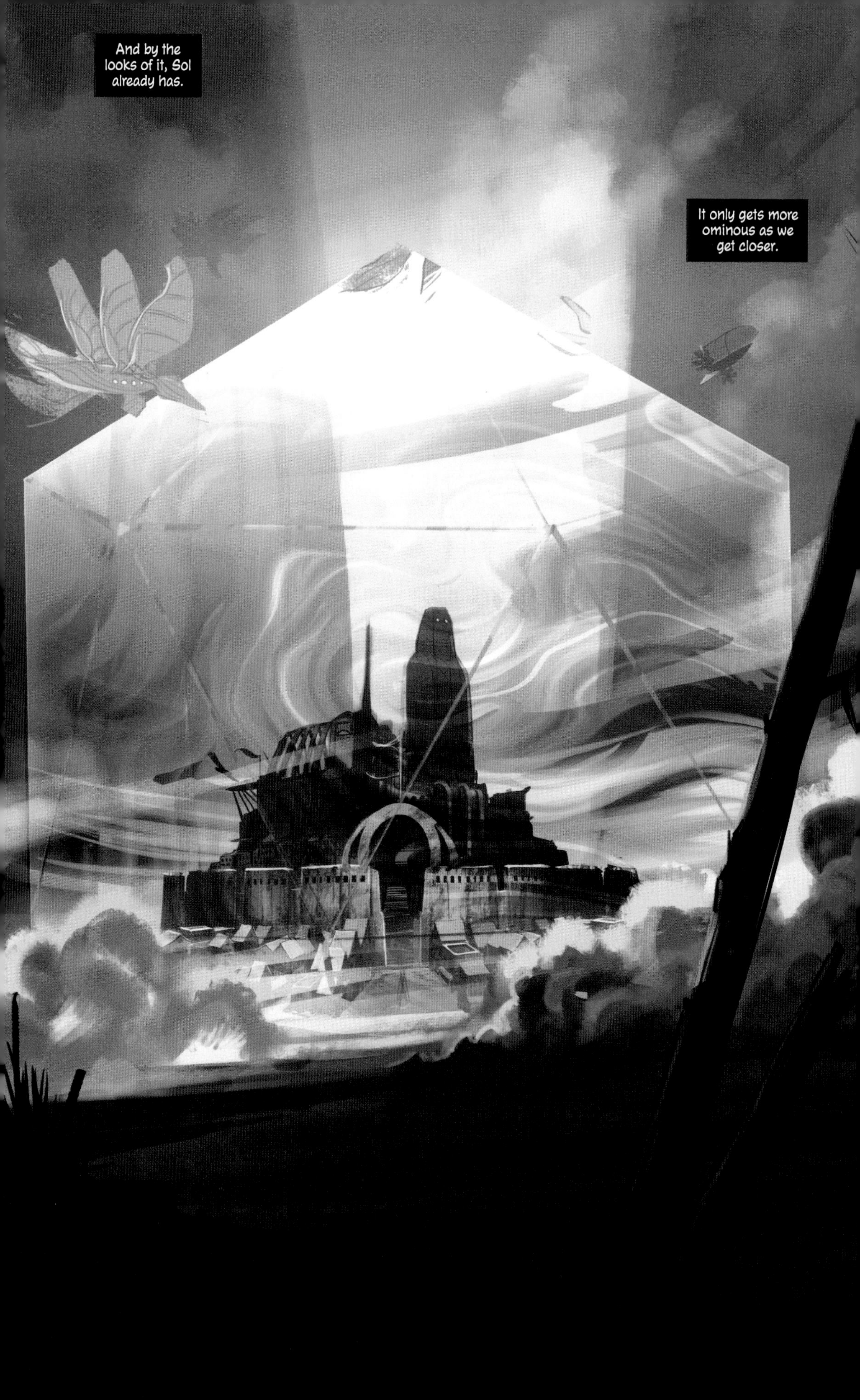
And by the looks of it, Sol already has.
It only gets more ominous as we get closer.

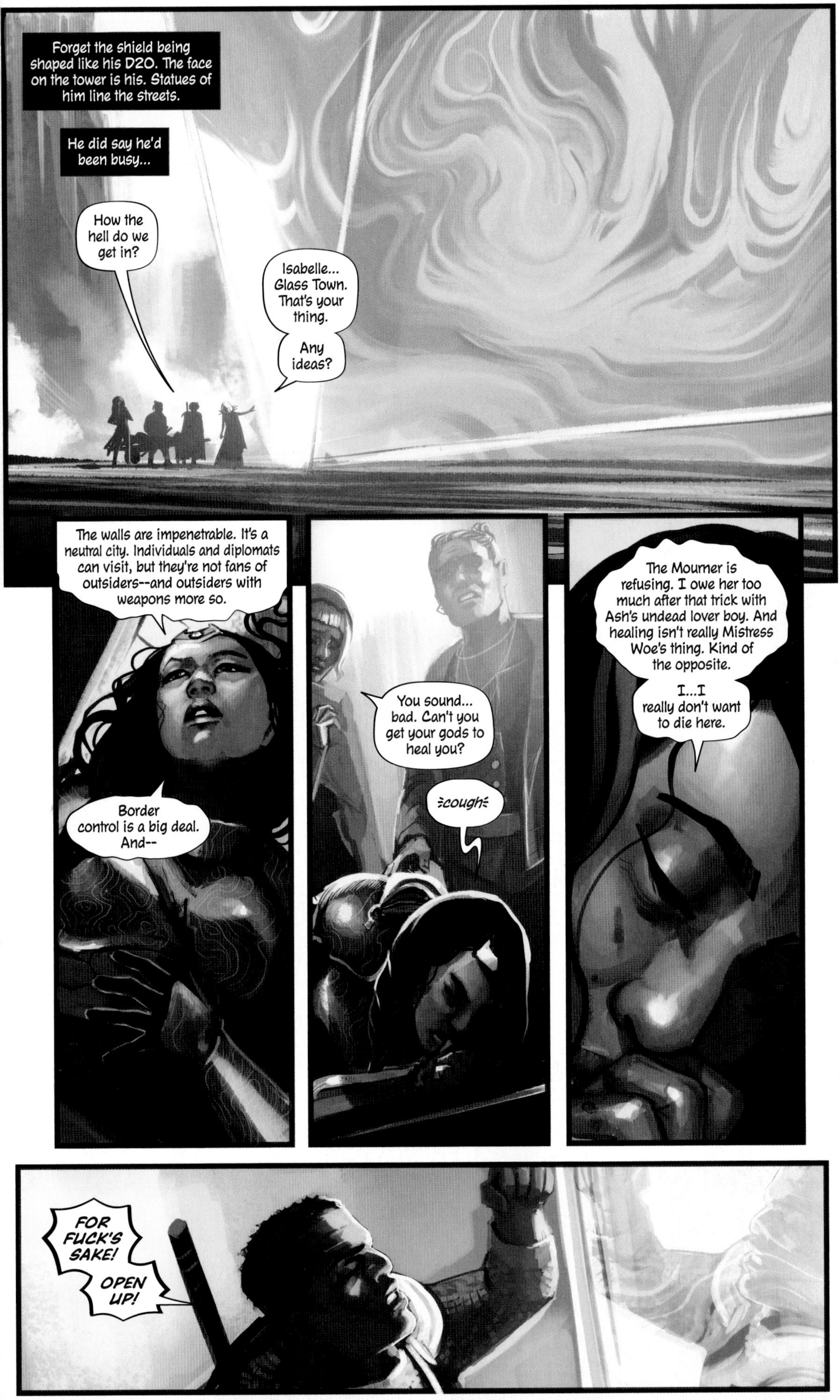
Forget the shield being shaped like his D20. The face on the tower is his. Statues of him line the streets.
He did say he'd been busy...
How the hell do we get in?
Isabelle... Glass Town. That's your thing.
Any ideas?
The walls are impenetrable. It's a neutral city. Individuals and diplomats can visit, but they're not fans of outsiders--and outsiders with weapons more so.
Border control is a big deal. And--
You sound... bad. Can't you get your gods to heal you?
cough
The Mourner is refusing. I owe her too much after that trick with Ash's undead lover boy. And healing isn't really Mistress Woe's thing. Kind of the opposite.
I...I really don't want to die here.
FOR FUCK'S SAKE!
OPEN UP!

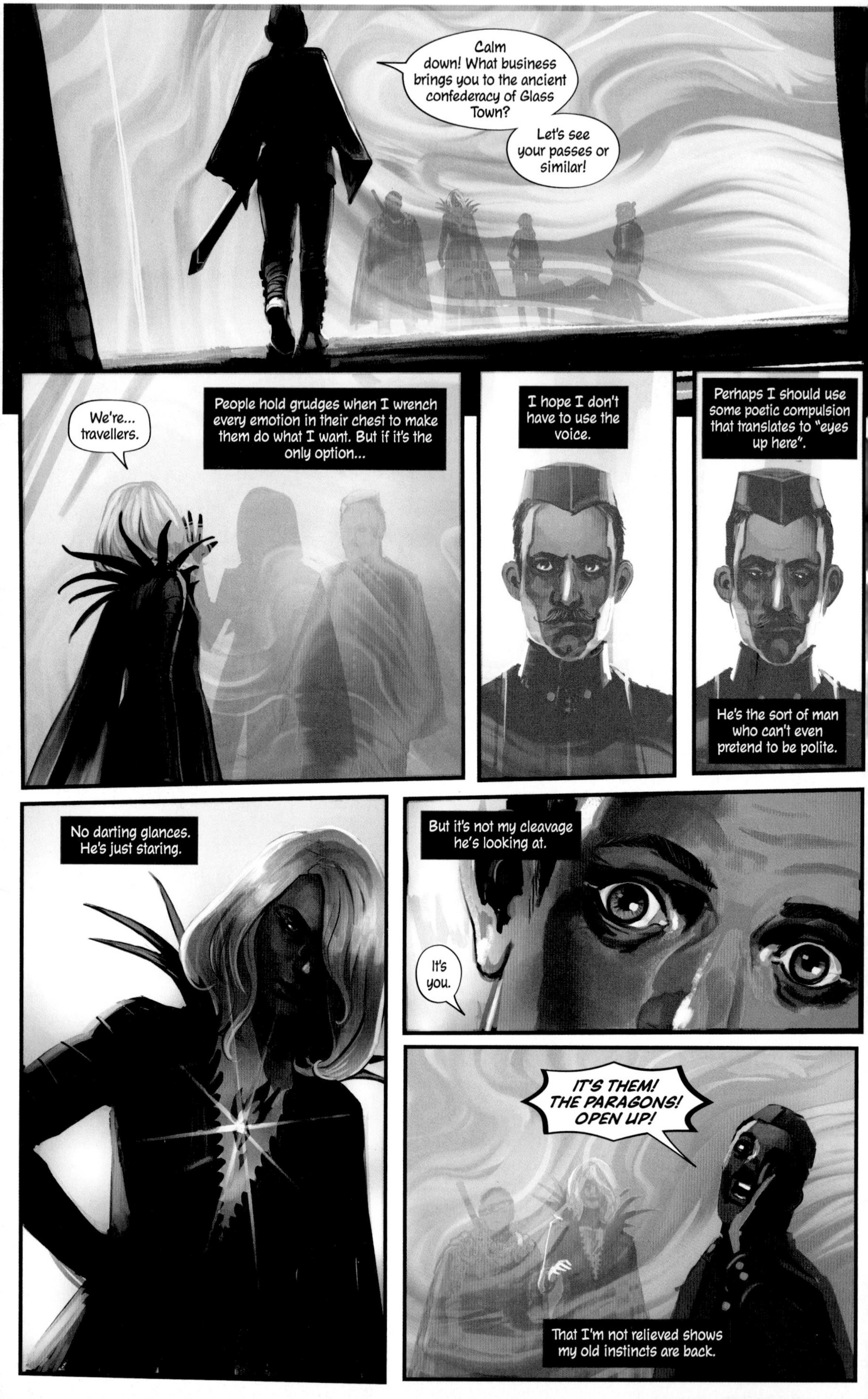

Calm down! What business brings you to the ancient confederacy of Glass Town?
Let's see your passes or similar!
We're... travellers.
People hold grudges when I wrench every emotion in their chest to make them do what I want. But if it's the only option...
I hope I don't have to use the voice.
Perhaps I should use some poetic compulsion that translates to "eyes up here".
He's the sort of man who can't even pretend to be polite.
No darting glances. He's just staring.
But it's not my cleavage he's looking at.
It's you.
IT'S THEM! THE PARAGONS! OPEN UP!
That I'm not relieved shows my old instincts are back.

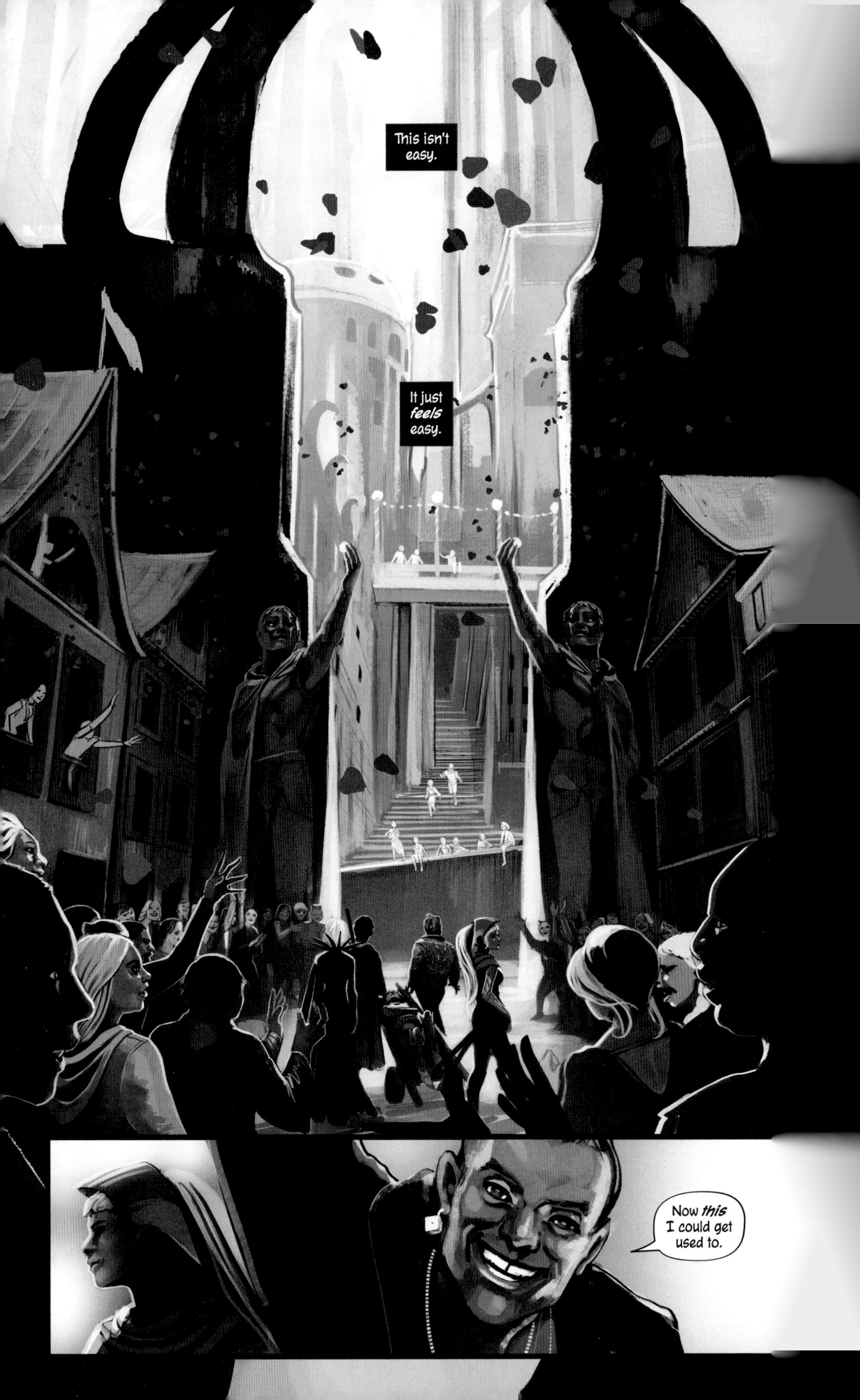
This isn't easy.
It just *feels* easy.
Now *this* I could get used to.

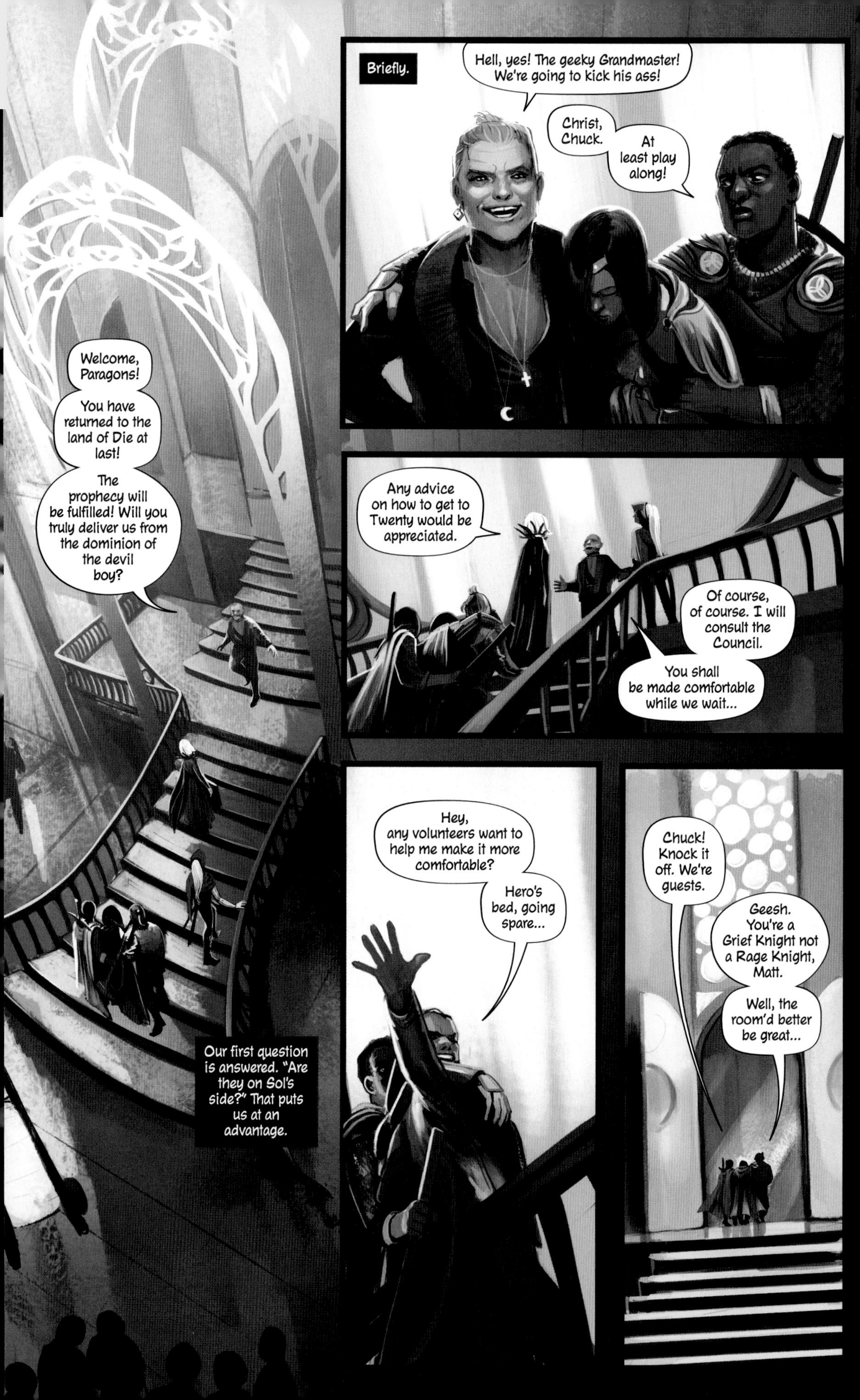

Welcome, Paragons!
You have returned to the land of Die at last!
The prophecy will be fulfilled! Will you truly deliver us from the dominion of the devil boy?
Our first question is answered. "Are they on Sol's side?" That puts us at an advantage.
Briefly.
Hell, yes! The geeky Grandmaster! We're going to kick his ass!
Christ, Chuck.
At least play along!
Any advice on how to get to Twenty would be appreciated.
Of course, of course. I will consult the Council.
You shall be made comfortable while we wait...
Hey, any volunteers want to help me make it more comfortable?
Hero's bed, going spare...
Chuck! Knock it off. We're guests.
Geesh. You're a Grief Knight not a Rage Knight, Matt.
Well, the room'd better be great...

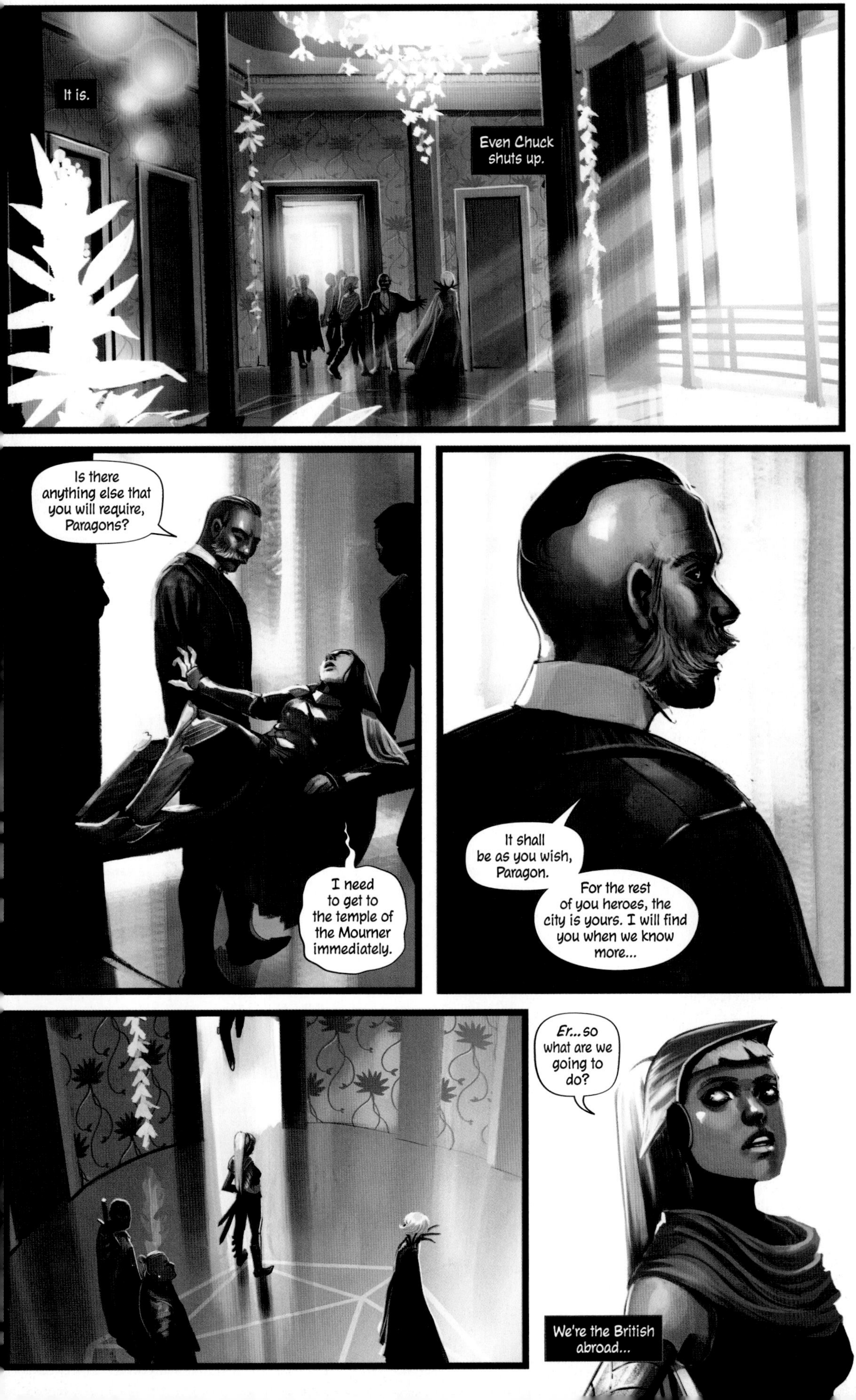
It is.
Even Chuck shuts up.
Is there anything else that you will require, Paragons?
I need to get to the temple of the Mourner immediately.
It shall be as you wish, Paragon.
For the rest of you heroes, the city is yours. I will find you when we know more...
Er... so what are we going to do?
We're the British abroad...

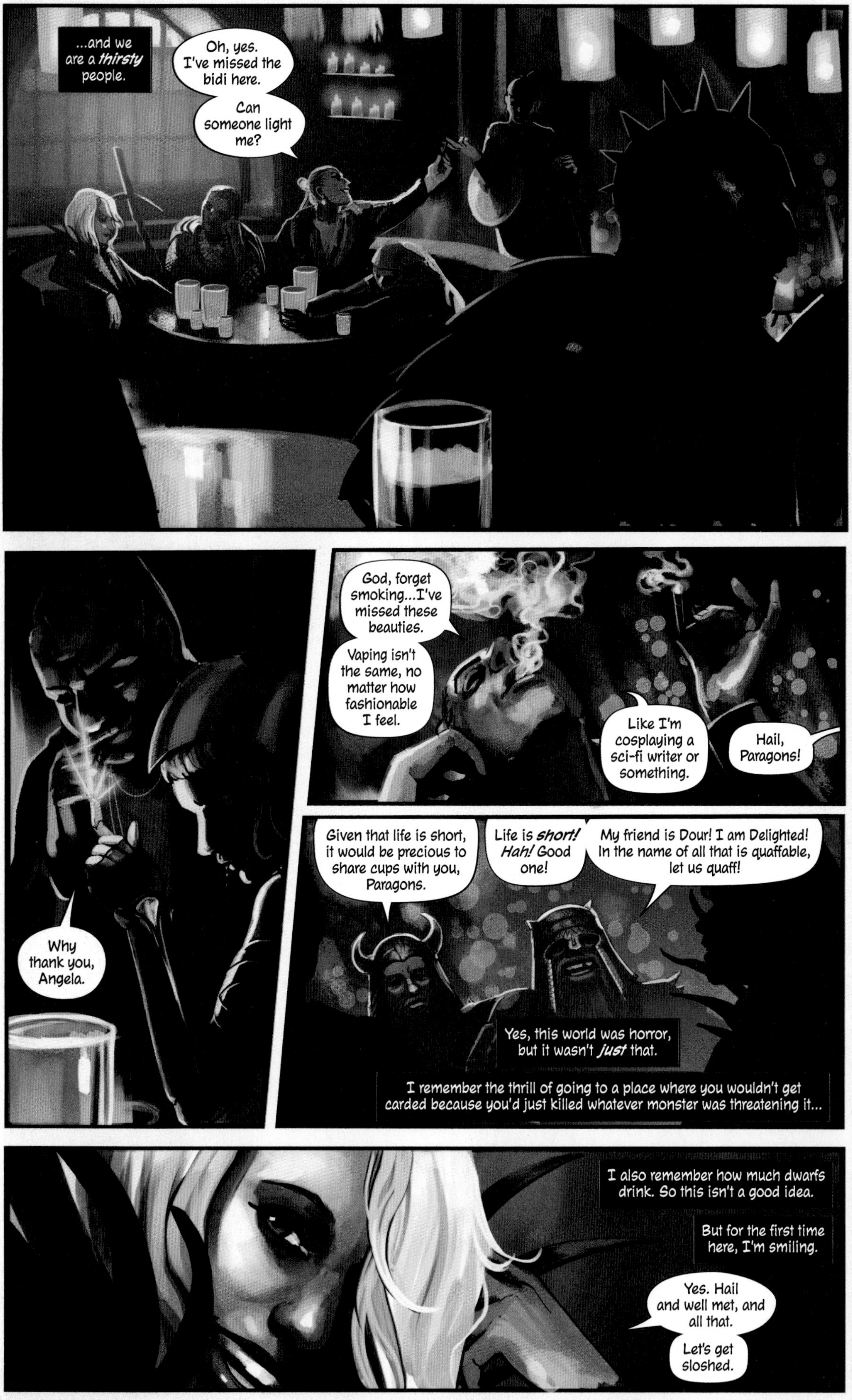
...and we are a *thirsty* people.
Oh, yes. I've missed the bidi here.
Can someone light me?
Why thank you, Angela.
God, forget smoking...I've missed these beauties.
Vaping isn't the same, no matter how fashionable I feel.
Like I'm cosplaying a sci-fi writer or something.
Hail, Paragons!
Given that life is short, it would be precious to share cups with you, Paragons.
Life is *short! Hah!* Good one!
My friend is Dour! I am Delighted! In the name of all that is quaffable, let us quaff!
Yes, this world was horror, but it wasn't *just* that.
I remember the thrill of going to a place where you wouldn't get carded because you'd just killed whatever monster was threatening it...
I also remember how much dwarfs drink. So this isn't a good idea.
But for the first time here, I'm smiling.
Yes. Hail and well met, and all that.
Let's get sloshed.

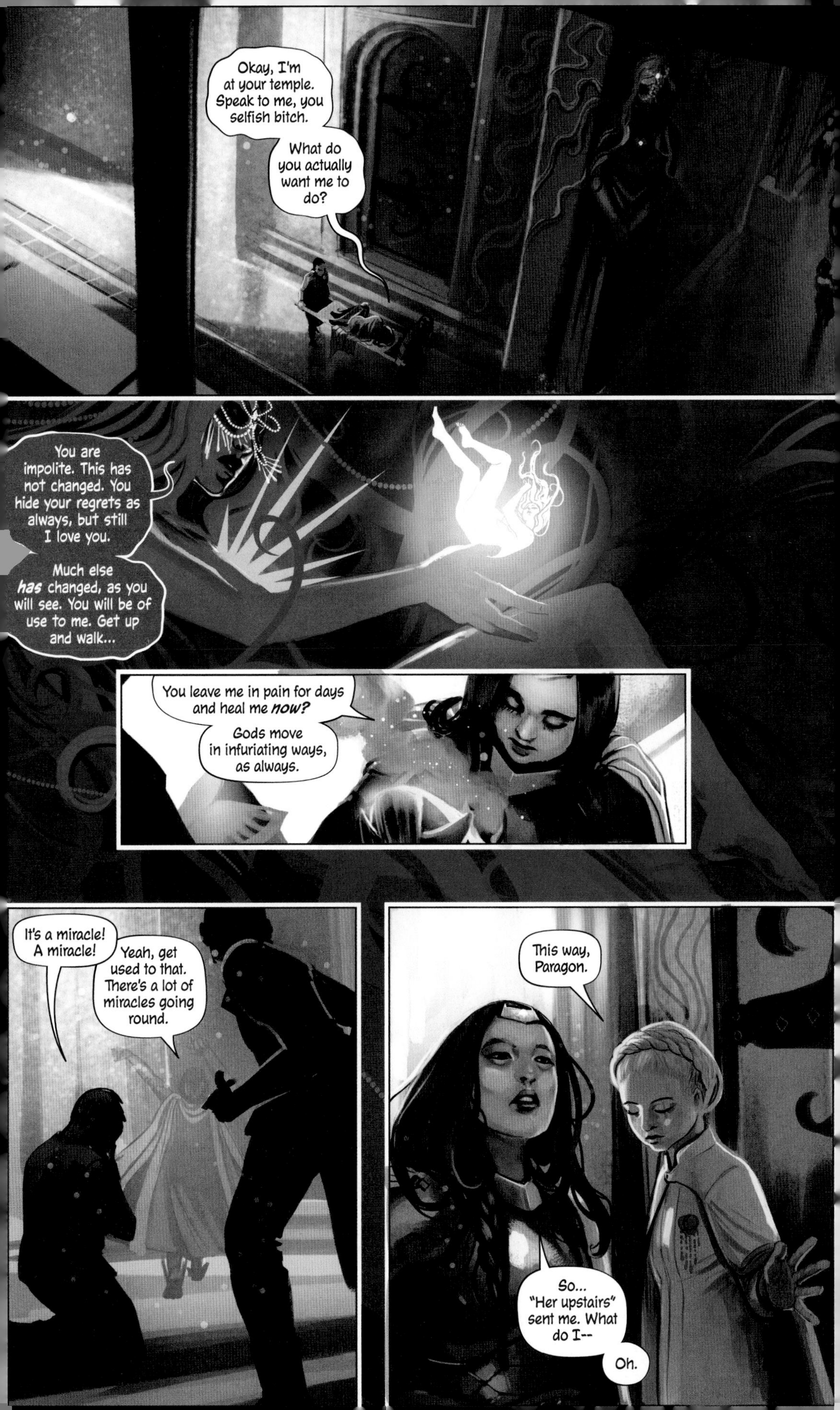
Okay, I'm at your temple. Speak to me, you selfish bitch.
What do you actually want me to do?
You are impolite. This has not changed. You hide your regrets as always, but still I love you.
Much else *has* changed, as you will see. You will be of use to me. Get up and walk...
You leave me in pain for days and heal me *now?*
Gods move in infuriating ways, as always.
It's a miracle! A miracle!
Yeah, get used to that. There's a lot of miracles going round.
This way, Paragon.
So... "Her upstairs" sent me. What do I--
Oh.

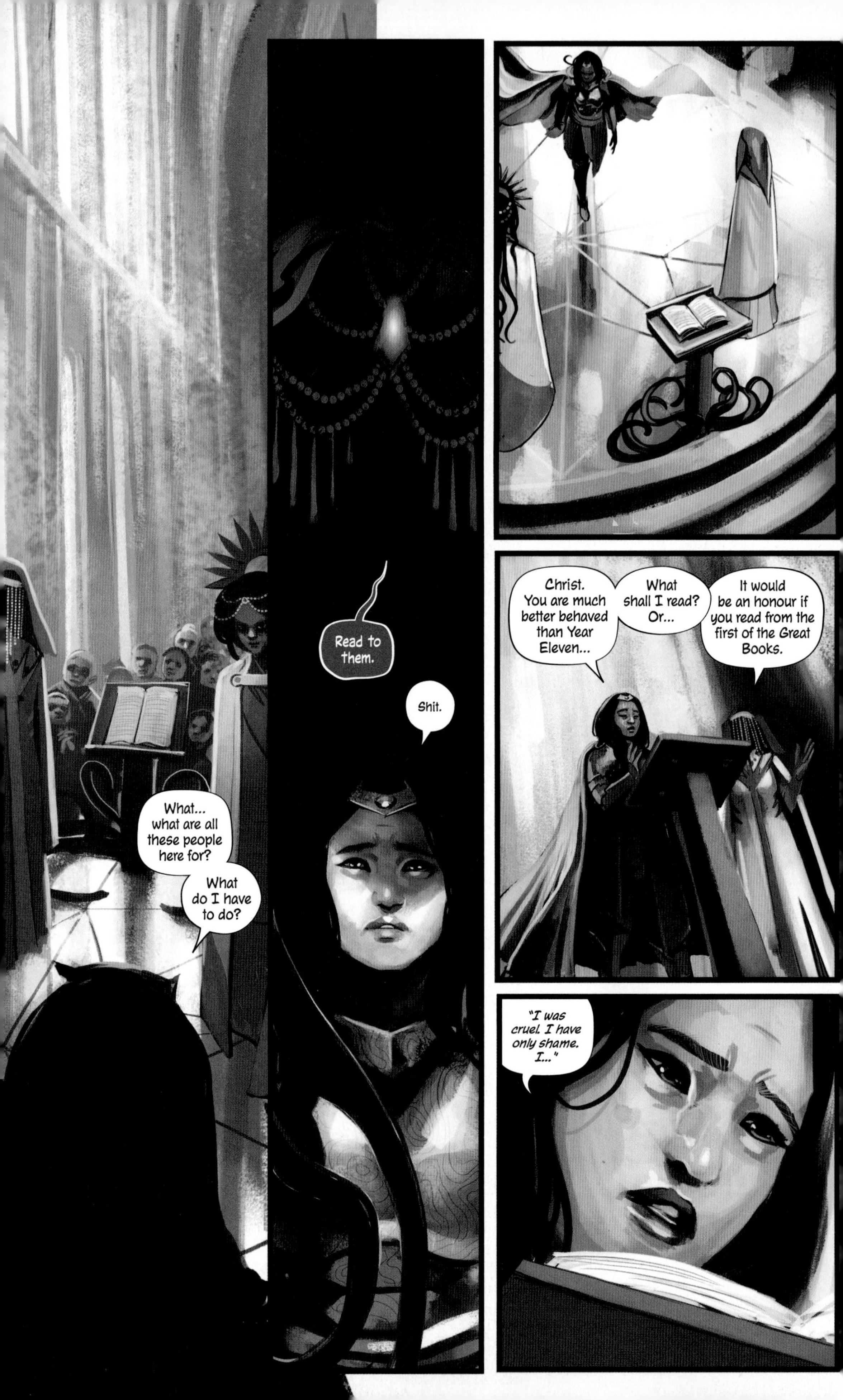
What... what are all these people here for?
What do I have to do?
Read to them.
Shit.
Christ. You are much better behaved than Year Eleven...
What shall I read? Or...
It would be an honour if you read from the first of the Great Books.
"I was cruel. I have only shame. I..."

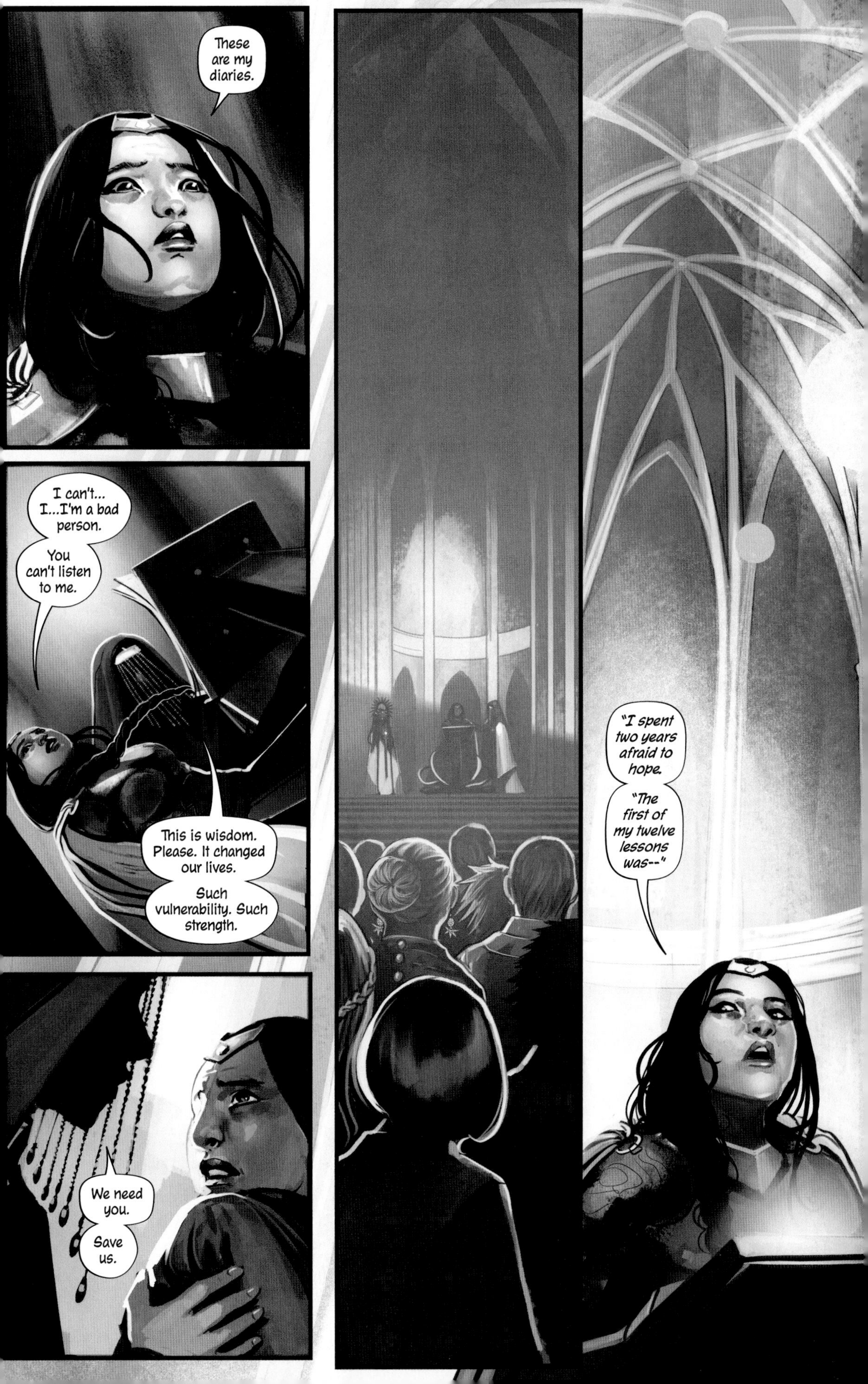
These are my diaries.
I can't... I...I'm a bad person.
You can't listen to me.
This is wisdom. Please. It changed our lives.
Such vulnerability. Such strength.
We need you.
Save us.
"I spent two years afraid to hope.
"The first of my twelve lessons was--"

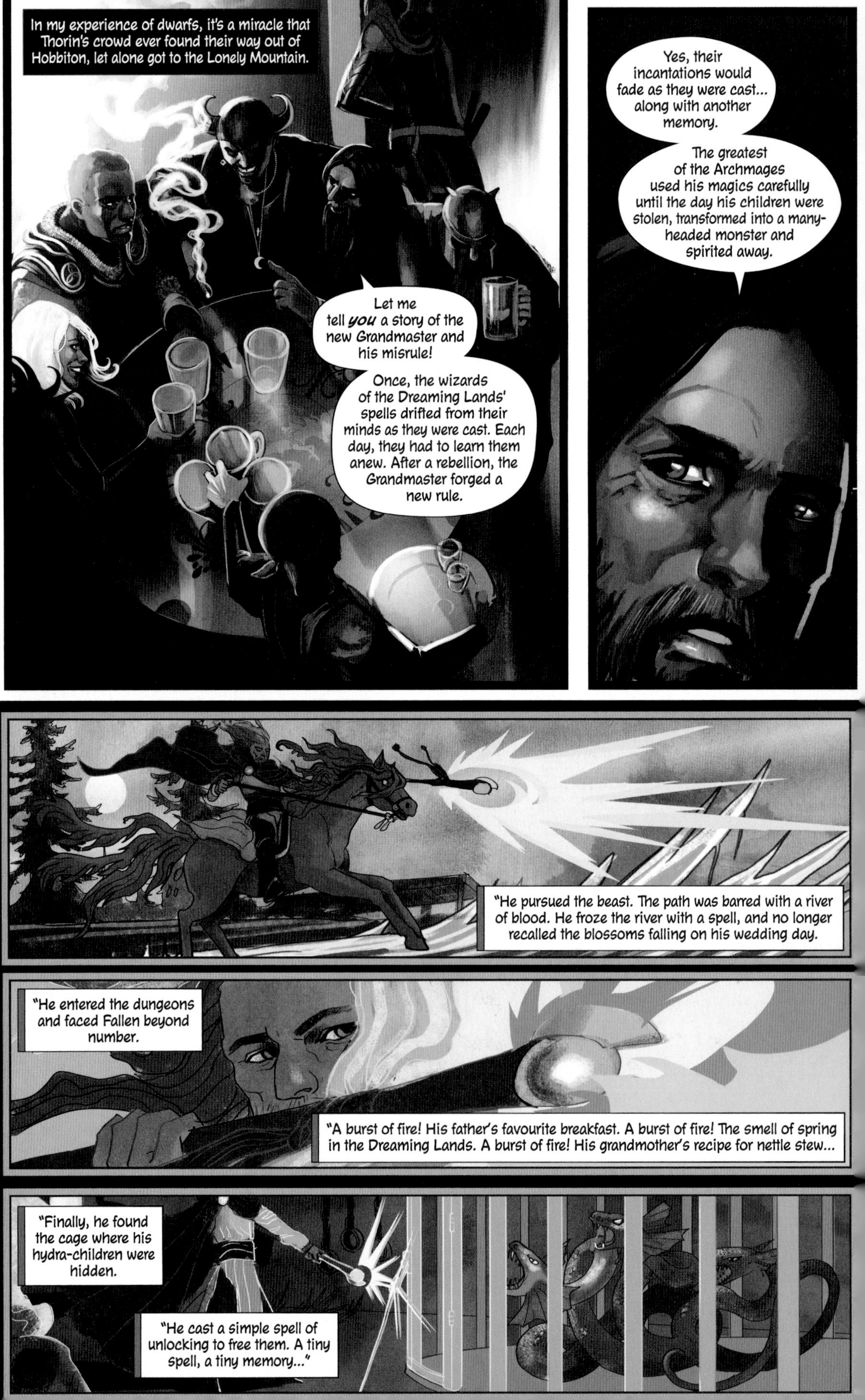
In my experience of dwarfs, it's a miracle that Thorin's crowd ever found their way out of Hobbiton, let alone got to the Lonely Mountain.
Let me tell *you* a story of the new Grandmaster and his misrule!
Once, the wizards of the Dreaming Lands' spells drifted from their minds as they were cast. Each day, they had to learn them anew. After a rebellion, the Grandmaster forged a new rule.
Yes, their incantations would fade as they were cast... along with another memory.
The greatest of the Archmages used his magics carefully until the day his children were stolen, transformed into a many-headed monster and spirited away.
"He pursued the beast. The path was barred with a river of blood. He froze the river with a spell, and no longer recalled the blossoms falling on his wedding day.
"He entered the dungeons and faced Fallen beyond number.
"A burst of fire! His father's favourite breakfast. A burst of fire! The smell of spring in the Dreaming Lands. A burst of fire! His grandmother's recipe for nettle stew...
"Finally, he found the cage where his hydra-children were hidden.
"He cast a simple spell of unlocking to free them. A tiny spell, a tiny memory..."

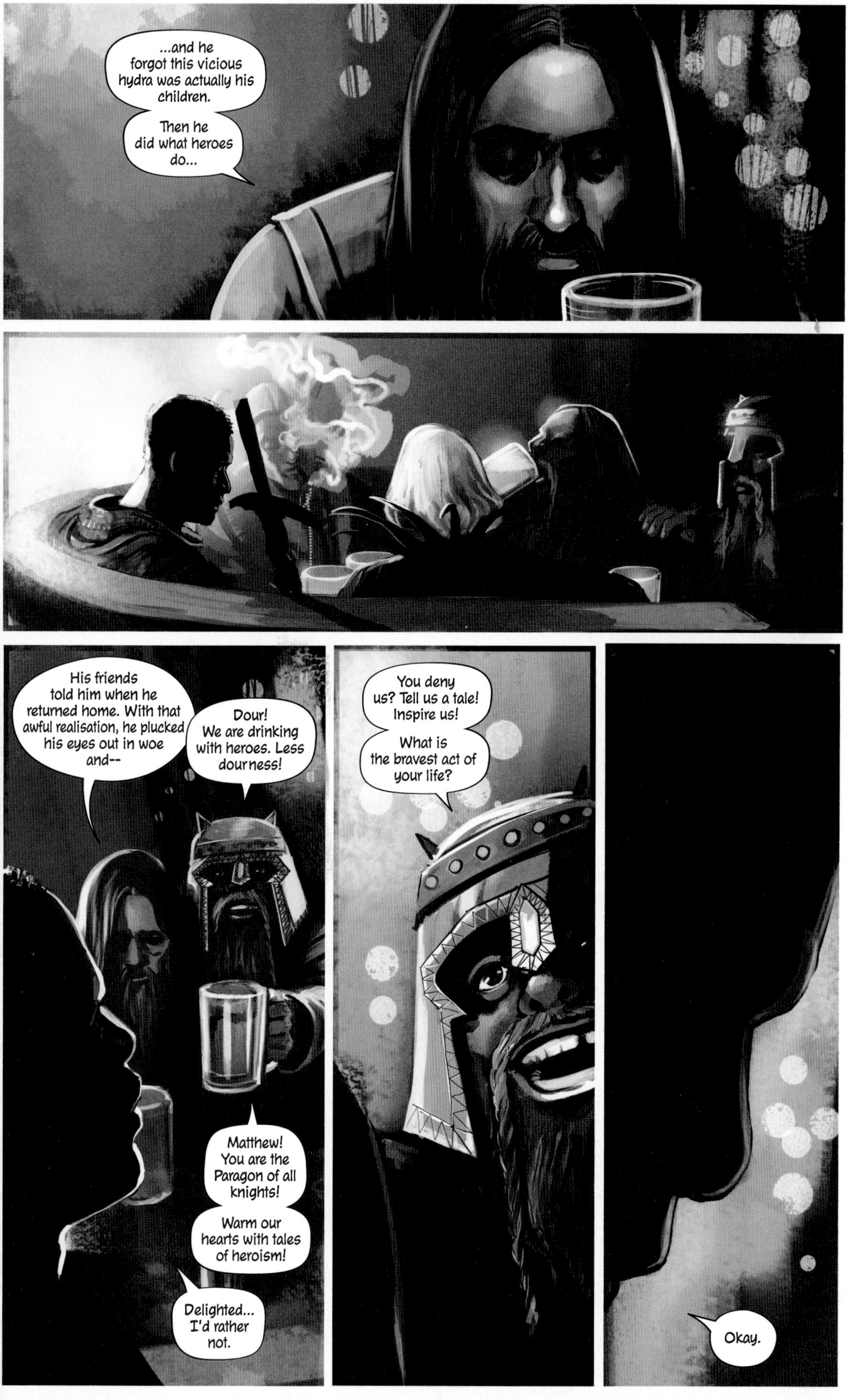
...and he forgot this vicious hydra was actually his children.
Then he did what heroes do...
His friends told him when he returned home. With that awful realisation, he plucked his eyes out in woe and--
Dour! We are drinking with heroes. Less dourness!
Matthew! You are the Paragon of all knights!
Warm our hearts with tales of heroism!
Delighted... I'd rather not.
You deny us? Tell us a tale! Inspire us!
What is the bravest act of your life?
Okay.

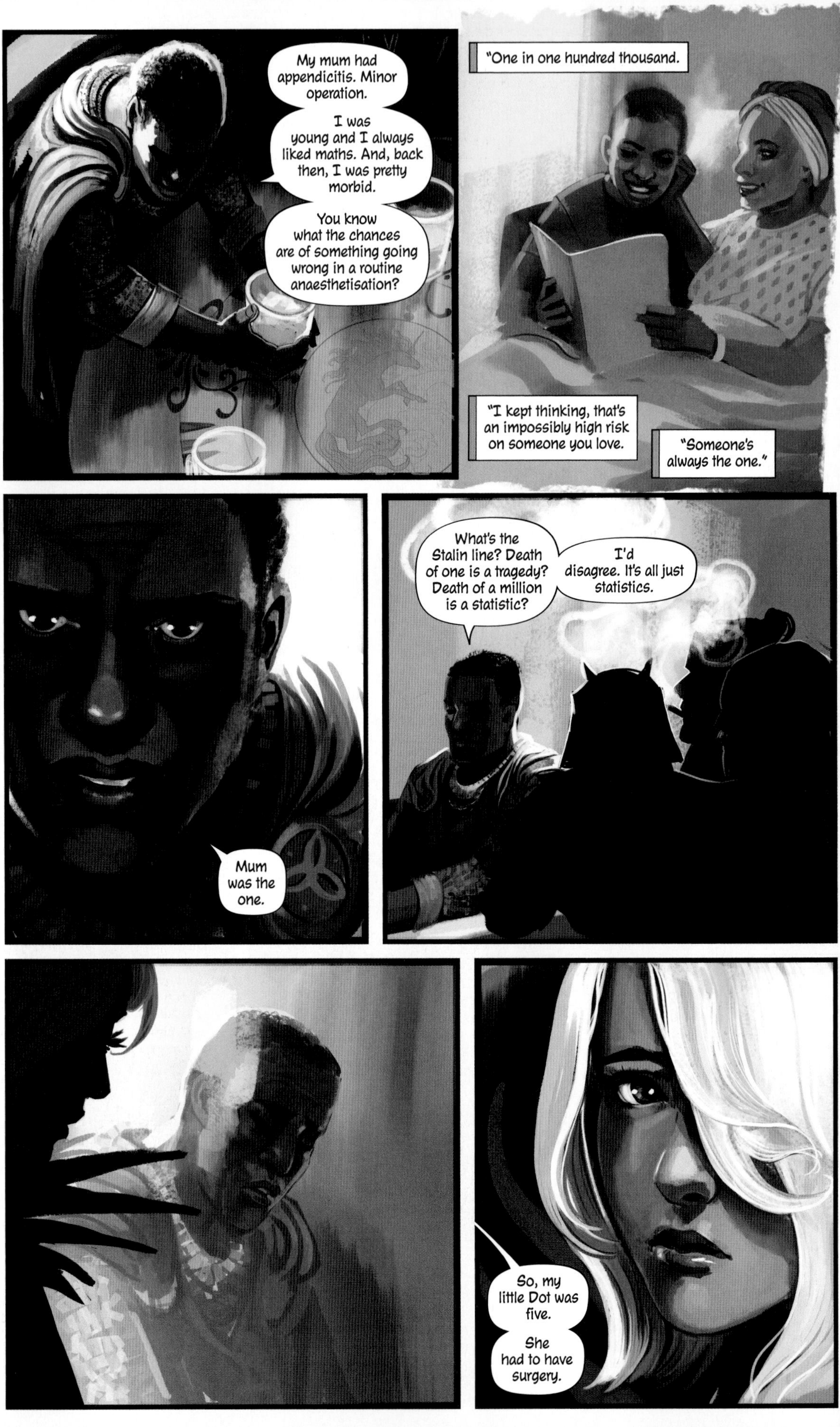
My mum had appendicitis. Minor operation.
I was young and I always liked maths. And, back then, I was pretty morbid.
You know what the chances are of something going wrong in a routine anaesthetisation?
"One in one hundred thousand.
"I kept thinking, that's an impossibly high risk on someone you love.
"Someone's always the one."
Mum was the one.
What's the Stalin line? Death of one is a tragedy? Death of a million is a statistic?
I'd disagree. It's all just statistics.
So, my little Dot was five.
She had to have surgery.

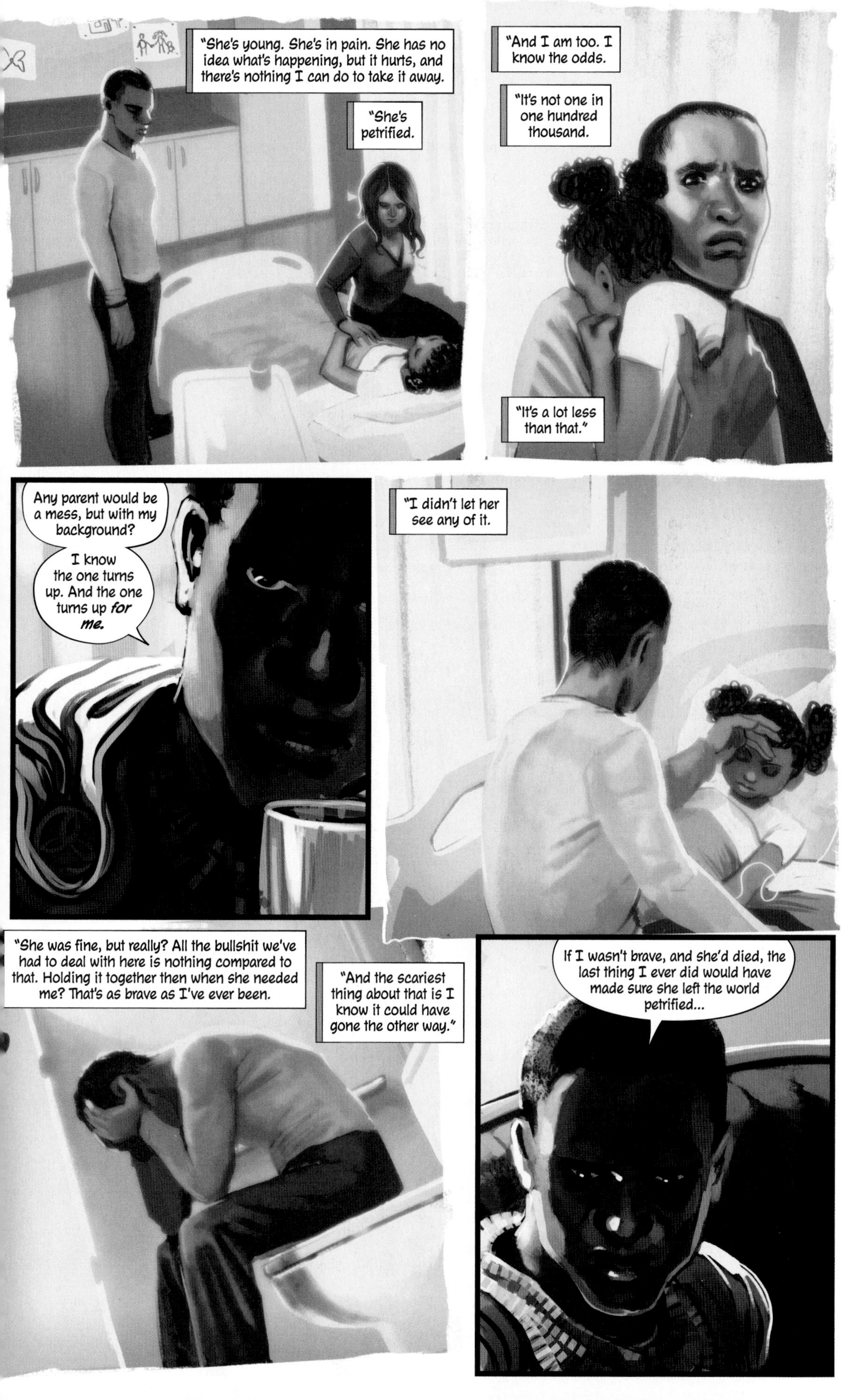
"She's young. She's in pain. She has no idea what's happening, but it hurts, and there's nothing I can do to take it away.
"She's petrified.
"And I am too. I know the odds.
"It's not one in one hundred thousand.
"It's a lot less than that."
Any parent would be a mess, but with my background?
I know the one turns up. And the one turns up *for me.*
"I didn't let her see any of it.
"She was fine, but really? All the bullshit we've had to deal with here is nothing compared to that. Holding it together then when she needed me? That's as brave as I've ever been.
"And the scariest thing about that is I know it could have gone the other way."
If I wasn't brave, and she'd died, the last thing I ever did would have made sure she left the world petrified...

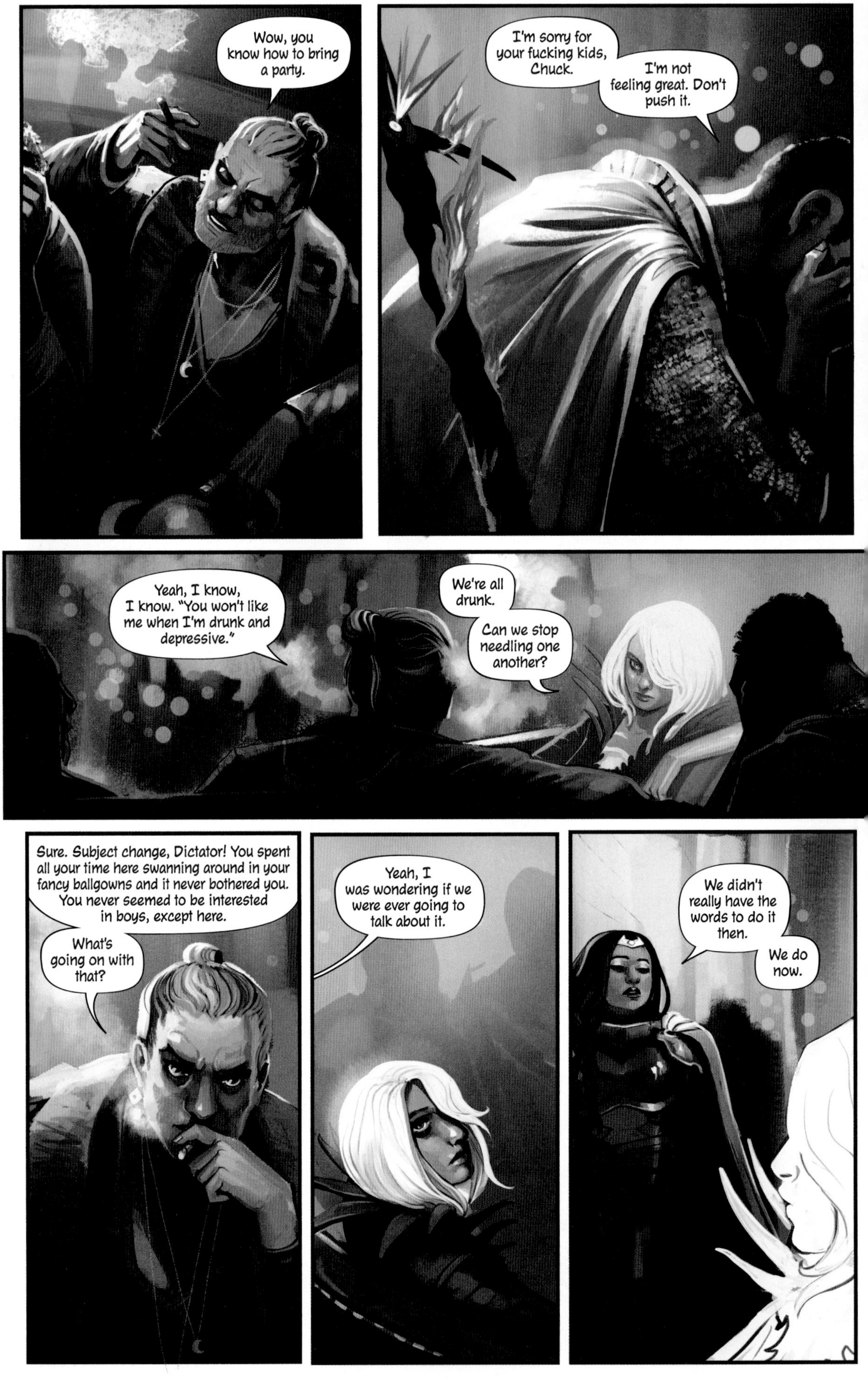
Wow, you know how to bring a party.
I'm sorry for your fucking kids, Chuck.
I'm not feeling great. Don't push it.
Yeah, I know, I know. "You won't like me when I'm drunk and depressive."
We're all drunk.
Can we stop needling one another?
Sure. Subject change, Dictator! You spent all your time here swanning around in your fancy ballgowns and it never bothered you. You never seemed to be interested in boys, except here.
What's going on with that?
Yeah, I was wondering if we were ever going to talk about it.
We didn't really have the words to do it then.
We do now.

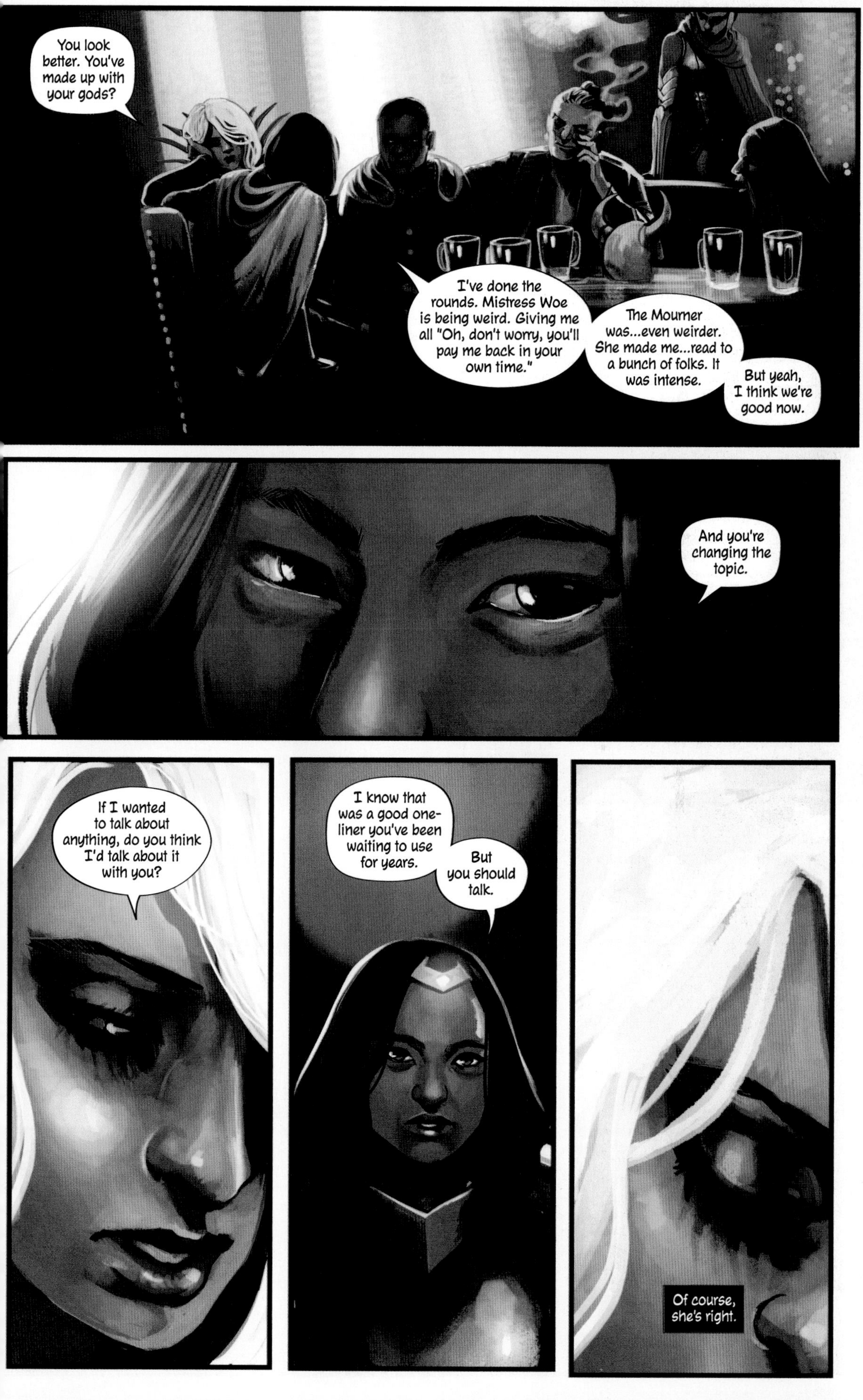
You look better. You've made up with your gods?
I've done the rounds. Mistress Woe is being weird. Giving me all "Oh, don't worry, you'll pay me back in your own time."
The Mourner was...even weirder. She made me...read to a bunch of folks. It was intense.
But yeah, I think we're good now.
And you're changing the topic.
If I wanted to talk about anything, do you think I'd talk about it with you?
I know that was a good one-liner you've been waiting to use for years.
But you should talk.
Of course, she's right.

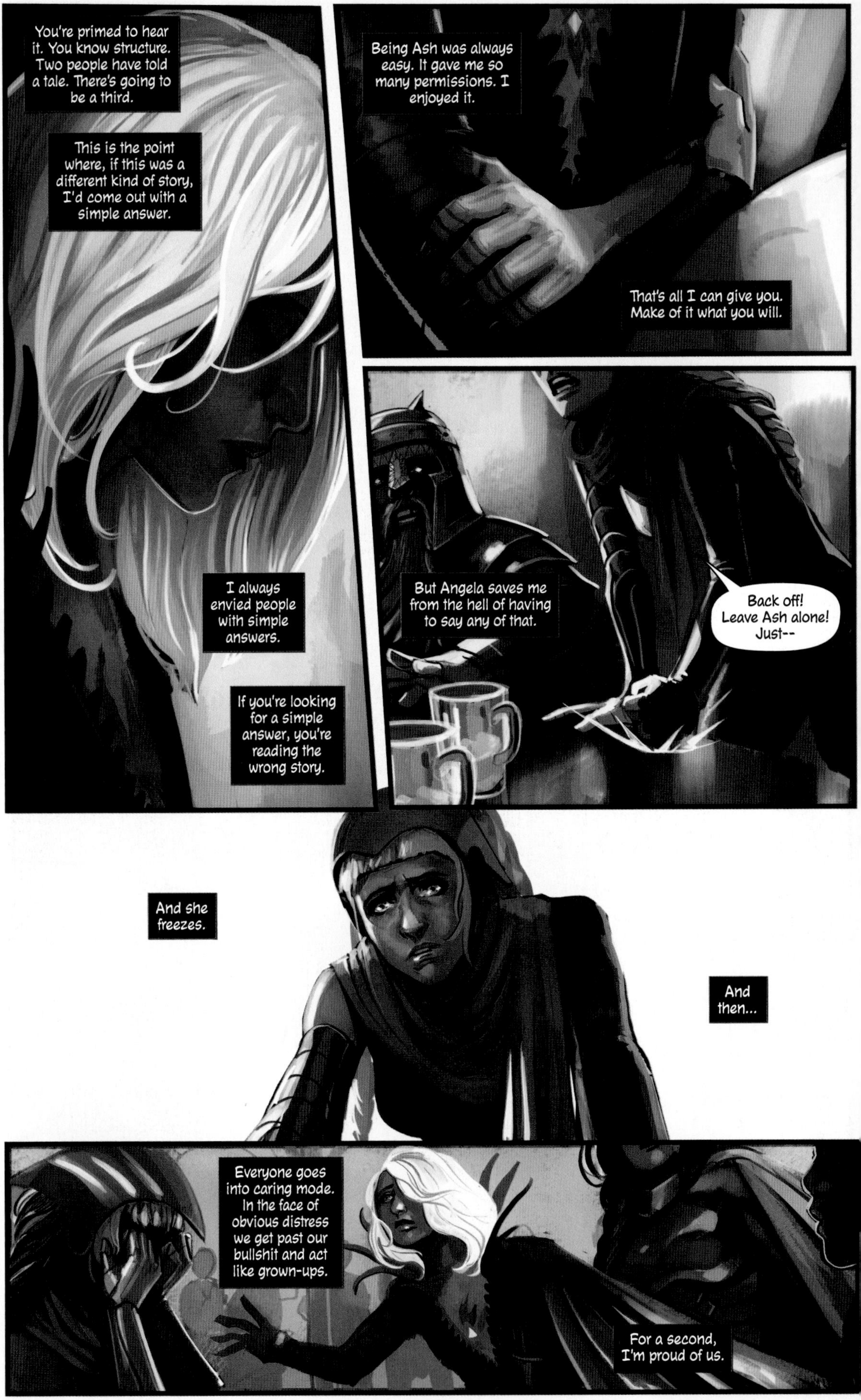
You're primed to hear it. You know structure. Two people have told a tale. There's going to be a third.
This is the point where, if this was a different kind of story, I'd come out with a simple answer.
Being Ash was always easy. It gave me so many permissions. I enjoyed it.
That's all I can give you. Make of it what you will.
I always envied people with simple answers.
If you're looking for a simple answer, you're reading the wrong story.
But Angela saves me from the hell of having to say any of that.
Back off! Leave Ash alone! Just--
And she freezes.
And then...
Everyone goes into caring mode. In the face of obvious distress we get past our bullshit and act like grown-ups.
For a second, I'm proud of us.

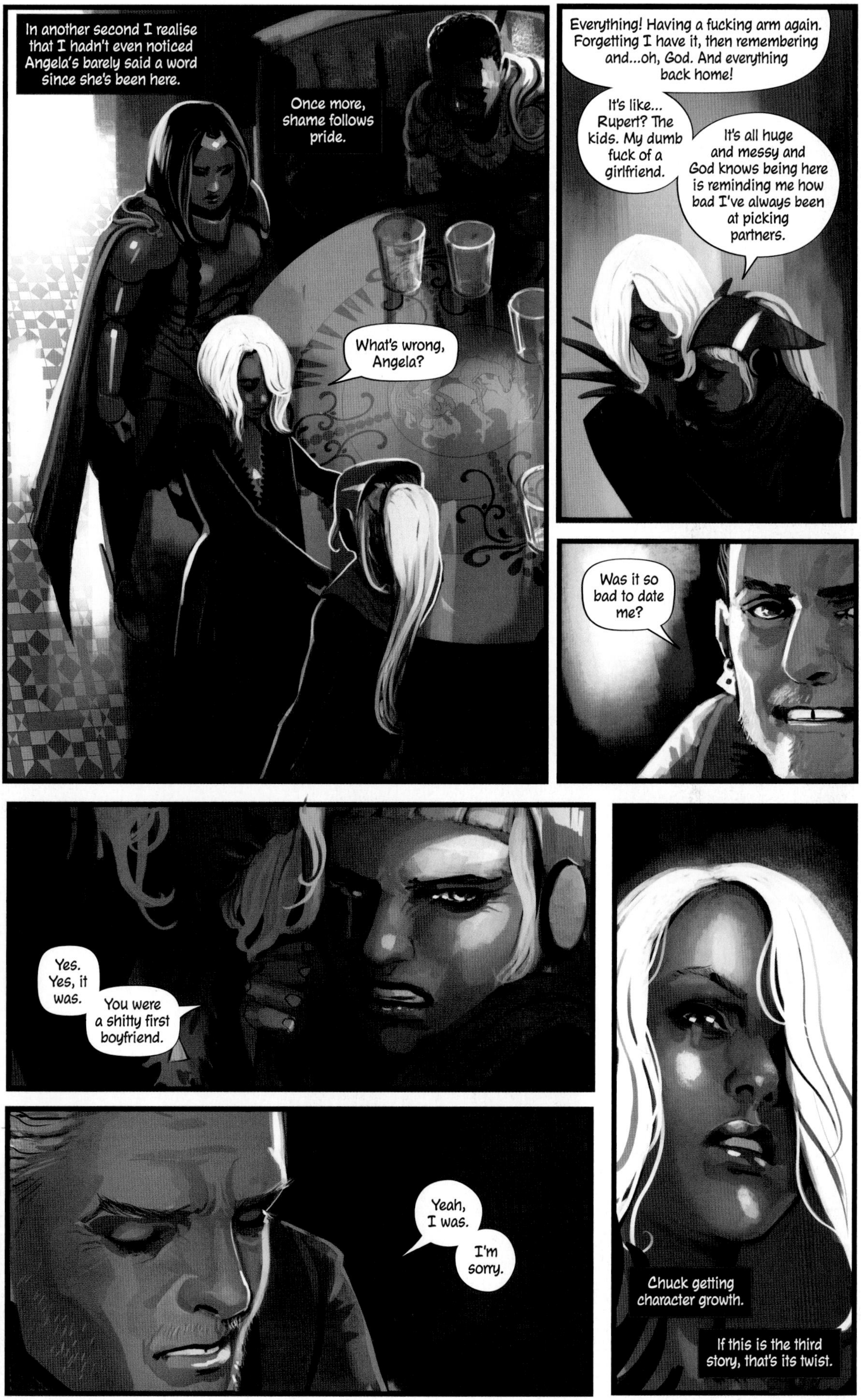
In another second I realise that I hadn't even noticed Angela's barely said a word since she's been here.
Once more, shame follows pride.
What's wrong, Angela?
Everything! Having a fucking arm again. Forgetting I have it, then remembering and...oh, God. And everything back home!
It's like... Rupert? The kids. My dumb fuck of a girlfriend.
It's all huge and messy and God knows being here is reminding me how bad I've always been at picking partners.
Was it so bad to date me?
Yes. Yes, it was.
You were a shitty first boyfriend.
Yeah, I was.
I'm sorry.
Chuck getting character growth.
If this is the third story, that's its twist.

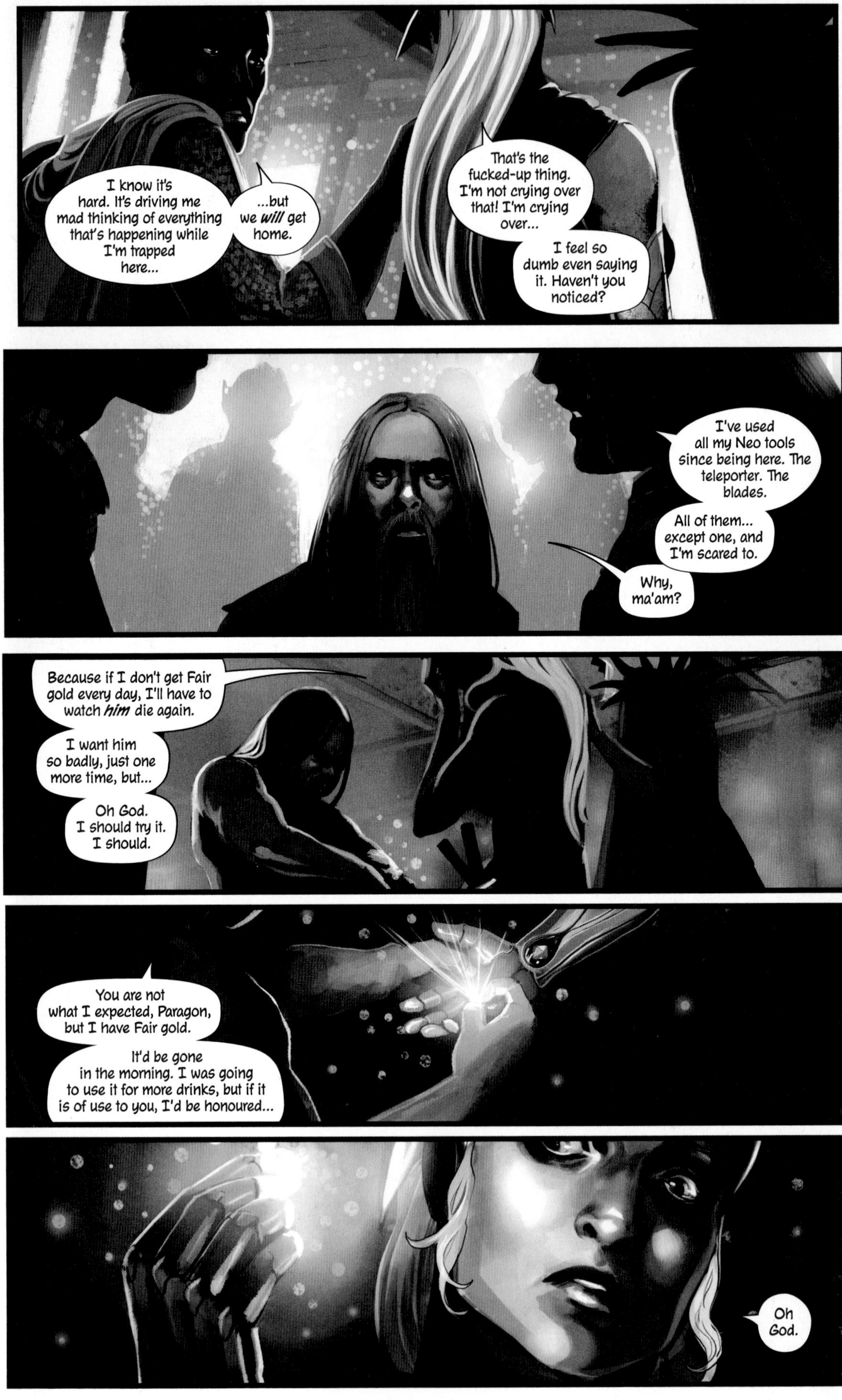
I know it's hard. It's driving me mad thinking of everything that's happening while I'm trapped here...
...but we *will* get home.
That's the fucked-up thing. I'm not crying over that! I'm crying over...
I feel so dumb even saying it. Haven't you noticed?
I've used all my Neo tools since being here. The teleporter. The blades.
All of them... except one, and I'm scared to.
Why, ma'am?
Because if I don't get Fair gold every day, I'll have to watch *him* die again.
I want him so badly, just one more time, but...
Oh God. I should try it. I should.
You are not what I expected, Paragon, but I have Fair gold.
It'd be gone in the morning. I was going to use it for more drinks, but if it is of use to you, I'd be honoured...
Oh God.

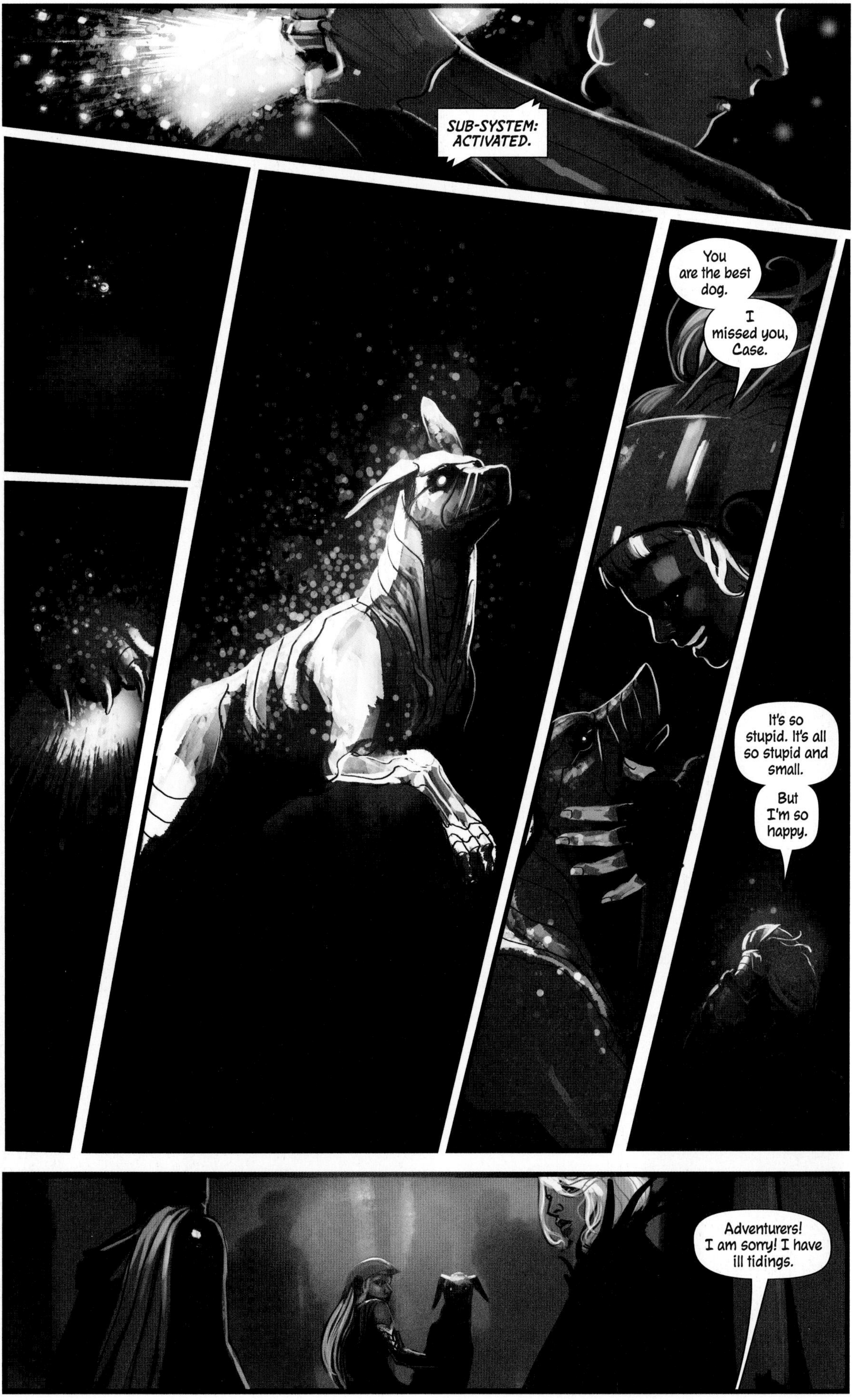
SUB-SYSTEM:
ACTIVATED.
You are the best dog.
I missed you, Case.
It's so stupid. It's all so stupid and small.
But I'm so happy.
Adventurers! I am sorry! I have ill tidings.

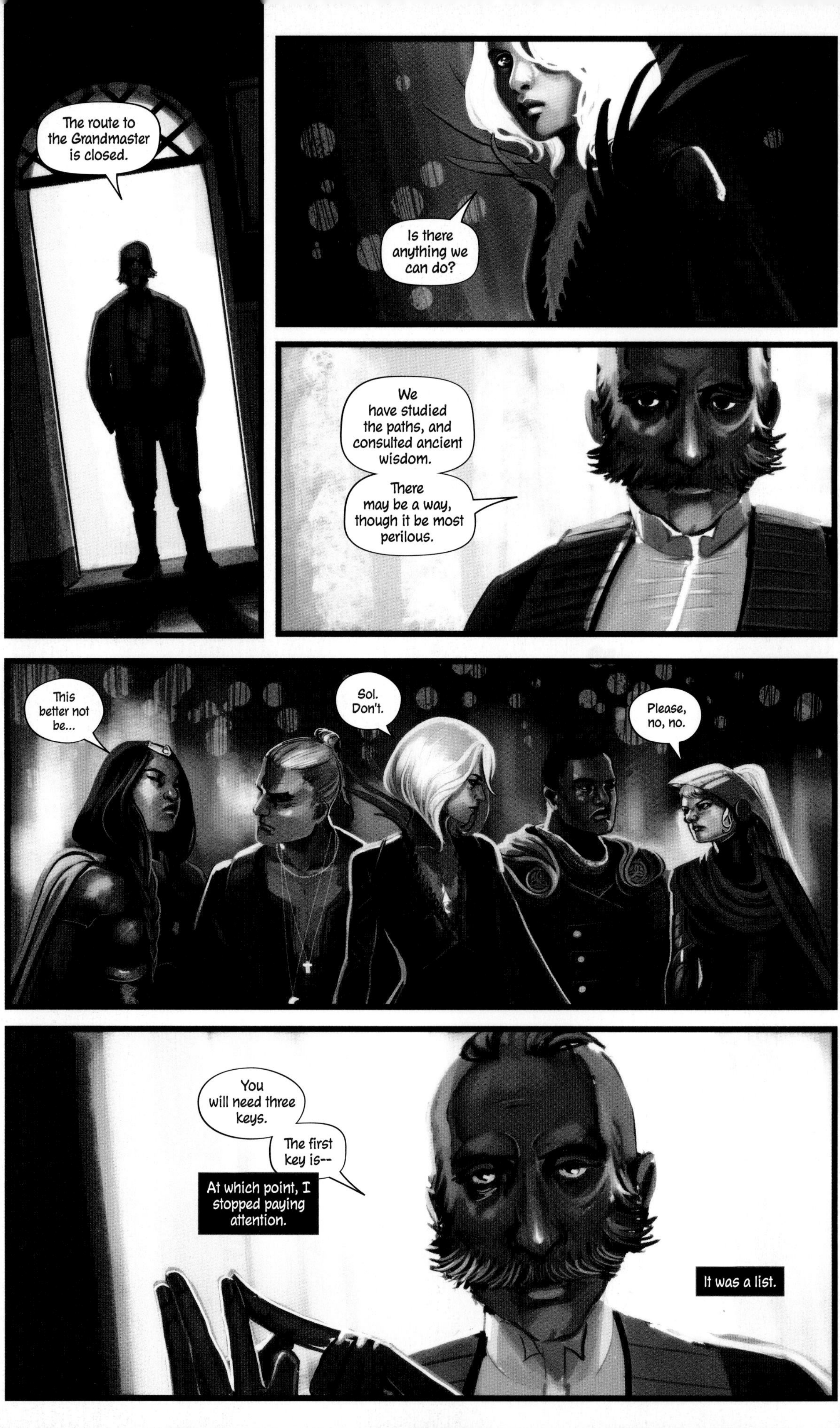
The route to the Grandmaster is closed.
Is there anything we can do?
We have studied the paths, and consulted ancient wisdom.
There may be a way, though it be most perilous.
This better not be...
Sol. Don't.
Please, no, no.
You will need three keys.
The first key is--
At which point, I stopped paying attention.
It was a list.

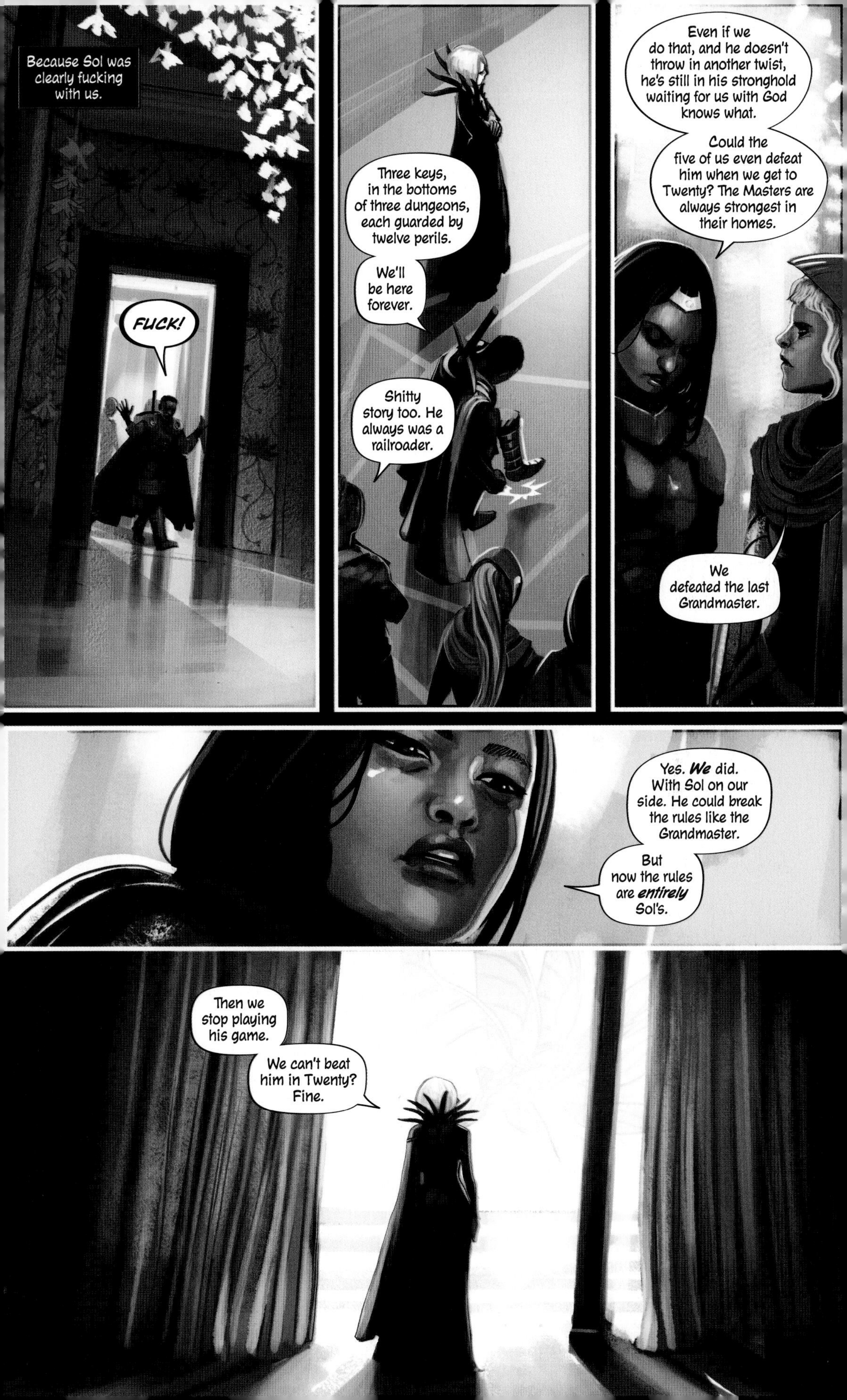
Because Sol was clearly fucking with us.
FUCK!
Three keys, in the bottoms of three dungeons, each guarded by twelve perils.
We'll be here forever.
Shitty story too. He always was a railroader.
Even if we do that, and he doesn't throw in another twist, he's still in his stronghold waiting for us with God knows what.
Could the five of us even defeat him when we get to Twenty? The Masters are always strongest in their homes.
We defeated the last Grandmaster.
Yes. We did. With Sol on our side. He could break the rules like the Grandmaster.
But now the rules are entirely Sol's.
Then we stop playing his game.
We can't beat him in Twenty? Fine.

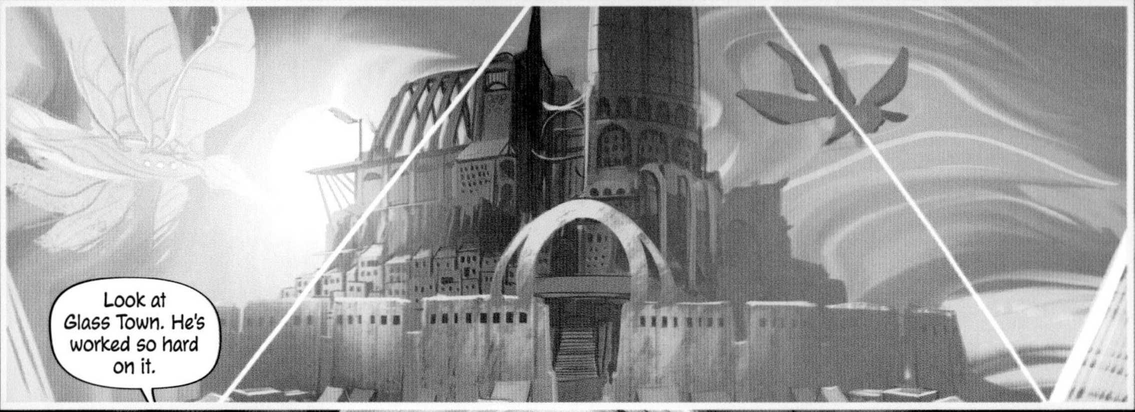
Look at Glass Town. He's worked so hard on it.

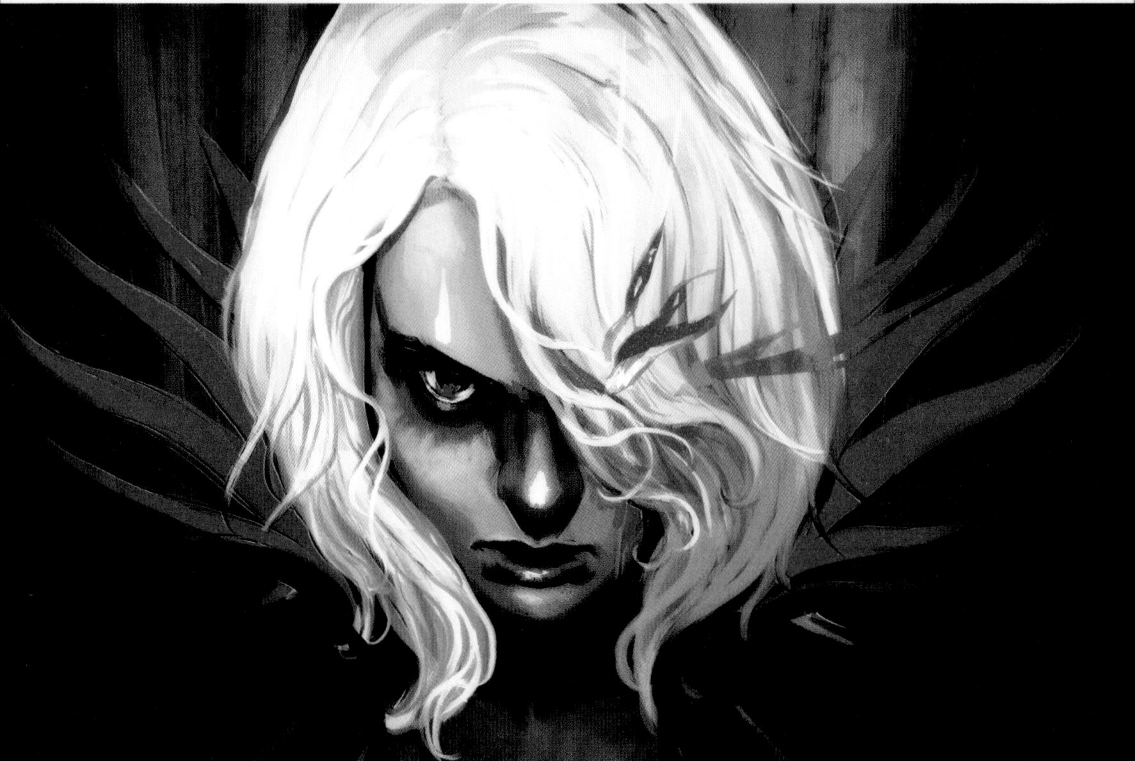

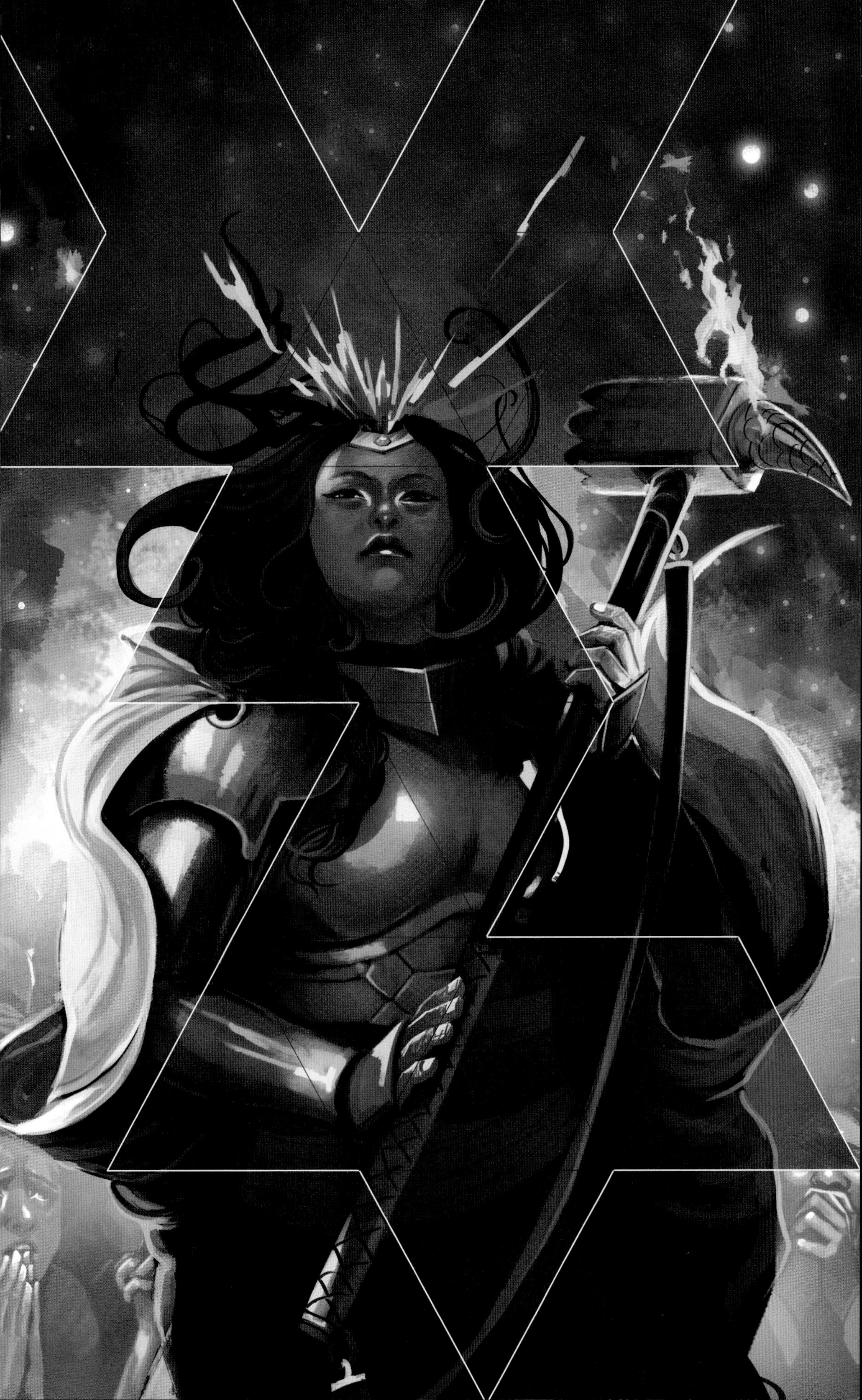

5:
PREMISE
REJECTION

"I'm very sorry, Mr Tumnus," said Lucy.
"But please let me go home."
– CS Lewis,
The Lion, the Witch and the Wardrobe

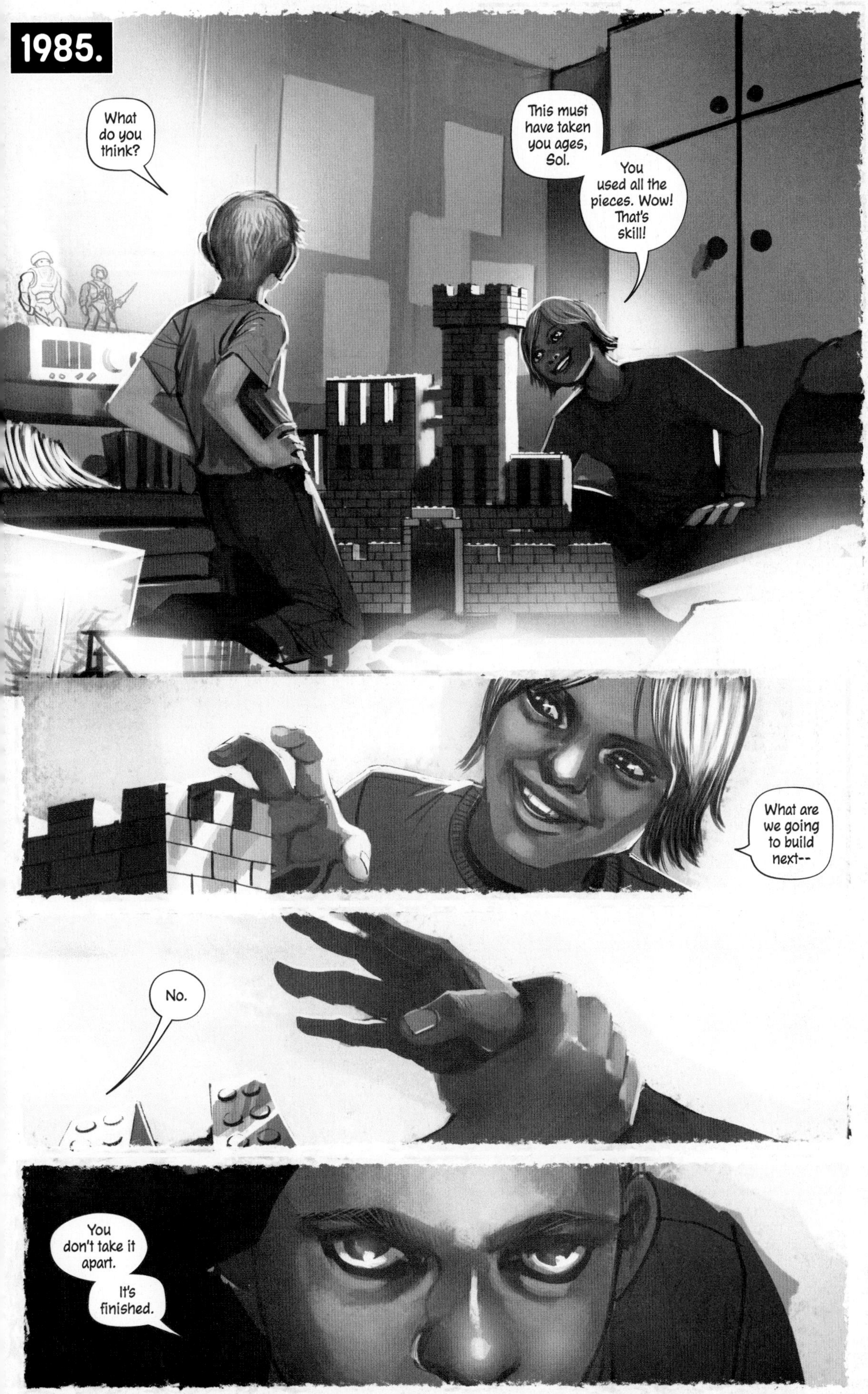
1985.
What do you think?
This must have taken you ages, Sol.
You used all the pieces. Wow! That's skill!
What are we going to build next--
No.
You don't take it apart.
It's finished.

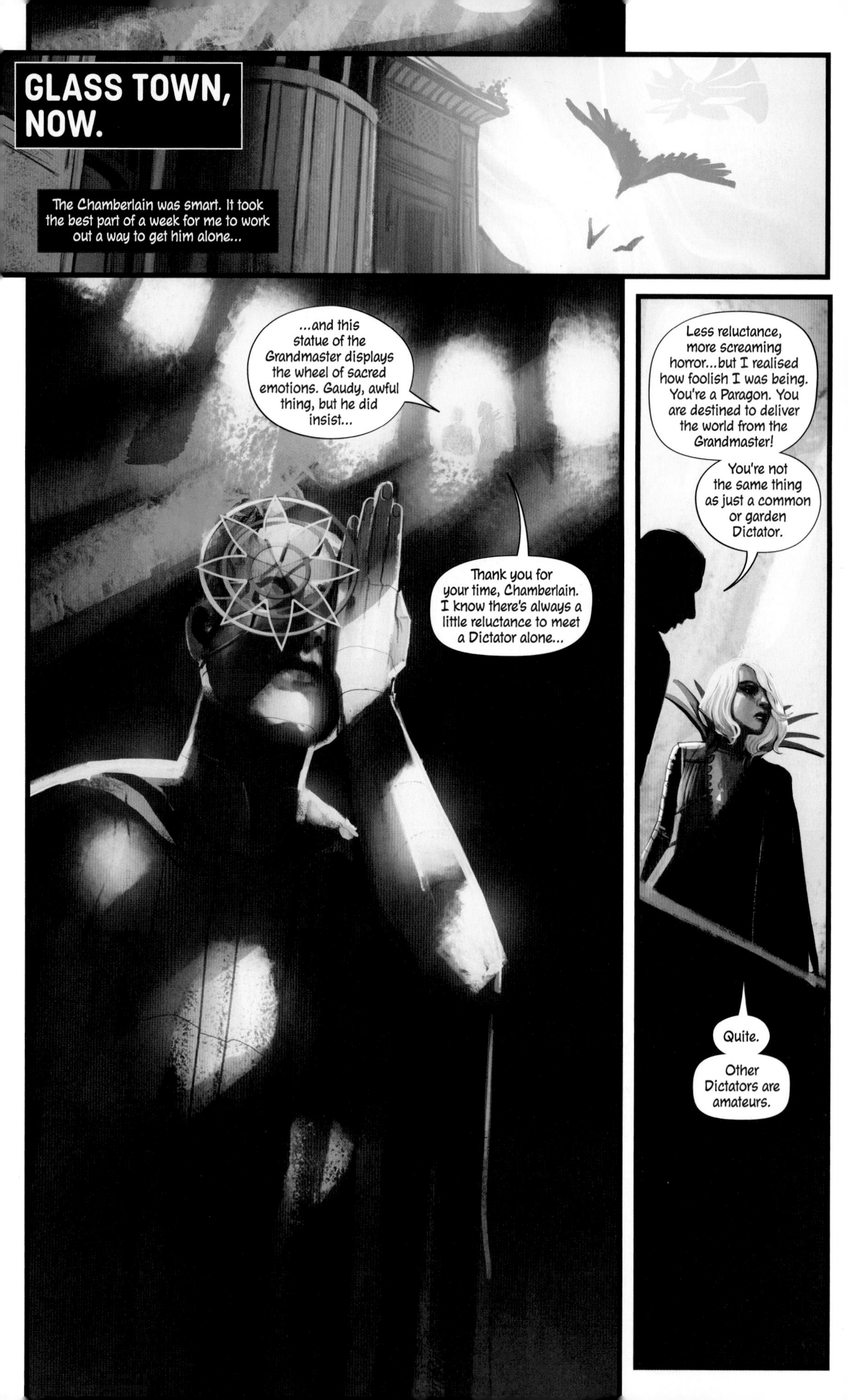
GLASS TOWN, NOW.
The Chamberlain was smart. It took the best part of a week for me to work out a way to get him alone...
...and this statue of the Grandmaster displays the wheel of sacred emotions. Gaudy, awful thing, but he did insist...
Thank you for your time, Chamberlain. I know there's always a little reluctance to meet a Dictator alone...
Less reluctance, more screaming horror...but I realised how foolish I was being. You're a Paragon. You are destined to deliver the world from the Grandmaster!
You're not the same thing as just a common or garden Dictator.
Quite.
Other Dictators are amateurs.

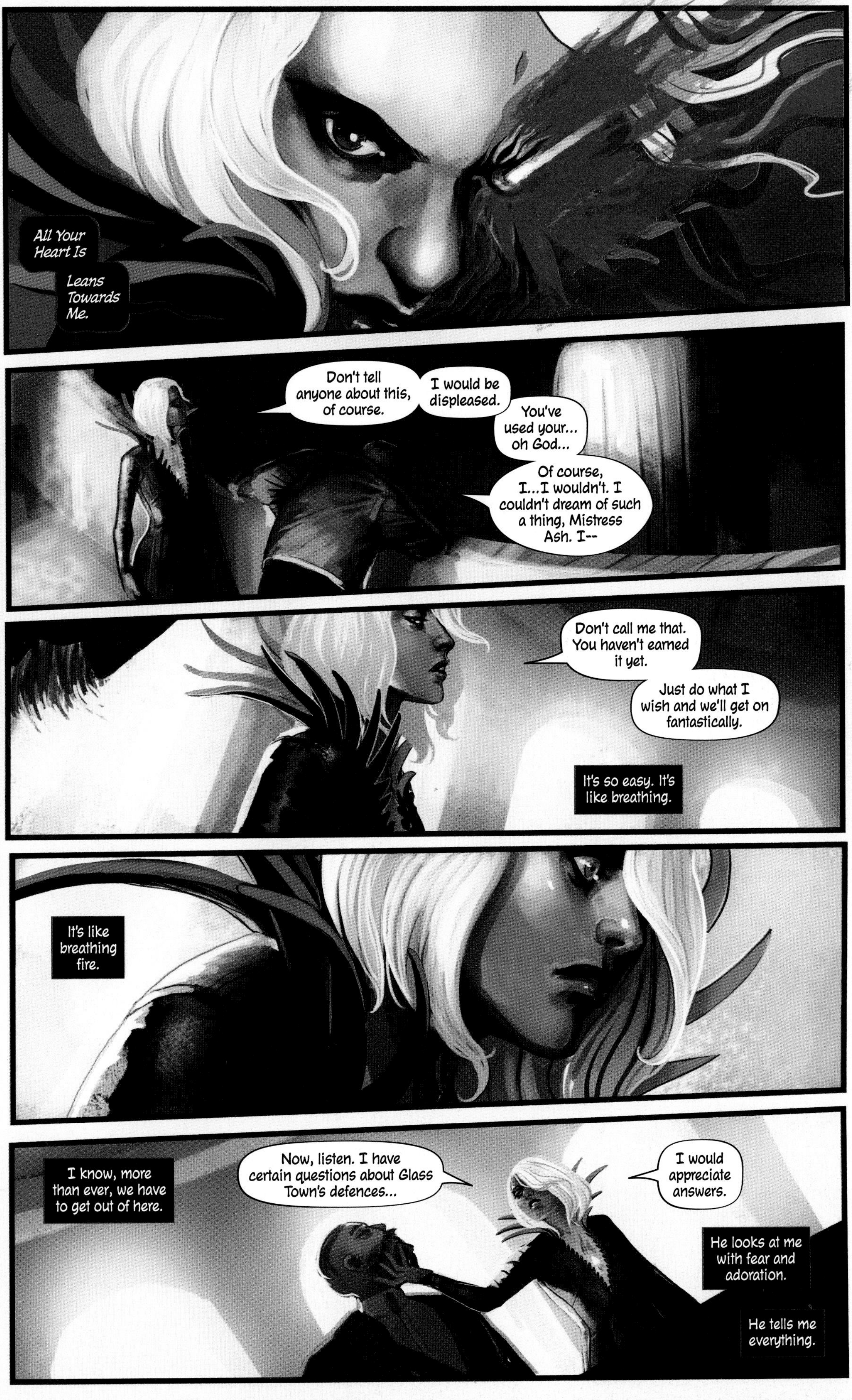
All Your Heart Is
Leans Towards Me.
Don't tell anyone about this, of course.
I would be displeased.
You've used your... oh God...
Of course, I...I wouldn't. I couldn't dream of such a thing, Mistress Ash. I--
Don't call me that. You haven't earned it yet.
Just do what I wish and we'll get on fantastically.
It's so easy. It's like breathing.
It's like breathing fire.
I know, more than ever, we have to get out of here.
Now, listen. I have certain questions about Glass Town's defences...
I would appreciate answers.
He looks at me with fear and adoration.
He tells me everything.

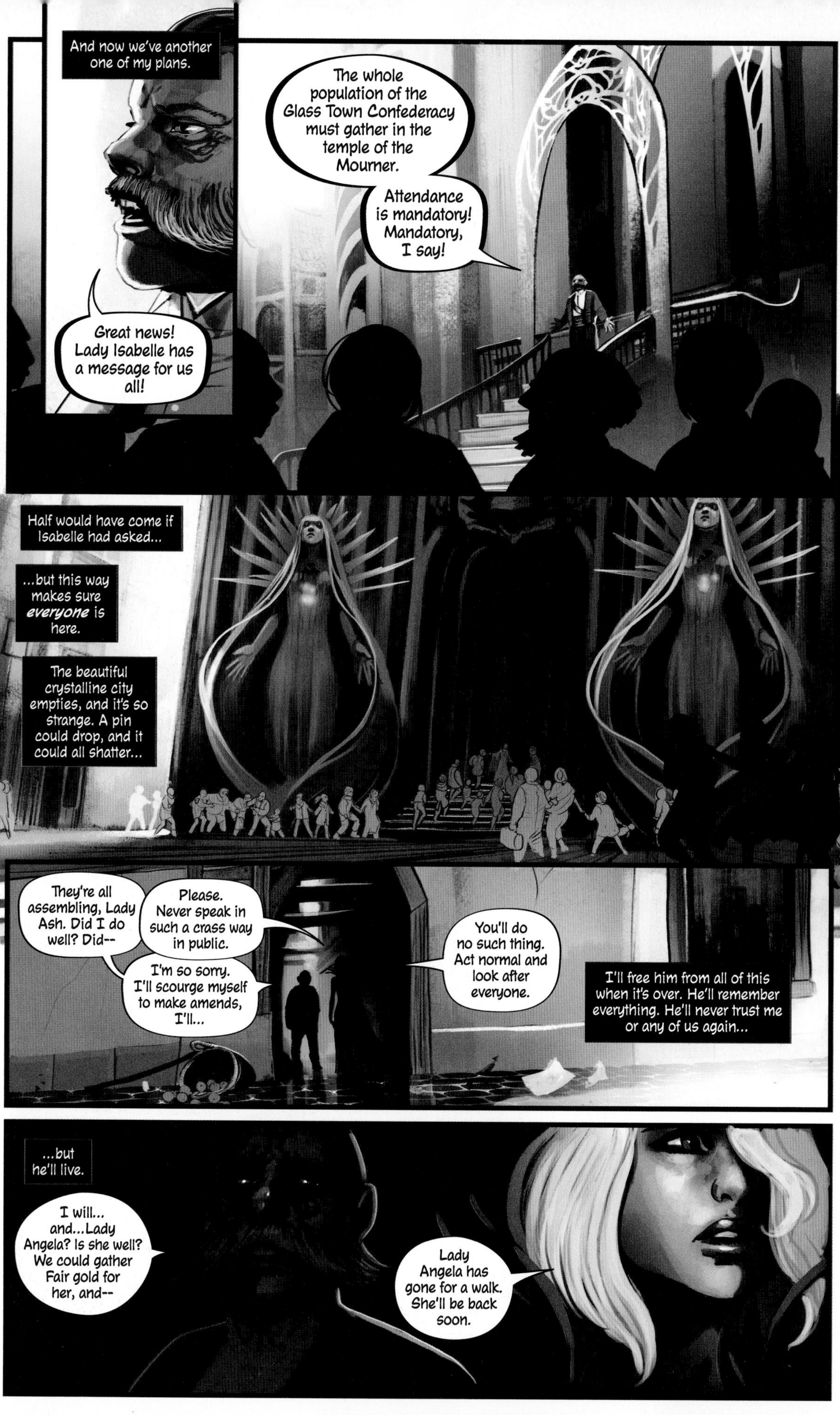
And now we've another one of my plans.
The whole population of the Glass Town Confederacy must gather in the temple of the Mourner.
Attendance is mandatory! Mandatory, I say!
Great news! Lady Isabelle has a message for us all!
Half would have come if Isabelle had asked...
...but this way makes sure *everyone* is here.
The beautiful crystalline city empties, and it's so strange. A pin could drop, and it could all shatter...
They're all assembling, Lady Ash. Did I do well? Did--
Please. Never speak in such a crass way in public.
I'm so sorry. I'll scourge myself to make amends, I'll...
You'll do no such thing. Act normal and look after everyone.
I'll free him from all of this when it's over. He'll remember everything. He'll never trust me or any of us again...
...but he'll live.
I will... and...Lady Angela? Is she well? We could gather Fair gold for her, and--
Lady Angela has gone for a walk. She'll be back soon.

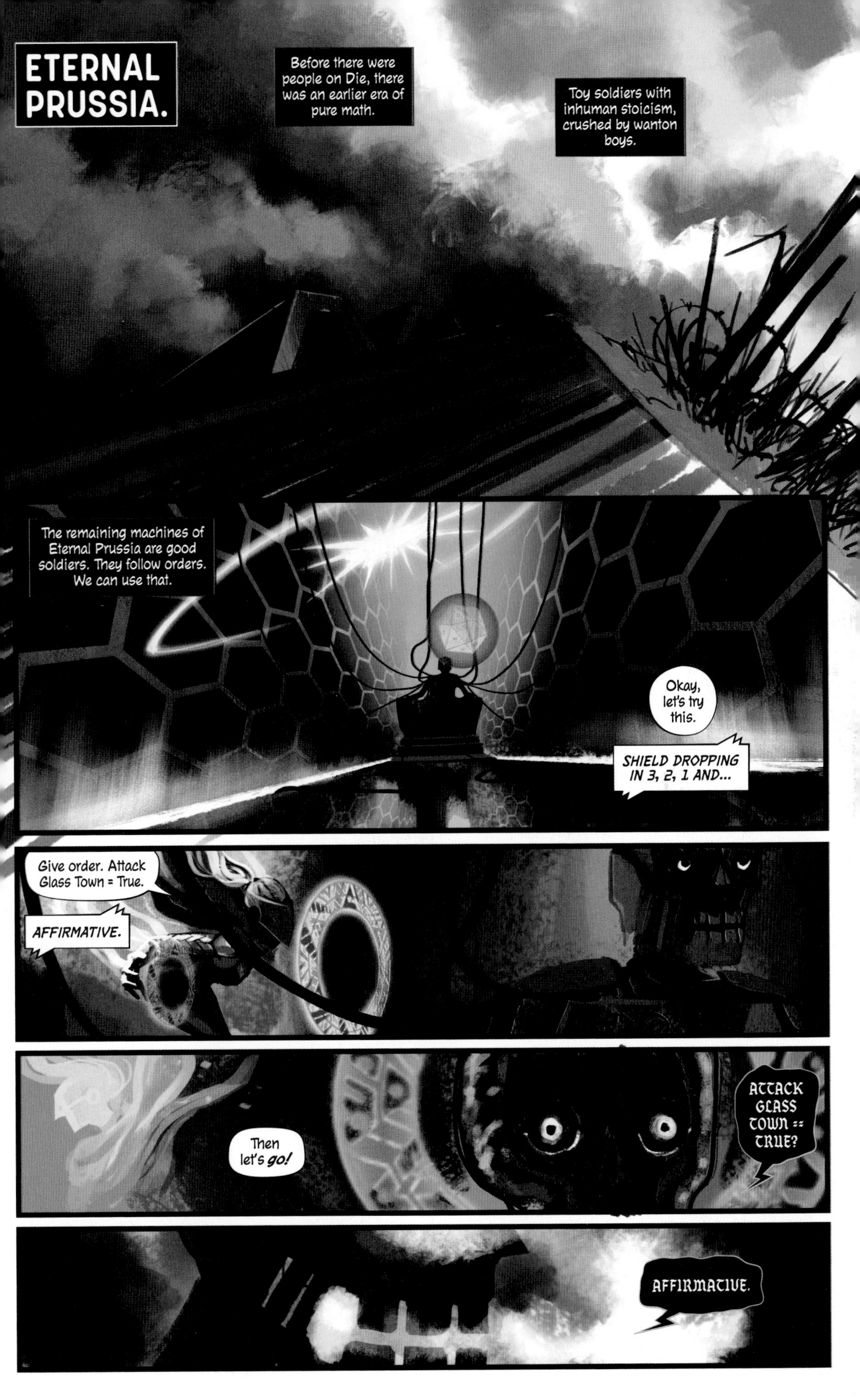
ETERNAL PRUSSIA.
Before there were people on Die, there was an earlier era of pure math.
Toy soldiers with inhuman stoicism, crushed by wanton boys.
The remaining machines of Eternal Prussia are good soldiers. They follow orders. We can use that.
Okay, let's try this.
SHIELD DROPPING IN 3, 2, 1 AND...
Give order. Attack Glass Town = True.
AFFIRMATIVE.
Then let's go!
ATTACK GLASS TOWN == TRUE?
AFFIRMATIVE.

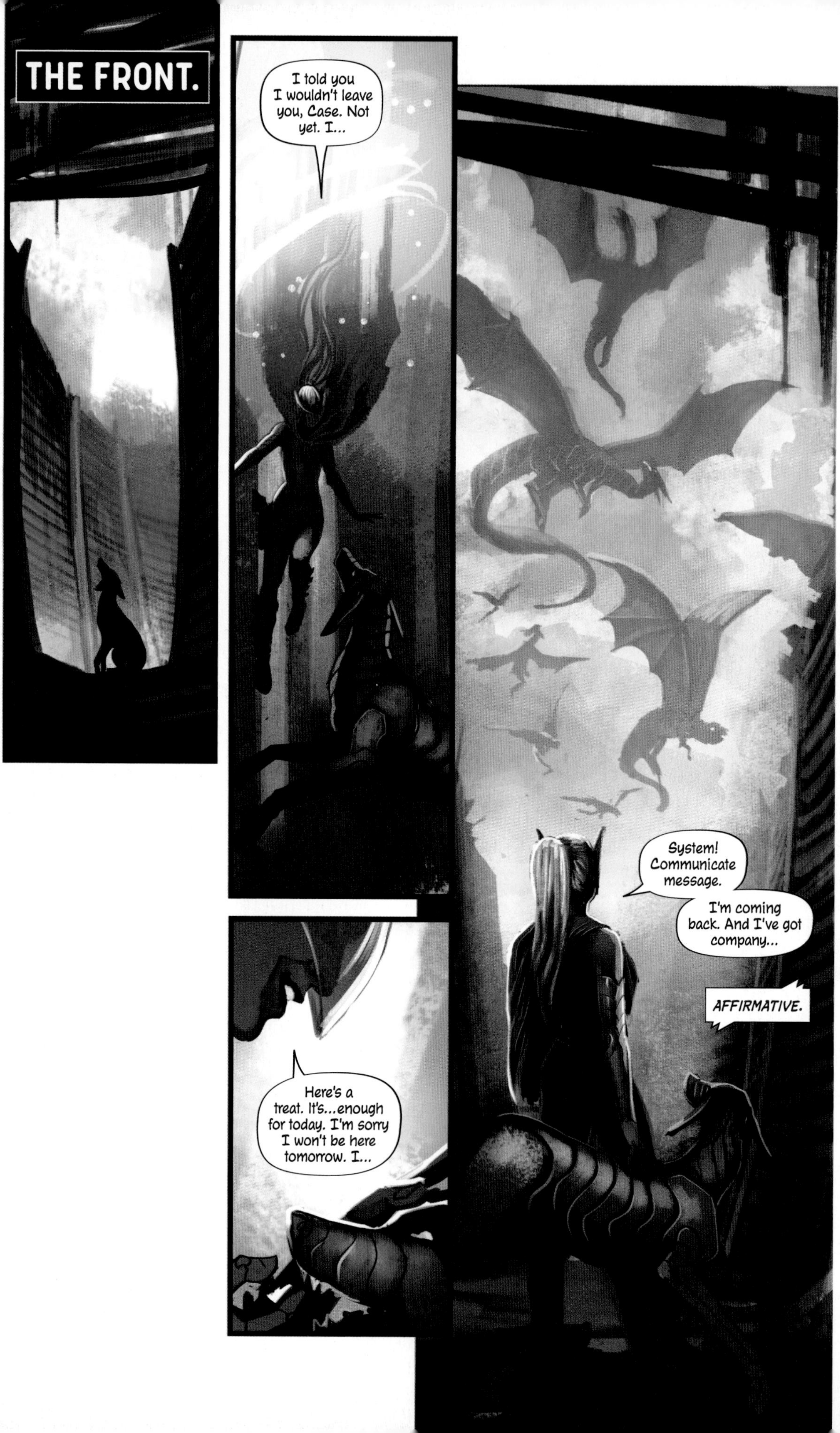
THE FRONT.
I told you I wouldn't leave you, Case. Not yet. I...
Here's a treat. It's...enough for today. I'm sorry I won't be here tomorrow. I...
System! Communicate message.
I'm coming back. And I've got company...
AFFIRMATIVE.

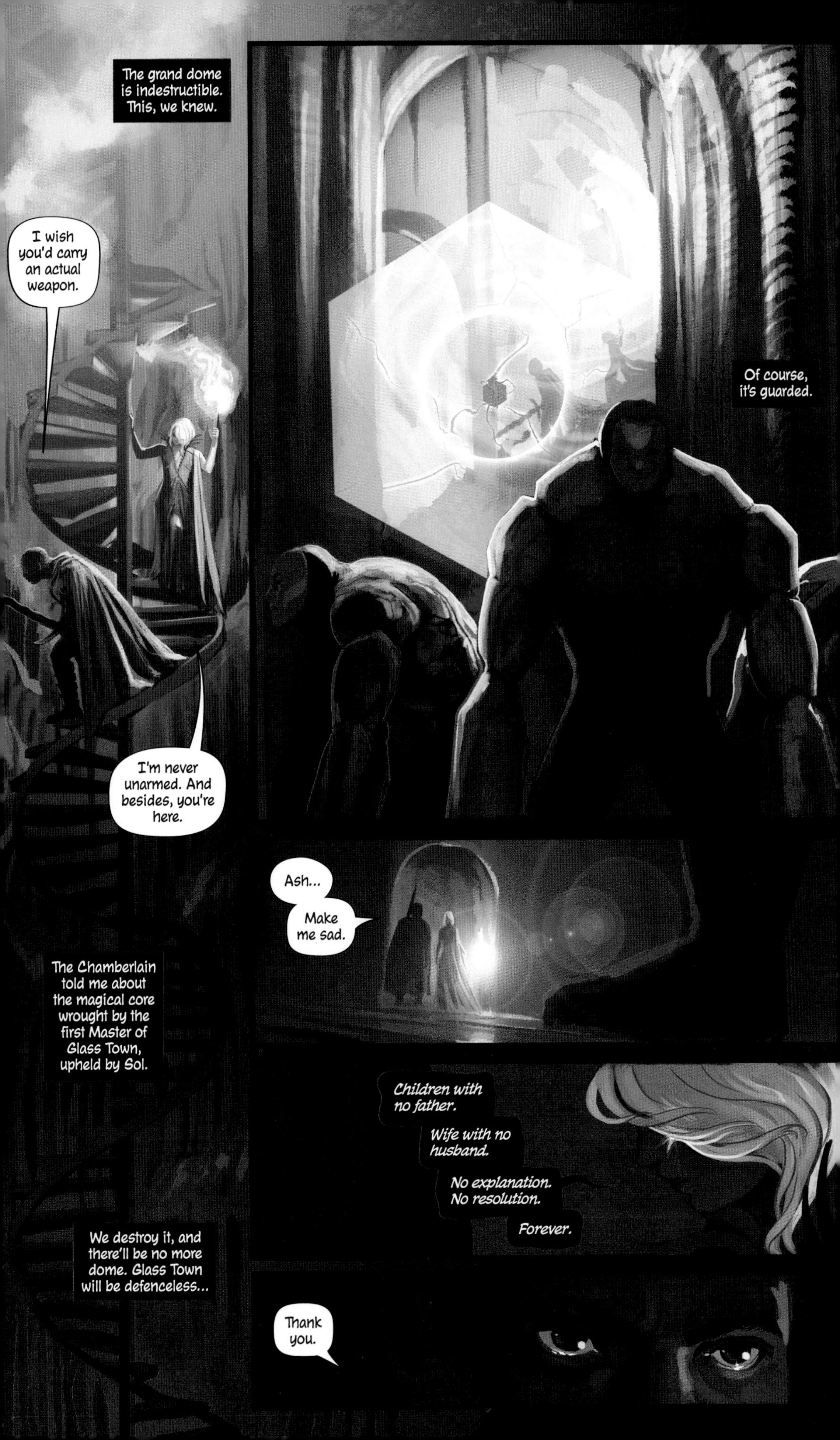

The grand dome is indestructible. This, we knew.
I wish you'd carry an actual weapon.
I'm never unarmed. And besides, you're here.
Of course, it's guarded.
The Chamberlain told me about the magical core wrought by the first Master of Glass Town, upheld by Sol.
Ash...
Make me sad.
We destroy it, and there'll be no more dome. Glass Town will be defenceless...
Children with no father.
Wife with no husband.
No explanation. No resolution.
Forever.
Thank you.

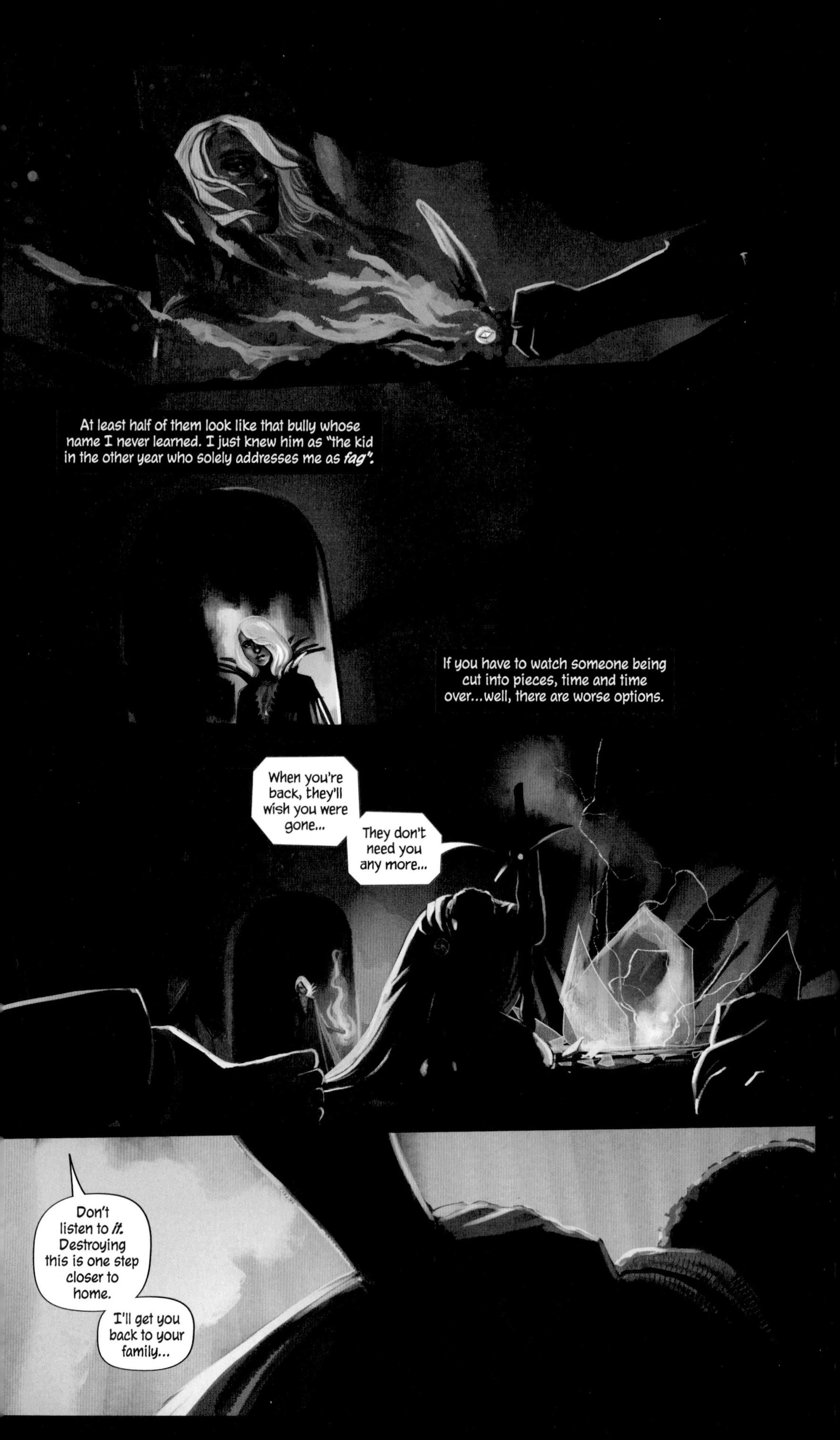
At least half of them look like that bully whose name I never learned. I just knew him as "the kid in the other year who solely addresses me as *fag*".
If you have to watch someone being cut into pieces, time and time over...well, there are worse options.
When you're back, they'll wish you were gone...
They don't need you any more...
Don't listen to *it*. Destroying this is one step closer to home.
I'll get you back to your family...

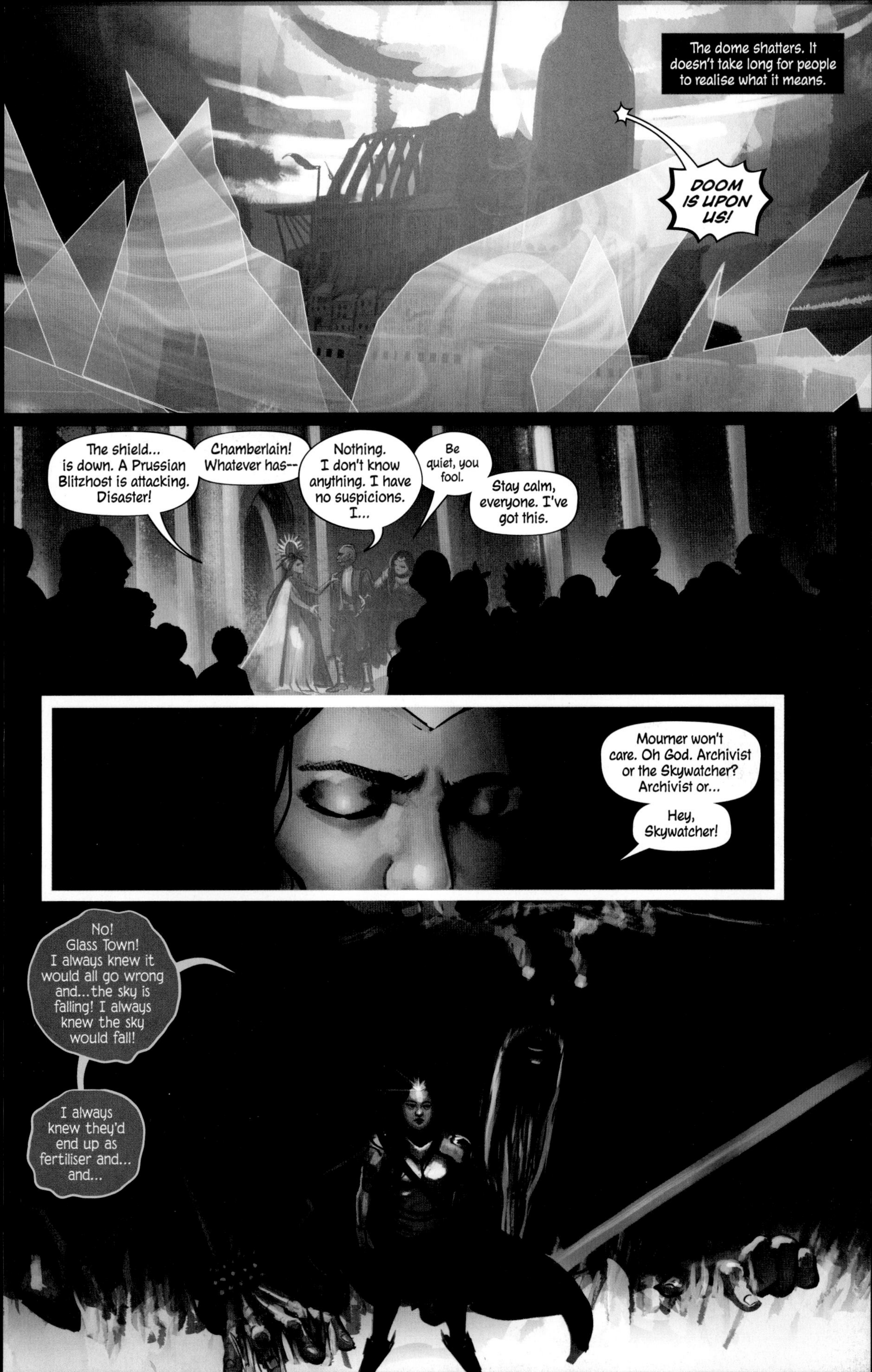

The dome shatters. It doesn't take long for people to realise what it means.
DOOM IS UPON US!
The shield... is down. A Prussian Blitzhost is attacking. Disaster!
Chamberlain! Whatever has--
Nothing. I don't know anything. I have no suspicions. I...
Be quiet, you fool.
Stay calm, everyone. I've got this.
Mourner won't care. Oh God. Archivist or the Skywatcher? Archivist or...
Hey, Skywatcher!
No! Glass Town! I always knew it would all go wrong and...the sky is falling! I always knew the sky would fall!
I always knew they'd end up as fertiliser and... and...

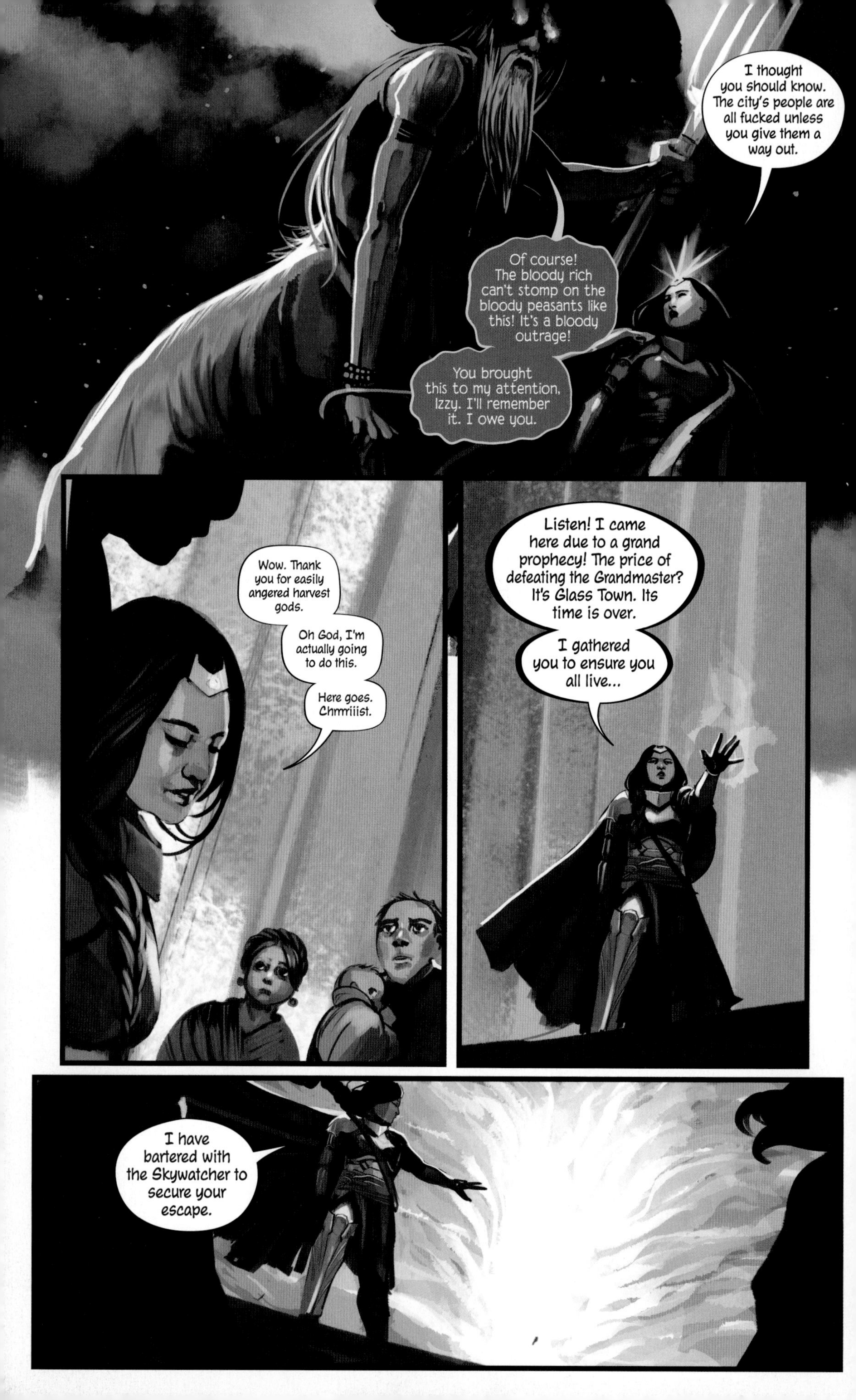
I thought you should know. The city's people are all fucked unless you give them a way out.
Of course! The bloody rich can't stomp on the bloody peasants like this! It's a bloody outrage!
You brought this to my attention, Izzy. I'll remember it. I owe you.
Wow. Thank you for easily angered harvest gods.
Oh God, I'm actually going to do this.
Here goes. Chmmiiist.
Listen! I came here due to a grand prophecy! The price of defeating the Grandmaster? It's Glass Town. Its time is over.
I gathered you to ensure you all live...
I have bartered with the Skywatcher to secure your escape.

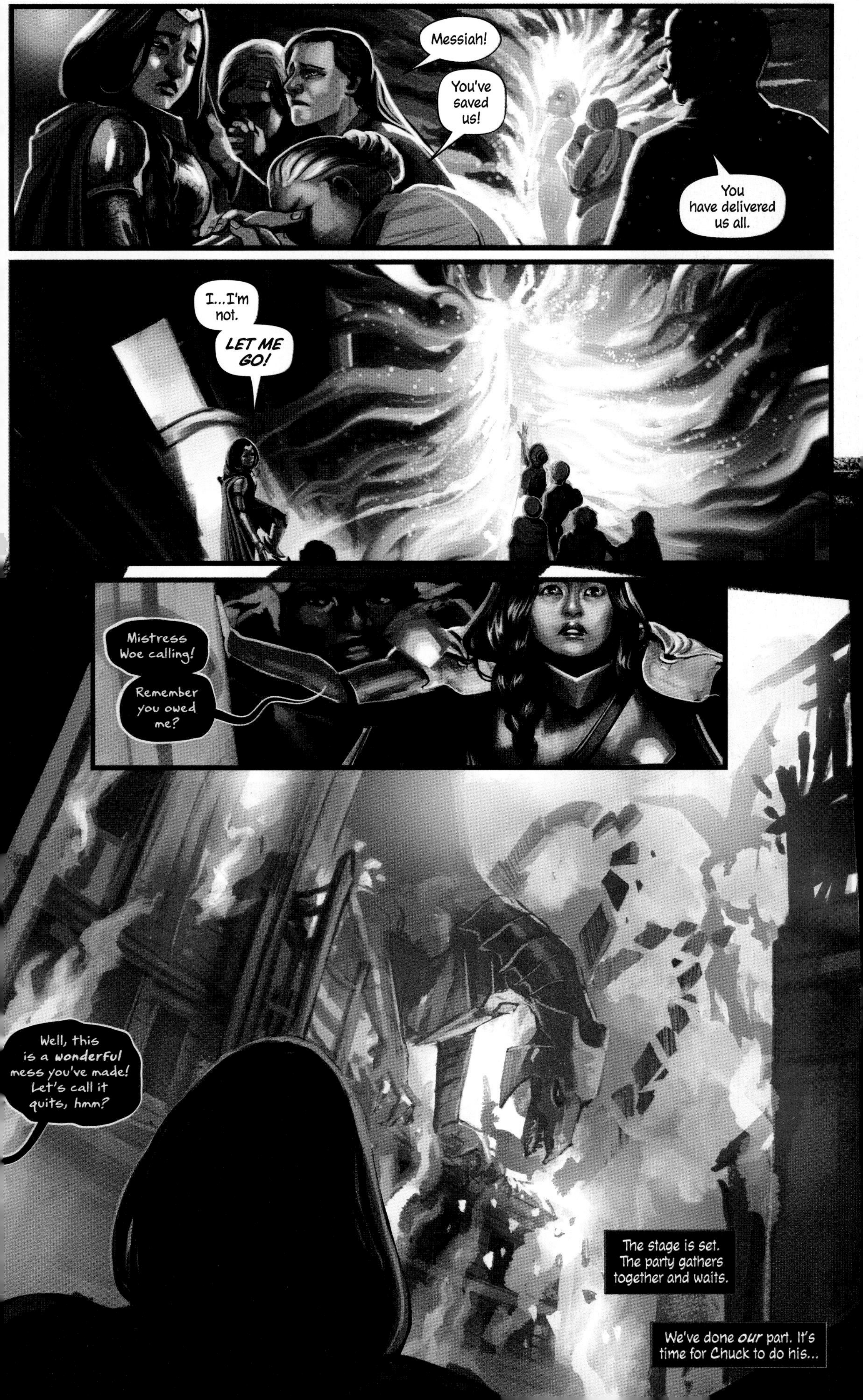
Messiah!
You've saved us!
You have delivered us all.
I...I'm not.
LET ME GO!
Mistress Woe calling!
Remember you owed me?
Well, this is a wonderful mess you've made! Let's call it quits, hmm?
The stage is set. The party gathers together and waits.
We've done our part. It's time for Chuck to do his...

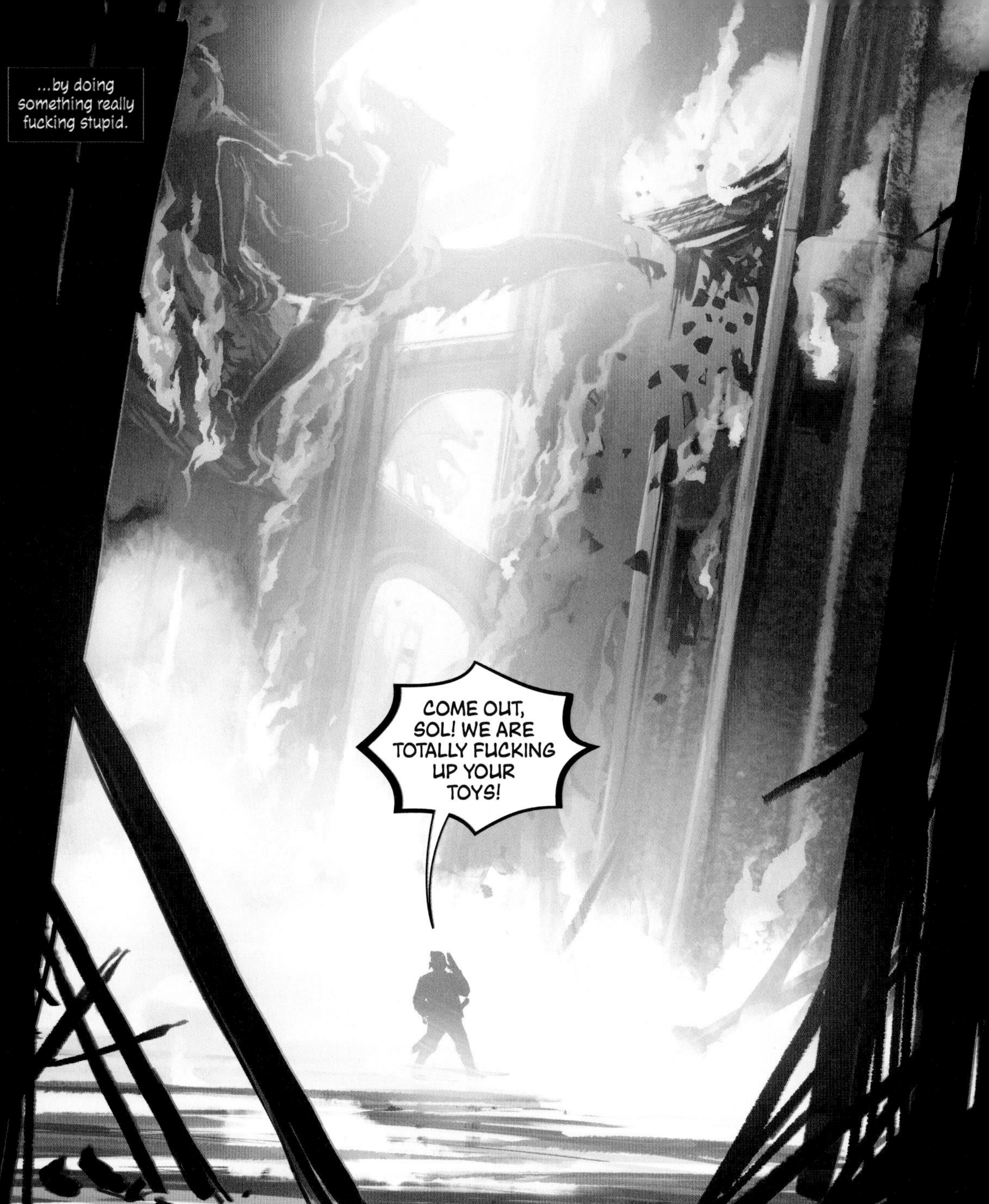
...by doing something really fucking stupid.
COME OUT, SOL! WE ARE TOTALLY FUCKING UP YOUR TOYS!

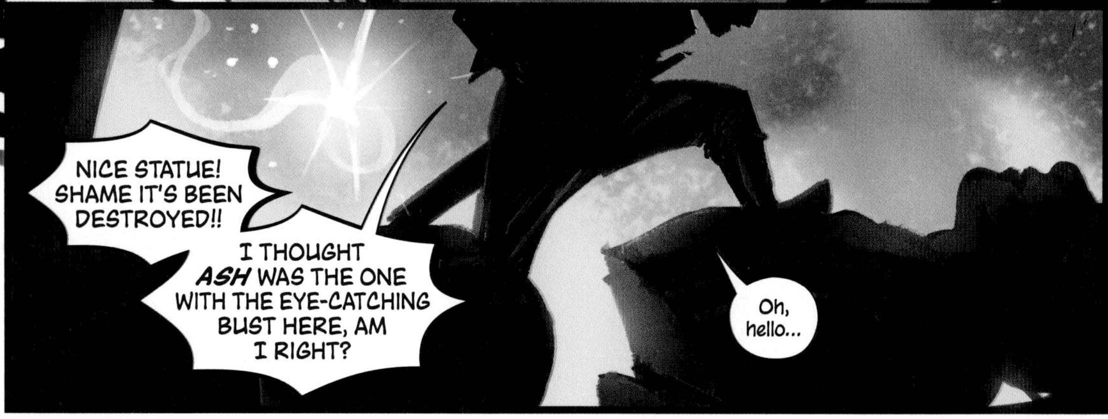
NICE STATUE! SHAME IT'S BEEN DESTROYED!!
I THOUGHT *ASH* WAS THE ONE WITH THE EYE-CATCHING BUST HERE, AM I RIGHT?
Oh, hello...

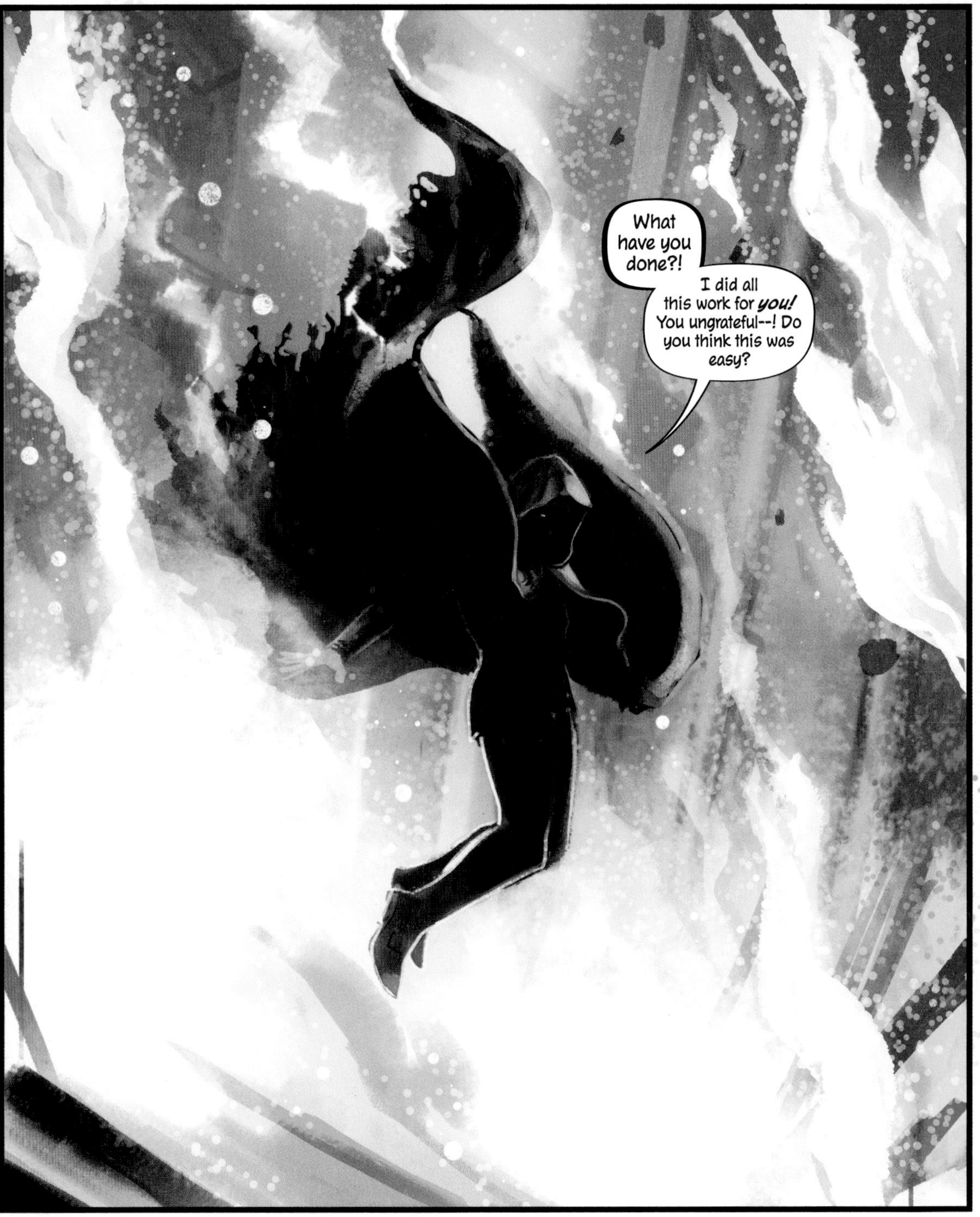
What have you done?!
I did all this work for ***you!*** You ungrateful--! Do you think this was easy?

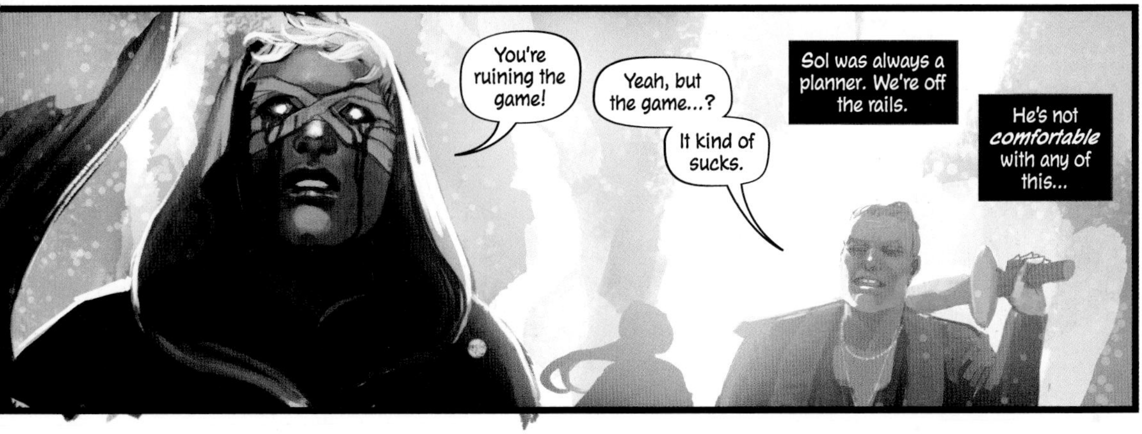
You're ruining the game!
Yeah, but the game...?
It kind of sucks.
Sol was always a planner. We're off the rails.
He's not ***comfortable*** with any of this...

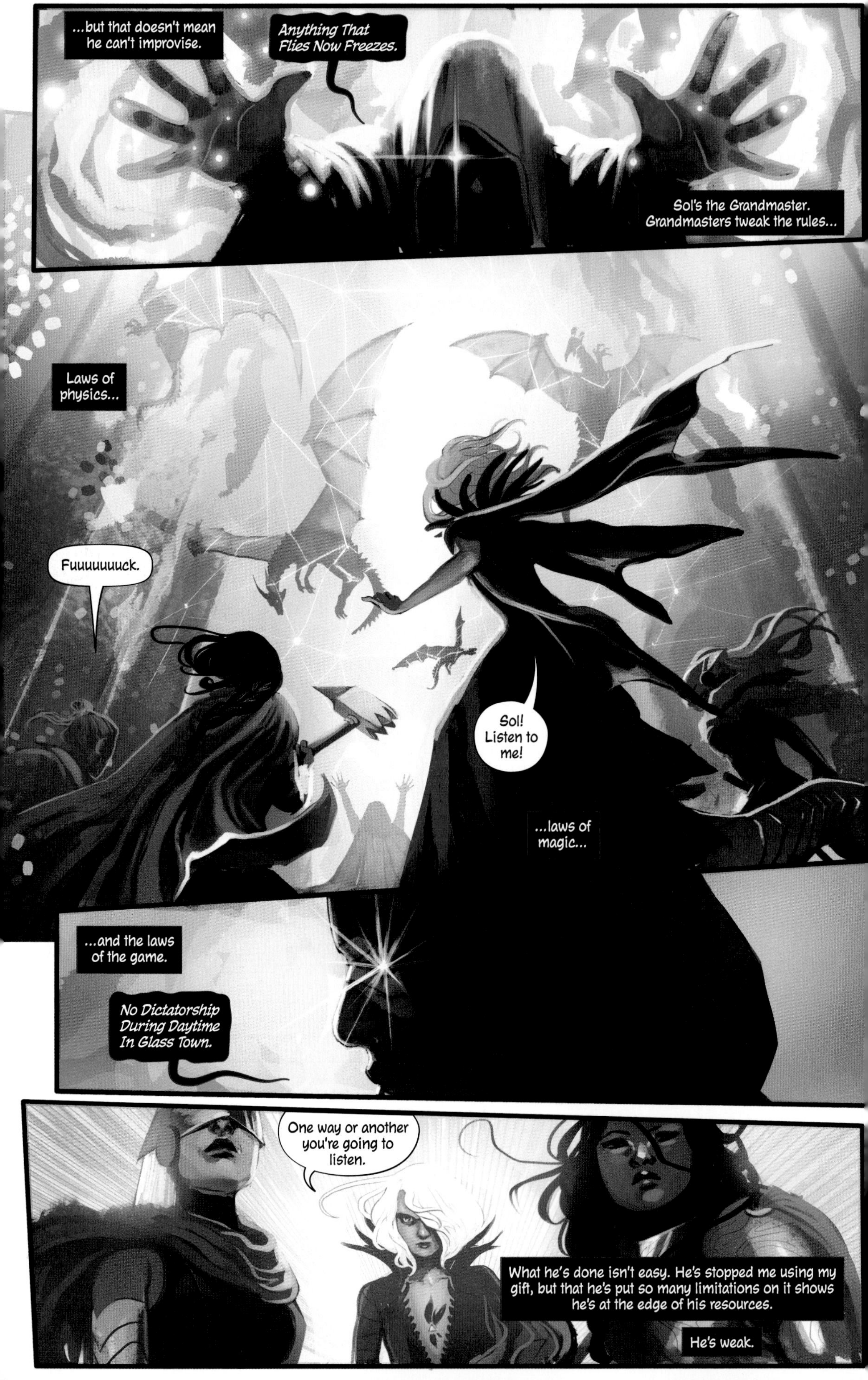
...but that doesn't mean he can't improvise.
Anything That Flies Now Freezes.
Sol's the Grandmaster. Grandmasters tweak the rules...
Laws of physics...
Fuuuuuuuck.
Sol! Listen to me!
...laws of magic...
...and the laws of the game.
No Dictatorship During Daytime In Glass Town.
One way or another you're going to listen.
What he's done isn't easy. He's stopped me using my gift, but that he's put so many limitations on it shows he's at the edge of his resources.
He's weak.

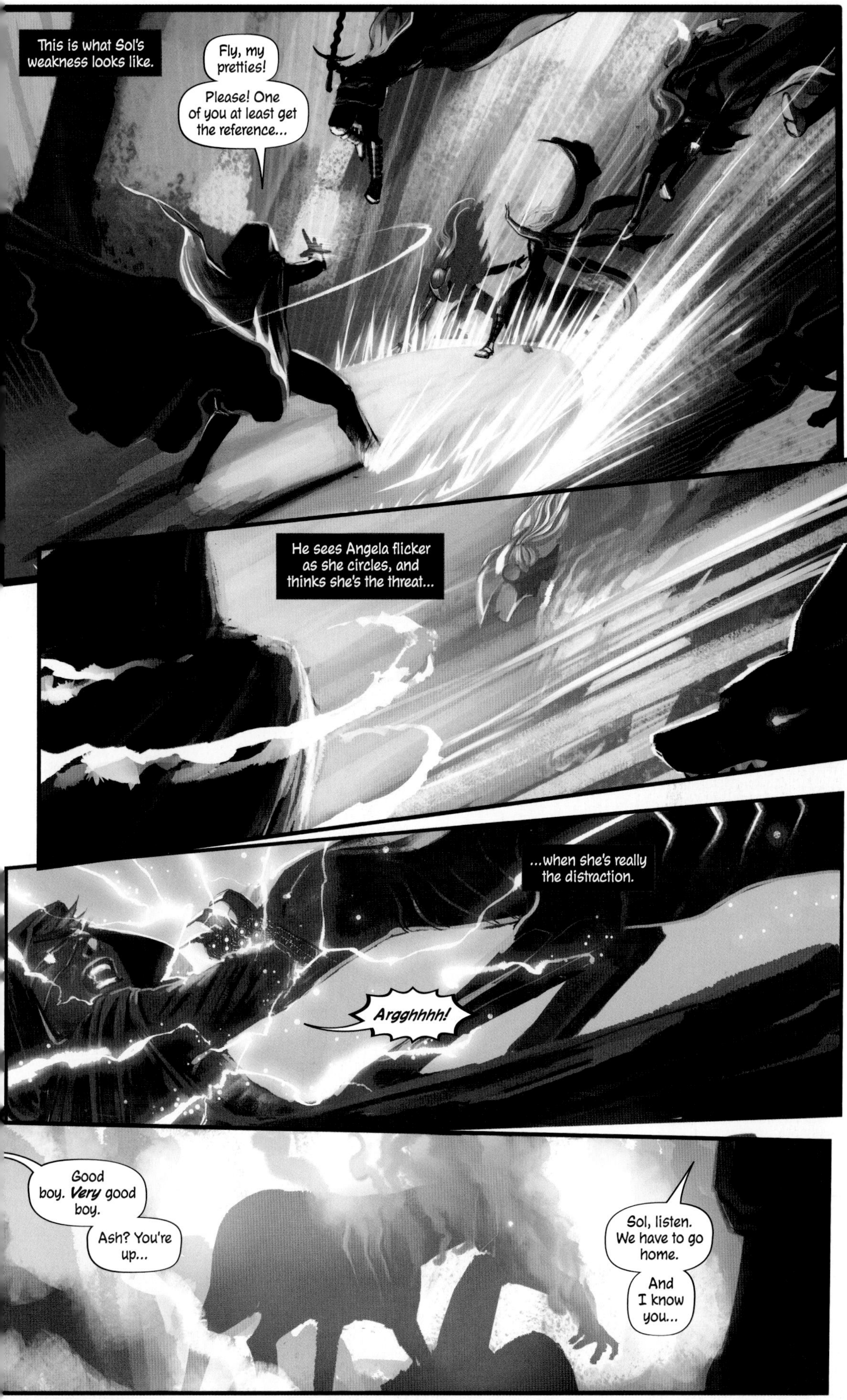
This is what Sol's weakness looks like.
Fly, my pretties!
Please! One of you at least get the reference...
He sees Angela flicker as she circles, and thinks she's the threat...
...when she's really the distraction.
Argghhhh!
Good boy. *Very* good boy.
Ash? You're up...
Sol, listen. We have to go home.
And I know you...

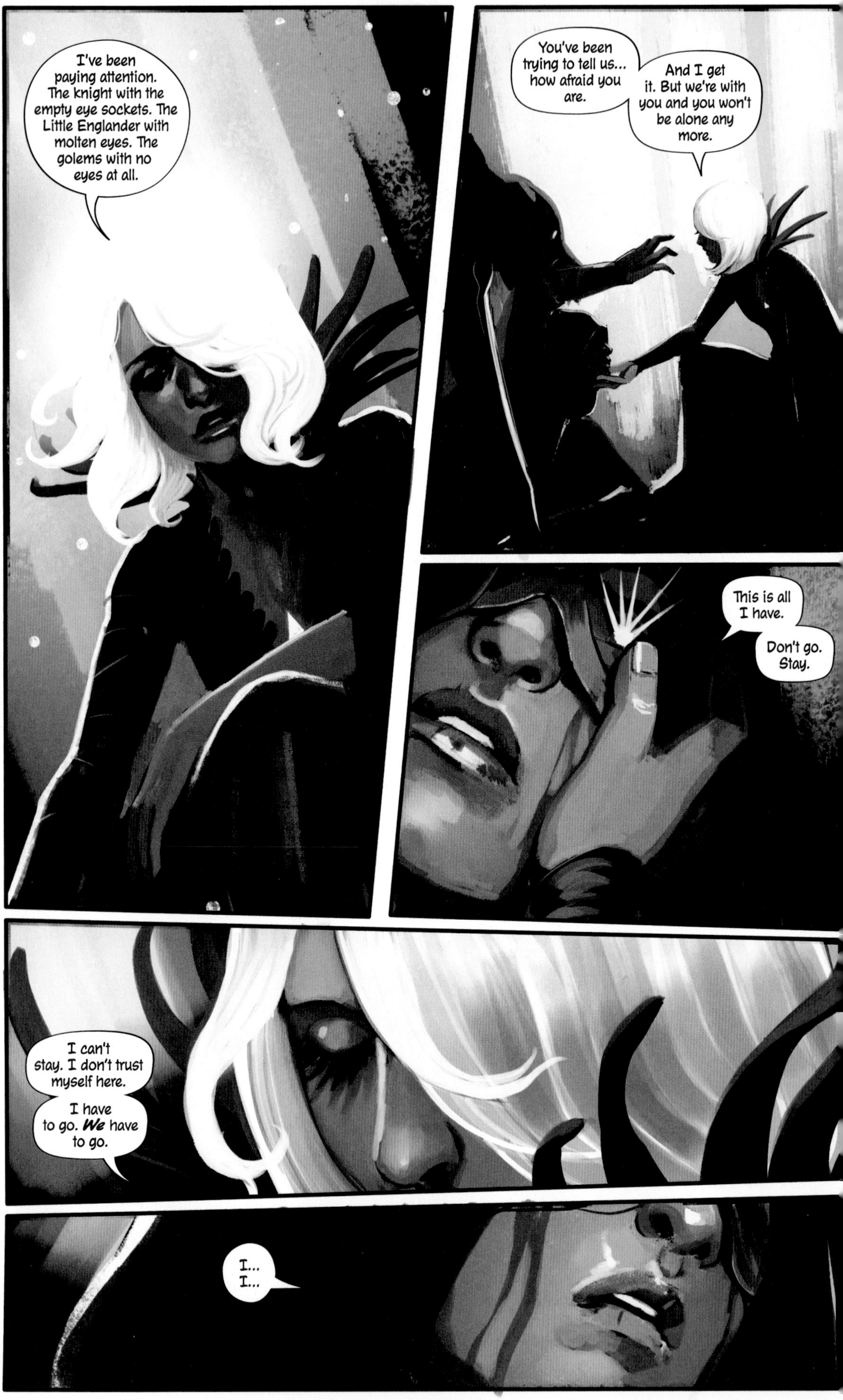

I've been paying attention. The knight with the empty eye sockets. The Little Englander with molten eyes. The golems with no eyes at all.
You've been trying to tell us... how afraid you are.
And I get it. But we're with you and you won't be alone any more.
This is all I have.
Don't go. Stay.
I can't stay. I don't trust myself here.
I have to go. *We* have to go.
I...
I...

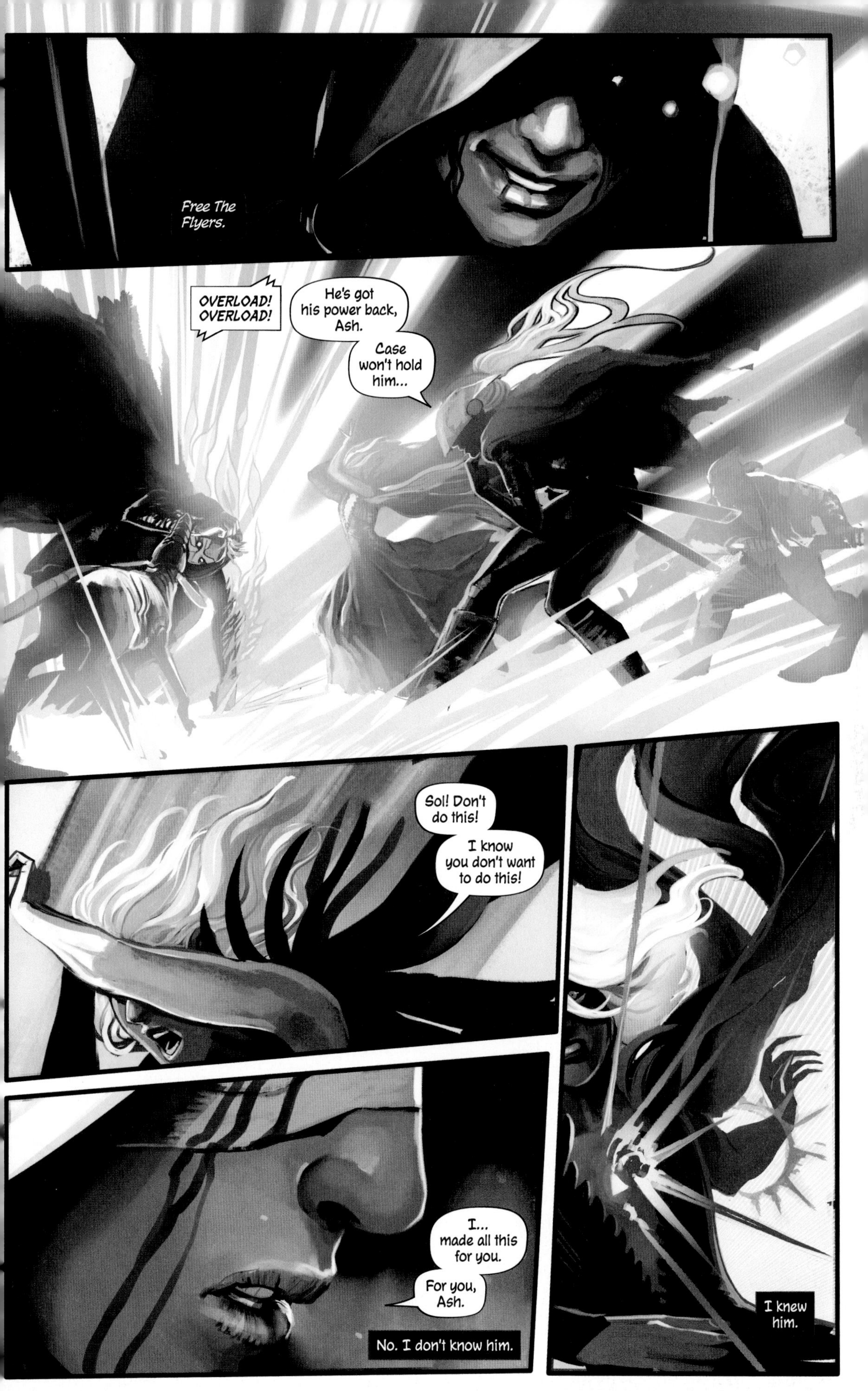
Free The Flyers.
OVERLOAD! OVERLOAD!
He's got his power back, Ash.
Case won't hold him...
Sol! Don't do this!
I know you don't want to do this!
I... made all this for you.
For you, Ash.
No. I don't know him.
I knew him.

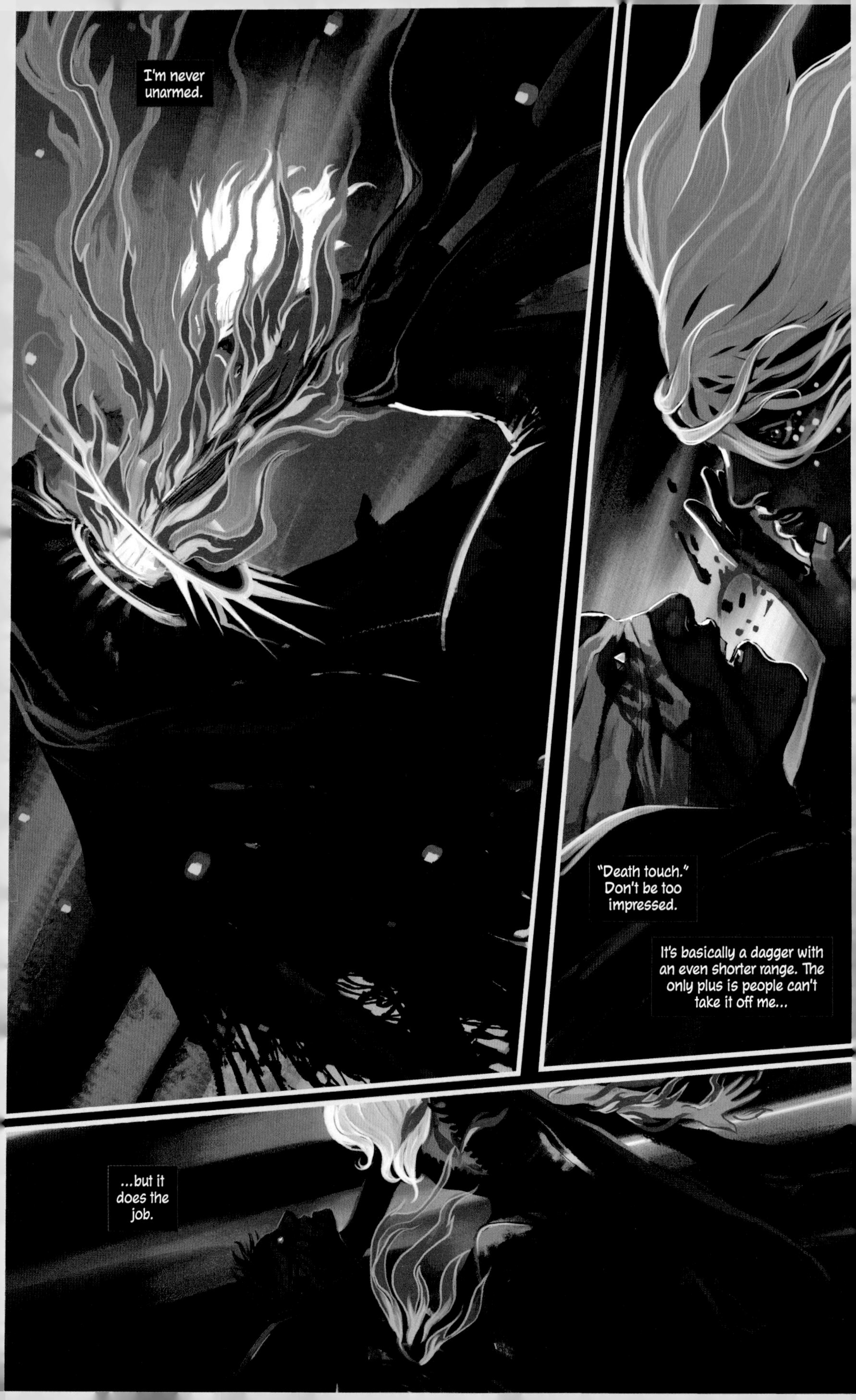
I'm never unarmed.
"Death touch." Don't be too impressed.
It's basically a dagger with an even shorter range. The only plus is people can't take it off me...
...but it does the job.

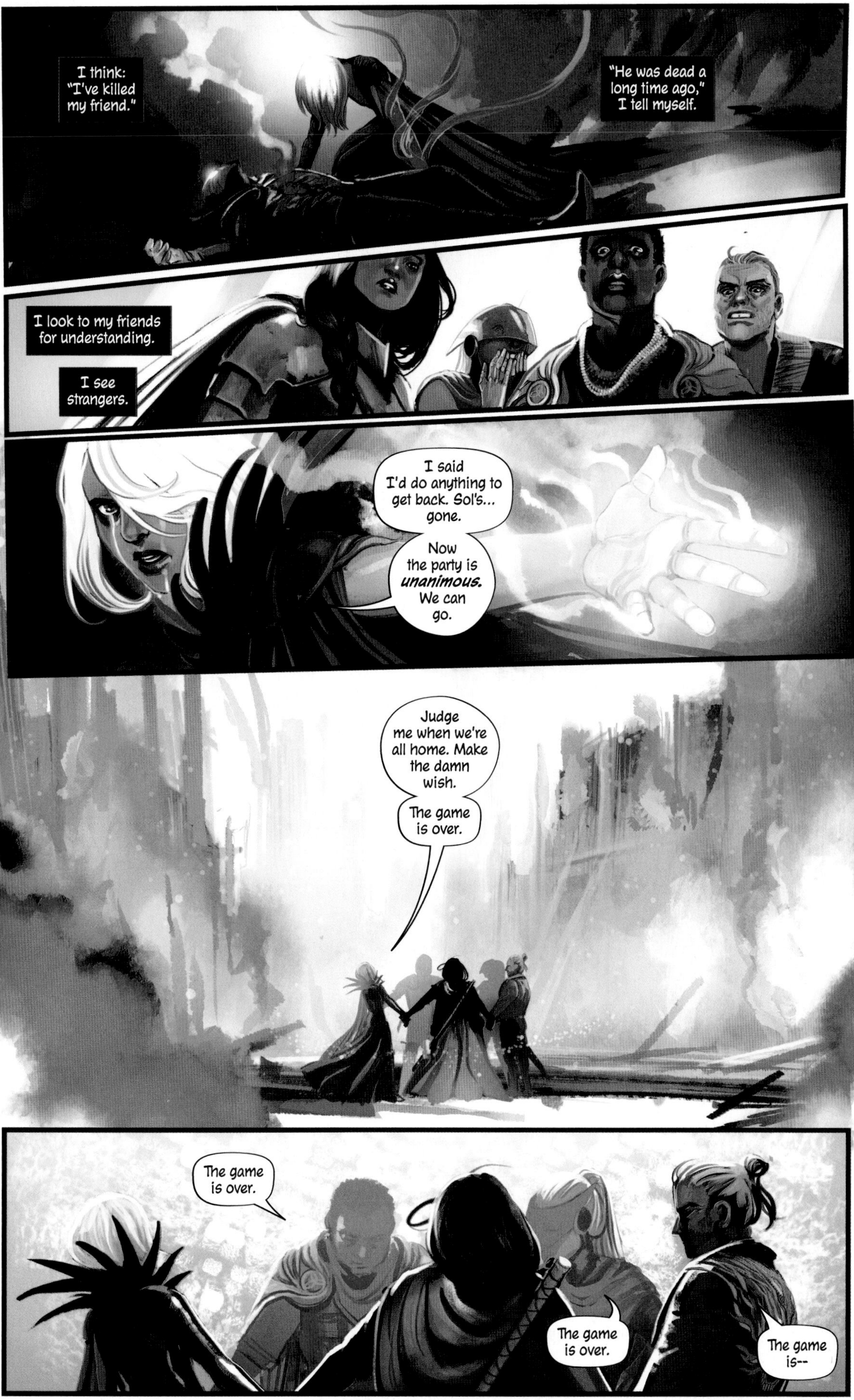
I think:
"I've killed my friend."
"He was dead a long time ago," I tell myself.
I look to my friends for understanding.
I see strangers.
I said I'd do anything to get back. Sol's... gone.
Now the party is ***unanimous.*** We can go.
Judge me when we're all home. Make the damn wish.
The game is over.
The game is over.
The game is over.
The game is--

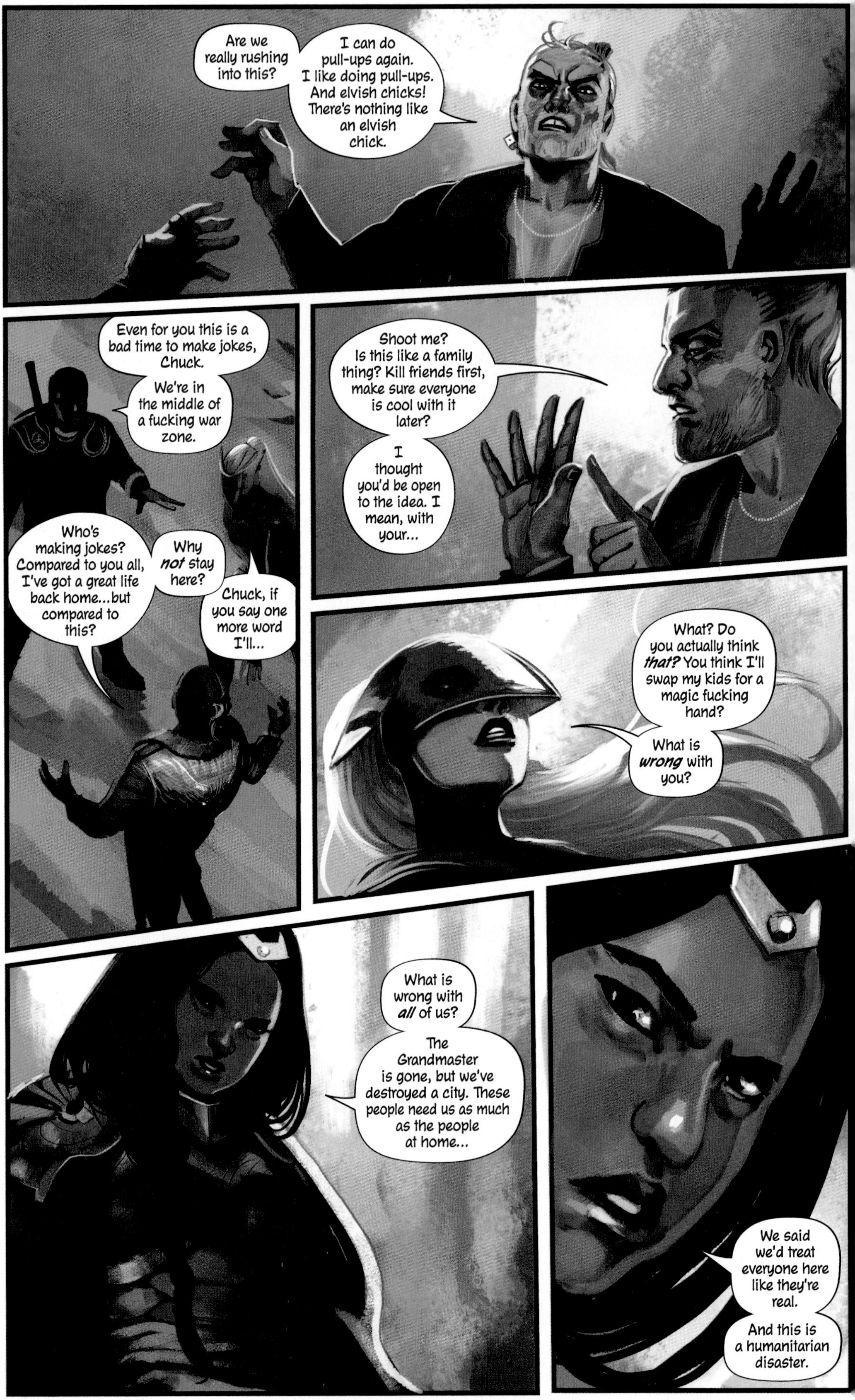
Are we really rushing into this?
I can do pull-ups again. I like doing pull-ups. And elvish chicks! There's nothing like an elvish chick.
Even for you this is a bad time to make jokes, Chuck.
We're in the middle of a fucking war zone.
Who's making jokes? Compared to you all, I've got a great life back home...but compared to this?
Why *not* stay here?
Chuck, if you say one more word I'll...
Shoot me? Is this like a family thing? Kill friends first, make sure everyone is cool with it later?
I thought you'd be open to the idea. I mean, with your...
What? Do you actually think *that?* You think I'll swap my kids for a magic fucking hand?
What is *wrong* with you?
What is wrong with *all* of us?
The Grandmaster is gone, but we've destroyed a city. These people need us as much as the people at home...
We said we'd treat everyone here like they're real.
And this is a humanitarian disaster.

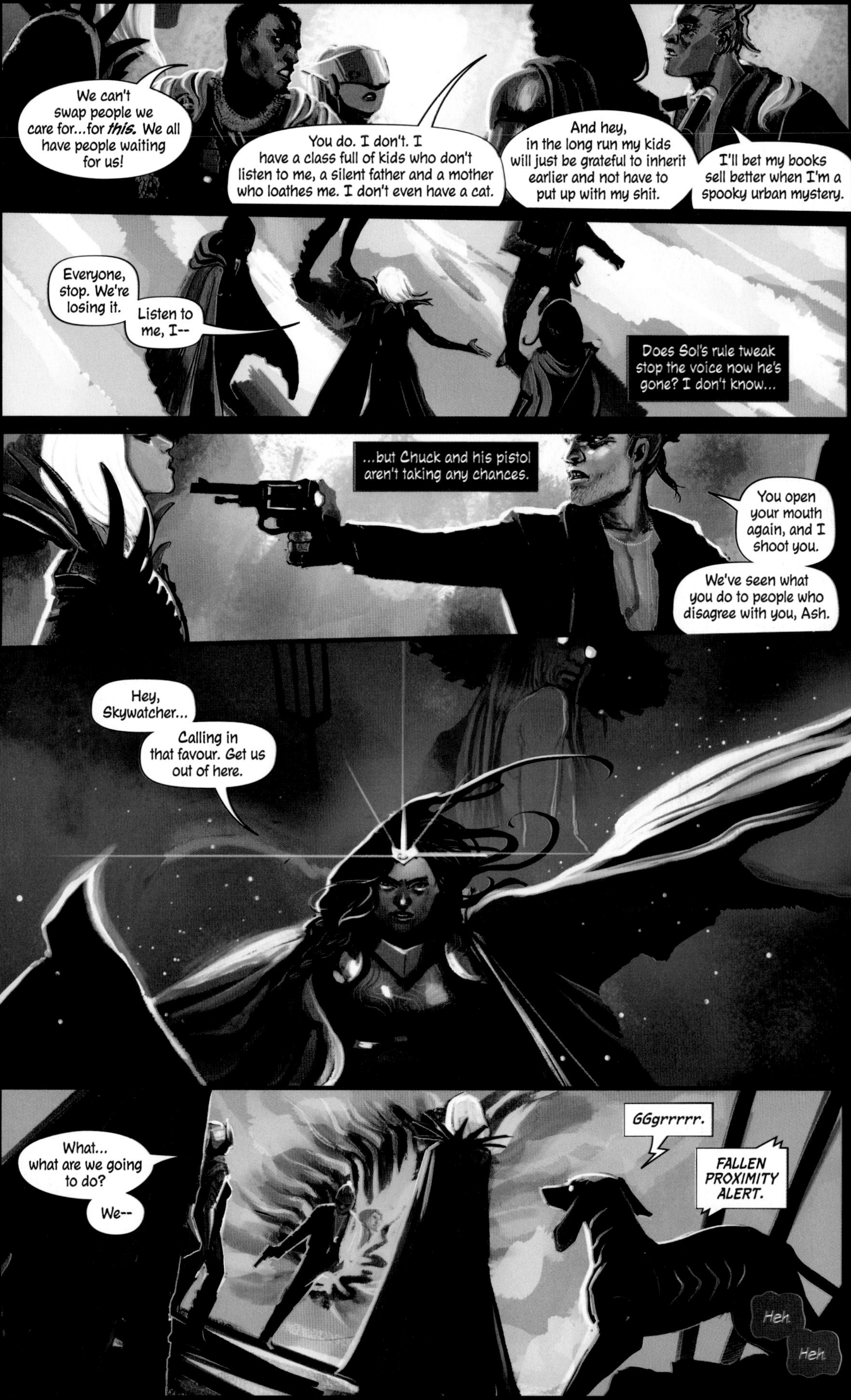
We can't swap people we care for...for *this.* We all have people waiting for us!
You do. I don't. I have a class full of kids who don't listen to me, a silent father and a mother who loathes me. I don't even have a cat.
And hey, in the long run my kids will just be grateful to inherit earlier and not have to put up with my shit.
I'll bet my books sell better when I'm a spooky urban mystery.
Everyone, stop. We're losing it.
Listen to me, I--
Does Sol's rule tweak stop the voice now he's gone? I don't know...
...but Chuck and his pistol aren't taking any chances.
You open your mouth again, and I shoot you.
We've seen what you do to people who disagree with you, Ash.
Hey, Skywatcher...
Calling in that favour. Get us out of here.
What... what are we going to do?
We--
GGgrrrrr.
FALLEN PROXIMITY ALERT.
Heh.
Heh.

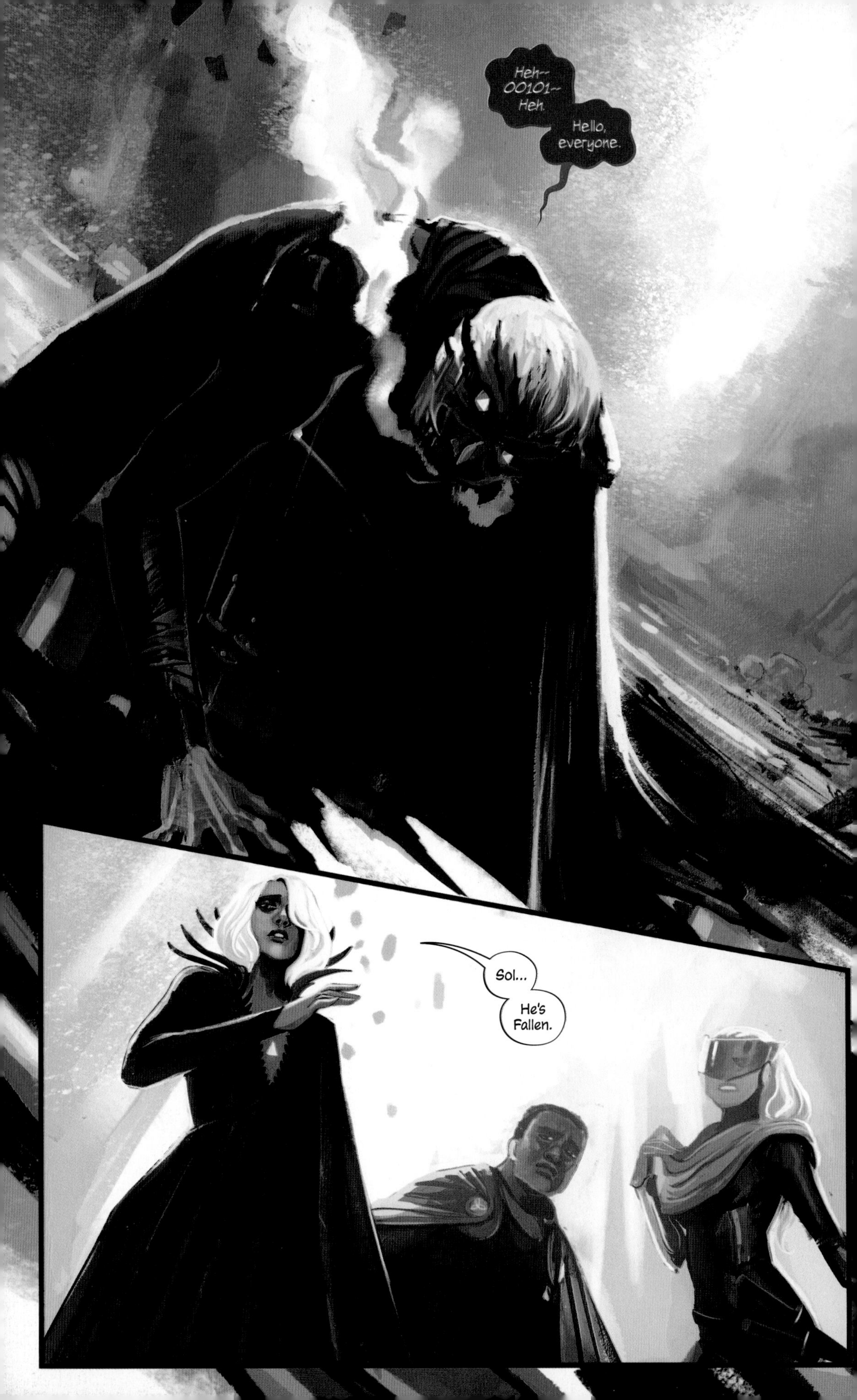
Heh--
00101--
Heh.
Hello,
everyone.
Sol...
He's
Fallen.

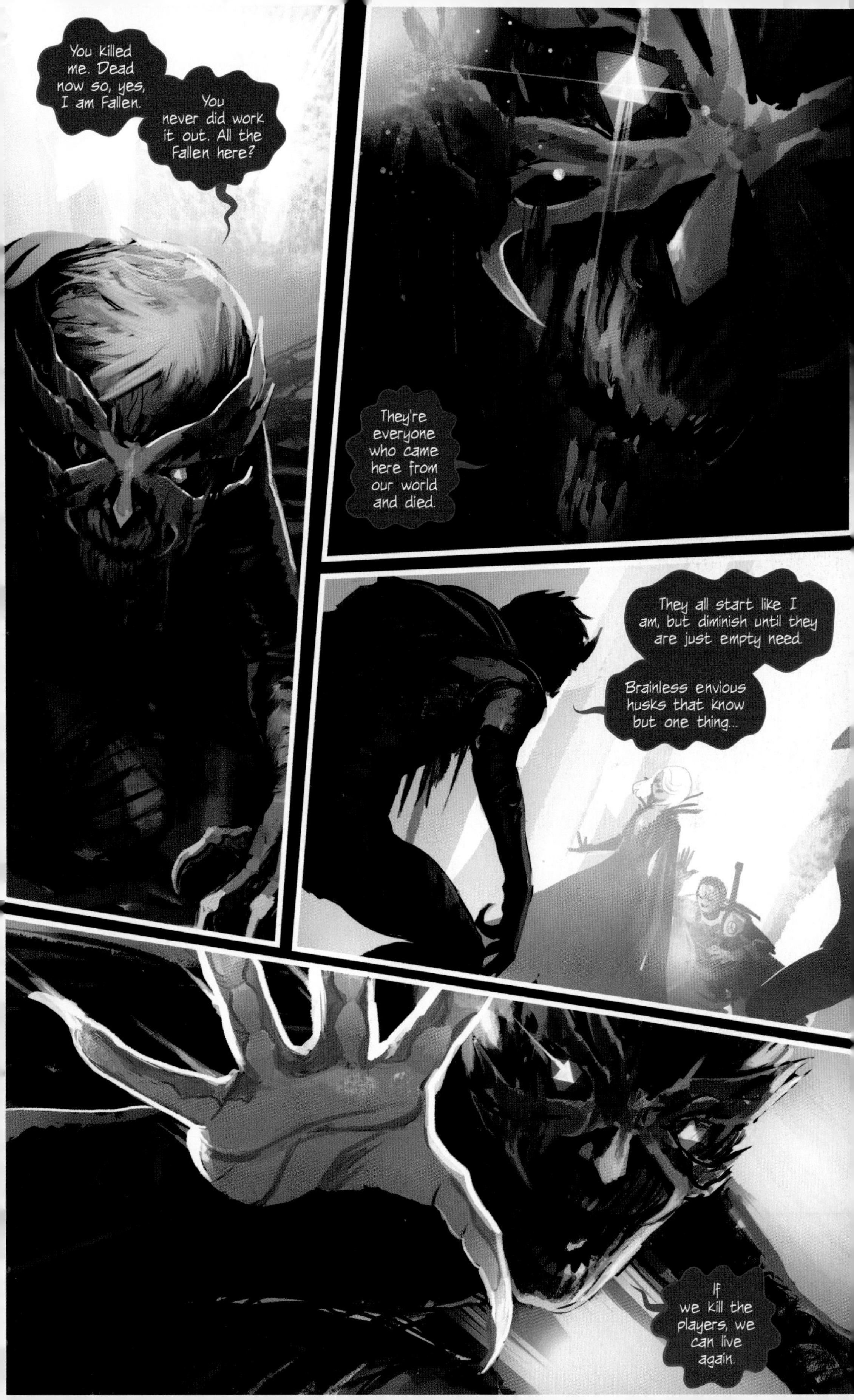

You killed me. Dead now so, yes, I am Fallen.
You never did work it out. All the Fallen here?
They're everyone who came here from our world and died.
They all start like I am, but diminish until they are just empty need.
Brainless envious husks that know but one thing...
If we kill the players, we can live again.

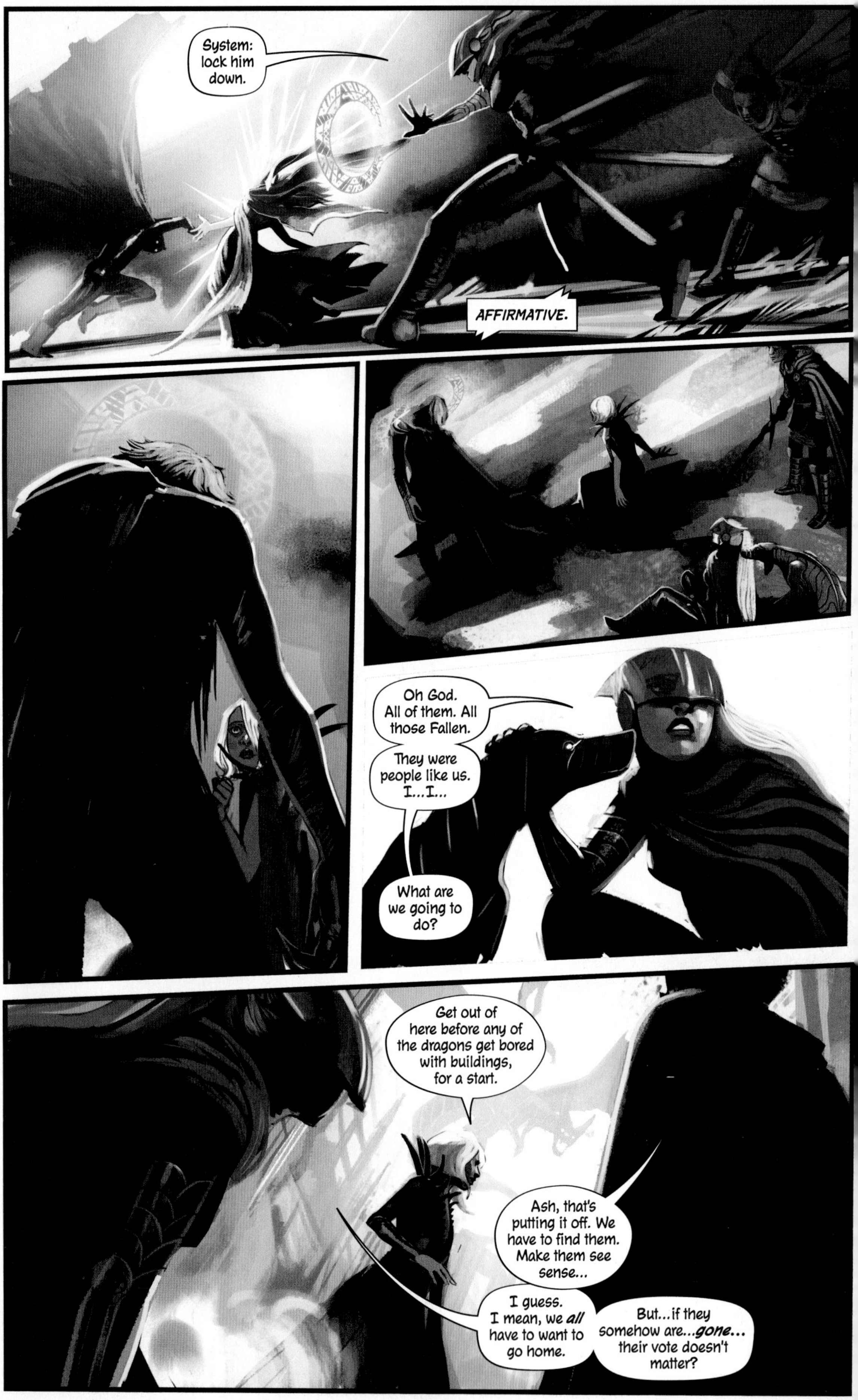
System: lock him down.
AFFIRMATIVE.
Oh God. All of them. All those Fallen.
They were people like us. I...I...
What are we going to do?
Get out of here before any of the dragons get bored with buildings, for a start.
Ash, that's putting it off. We have to find them. Make them see sense...
I guess. I mean, we *all* have to want to go home.
But...if they somehow are...***gone...*** their vote doesn't matter?

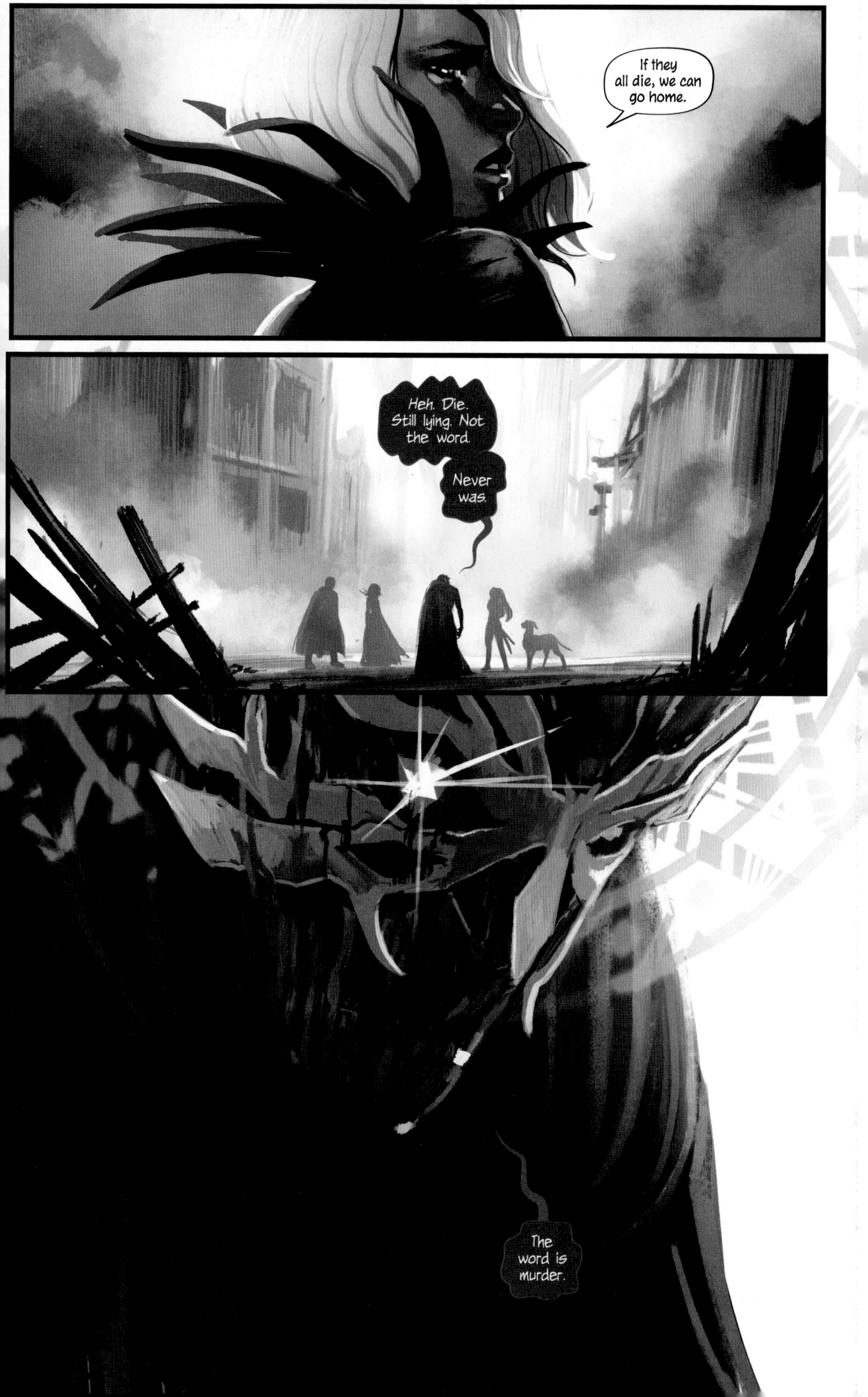
If they all die, we can go home.
Heh. Die. Still lying. Not the word.
Never was.
The word is murder.

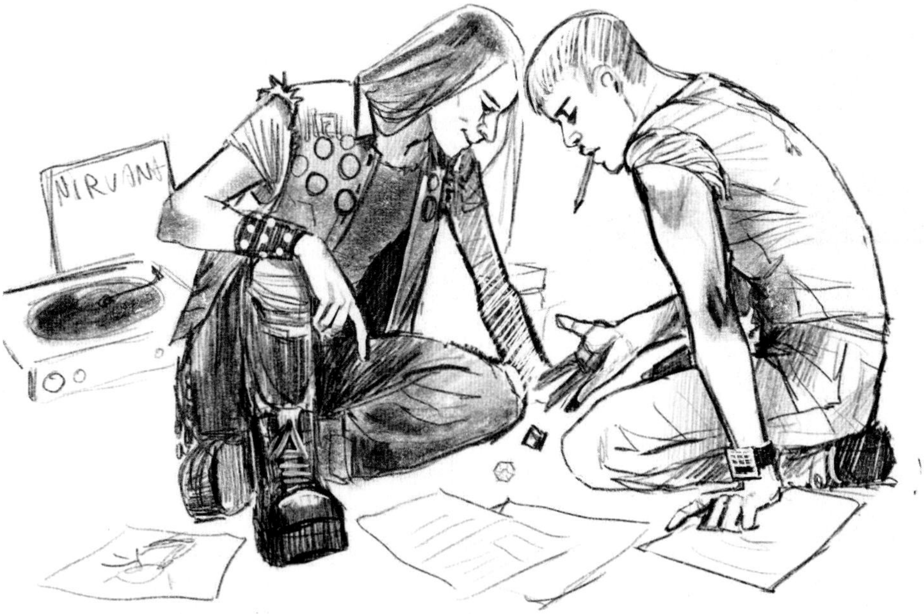
NIRVANA

DIE: THE RPG

Kieron, as part of writing the volume you're presently reading, wrote a role-playing game. It's available now - go here to find out how to get hold of it:

www.diecomic.com/rpg

These are the beta rules. They let you basically recreate your very own version of the story you've just read. As in, you create a messed up social group, generate some game characters for them, and then drag them into a fantasy world and see if they come home or not. It's designed to take a group of up to six people (including the person running the game) between two and four sessions to play. It's also designed to be a replayable game, so there's a lot of content here and we're very proud of it.

However, it is a set of beta rules by a complete amateur (me). They've been playtested a bunch, by some lovely folks, but they remain a work in progress. If people seem interested in them, we'll continue to develop them, and ideally have a fancy edition made down the line. There's certainly a lot more we'd like to include, no least a lot more about the *DIE* world and campaign structures and all the rest.

Those who have no interest in tabletop RPGs may find them amusing too. If you've any fondness for me going off on rants, there's a lot of musing about narrative structure plus at least three good jokes. Download and nose. Bandwidth is cheap these days, right?

If you've any thoughts, hit us up at dierpgplaytest@gmail.com.

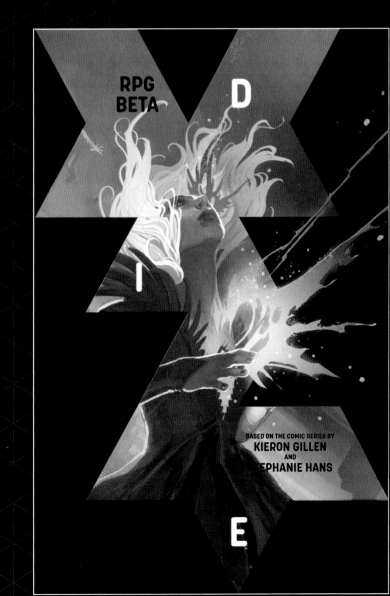

RPG
BETA

D
I
E

BASED ON THE COMIC SERIES BY
KIERON GILLEN
AND
STEPHANIE HANS

VARIANT COVERS

We've created a fantasy world here. As such, it's fun to invite our talented friends to bring their vision to the page. Equally, if Stephanie has a spare three seconds, she'll inevitably conjure another amazing image off the top of her Gallic noggin. Hail her and hail everyone who drew any of the following. They're great. Kieron has trouble drawing stick figures.

Jamie McKelvie
Issue 1 variant

Emma Vieceli
Issue 1 cover for One Stop Shop

Stephanie Hans
Issue 1 cover for The Comic Mint

Mike Rooth
Issue 1 cover for Sad Lemon Comics

Mike Rooth
Issue 1 cover for Sad Lemon Comics

Stephanie Hans
Issue 1 fourth printing cover

Jana Schirmer
Issue 2 variant

Stephanie Hans
Issue 2 second printing cover

Jen Bartel
Issue 3 variant

Stephanie Hans
Issue 3 second printing cover

Christian Ward
Issue 4 variant

David Mack
Issue 5 variant

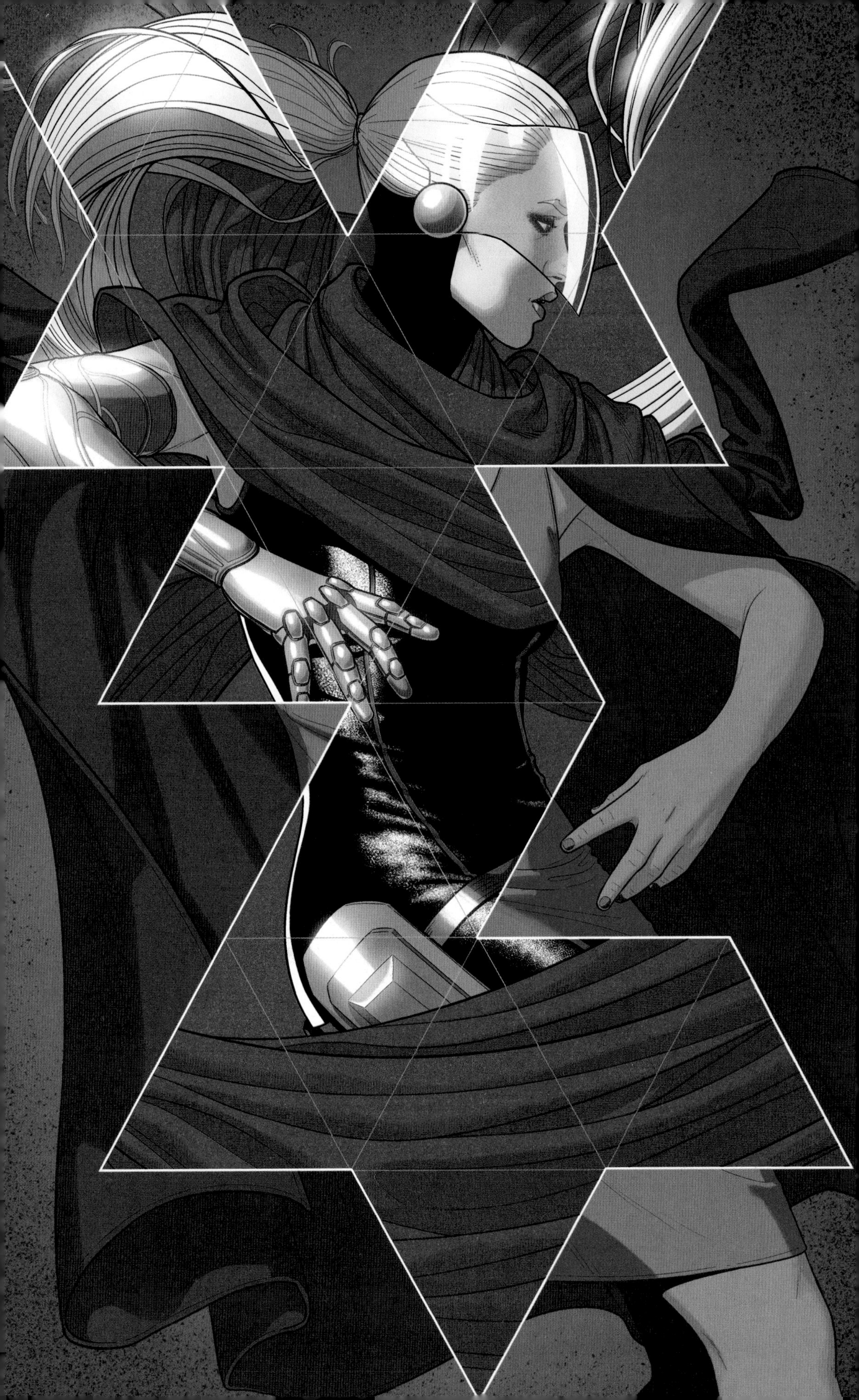

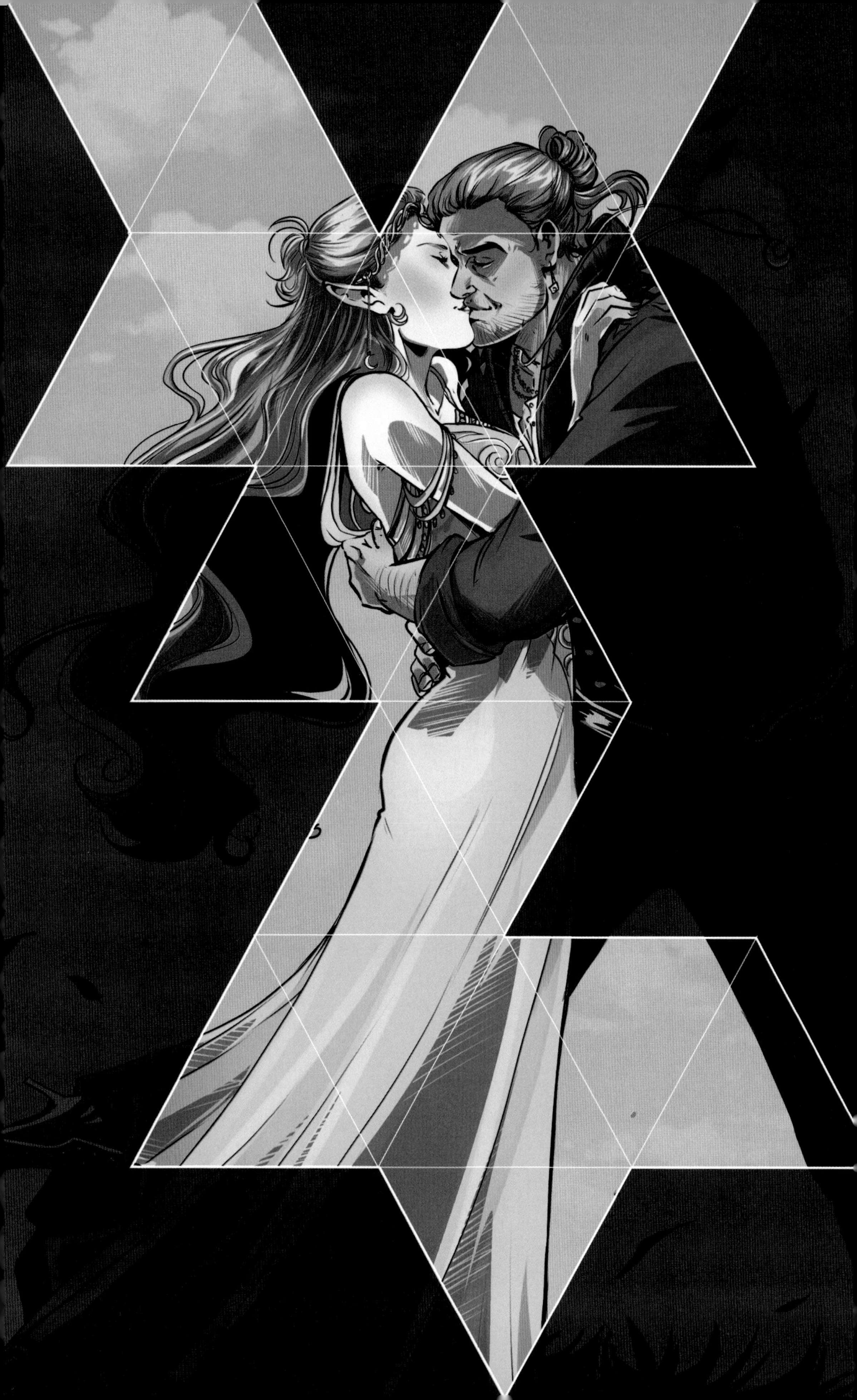

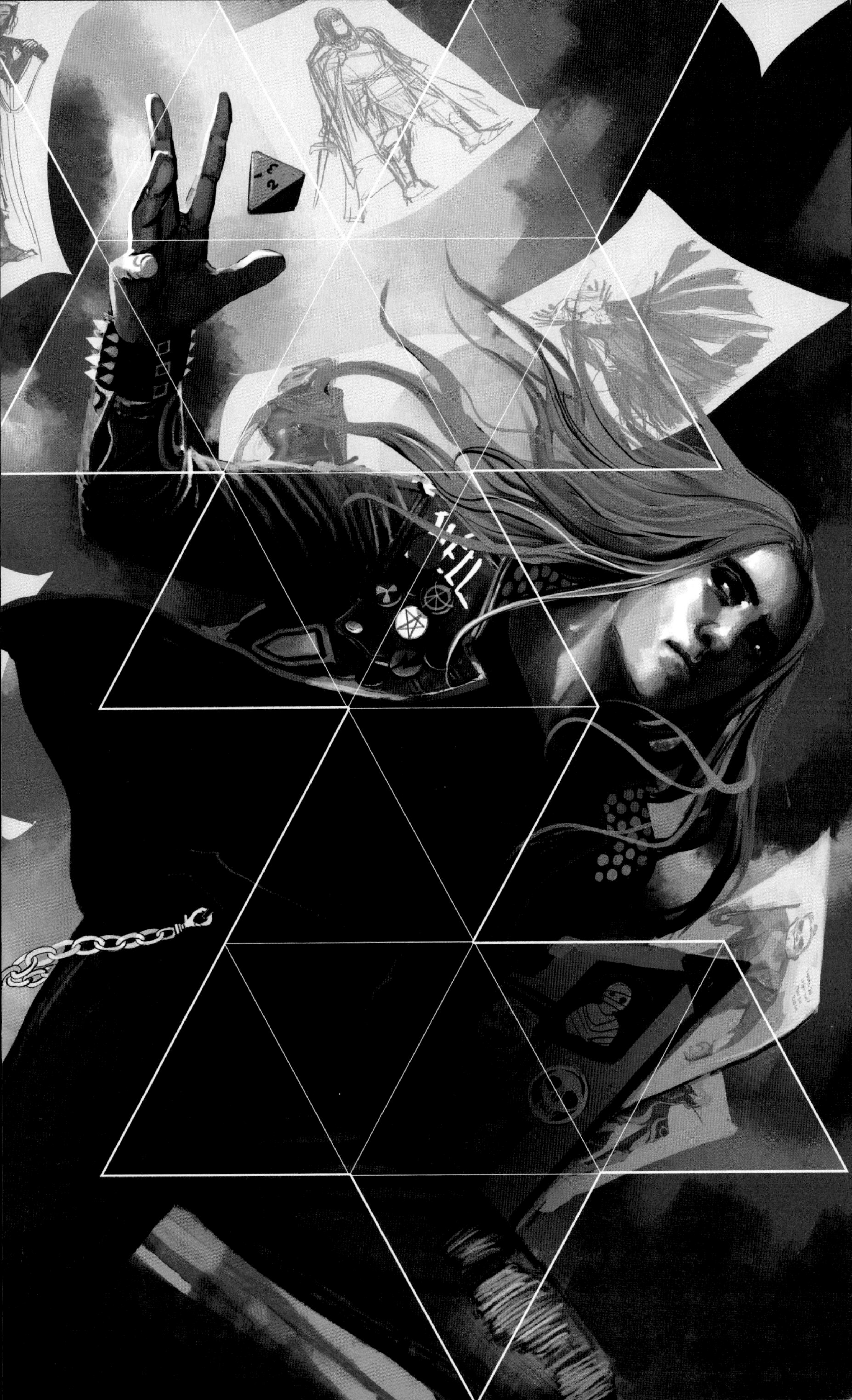

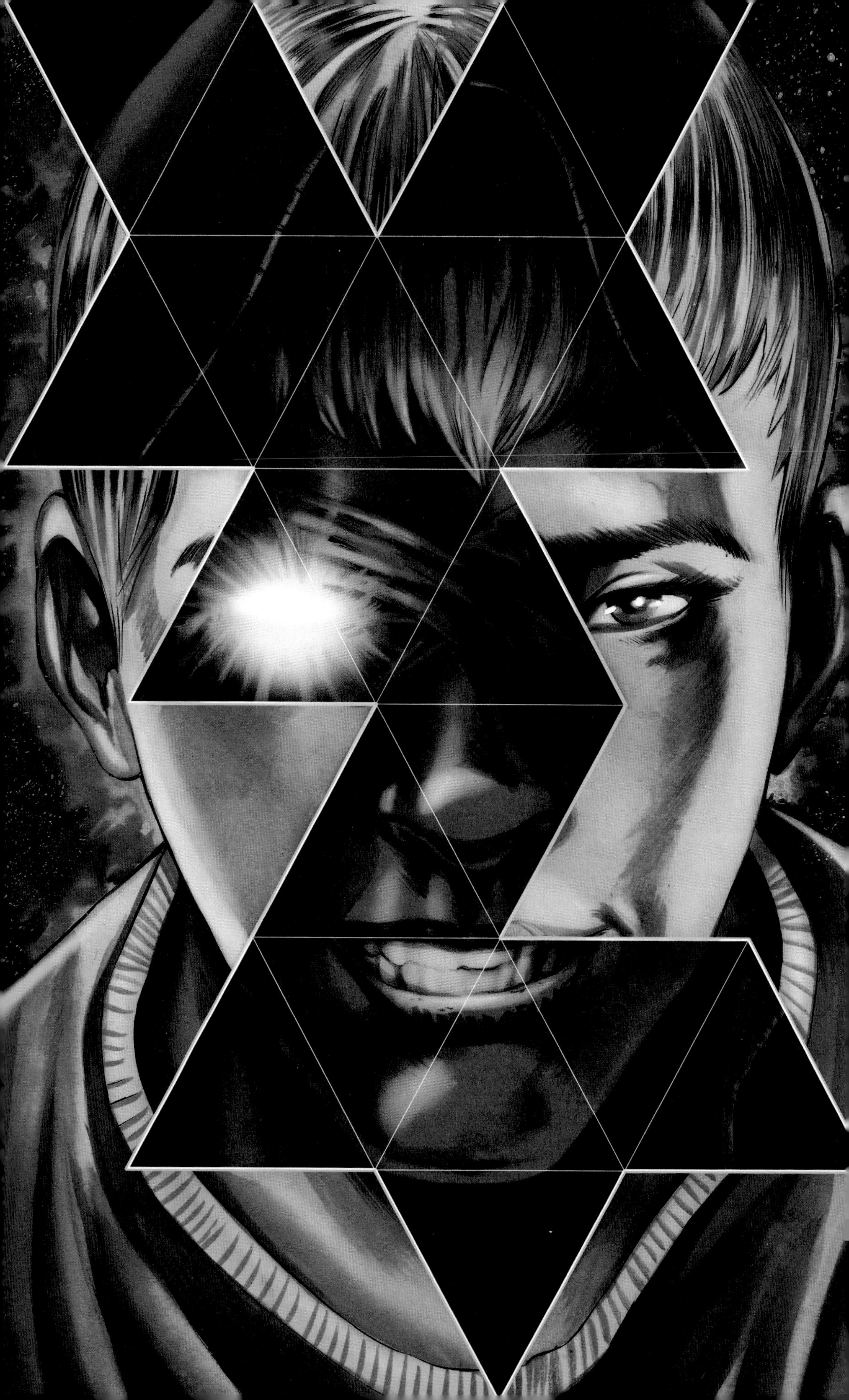

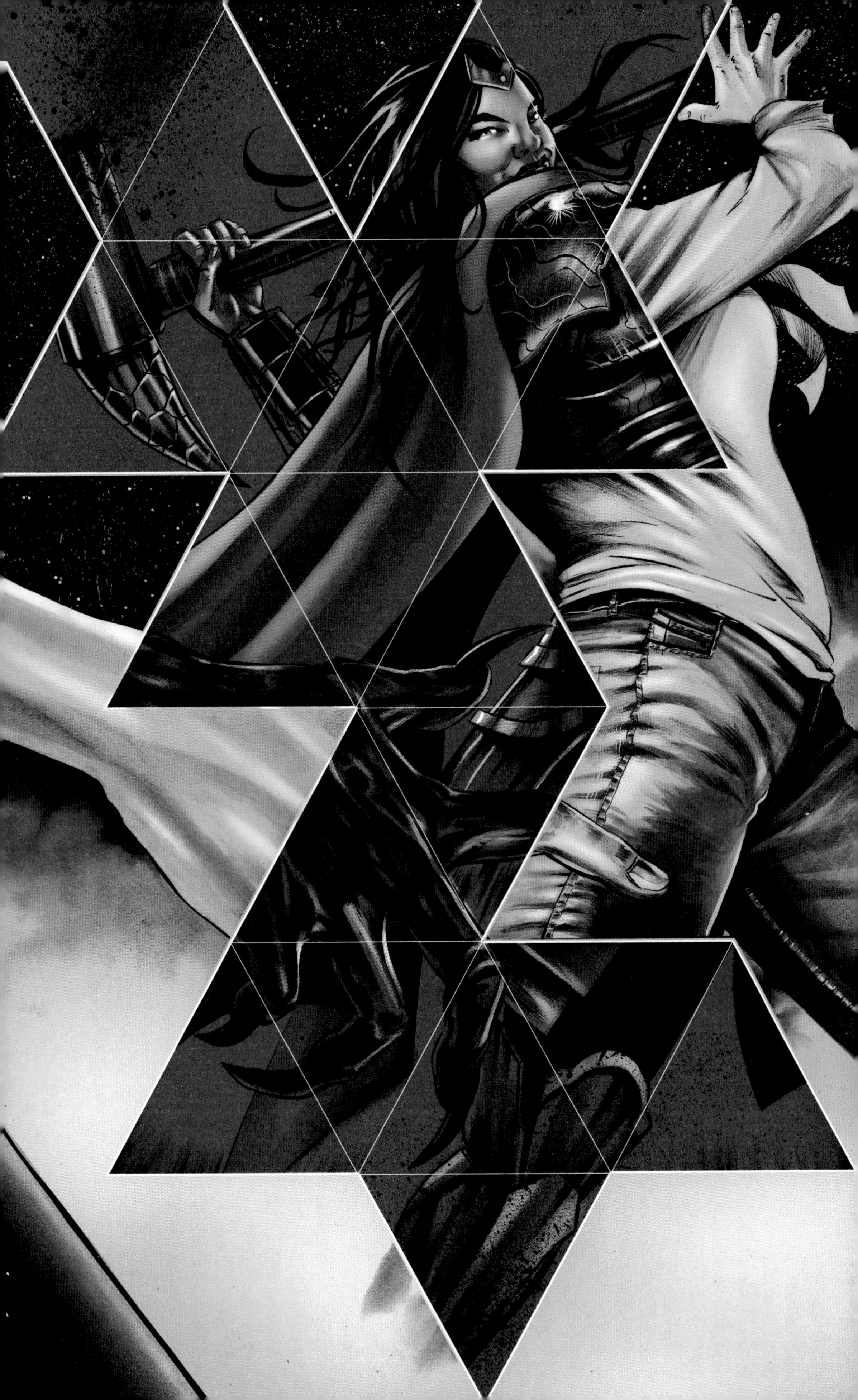

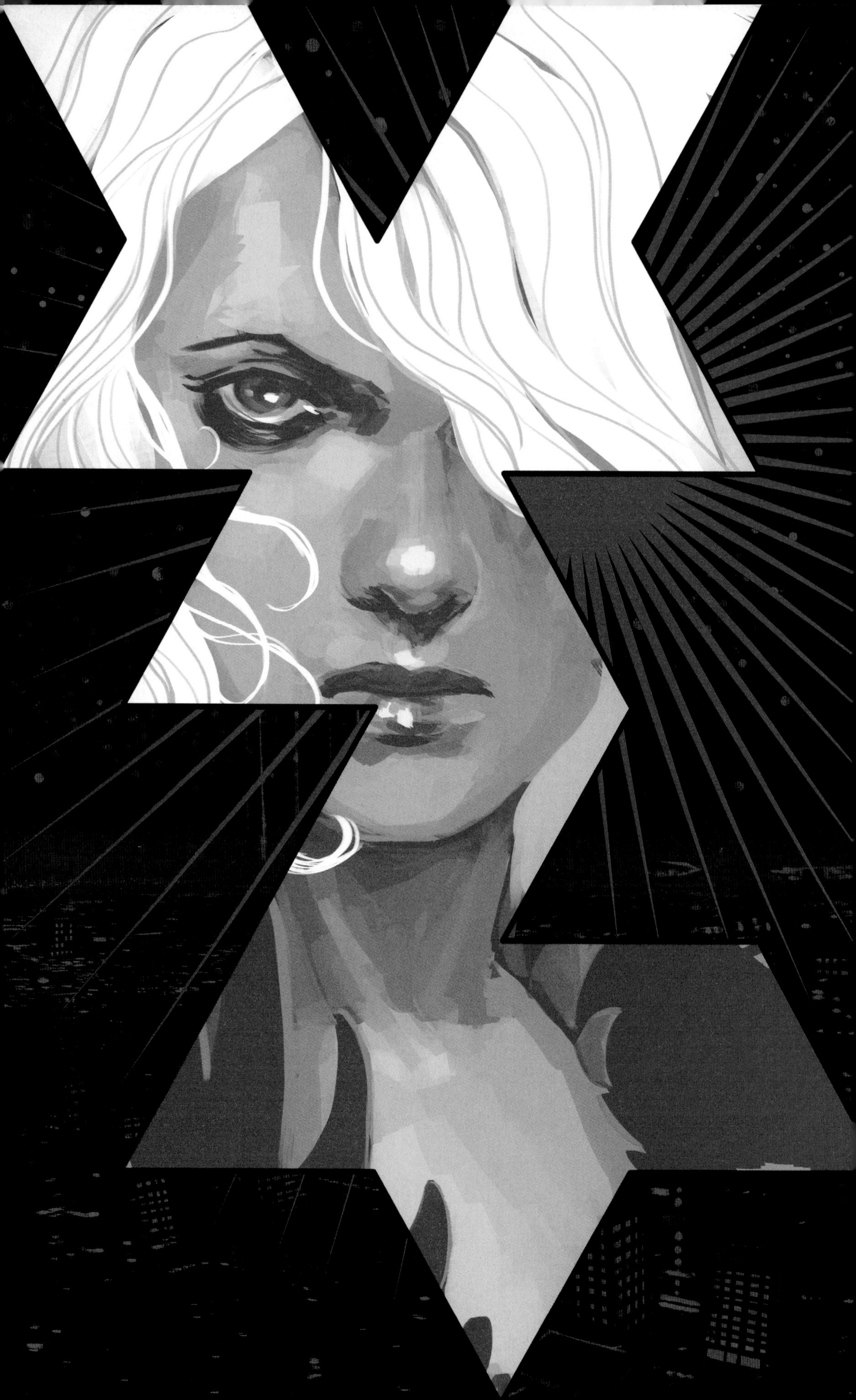

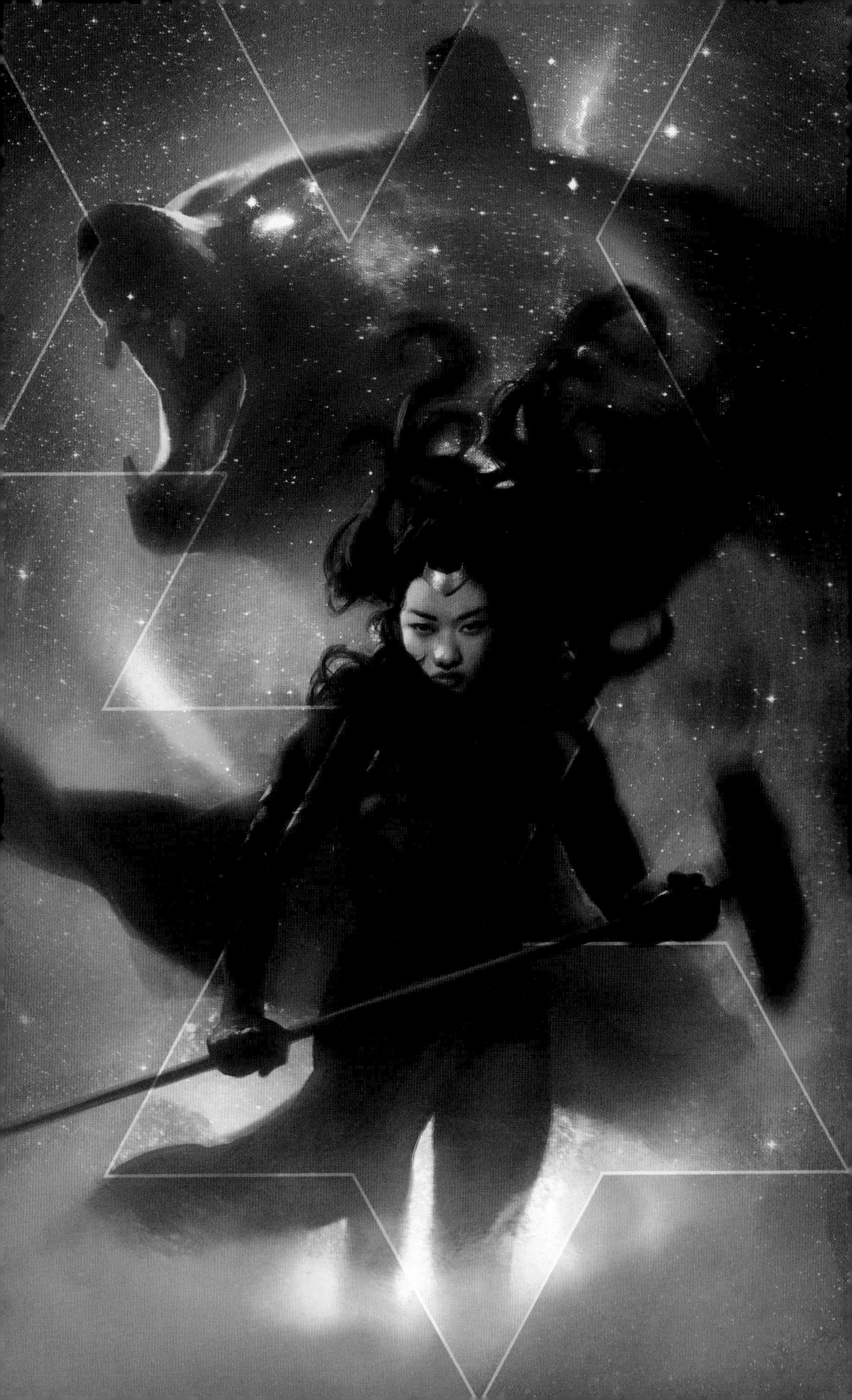

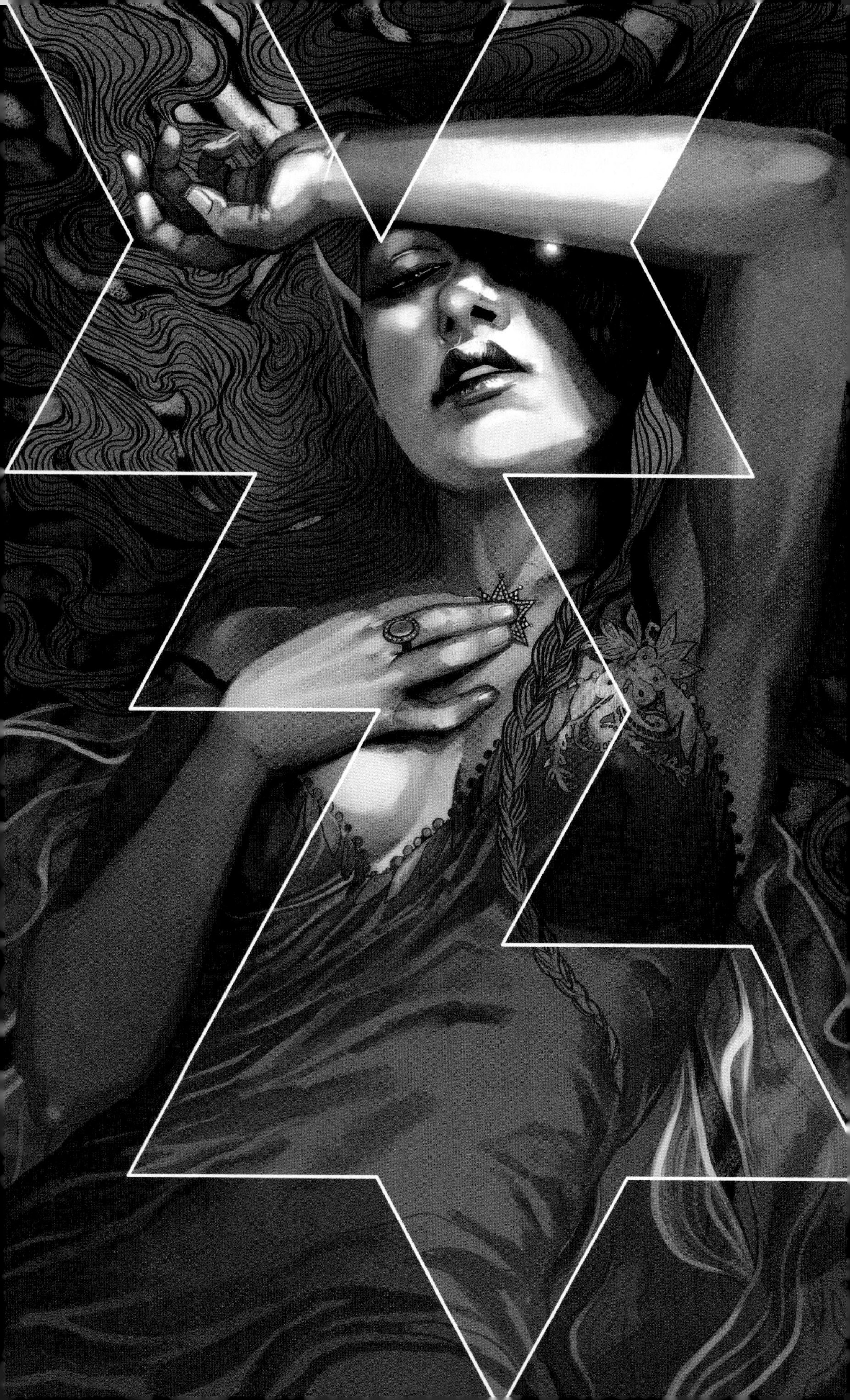

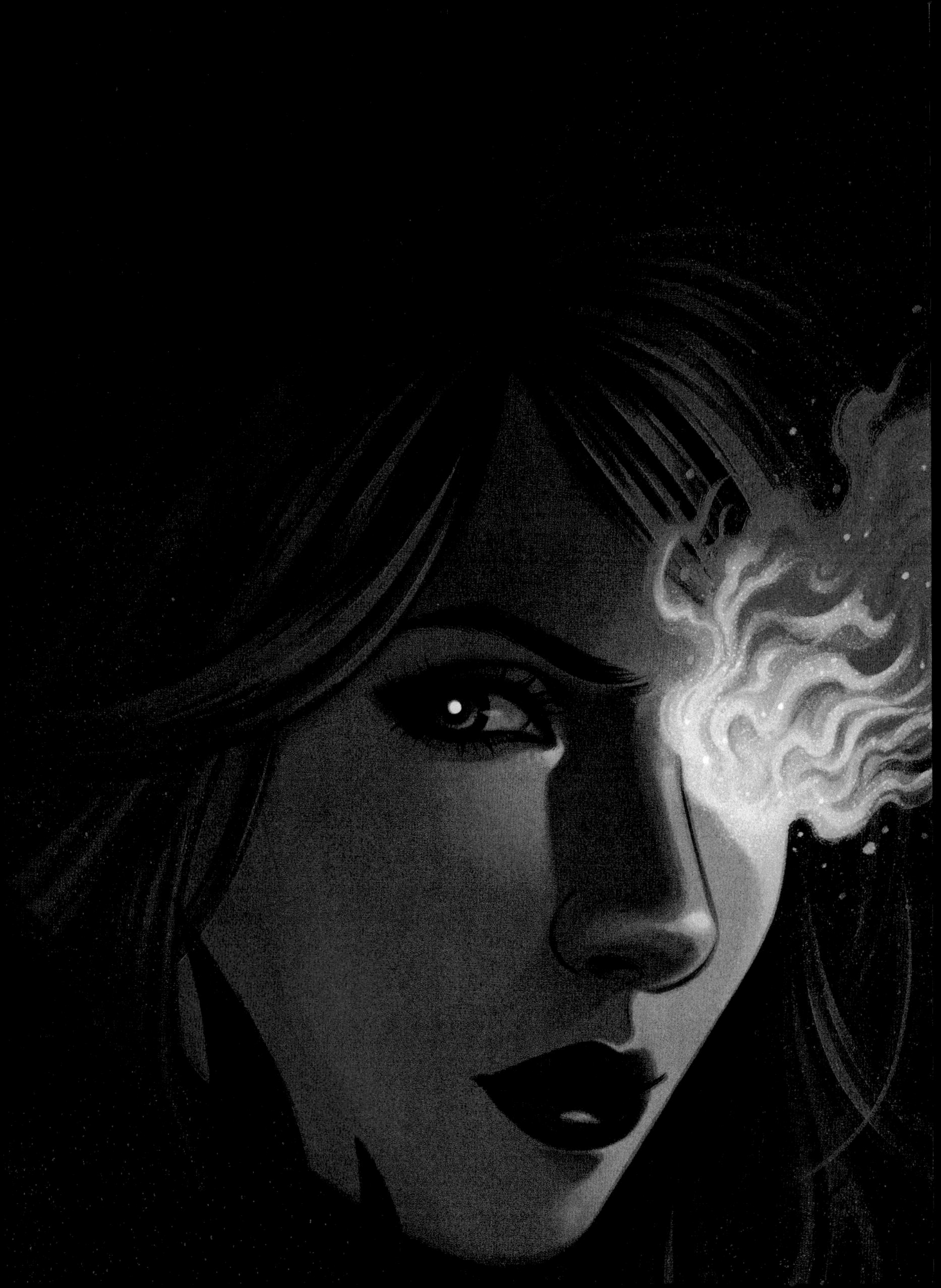

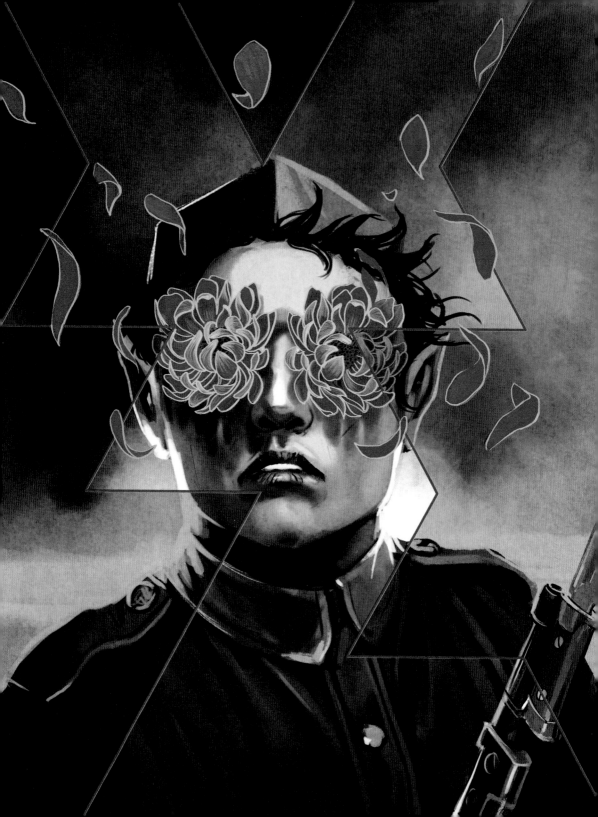

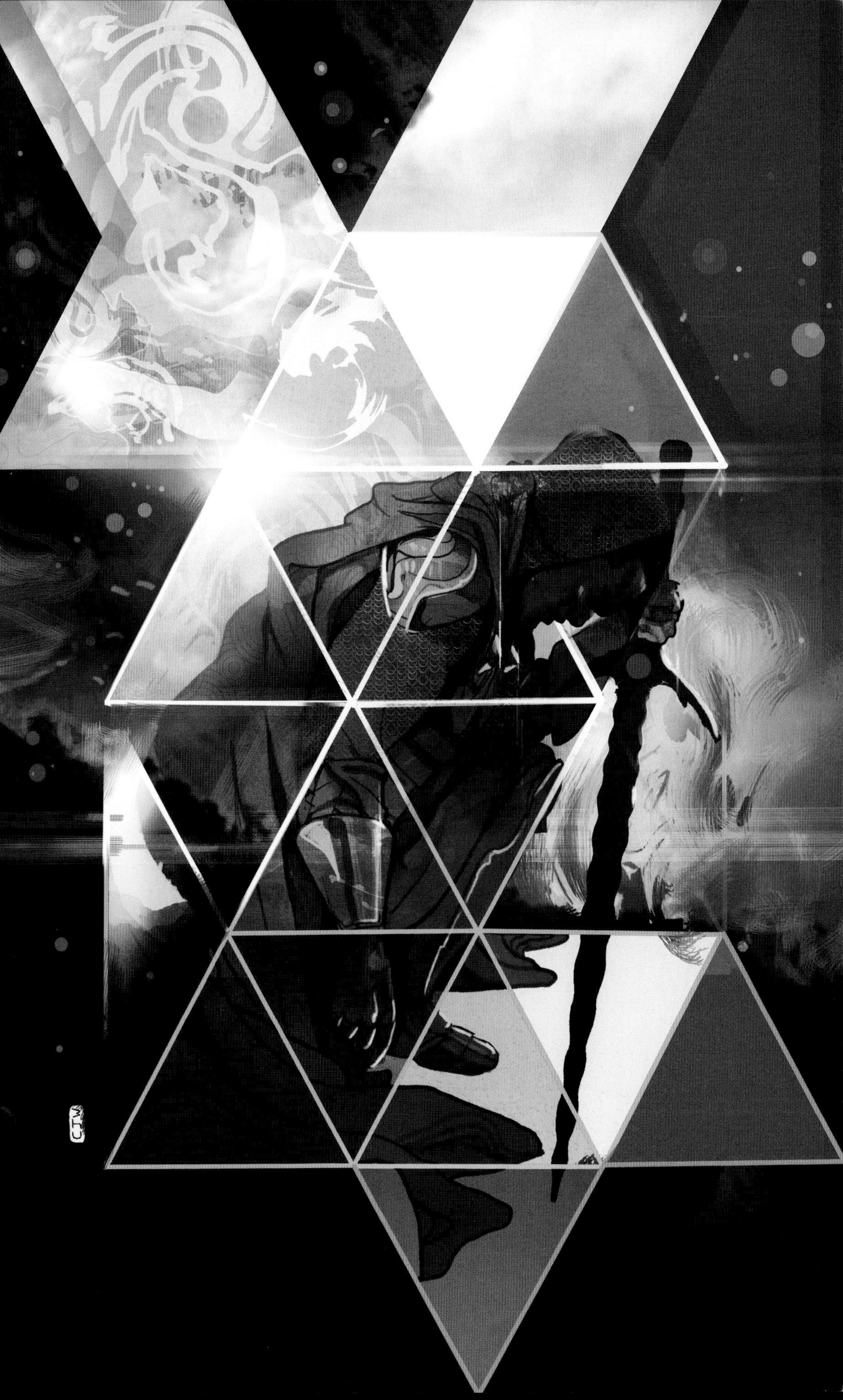

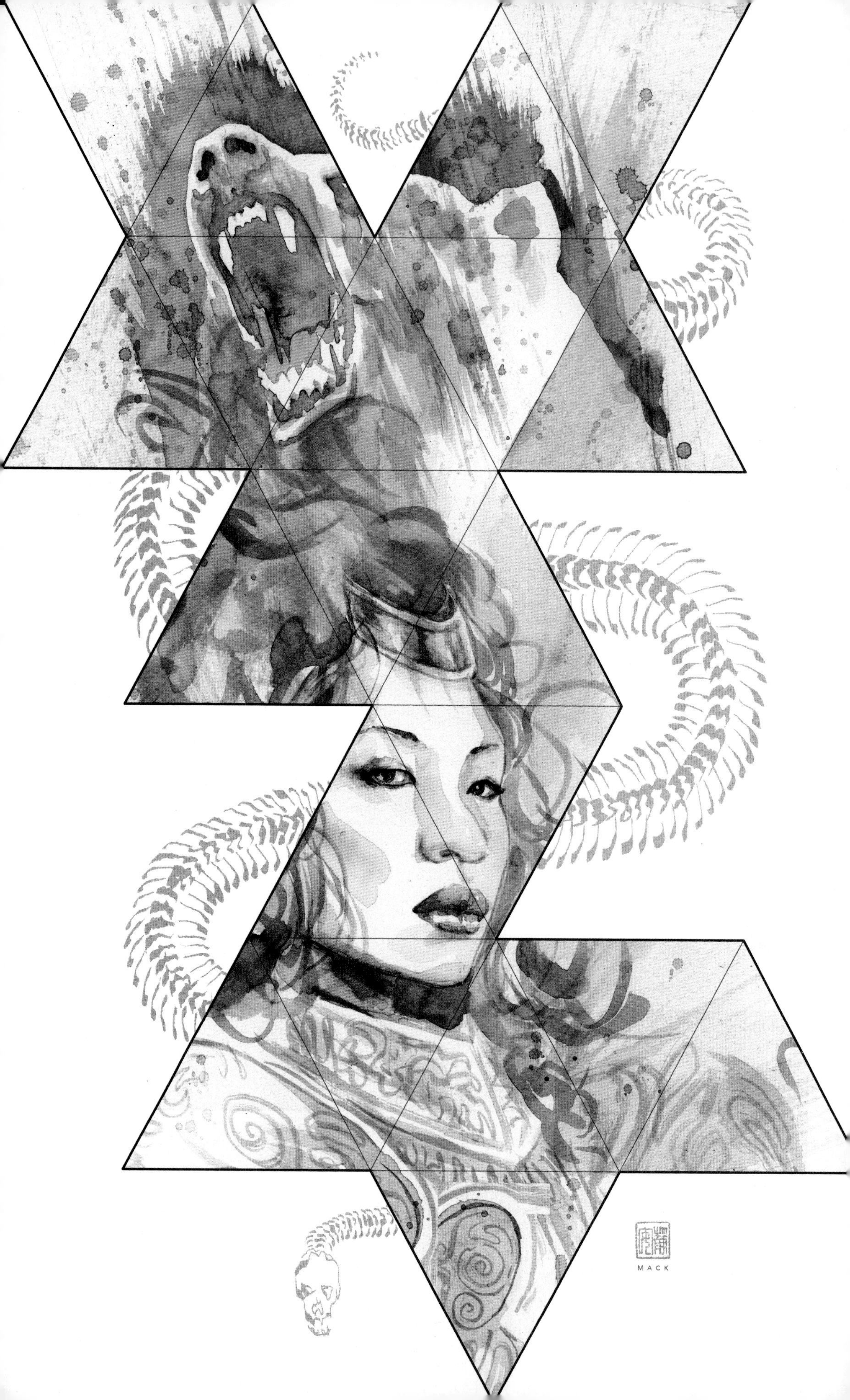
MACK

CHARACTER DESIGN

When it comes to the creation of *DIE*'s characters, quite a lot of inspiration came from random places. I started working on them when I was still a nomad artist. I remember sketching the first drafts in Kyoto, in the heat of the Asian summer, talking to Kieron on Skype and pretending the connection was bad, because his accent makes everything more difficult than it should for this French artist.

You can read more about all this in my essay on p181.

ASH

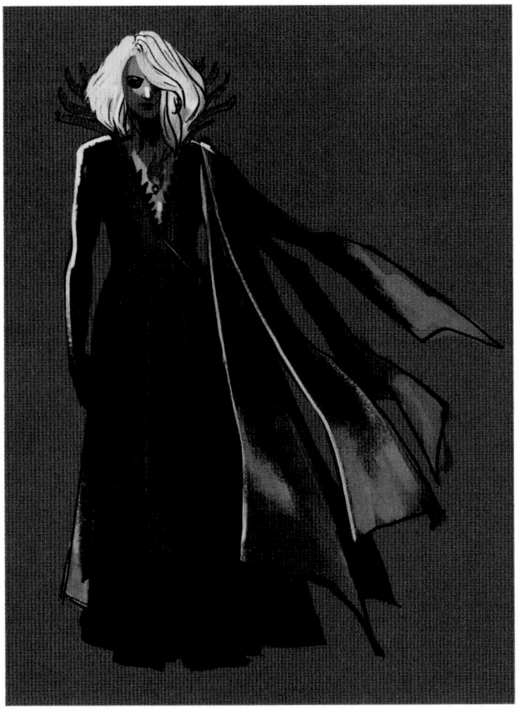

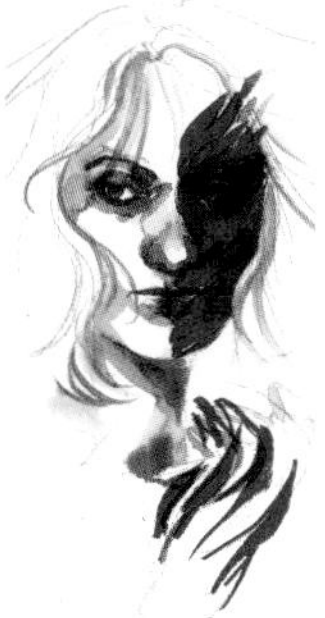

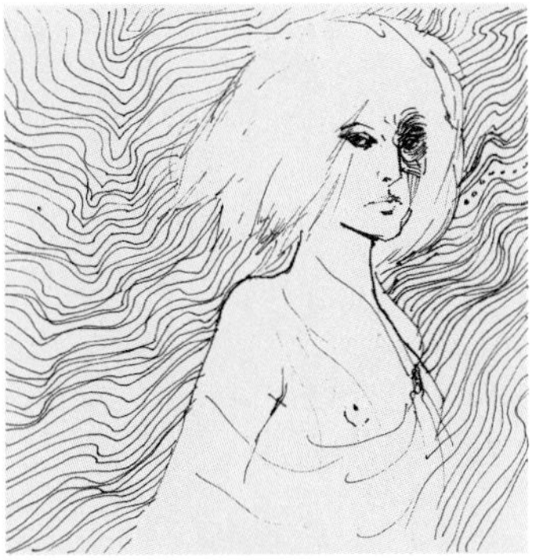

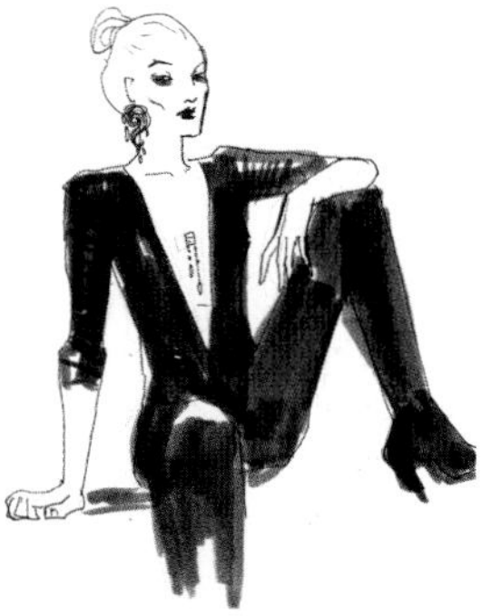

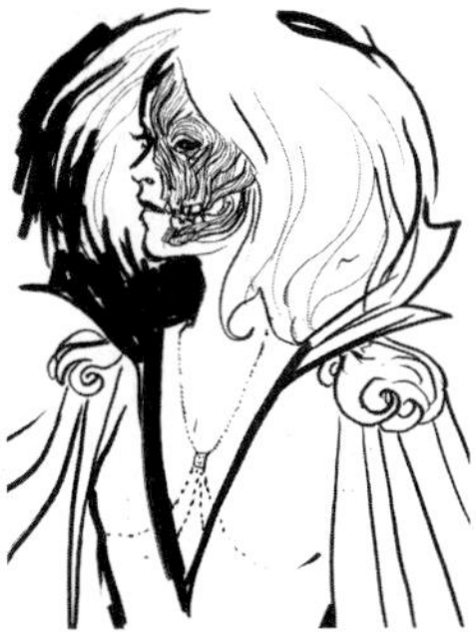

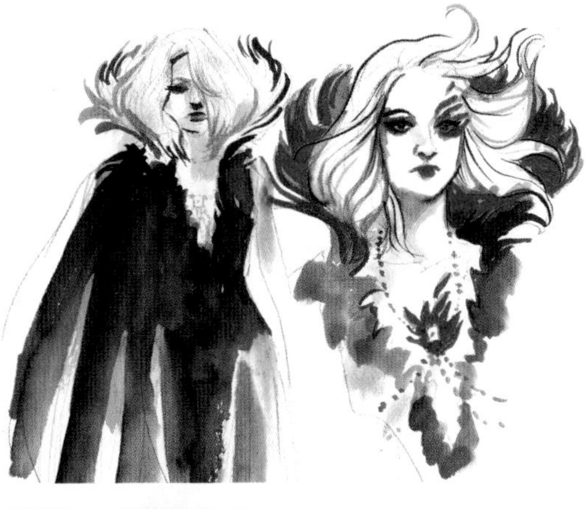

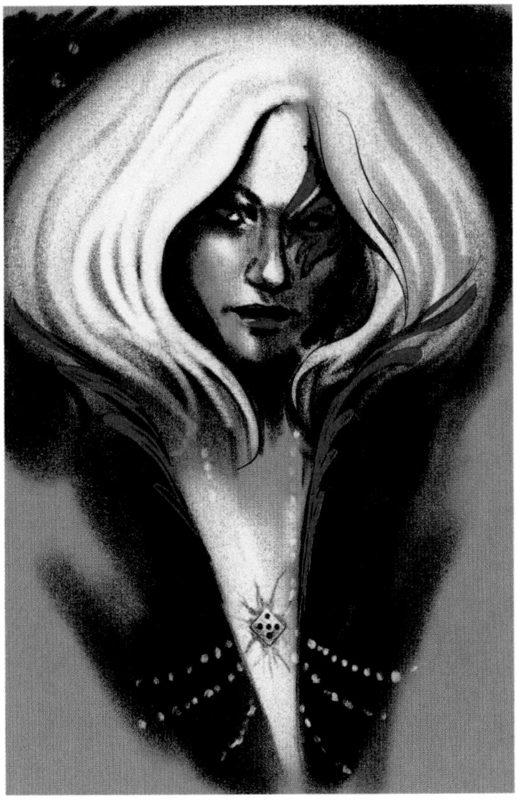

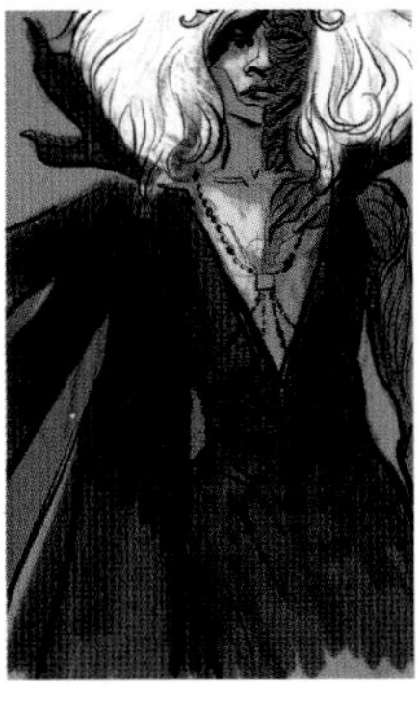

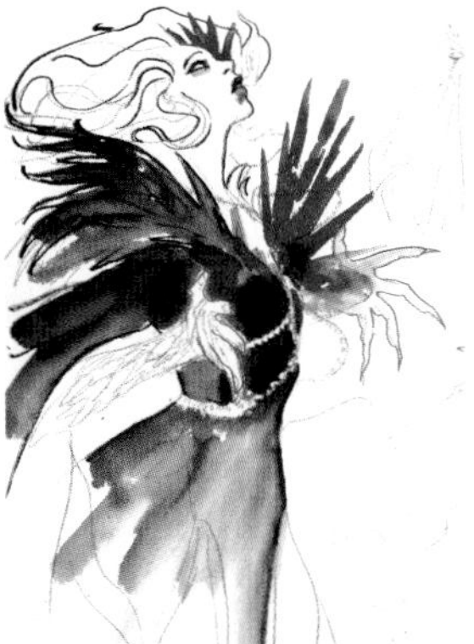

ANGELA

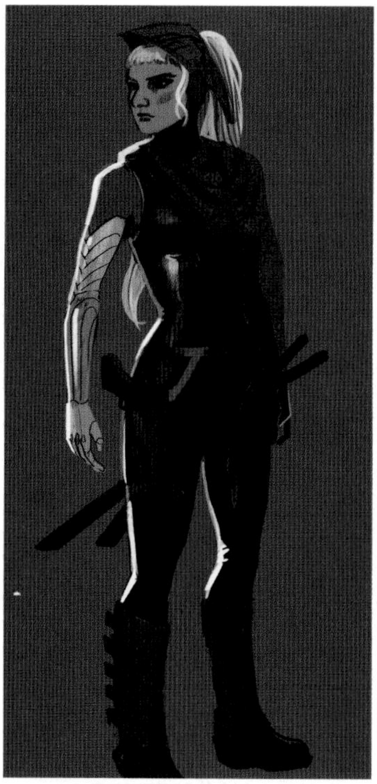

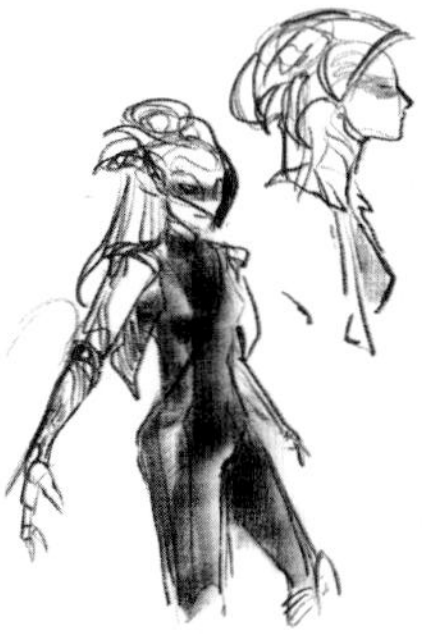

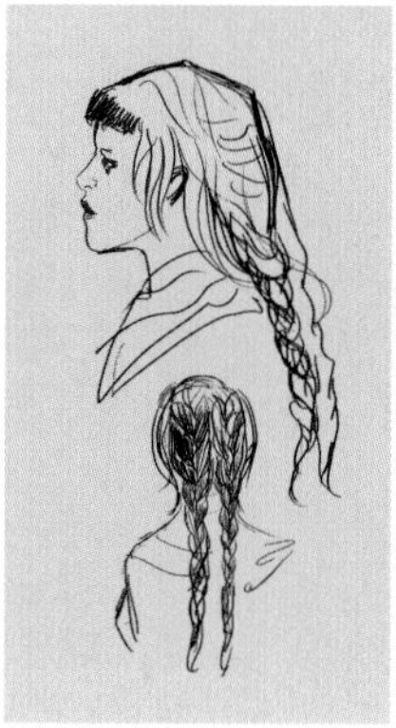

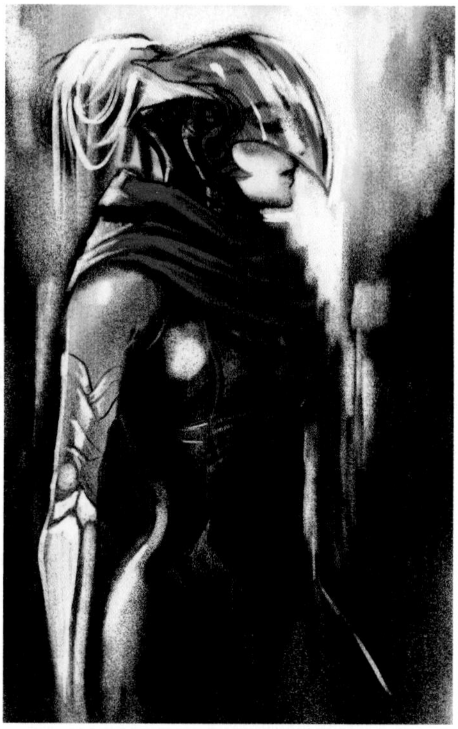

ISABELLE

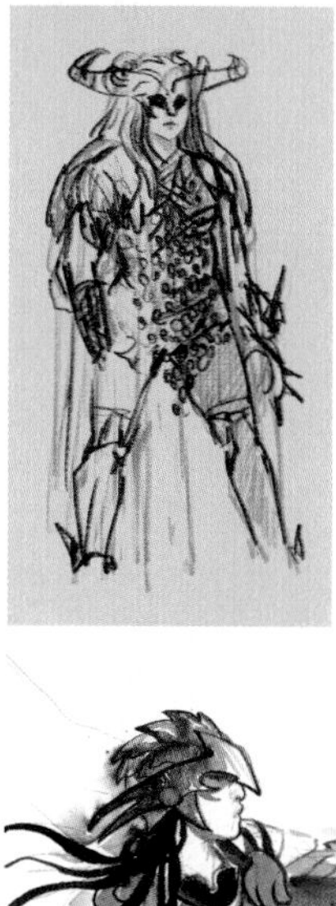

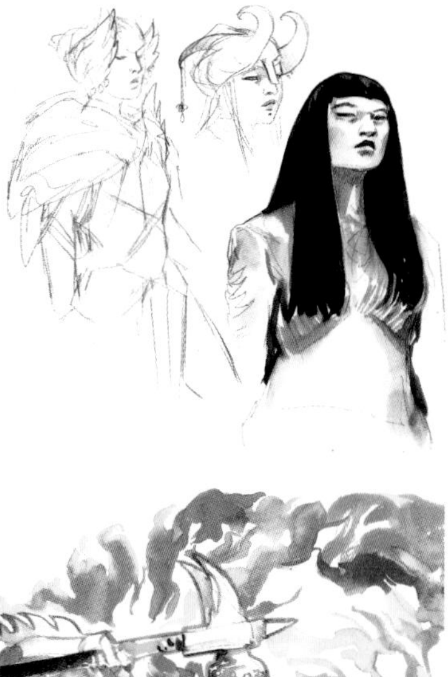

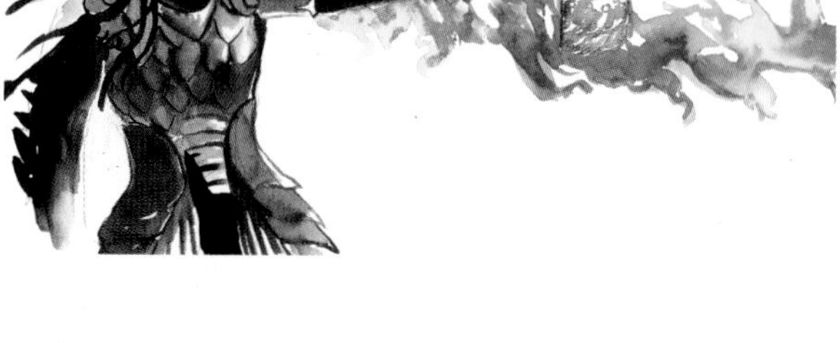

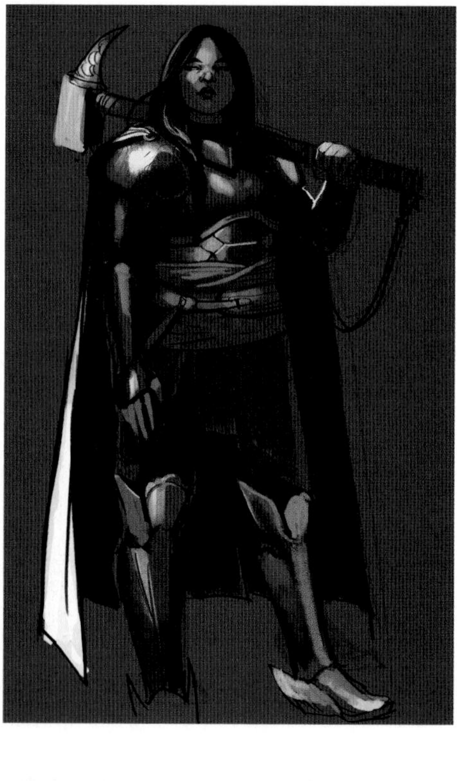

MATT

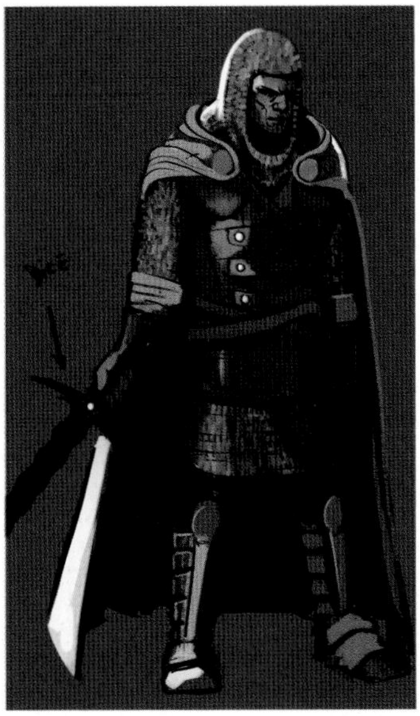

CHUCK

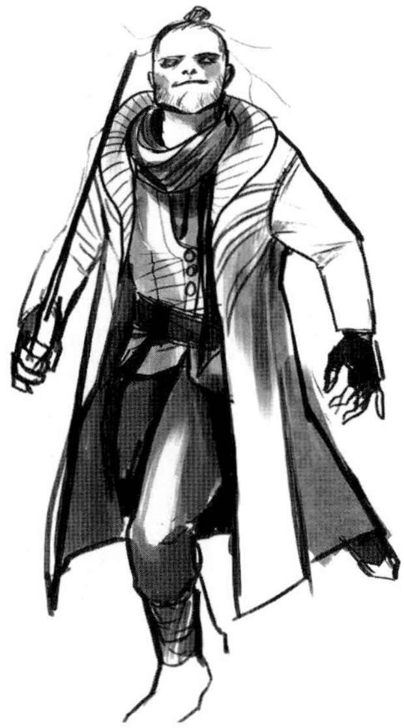

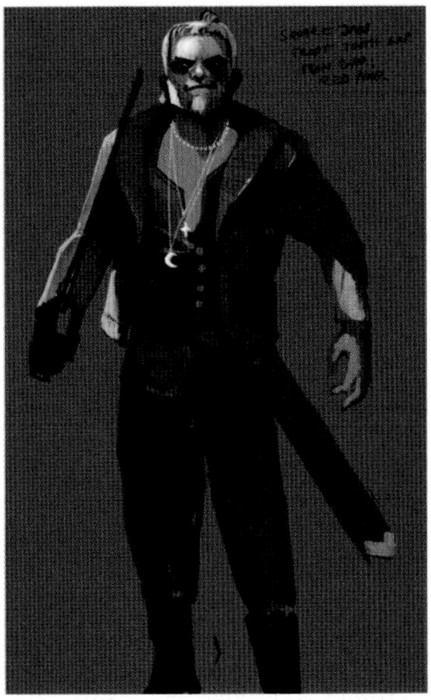

ELF QUEEN

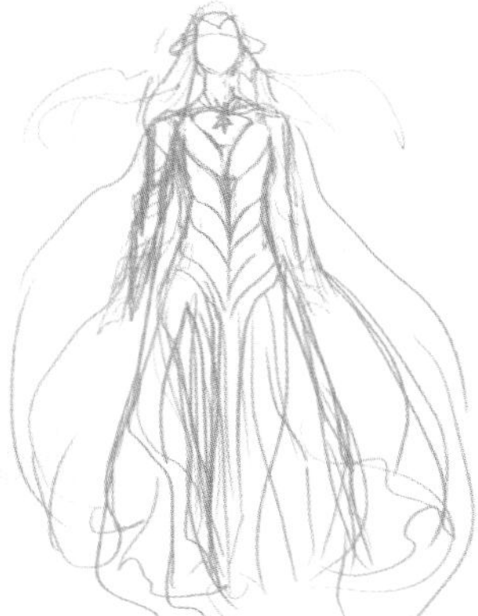

SKYWATCHER

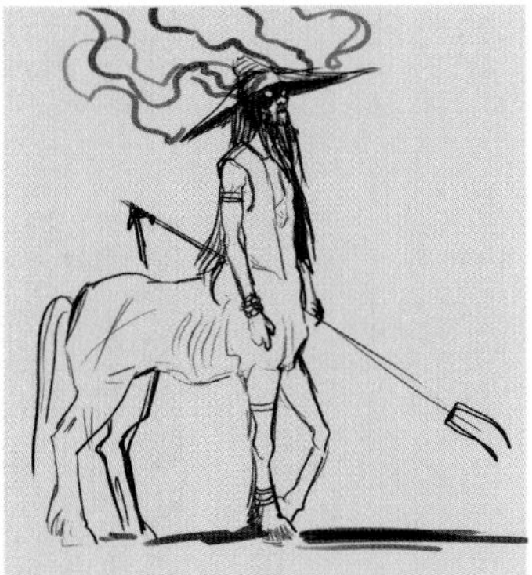

MOURNERS

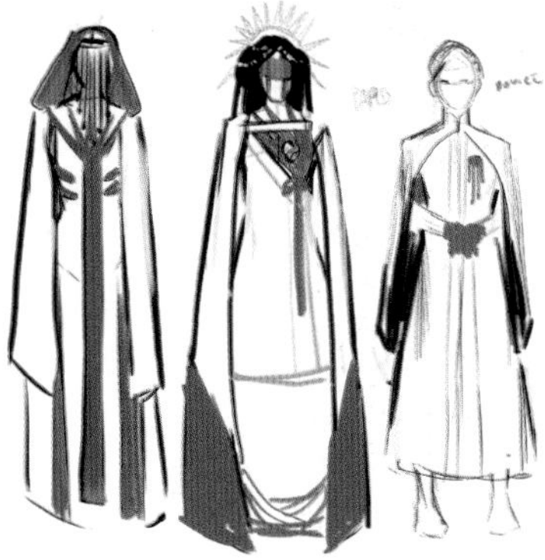

SOL

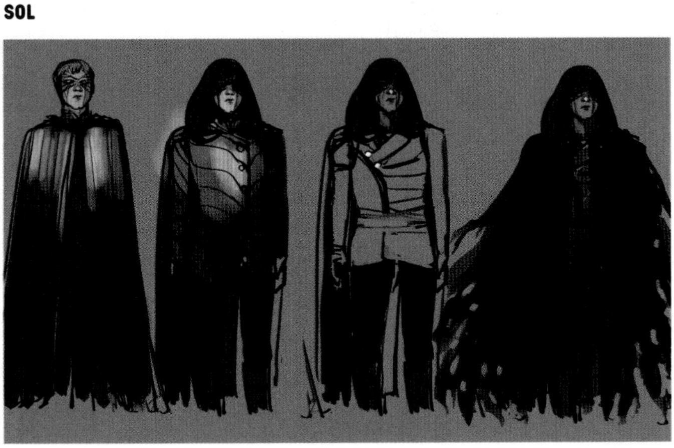

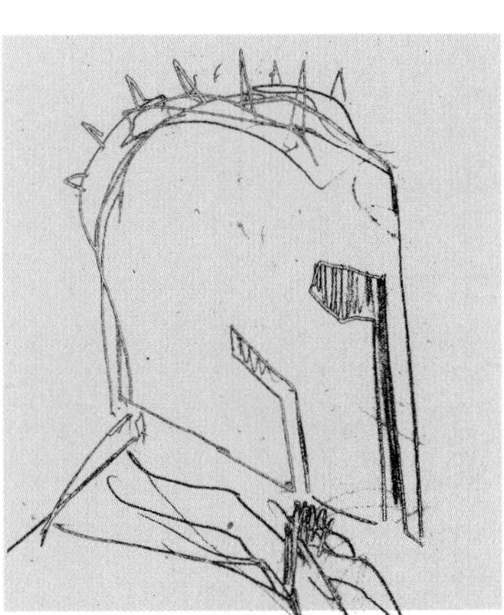

ESSAYS

Normally Kieron wouldn't include even cut-down versions of the essays from the back of a comic in the trade. *DIE* seemed to be an exception. As such, we're getting our Tolkien on and including some appendix essays, one for each of the five chapters in this volume. And, encouraged by her creative partner's hypergraphic tendency, Stephanie's written an essay about her influences too.

INTO THE DUNGEON

It's San Diego Comic Con. We're walking around Springfield Mall. We're talking nonsense.

The "We" is Jamie McKelvie, Ray Fawkes and myself. Someone - I forget who - mentions the 1980s *Dungeons & Dragons* cartoon. We start riffing. It's a fascinating thing, culturally speaking. A group of kids go on a *Dungeons & Dragons*-themed ride and get transported into a fantasy world, and transformed into the character classes. The "ride" is clearly to create distance from the actual game. I suspect it came from a mixture of trying to not turn off the less geeky kids, and partially to avoid the Satanic Panic scare that was happening at the time. They spend the rest of its three-season run trying to get home. They never do. Jamie tells us that they would have in the final episode. It was written but never filmed.

"I wonder what ever happened to them?" I say, and get back to the serious business of accidentally buying the identical sneakers to Jamie.

That evening, we're having dinner. I'm distracted. The idea of "whatever happened to the *D&D* cartoon kids?" has been nagging at me. This is distinctly annoying. I don't need the idea for a new book. I'm already deep in the world building on two large-scale fantasy projects. Yet still, it burrows, and I'm just idly pushing the pieces around in my head. Two connect. A little Promethean spark. I burst into tears.

I get it. I get why this has got to me. I just see the whole story sprawl out in front of me - the real meaty, awful things that this would let me write about, that I'd never really written about before, at least not like this. I instantly know it has to be my next book.

Stephanie Hans and I have been talking about doing a book together since 2013. We met when she was painting the atmospheric, iconic covers for *Journey Into Mystery*. I had no idea she also drew sequential art until she did the final issue of the run, which is just virtuoso stuff. Since then, we've done some small pieces of work together - for various incarnations of *Angela* for Marvel and a couple of issues of Jamie's and my own *The Wicked + The Divine*. She's been magnificent in all of them, mixing epic romance with operatic intensity.

I knew that the 21st century was in desperate need of a fantasy world as conceived of by Stephanie Hans.

I told her about the idea and why I cared. She reciprocated, opening up about her own teenage experiences with games, and her own journey through the fantastical. She was in.

And so started a couple of years of ludicrous research, because we never make it easy on ourselves. This is my first book after my own *The Wicked + The Divine*. It's Stephanie's first ongoing comic. We are emotionally overcommitted, which is lucky, because it's the only way I ever create anything. I dunno about Stephanie. I hope she's more sensible than me. Someone has to be the sensible one on a team.

We recruited Clayton early. He's lettered literally almost every single issue of my best work. He's wrestled with captions the size of novels in *Journey Into Mystery*. He's made a half-dozen custom balloon styles in *WicDiv*. He's the only option for me. Thankfully he said yes, and that means I didn't have to kidnap him and keep him in my basement until he relented. Only joking. I don't have a basement. I'd keep him in my shed.

We recruited Rian late. I've admired Rian's design and comics work for longer than I've loved design and comics. From the tangential glimpses, it was stark and fresh. I found myself in the pub, and mentioned that I was looking for a logo design. Conversations balloon and now Rian's designing it, bringing stark modernist thinking to this project.

The "modernist" part was key to us. There's a lot of history, postmodernism and even nostalgia in the mix here, but it's not a book which is interested in being comforting. We are taking you to a fantasy world, but it tries to reject pastiche. We simultaneously are a deconstructionary critique of Fantasy, while also trying to create something so vibrantly pure as to remind people why anyone fell in love with the idea of there being a land at the back of the wardrobe in the first place.

That's the setting. The emotional core of the book? The thing which tore tears from me in the Japanese restaurant, was the simple idea of six forty-something adults contrasting their teenage fantasies with the realities of where their lives ended up. It's a pure midlife crisis scream of a book. And the bit that got me? The idea that maybe part of me did disappear into a fantasy world at the age of sixteen and never came out. How has my love of all this hurt everyone around me and myself?

Yeah, bleak. It is called *DIE*. The name was the first of several bits of oddly untouched low-hanging fruit which intersected with this book. That it appeared that no one had done an RPG-themed horror comic called *DIE* seemed startlingly unlikely.

It's a book born of obsession, committed to be exactly too much. Hell, I've been working on my own bespoke role-playing system for it, translating the comic into a game. I was originally going to include it in the backmatter of the issues, but soon realised that the game in its smallest state is just too big. I was then going to lob it out as a PDF when this issue dropped, but realised that it includes spoilers for issue 5 in it. I've decided to hopefully release it when the first trade drops [*Ed. note: See page 155 of this volume!*]. Until then, I'll be using the backmatter to talk about the thinking which went into it, which handily doubles as the thinking that went into the world building, so shouldn't bore anyone who is just here for the dark fantasy adventure.

That's the plan, anyway. Everything is subject to change.

So. This is a different beast than usual for me. That said, *D&D* villain Venger is namechecked on the sleeve of seminal 1990s indie pop band Kenickie. No, regular readers, I haven't quite escaped my traditional pop-music obsessions entirely. Rest assured, I'll be telling RPG stories about being a warped child of *Paranoia* and *MERPS* next time.

CHARGEN

When doing our first thinking about *DIE*, I knew there was something we had to do. It'd be easy to just drop them into a standard fantasy world. Easy, and likely smart - it ups the nostalgia aspect, and people always like nostalgia. Conversely, I am suspicious of nostalgia, even when writing about it.

I knew that for *DIE* to do what I wanted it to do, it had to be both familiar and new. You'd recognise things, but they'd come at an angle which made you reevaluate them. I wanted to be deconstructionary (as in, the world takes apart some common RPG tropes) while also reconstructionary (as in, creating a whole fantasy that is seductive and enchanting). I wanted character types that could be commentary on your Cleric and Paladin and the rest... while having the potential to operate by themselves as their own iconic sense. A Godbinder is a commentary on a Cleric, but it's also something that works as a fantasy by itself.

I came at it methodically. It all started with the dice. That was my core idea - *the dice changed people*. As such, the dice should speak to what they become.

There is a lot in *DIE* - both the comic and the spinoff RPG - about the fetishism of those six polyhedral dice. They're still somewhat alien objects now. In the 1980s, they may as well have been Lovecraftian artefacts. Part of me doesn't blame parents for being concerned when they saw these euclidean nightmares bouncing across tables...

So a lot became about what those dice *meant*. This was in the widest possible sense. I looked all over the place for things to turn into their mythology, and then cast the archetypes to the dice.

(In passing, the proper terminology is d6, d10 and so on. We're using D6 for two reasons. Firstly, these aren't d20. This is a D20 - a magical artefact. A totally different thing. Secondly, our designer would kill us if we did something so typographically ugly as "d6". So we'll use "D" throughout as a stylistic choice.)

The D20 was the first, as it was easiest. The symbolism of the D20 is simple. D20 is D&D. D20 is RPGs. You show a D20 to someone, and people think "D&D". It's not entirely fair or true - Egyptians had D20s, and if you went back to ancient Rome, you could pick up some excellent glass D20s that would still turn heads today. But in the modern age, this became an icon of the art form. The D20 is *everything*.

This is true in a literal way in *DIE*. The world is a D20. As such, the D20 acolytes have control over the world. A very literal control - they're reality warpers who can tweak the rules on the fly. This gave us our Mage archetype and our Dungeon Master archetype in a single stroke.

If the Master was easy, the rest were hard. They came in bits and pieces, and there were definitely times when I was considering other possibilities - hell, that the D4 is a foot-puncturing deathtrap if you drop it on the floor made me consider to use it for the Rogue analogue. Sometimes the theory came first. Sometimes the die was left over, and we scrambled to make the theory fit. Like all magic, there is a lot of waving your hands to distract folks.

The Godbinder's die is the D12. The second-largest die after the D20, representing the gods' power within the nature of creation. The 12 turns up in religion a bunch, not least in the 12 Olympians. It's also the dual-polyhedra of the D20. In other words, it is the opposite in terms of points-in-space as D20, with all the faces and vertices interchanged. As in, everything that is not a D20, *is* a D12. If D20 is reality, the D12 is everything that is *not* reality. The D20 is the natural, and the D12 is the supernatural.

So the D12 will be our Cleric riff, and Clerics are always one of those interesting sidesteps in *D&D*. Mages do their spells by themselves. Clerics ask their gods to do spells for them and, in their god's name, perform miracles. Depending on the world or system, you can analyse this (as in, does the faith allow people to access their own inner power?) but the core is "my god has given me power" rather than "this power is my own".

And what are gods in these games? In our world, there are constant prayers for miracles, but god isn't exactly quick on picking up the phone. In a *D&D* world, gods are kind of the equivalent of a call centre or tech support, sending off minor miracles ("I'll heal you, but only D8 wounds") constantly. How incredibly compliant are gods in *D&D*? And, when gods tend towards the Olympian mythological mode, where they have strong personalities, "compliant" isn't exactly how they come across. Can you imagine Zeus doing anything if you ask him to, unless it's turn into a goose and have sex with you?

Now, there's usually some lip service in the game that a Cleric's miracles will only be answered if they're sufficiently religious, but in practise, the Cleric is a Christian who views Christ's main merit as basically how good he is at catering for large crowds in the middle of a desert. Really, Clerics aren't like holy men. Clerics are entitled shits shouting at a company until they get what they want. If the miracles are being done by these extra-planar entities, the Clerics are summoning them for a set task, and then dismissing them.

And you know what? There's a name for people who summon extra-planar creatures and bully them into obeying them. It's "demonologist". Having a Cleric who has a more personal I-talk-to-god-and-god-talks-back-*constantly* relationship is a lot fun. We can do a lot with that, especially when the woman in question is an atheist. It's hard to believe in gods in the same way once you've met them and had them clean your toilet.

The D10 is the Neo. That was one of the first dice to be settled. I tried a few names before settling on Neo, for the simple fact it means new and that's one of the core parts of the class. The D10 is literally the new. It wasn't in common use until the 1980s. Previously 1-10 numbers were generated by other methods, like by rolling a twenty-sided die that had two sets of 1-10 on it, or rolling a second die alongside the D20. It's also the die that isn't *a platonic* solid. It's something else. As well as all that, the 10 is a 1 and 0, which is (of course) binary. And 1 and 0 being the two sides of a coin. Coins, binary, the new...

When trying to work out what a 1991 era cyberpunk-loving GM may do to make their world interesting, I hit upon the idea of flipping what a bunch of people - but most famously, *Shadowrun* - did. Instead of bringing magic to the cyberpunk, let's do cyberpunk tech in fantasy. This rapidly became the Thief class. In the game, you can play them as more martial sorts, but the mercenary aspect is hard baked into them, and works explicitly as explained in the issue: they actively need this specific treasure in a way that no one else does.

The D8 is the damage a standard longsword does in *D&D*. That alone seemed enough to put my Fighter analogue here. But, after a weirdly rambling road of research, I found another reason. All this was in answer to two problems: 1) we clearly needed a Fighter class - no classical RPG can live without one; 2) equally clearly, Fighters are boring.

I couldn't have that. There's other sorts of Fighters, of course - Barbarians (with their berserker rage) and Paladins (with their ability to induce rage in all other players by being so tedious). The latter interested me. Paladins, in old skool games, could only be Lawful Good. Which, for those who don't know old RPG lingo (or follow internet memes), means they were meant to be word-keeping good-hearted lovely sweethearts of ethical paragons. Superman, basically. Sadly, a common fault is people tend to play Lawful Good as either Shithead Good or Stupid As Balls Good.

As a kid, it never made much sense to me. If a Paladin is a fancy religious warrior, and religions were aligned with alignments, then all religions should have some kind of Paladin. Obviously, this is the way game design went - current *D&D* lets you have your Paladins be any alignment you want. As there's eight actual "directions" in an alignment grid (putting aside neutral) and our fighter class is based on the D8 so... it all seems to line up? Except there was another problem: alignment is rubbish. Fuck alignment. I'd rather die than make *DIE* have alignments.

Then, when down another research hole, I hit the contemporary-to-1991 work of Robert Plutchik who argued all emotions were created by varying their intensity and mixing eight primary emotions. You can imagine me leaning forward in my seat, steepling my fingers and smiling. Oh, Dr Plutchik. Do tell me more.

Instantly, we have eight knightly orders, each powered by one of the eight emotions, each whose abilities operate off the same principles, but with radically different implications. This is one of the moments when you may realise exactly how overreaching this whole world is. The Grief Knight? That's one of *eight* entirely developed options I could have picked. There's a lot of fun here. And sadness. Trust me, Joy Knights are some of the worst people you will ever meet. Also, in a roundabout way, by having Rage Knights, I recreate a Barbarian/ Berserker class, so it's even efficient.

So we've got our Wizard, Cleric, Thief and Fighter archetypes. Which left me two classes which are (er) both a riff on Bards. Bards are a jack-of-all-trades class in most games, with the sole ability that is theirs alone being "play music to have magical effects". They're generally considered a marginal class at best and a joke class at worst. That someone who is best known for a series of music-is-magic comics has turned them into two archetypes is a very me thing to do.

The Fool is more the style than the content, and basically them as gleeful swashbucklers - but the soul of the Bard is in there. Because, while I'm talking *character* archetypes in this column, there is also an element of me casting *player* archetypes. And almost every game has someone (or someones) who really doesn't care about being there. They're there for social reasons, to have fun, to mess around. They don't take it that seriously. They want to take it more lightly.

As a designer, I wanted to have a class that was a little simpler than the rest. The Dictator and the Master are ones for experienced players (both in terms of rules and emotional maturity required to make them work). The Godbinder, the Neo and the Emotion Knights fall in between, in roughly descending order of complexity. There has to be something beneath that. Something more... casual. Something less threatening.

The D6 is the what people think of when they think of dice. It has the common touch. It is everywhere. It is universal. You show a D20 or a D4 or any of the rest, they think *D&D*. If you show a D6, they say it's a die. It is what a normal die looks like. And "normal" is always a loaded word.

Following the comic, each player in *DIE* gets sole ownership of a die. As in, the Godbinder gets the only D12 in the whole game. No one else gets to touch it. However, the rest of the game runs off normal six-side dice. You do anything, you'll use a few D6 to see if you succeed or fail. And the Fool? They just get given this normal D6 at the start. Everyone laughs. And then the Fool, when no one's looking, gets to write on their D6 to change the numbers.

There is distinctly less symbology here, because it is a more shallow character class. Simultaneously, despite that, they're *also* more than they seem. I liked that contradiction. Something can be shallow, yet deeper than you actually think.

Let's be honest - they're also weaponized early-00s-*World- of-Warcraft*-meme-Leeroy- Jenkins as a superpower.

And finally, the official worst die of all time, the D4, the *other* half of the Bard.

The D4 is the smallest regularly used die in a game of traditional *D&D*. It is, as such, as far as any die is from the D20 - the physics die, the die of reality. The D4 therefore embodies the opposite part of a game of *D&D*, namely the soft parts, namely the *role playing*. In a meta way, the D20 is about manipulating the rules of the game... the D4 is about manipulating everything which is part of the game, but not part of the rules. In actual shape, the D4 is connected to the D8 - the other class based explicitly on emotions. It also represents power structures, with the player at the tip of the pyramid and everyone beneath them. Hence, Dictators.

Put it like this: you listen to an upbeat song. You feel happy. You read a depressing story. You feel sad. Does that ever strike you as sinister? As if someone has magically taken control of your emotions and should be shunned and feared? Of course not. That's just what artists do. It's natural.

No, it's not. It's unnatural, sinister magic.

Dictators, by performing their art, are capable of altering other creatures' emotional states. Dictators can play emotions like an earth musician would play a harp. They can pluck the strings. They can snap them.

In other words, Dictators are like Bards, if everyone was fucking petrified of Bards.

DIE is a dark fantasy game. It can (and often does) edge towards horror. That's not just the world you're moving through. It's also you. Sometimes the horror is what using your abilities does to you. With others, it can be about what using your abilities does to everyone around you. You can likely imagine which pole the Dictators tend towards.

That's our core six, or at least a slice of the thinking behind them. The document which had my initial thoughts on this is a clear eight thousand words of download, and they've developed a bunch since. And, as you can likely see, I switch between the literary mode of the *DIE* comic and the ludic mode of the *DIE* game freely when I'm talking about this. And I've also used the "I" a lot, because this is definitely part of the planning where I was like Sol, locked inside my own head, beavering away at my obsessions...

Next time, I suspect I'll write a little about the world-building of *DIE* generally, and if all goes well, something other than me blithering on about what's been eating my mind alive for over two years (or 33 years, if you want to look at it in that way).

Oh - and something I wanted to mention. Sally Couch has been helping me as a sensitivity consultant on *DIE*, regarding Angela's missing limb. Firstly, I wanted to thank her (as she is amazing) but she mentioned that she'd like to help more creators with this sort of thing, so if anyone is looking, she's letsflyfree on Twitter and Instagram, or salcouchconsultancy@gmail.com.

WORLDGEN

By now, you hopefully know what *DIE* is like. Issue one is the pitch, written to sell the core fantasy and cast. It's a mix of stately and intense. It hits everything you absolutely need to know immediately. Issue 2 is frenzied - its purpose is to hit everything *else* you need to know. It's a tasting platter of the sorts of flavours *DIE* serves - the adventure elements, the relationship with Sol, the real-world-stuff-becomes-horrific idea, the their-past-adventure-in-Die-comes-back-to-mess-with-them and so on. These are the main refrains of our series. Ideally you come out of issue 2 thinking you know the book.

And then issue 3 is a "Oh - we're also this."

I've referenced Ellis/Cassaday's *Planetary* a few times in interviews, which used the device of a group of archaeologists to explore the history of the superhero. The Planetary organisation's conspiratorial nature was the backbone of the ongoing series, but each adventure illuminated one of the elements of pop fiction that was subsumed into superhero comics. So you had the pulp adventurer issue, the 19th century penny dreadful issue, the Japanese monster movie issue and so on. I reread *Planetary* when doing my thinking on *DIE* and realised that it showed one way that this could work - that rather than using archaeologists sifting through the rubble, an adventuring party moving across the right kind of fantasy world could be a device to encounter the constituent elements of a genre. As you pass through a region, you can do a story about that.

We do it less than *Planetary*, as the character drama and other elements are more key to the power of the beast, but it's certainly there. This is a thing we do. Sometimes we'll just do an episode like this, and so the world-building of *DIE* would have to support it.

And if we're talking world-building, it's appropriate this is the Tolkien issue.

World-building is a kind of dirty word. If you're listening to the general thrust of writing advice, the "don't get lost in world-building" is a common refrain. Sometimes you hear it taken further, into "world-building is a waste of time". The latter is many things, but at least seems to be an echo of Moorcock's seminal anti-Tolkien essay 'Epic Pooh'. As in, a 'Down With Tolkien And His Impersonators' writ large.

I love 'Epic Pooh', but the research for this issue got me thinking on lines I wasn't expecting.

I've done a lot of world-building, in various modes. A WW2 comic like *Über* is hard and mechanical based upon a rock-solid formula. The point of that book was the sense that everything ran off blueprints. At the other end was *Phonogram*, whose world-building all came from its literary pretensions - magic in our story is a metaphor for what music really does to people. The magic is a device for talking about music, not a thing in and of itself.

DIE's world-building is kind of both - it's mechanised in a way that would make *Über* blanche. I've just finished a draft of the RPG I want to lob online circa the trade, which is currently 60,000 words. That's a novel's worth of material I've done as a weird side-project. In the *Phonogram* corner, the literary mode of *DIE* is also way up in the mix. The low-level structure of the book - the Godbinders and Dictators and all the rest - is like *Über*. The high-level structure of the book - the *setting* - leans closer to *Phonogram*.

In other words, *DIE*'s world-building had to support the meta-fantasy aspect of the comic. As in, it's a world made up of everything that went into the RPG, which then went on to influence the world. At least part of *DIE*'s concept is tracing not just the influences leading into the RPG, but RPGs' impact on the world. We had to find a way to be able to include anything I wanted to.

I had the idea of a 20-sided world - as I put it in the manual: "Die is a planet-sized 20-sided polyhedron consisting of 20 equal-sized triangular planes. It tumbles, though does not move. Despite this, gravity appears to operate as it would on Earth. It is fun to be a physicist in the world of Die." As such, I have 20 regions, and needed to populate the world and generate its politics based upon the history of the form.

I knew much of this before starting. I used to be a games critic. My thinking then was that it's interesting that RPGs took forever to develop. It would seem that we've had the technology forever - as I said, the Egyptians had D20s. What's to stop people from sitting down and just making it up earlier? My basic take then was games were in part a child of postmodernism - as in, you have to have a cultural understanding of the mutability of texts before you can really go where RPGs went. I was certainly aware of the fun prehistory - 19th century German wargames inspired HG Wells' *Little Wars* which inspired the hobby games industry, leading to the emergence of *D&D*. But I also knew I wanted to research it a damn sight more. Suffice to say, my take is somewhat different now.

The reading has been considerable, but if you only read one book about RPG history, read *Playing at the World* by Jon Peterson. I say "one book" but it's at least four or five books tied together with string. "A history of simulating wars, people and fantastic adventures, from chess to role-playing games" which feels like the sort of subtitle which a publisher adds when they feel "a history of role-playing games" lacks sufficient grandeur. Frankly, to hold it gives it all the grandeur required. It's a tome. Not a tome as a "mysterious grimoire" but tome as in "serious academic-looking book that professors use to frighten their undergraduates".

Playing at the World's main thesis is that *D&D* emerged through the intersection of three traditions - the shared paracosm, the refereed games of German Kriegsspiel, and the fantasy genre. The intersection of Kriegsspiel with the fantasy genre - knowing that hobby gaming was born of the creator of modern science fiction - is one of those things which has always obsessed me, but his take on paracosms was new and is one of the main influences on the book. Those who have spotted the Brontë nods may suspect where we're going.

But I was always going to include Tolkien. The image of this story was one of the first things which came to mind when constructing *DIE*: Hobbiton on the Western Front, Bag End's door embedded in a Somme trench. That was horrible, and also true. I had to write it, and I had to write it properly.

That led to me wrestling with Tolkien seriously for the first time since I was a teenager, and likely a pre-teen. It proved illuminating, and a little humbling. This research on Tolkien also led to me being unbearable, which was thankfully mocked relentlessly by my friends. Before last Christmas we had a marathon watching of the *Lord of the Rings* extended editions. Early on, I make the mistake of mentioning "Did you know that Tolkien was attacked by a tarantula when he was young, which probably explains Shelob". For the next twelve hours, every plot element was heralded by a "Did you know that Tolkien's house had a sticky front door? That was the inspiration the Moria gate" or "Did you know Tolkien was attacked by trolls while walking in the park at Oxford? Well, that's the inspiration for, etc, etc." Humbling. And not just in *that* way.

One of my favourite comments on my work - and yes, that's a horrible sentence that says terrible things about me - was Douglas Wolk saying something off-hand about *Journey Into Mystery*: "The most affectionate act of slaying the father I've seen in comics lately." I like that as it both recognises what the book is doing and also notes the lightness it employs. *Journey Into Mystery* is a pop-*Sandman*, a playful dance with the core Vertigo books - Moore's and Gaiman's especially - and mocks them, but without malice. It's as impish as Loki. I like that, as it shows I have oedipal issues tightly under check. It's only when seriously thinking about Tolkien I realise I'm full of shit.

One of Jamie McKelvie's favourite stories about me is the time I explained, at length, that elves were basically "what if there actually was a master race" racial supremacists *to a group of people cosplaying Tolkien elves*. I'm annoyed at the Know Your Place implicit in Middle-earth, the hatred of the industrial world and the working class who inhabit it. My standard line is "If I was in Middle-earth, I would clearly be an orc" and I still believe that. But feel the simmering *resentment* there. I quickly realise why. I came to comics as an adult. As such, my comic influences are all adult influences. I'm chill about them. Conversely, Tolkien was what got me into this world. *He's* the father figure I have oedipal rage towards. As such, the research was my process of forgiving Tolkien. After

his father dies in South Africa, he settles in Britain. After his mother dies, he moves to Birmingham. All his happy young memories are rural memories. Of course his stories speak to that.

While a study of a creative through an autobiographical filter is always questionable and does not remove any critique of the work, it does engender empathy. It was a process of not seeing him as this patriarchal statue but a human being - a creative responding in natural ways to the life he lived.

This issue came from that. It's the sort of thing which I suspect is either very good or very bad. I hope you like it. It means the world to me.

One angle in my research led me to think about the *why* of these worlds. Tolkien's worlds were arguably a property emerging from his home-cooked fanfic languages. As in, a language speaks to the stories you tell with it. A creator's interests are not just decoration, but what it grows from - Greg Stafford's *Glorantha* is powered by his interest in mythological structure, for example. These are not surface concerns, but core.

All of which got me thinking about what lies at the core of *DIE*. I know what its purpose is, as described above. But what is it *for*? *Why DIE*? What drives us to even do this thing? All of which are questions worth pursuing. *DIE* as an equation for solving itself appeals to me enormously.

Right - I've hit my word limit, and haven't even talked about how I plan to allow the obviously somewhat idiosyncratic setting of *DIE* to work with everyone's own individual games. The short version is that we have lesser Masters with their own pocket-dimensions inside *DIE*, each of which has their own playground. In other words, everyone has complete freedom to do whatever they want, and the place where all these dimensions exist is in my world-building too. *DIE* has room for everyone. And yes, that simultaneously sounds both welcoming and like a threat. That's how we roll.

COMMUNITY

The first issue was a general introduction. The second issue was a deep dive into the crunchy world-building. The third issue was a soar into the *fluffy* world-building. What other core parts are there to role-playing games?

Well, it's the people you do it with. In the case of *DIE* the comic, it's you lot, with Stephanie and me as the Masters leading you into this world. In the case of the comic itself, it's the six people Sol gathered back in 1991. In the case of every game, it's the people you can get together. When you hear people talk about how they can't run a game, there's two perpetual problems. Firstly, it's not having time. Secondly, it's not having the people.

One of the fascinating things about the growth of RPGs' profile in public conversation is the increasing ease of the latter. The problem with getting people isn't that there's no people - it's that there's no people who would be interested in playing a game. The biggest block to playing was the conceptual leap to sitting down with those funny dice. That fundamental alienation. That's changed, and that's due to all manner of increased cultural representation. *DIE* Editor Chrissy decided she'd like to try it out one day after enjoying the jokey *D&D* game that used to end all the Harmontown podcasts. She heard it, she realised what it was, and thus it became something she could imagine herself doing. That's everywhere now, with *Critical Role* and *Adventure Zone* inventing stadium *D&D*. All these are acts of necessary demystification. RPGs are games about an embodiment in fantasy, to see yourself in another place. Ironically, one of the biggest things preventing people playing was their inability to see themselves in the place of playing the game, as they had no idea what it really entailed. That's gone now.

The other, of course, was stigma, the whole Jocks versus Nerds thing. Unpacking that is somewhat tricky.

Partially as I'm British, and we didn't do that in-school regimented class-system thing, in favour for turning our *whole country* into a quasi-feudal monstrosity. Shame was never a thing for me. I was never significantly embarrassed doing this.

(Except jokingly when I was at university, referring to "role-playing" as "vole-flaying" as admitting you were off playing fantasy games was more embarrassing than confessing you were tearing the skin from helpless rodents.)

I can't say how much was me, and how much the people I found myself surrounded by. I know there's something of the former. I am a creature of shameless steamroller enthusiasm, but having a critical mass of trench-coated Games Workshop fans in my class helped. As in, we never felt isolated because of our interests. I was surrounded with a surfeit of smart people with overlapping interests that covered most of what we wanted to do. In fact, more than we "needed". When thinking of those teenage crowds, I realised that in the various RPGs I played in my teenage years, there wasn't an entirely steady core group. There were enough people that all those games had their own players and so their own tone and character.

Sometimes they were my best friends. Regular readers of my work may wish, at this point, to imagine a teenage Kid-With-Knife from *Phonogram* turning up to a game of *Cyberpunk* wearing a bulletproof jacket. Yes, perhaps it would have been better if we were more capable of embarrassment.

However, sometimes they weren't, at least when we started. Other people got dragged in. We didn't know each other much when we sat down to play. By the end of a campaign we did. Some of my closest friends have been forged in that shared experience.

But weirder? There's people I didn't. There's people I spent the best part of two years with in the same room most Saturdays, mashing our way through the entirety of *The Enemy Within* campaign, whose names I can't remember. I only dimly recall their faces. I can't even recall how I knew them. It's as if they disappeared, or have been written out of history, and only really existed in the context of that world...

Sol was perhaps the first character in *DIE* to coalesce, so I was already thinking along such lines, but when I remembered not-remembering some people, it felt uncanny. I valued those experiences. That campaign was the most formative in my gaming history, where I changed from one sort of gamer to another. It's the one which most influences the comic you're reading. *But who the hell was that person?* Weirder, none of my friends I've asked remember either. Shiver.

The beta rules of *DIE* presently have a list of components the Master will need to run it. One of them is "1-5 friends or at least people you can bear being in the same room as for a couple of sessions." That's obviously a joke, but sitting here and now I'm thinking of how gaming groups have worked across history. Sometimes it's getting together with your friends. Sometimes it's getting together with whoever wants to do the thing so you can all do this thing. Sometimes you become friends and sometimes you don't. But something happens, and it can be magical, either way. We share stories.

That's what this issue is about. The "adventurers arrive in the pub" is a stereotypical start to any game, and it's playing with that. I found myself thinking of the times you went to a pub, and never went anywhere else, as you'd all had adventures already (of one kind or another) and wanted to share them.

I talked a little (ie a lot) in issue two about the character classes. As we're talking people, it may be worth noting how our core cast are all different kinds of *players* - I'm mainly writing from experience, but Robin D Laws' *Robin's Laws of Good Games Mastering* does a useful taxonomy of what he considers the core player types are. I suspect it could do with an updating from the early 00s with the explosion of more story-led indie games, and the two less ludic sorts of players may be worth being refined into other categories... but as I can't think how I'd do it off the top of my head, I'm likely wrong. If you're interested in this kind of stuff, it's worth your time. Suffice to say, any RPG is a negotiation between what different players want, and the players' ability to compromise and (to some degree) the GM's ability to keep all those different players happy.

MECHANICS

Right. Let's do this.

The title of issue 5 ('Premise Rejection') is a nod to Robin D Laws' phrase, used to describe when a group of players explicitly reject the concept of the game. The players don't want to take the ring to Mordor. The players want to bum around Hobbiton and hit on Rosie.

This is closely linked to another concept - namely, a failure to get "Buy In". Buy In signals to a group the game we're going to be playing, and asks them to enter a social contract to do that. If you're playing a game of heroic adventure, you play heroic adventurers. If you don't want to be a heroic adventurer, we play a different game. There's philosophies that reject this, of course, which leans towards the idea of complete player agency and a pure sandbox experience. You can't reject the premise when there's no premise.

This is actually an experience we can easily see in traditional, linear, non-interactive storytelling, but it's inverted. The audience buys in when they start experiencing a story. The story has signalled to some degree what it is - either in its marketing, or simply by elements it displays early in the story. The story makes promises. If it breaks its promises, it's one of the easiest ways to lose the audience. Navigating that space is just difficult, and the attempt to make multiple sorts of promises to signal that this isn't just going to be a surface reading is key.

I hope we did that. This is the issue where the book's mechanics are revealed, in terms of what our engine of drama is.

Of course, our cast's rejection of Sol's game mirrors my own rejection of the core fantasy that I devoured as a teen. If you've seen interviews with me, you've likely seen me talk about the slow and awful realisation I was a fantasy writer. When I started writing comics, I tended to describe myself as a speculative fiction writer. My partner

at the time noted this was full of shit. "When your speculations are 'What if music is magic?' you're a fucking fantasy writer," she noted. Rumbled. You can imagine me wailing, "I don't want to be one of them!", falling to the ground and having a tantrum.

The problem was that I had burned out on what I termed travelogue fantasy back in my teenage years, due to terminal overexposure. The idea of the books with a map at the front and the heroes trekking between every mysterious blob on the map, before ending the book (or multiple series of books)? No. I'm nothing to do with that.

This is a pretty common stance. I mentioned 'Epic Pooh' a couple of issues back. The tradition of anti-fantasy fantasy writers is as long as the current mode of the genre. It took me a while to realise that, and it's percolated into my work since. I'm a fantasy writer. I tweak reality into explicit unreality to better talk about reality. It's my major mode. Frankly, the realisation isn't always comfortable. Scanning around a Marvel summit and realising I'm the only fantasy writer in the room is one of the things which makes you realise you're likely going to be found out sooner rather than later.

(This is one my pet theories - as in, while everyone is flexible, most writers have a core genre they gravitate towards. Brubaker is at heart a crime writer, as is Bendis. Ellis is a science fiction writer. Remender is too - though the lurid pulp side of it. The tell is "what does this writer do when they're doing a creator-owned book?" As in, if you remember the limitations of the two main superhero universes, what comic do they write? It's for this reason that despite all his wonderful work on *Thor* and *Conan*, I think of Jason Aaron as a crime writer.)

For all the literary elements of *DIE*, which I talked about in issue 3, the pure cold mechanics of the world click into place here. This is what, we hope, grounds you as we progress. "Can these people come to an agreement?"

It's the reason why I couldn't release the rules before this point. The "if everyone agrees to go home, you go home" is there in the second issue. The "if someone dies, they lose their vote, and can only regain their life by killing one of their party members" is also there, lurking in the subtext. But

the "players come back as Fallen, and then can reclaim their vote by killing someone else" only appears here.

This is a storytelling mechanic - you all know the rules, so you can use it to orientate yourself. But it's also a game mechanic. This dilemma is right out of a brutal TV reality show, existential survivor. Mechanics are interesting with *DIE*.

It's one of the parts where creating *DIE*'s back and forth between the game system and the comic starts to become the ouroboros, eating itself. I was looking for meaningful mechanics to use death in the game, and hit upon the idea of the Fallen being dead players. But the Fallen were already in the story - our generic enemy. It was only then, by approaching them in a completely indirect way, that I realised why they were called Fallen. It was just sitting there.

The human subconscious is a strange thing. I'll come back to that at the end.

(I'll say this - the major advantage to doing this game system means it's something else that makes me think about the material from a completely different angle.)

Oh, the game. Let's say what actually happens in our game. It basically recapitulates in a single scenario the first five issues. It works like this. You generate a social group. As in, a group of people who know each other. You decide who they are, what they want, how they interact, their hopes, their fears. This includes the person who's running the game. It's likely the majority of the characters (or "personas" as the game puts it - with multiple levels of reality, clearly this can be tricky) will have played a role-playing game as teenagers, and now have got back together as adults.

You then step away from the table, and sit back down. You're now actively playing the people you've generated, who have sat down to play a role-playing game, at the behest of the GM's persona. Then everyone generates one of the fantasy characters in our six character classes, on handy sheets, as we see in issue one. Yes, this sequence is you role-playing someone playing a role-playing game.

Shortly, you're all transported into a fantasy world by the GM's persona.

You are likely transformed into the hero you generated - this real-world normal person with the abilities of a fantasy hero. And then? An adventure.

You know the rules. You've read the comic. If you all agree to go home, you go home. Your friend who dragged you here? They've clearly got reasons they want to stay. Can you talk them out of it? What are you going to do if you can't change their mind? More so - what are you going to do if your friends start to change their minds?

I spend a lot of time in the rules, talking about story structure, and how to personalise this core arc for your group. There's a lot about how the personas they've generated can have their hopes and fears integrated into the game world. By which you may understand that it's not necessarily set in the large *DIE* you see in the comic - but it's set inside a smaller sub-dimension of *DIE*, which is all yours to personalise. That place where all these worlds are exists in *DIE*'s fiction, and I'm sure we'll get there eventually. "Eventually" is a key word.

Some games I've played have been pure fantasy romps, going through a series of challenges, confronting this shithead of a friend and everyone going home. Some games have turned into weird therapy sessions, for these broken people trying to help each other. It all depends on the players who sit down, and what they're looking for. As I said, you can't reject the premise when rejecting the premise has actually been built into the premise.

It's a single, flexible scenario, possible to play across as many sessions as you wish. I've mainly run it as one-offs and two-session games, though most players would have preferred it if I'd taken it to three or four. It's just your game, and will play radically differently depending what persona you drop in the end. Playing it with a twenty-something social group is a different thing from playing it with a group of seventy-year-olds in a home, to state the obvious. Playing it as a group of temp workers is different from playing it with an alcoholics anonymous group. It twists.

You go into a fantasy world, but it's your world. That's kind of the point of RPGs. It's the same thing for everyone. It's completely different. It's yours. That's what RPGs promise us, and it's

our meta game about exactly that. As I said earlier, I'll be releasing the beta rules when the trade drops [*Ed. note: See page 155 of this volume! You may want to skim the rest of this paragraph, but I've kept it in to show KG's thoughts about the playtest*]. There's a lot of me rambling about storytelling and art, so I hope folks who just like my stuff will find it entertaining even if they have no interest in RPGs per se. There are at least three good jokes. Down the line, assuming folks like it, we may do a larger edition - there's areas I'd like to do more with, to say the least. Until then, there's lots in the beta to amuse you. As said, it comes out circa the Trade. However, I'm considering doing a last larger playtest of the beta in the last months before then. I'm not 100% sure of this, but keep an eye on the *DIE* site and my Twitter around (er) now for info. There may be a chance to get involved for those with an urge to see the game in a rawer state, before it gets the final months' design and polish. You can only read something for the first time once though, and my writing is always much better in its final state than the earlier ones, so I urge you: if you can wait, do wait.

Before I go, one more weird story I'd forgotten. Last time I told you about the friend who I couldn't remember. I've got another one.

In my teenage years, among my random obsessions, was an arcade game called *Xain'd Sleena*. It was a cabinet on one of my holidays, which my brother and I funnelled coins into. It's a scrolling sci-fi action adventure, which kind brings to mind *Ghosts & Goblins*. Bar having an excellent name, its only notable feature was that you could choose which of its five levels you played first, meaning that even a crap player could see a fair selection of different stuff.

When it was released in the UK, it was renamed to *Soldier Of Light*. *Xain'd Sleena: Soldier of Light*. I never actually bought any of the conversions to the home computers, as it looked a bit duff. Still, it stuck in my head, and I started using the pen-name XAIN in a little of my early work. Programming, game writing, bits and pieces, but mainly in high score tables. I got a good score? I entered Xain.

Except a lot of high-score tables wouldn't let you enter more than

three letters. I wanted a reference, but Xain'd Sleena didn't seem to have any suitably punchy three letter acronym. Then I remembered the alternative name - *Soldier of Light*. Soldier. Of Light.

My name in those teenage high score tables?

"SOL."

THE SPACE BETWEEN WORDS

Hello everyone.

You may know me as the artist or, as someone once wrote, I am the Co. in Kieron & Co. At least in the *DIE* Team. The rest of the time, I am Stephanie Hans. Have we met? Nice to meet you anyway.

What am I doing here, playing with things as dangerous as words instead of arting, you ask? And in English no less? You're right, those things are sharp and I am indeed French but let's play together for just a little while. I promise I am nowhere near as wordy as my beloved writer. Not on paper that is, because in real life, I am a mouthy kid, and in French I am downright sassy. Cause, you know... French.

So what I am going to do right now is I am going to write a bit about the space between words, the space where I exist, and that I try my best to fill with colours and lines but also delicate feelings and raw emotions, and with myself, a bit, if I can be honest. I exist in that space, I put all I learnt in those last years as an artist, and I put all the emotions I usually keep to myself there.

People sometimes forget artists also bring something important in a comic, even if they don't write it. This is what I will try to show you today. You tell me after if I did a good job with that.

So, let's talk about *DIE*.

As my first ongoing and my first creator-owned project, I really am playing it by ear. Kieron and I wanted to work together for a while and I certainly never would have worked with another writer on such a big project. I had a fairly easy life, a good place in the comic book market as a cover artist and occasional interior artist for the big three.

I love working with Kieron. He gives me something precious: trust. We trust each other this way. I trust him to write me a beautiful story and I will do my best to be there when words are not necessary.

It's a dance really. There is no point in doing it if you don't enjoy yourself or aren't confident your partner will bring out the best of you and make it shine.

On *DIE* specifically what I did, beside the design, was to add a theory of colour to bring more meanings to scenes.

Basically I cut the book into sequences, to which I assigned a colour gradient. Each has a meaning but almost all of issue one is a preparation of the double-page spread with the big reveal of the *DIE* world with intoxicating reds and vivid pure colours... ho, and space. All the sequences before that are bleak, almost claustrophobic; air is heavy, dark. The only moment when it is not is the moment in the rain because, from my point of view, this is where the border between worlds is thinning.

Simple enough, right? First the book, then the sequence, then the page and lastly the panel. They all work like matryoshkas. They all have to exist perfectly within each other.

I see the relationship between me and my writer as a dance, but I see the book as a musical score, a melody that I need to organize. Action is fast: panels are small. Something happens that is important: big wide panel. Long action: long panel. Slow pace: strict panels, 90-degree angles but more diversity in their shape to keep them from being boring. They are notes. They need to make beautiful music.

I usually keep away from more spectacular effects like things getting out of panels. I believe in a strict slicing of my sequences. People don't need extra fanciness to make the book more likable. I love it in the work of other artists and won't rule out using it once in a while but, mostly, it will be a rarity.

DIE also brought me another rare treat which was to design characters and a world. We talked a lot about the characters before I started sketching anything. When I took up my pen, I felt like they were already there, I just had to find their shape.

As expected, Ash was the one who took most of our time. My main desire for them was to design them with influences from the time they created their avatars. And their own characters. You will have fun with that when you play the game yourself (cue: expect a lot of elves and the occasional Dark Elf).

So yeah, Ash is a woman when in the Die world. I brought the design of the dress in *Legend*, mixed with the first influence on her design, which was Eddie The Head from Van Halen. She kept the hair and the red horrifying skin that appears when she uses her powers. There also might be a bit of Captain Harlock, who was the first love of my life.

Isabelle is directly inspired by one of my best friends in France: Korean, adopted, French, all that and more. She also has a lot of me in her. Kieron wrote her as an elitist; she was the one most likely to get realistic armour. Mostly. She is a badass atheist.

Angela in real life and in her youth was inspired by Vanessa Paradis. Her Die-world design comes from *Gunnm* (*Alita*), *Battle of the Planets* and *Mother Sarah* with a touch of 90s Madonna. She and Ash have complementary outfits; they are siblings after all.

Matt as a teenager is inspired by the only black boy of my school from my youth. Worth noting, Kieron's school year group also only had one black boy in it. (It says a lot about the provincial nature of where we grew up). I remember a shy boy, always well dressed. It was important for him to fit in. He was designed in the Die world as the white knight with the heart on his shoulder. He is Aragorn. And he designed his outfit with the same seriousness he did everything else.

Chuck: Chuck is the child that is difficult to love. He is the fool. He most certainly manspreads. He will not take this seriously. I gave him a mixed style between a bosozoku and a hipster. His main appearance takes a lot from George Michael, 90s style, with a lot of bling mixed with extra bling. Worth saying: he is the only one showing his die off. Even though all the other characters are more connected to their dice, he treats his as mere jewellery. Told you, he is difficult to love, but we will get there, eventually.

Another thing I am trying to do in *DIE* is give you the desire to come back to look at the pages more. I am trying to give a nod to the fantasy artists that inspired me like Loisel, Bourgeon, Van Hamme, John Howe, Miyazaki (yes he also drew manga) or Moebius. Honestly there are too many of them to name them all and I know they are almost all French and not everyone may know them. But they brought the desire in me to do Fantasy someday and I am trying here to bring a little extra to the story in some old-school framing with foregrounds, details and, yes, a bit of poetry.

I don't know if I did a good job in explaining the things I do as an artist and I honestly don't know how other artists work. I suspect some of them like to just have to draw the thing without having to do the sequencing. To each his own, right? As long as it works and you never forget that someone will read it, I am sure you will be good.

I'll see you around. I will now crawl back to the artcave and resume arting.

Take care everyone.

FURTHER READING

Here are some things which Kieron has been looking at while researching *DIE*, and some works which directly inspired Stephanie on how she thinks and approaches fantasy. Go nose.

Kieron

Playing At The World by Jon Peterson: if you read one book about the history of the role-playing game, read this one, because it's basically five books tied together. I thought I knew the history of Kriegspiel leading into the hobby games well, but this has so many more angles. A hell of a thing.

The Monsters and the Critics and other Essays by J.R.R. Tolkien: obviously I read (and reread) a lot of Tolkien when writing the third issue, but hitting his critical writing was just as influential.

J.R.R. Tolkien: A Biography by Humphrey Carpenter: a short and excellent biography of Tolkien's life, and absolutely instrumental in freeing myself from my own ideas of him (as opposed to my ideas of his work).

Wizardry and Wild Romance by Michael Moorcock: includes the seminal anti-Tolkien rant, 'Epic Pooh'. Always good to see a master of the form go for it.

Planetary by Warren Ellis/John Cassaday/Laura Martin: I found myself rereading this genuine classic when thinking about *DIE*'s structure, and *Planetary*'s modular design connects deconstructionary standalone stories about the origins of the superhero genre with a conspiracy metaplot. We don't quite do the same thing, but being reminded such a thing was possible was a relief.

The Bones: Us and Our Dice edited by Will Hindmarch: a selection of personal and theoretical essays about gamers' relationship with their dice. Useful for thinking of the social history of such stuff.

Dangerous Games by Joseph P. Laycock: an academic look at the satanic panic, and theorises on more fundamental reasons why RPGs disturbed the fundamentalists. Some useful historical angles too.

Designers & Dragons by Shannon Appelcline (Volumes 1-4): if *Playing At The World* is the big theoretical text, this was the series which let me trace the history of each player in the development of the form.

Stephanie

Terry Pratchett: he is my god (especially with *Small Gods*). I keep his last book preciously, unread and unopened, for there will still be hope in dark times if I have another Pratchett to read.

Stephen King: the first author I had a passion for. I asked my mother to buy me all he wrote when I was 14 as a graduation present.
That was a lot of books.

Les Compagnons Du Crépuscule (The Dusk Companions): this was a French comic, in three parts, very very dark, between horrifying medieval realism and oneirism. Basically, three people meet and go on a quest together and at night they are linked in strange dreams. It doesn't end well.

La Quête de L'Oiseau du Temps (The Quest for the Time-Bird): first book of French comic book superstar Loisel. The story goes from entertaining to dark, ending in tears. Mine. It's also fascinating to see the transition from the 70s inking style, with a lot of lines everywhere to some pure and round clean lines in the end.

Nausicaä: manga from Miyazaki, who didn't do only anime movies. *Nausicaä* is particularly noticeable because of the will of the author to do pages with lots and lots of details, which is not the usual way to create manga. The universe is rich and graceful extremely creative. There was an anime by Studio Ghibli later.

Gunnm (Alita): everyone knows about *Alita* now with the movie, but when it came out, it was a revolution. With this incredible dystopian world and the elegant drawing, *Gunnm* is at the top of that kind of manga talking about a divided society and the fear of the future, with top-game fighting scenes.

ALSO BY THE SAME CREATORS

KIERON GILLEN & STEPHANIE HANS:

The Wicked + The Divine #15
Collected in *The Wicked + The Divine* Volume 3

The Wicked + The Divine 1831 #1
Collected in *The Wicked + The Divine* Volume 8

Journey Into Mystery
Collected in two volumes, with Stephanie providing covers and interiors on the final issue

Angela: Asgard's Assassin
with Marguerite Bennett and Phil Jimenez

1602 Witch Hunter Angela
with Marguerite Bennett and more

FOR FURTHER INFORMATION PLEASE VISIT:

www.diecomic.com
For comic and RPG news, new issues and updates

#diecomic
The hashtag for whatever social media you use

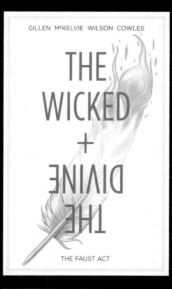

GILLEN McKELVIE WILSON COWLES
THE WICKED + THE DIVINE
THE FAUST ACT

The Wicked + The Divine
Volumes 1-8
With art by Stephanie Hans in Volumes 3 and 8

PHONOGRAM
RUE BRITANNIA
image
Kieron GILLEN
Jamie McKELVIE

Phonogram
Volumes 1-3

THREE
GILLEN KELLY BELLAIRE COWLES

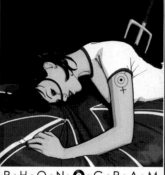

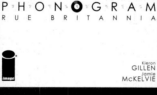

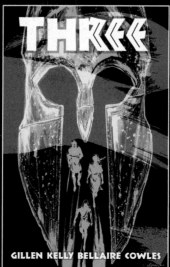

Three
Volume 1

TEAM BIOS

Kieron Gillen is a comic writer based in London, Britain. His previous work includes *The Wicked + The Divine, Phonogram* and *Young Avengers.* He mainly plays low intelligence Barbarians or high charisma Bards.

Photo: Mauricio de Souza

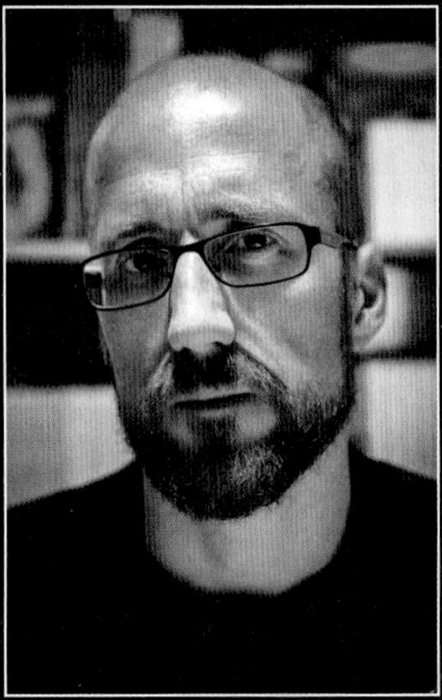

Stephanie Hans is a comic artist based in Toulouse, France. Her previous work includes issues of *The Wicked + The Divine, Journey Into Mystery* and *Batwoman.* She mainly plays Clerics and Wizards.

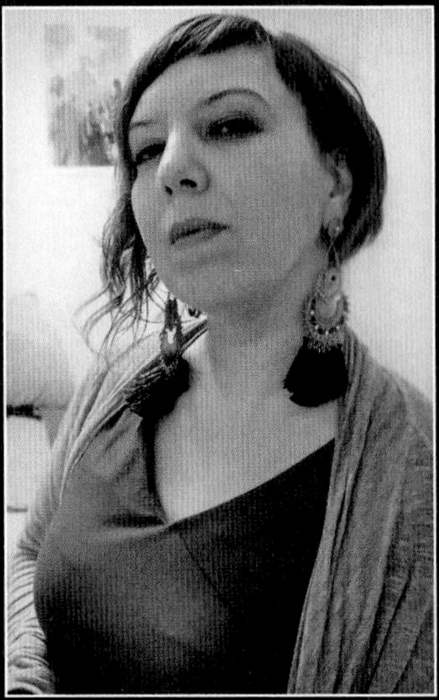

Clayton Cowles is an Eisner award-nominated letterer, based in Rochester, USA. His credits include everything. He has only played *D&D* once, and was a Bard.

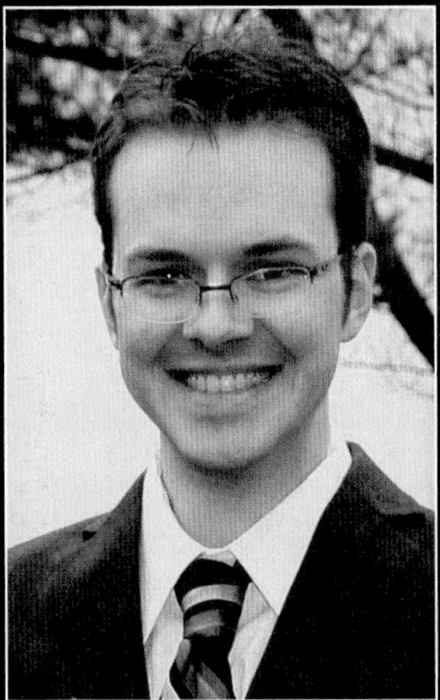